THE NEW PROPHECY
WARRIORS
MIDNIGHT

WARRIORS

WARRIORS: THE NEW PROPHECY

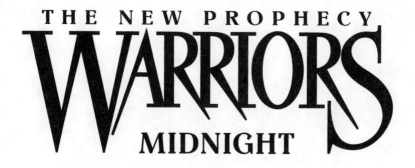

THE NEW PROPHECY

WARRIORS

MIDNIGHT

ERIN
HUNTER

HARPERCOLLINS*PUBLISHERS*

For Chris, Janet, and Louisa Haslum

Special thanks to Cherith Baldry

ALLEGIANCES

THUNDERCLAN

LEADER

FIRESTAR—ginger tom with a flame-colored pelt

DEPUTY

GRAYSTRIPE—long-haired gray tom

MEDICINE CAT

CINDERPELT—dark gray she-cat
APPRENTICE, LEAFPAW

WARRIORS

(toms, and she-cats without kits)

MOUSEFUR—small dusky brown she-cat
APPRENTICE, SPIDERPAW

DUSTPELT—dark brown tabby tom
APPRENTICE, SQUIRRELPAW

SANDSTORM—pale ginger she-cat
APPRENTICE, SORRELPAW

CLOUDTAIL—long-haired white tom

BRACKENFUR—golden brown tabby tom
APPRENTICE, WHITEPAW

THORNCLAW—golden brown tabby tom
APPRENTICE, SHREWPAW

BRIGHTHEART—white she-cat with ginger patches

BRAMBLECLAW—dark brown tabby tom with amber eyes

ASHFUR—pale gray (with darker flecks) tom, dark blue eyes

RAINWHISKER—dark gray tom with blue eyes

SOOTFUR—lighter gray tom with amber eyes

APPRENTICES (more than six moons old, in training to become warriors)

SORRELPAW—tortoiseshell and white she-cat with amber eyes

SQUIRRELPAW—dark ginger she-cat with green eyes

LEAFPAW—light brown tabby she-cat with amber eyes and white paws

SPIDERPAW—long-limbed black tom with brown underbelly and amber eyes

SHREWPAW—small dark brown tom with amber eyes

WHITEPAW—white she-cat with green eyes

QUEENS (she-cats expecting or nursing kits)

GOLDENFLOWER—pale ginger coat, the oldest nursery queen

FERNCLOUD—pale gray (with darker flecks) she-cat, green eyes

ELDERS (former warriors and queens, now retired)

FROSTFUR—beautiful white she-cat with blue eyes

DAPPLETAIL—once-pretty tortoiseshell she-cat, the oldest cat in ThunderClan

SPECKLETAIL—pale tabby she-cat

LONGTAIL—pale tabby tom with dark black stripes, retired early due to failing sight

SHADOWCLAN

LEADER   **BLACKSTAR**—large white tom with huge jet black paws

DEPUTY   **RUSSETFUR**—dark ginger she-cat

MEDICINE CAT   **LITTLECLOUD**—very small tabby tom

WARRIORS   **OAKFUR**—small brown tom
    APPRENTICE, SMOKEPAW

    TAWNYPELT—tortoiseshell she-cat with green eyes

    CEDARHEART—dark gray tom

    ROWANCLAW—ginger she-cat
    APPRENTICE, TALONPAW

    TALLPOPPY—long-legged light brown tabby she-cat

ELDERS   **RUNNINGNOSE**—small gray-and-white tom, formerly the medicine cat

WINDCLAN

LEADER   **TALLSTAR**—elderly black-and-white tom with a very long tail

DEPUTY MUDCLAW—mottled dark brown tom
APPRENTICE, CROWPAW—dark smoky
gray, almost black, tom with blue eyes

MEDICINE CAT BARKFACE—short-tailed brown tom

WARRIORS ONEWHISKER—brown tabby tom

WEBFOOT—dark gray tabby tom

TORNEAR—tabby tom

WHITETAIL—small white she-cat

ELDERS MORNINGFLOWER—tortoiseshell she-cat

RIVERCLAN

LEADER LEOPARDSTAR—unusually spotted golden
tabby she-cat

DEPUTY MISTYFOOT—gray she-cat with blue eyes

MEDICINE CAT MUDFUR—long-haired light brown tom
APPRENTICE, MOTHWING—beautiful
golden tabby she-cat with amber eyes

WARRIORS BLACKCLAW—smoky black tom

HEAVYSTEP—thickset tabby tom

STORMFUR—dark gray tom with amber
eyes

FEATHERTAIL—light gray she-cat with
blue eyes

HAWKFROST—broad-shouldered dark
brown tom

MOSSPELT—tortoiseshell she-cat

QUEENS

ELDERS

DAWNFLOWER—pale gray she-cat

SHADEPELT—very dark gray she-cat

LOUDBELLY—dark brown tom

CATS OUTSIDE CLANS

BARLEY—black-and-white tom that lives on a farm close to the forest

RAVENPAW—sleek black cat that lives on the farm with Barley

PURDY—elderly tabby tom that lives in woods near the sea

North Allerton
Amenity Tip

Windover Road

White Hart Woods

Chelford Forest

Chelford Mill

Chelford

Deciduous Woodland

Conifers

Marsh

Cliffs and Rocks

Hiking Trails

NORTH

PROLOGUE

Night lay upon the forest. *There* was no moon, but the stars of Silverpelt shed their frosty glitter over the trees. At the bottom of a rocky hollow, a pool reflected the starshine. The air was heavy with the scents of late greenleaf.

Wind sighed softly through the trees and ruffled the quiet surface of the pool. At the top of the hollow, the fronds of bracken parted to reveal a cat; her bluish gray fur glimmered as she stepped delicately from rock to rock, down to the water's edge.

Sitting on a flat stone that jutted out over the pool, she raised her head to look around. As if at a signal, more cats began to appear, slipping into the hollow from every direction. They padded down to sit as close to the water as they could, until the lower slopes were filled with lithe shapes gazing down into the pool.

The cat who had appeared first rose to her paws. "A new prophecy has come!" she meowed. "A doom that will change everything has been foretold in the stars."

On the opposite side of the pool, another cat bowed his tawny, bracken-colored head. "I have seen this too. There will be doubt, and a great challenge," he agreed.

"Darkness, air, water, and sky will come together, and shake the forest to its roots," the first cat went on. "Nothing will be as it is now, nor as it has been before."

"A great storm is coming," meowed another voice, and the word *storm* was taken up, repeated and passed around the circle until it seemed that thunder rumbled through the ranks of watching cats.

As the murmur died away a lean cat with a glossy black pelt spoke from near the water's edge. "Can nothing change what is about to happen? Not even the courage and spirit of the greatest warrior?"

"The doom will come," the blue-gray cat replied. "But if the Clans meet it like warriors, they may survive." Lifting her head, she let her luminous gaze travel around the hollow. "You have all seen what must befall," she meowed. "And you know what must be done. Four cats must be chosen to hold the fate of their Clans in their paws. Are you ready to make your choices before all of StarClan?"

As she finished speaking, the surface of the pool shivered, though there was no wind to disturb it, then was still again.

The bracken-colored tom rose to his paws, starlight turning the fur on his broad shoulders to silver. "I will begin," he meowed. He glanced sideways to meet the gaze of a light-colored tabby with a twisted jaw. "Crookedstar, do I have your permission to speak for RiverClan?" The tabby bowed his head in agreement, and the first cat went on, "Then I invite you all to see and approve my choice."

He stared down into the water, as motionless as the rocks around him. A pale gray blur appeared on the surface of the pool, and all the cats craned forward to see it more clearly.

"That one?" murmured the blue-gray cat, staring at the shape in the water. "Are you sure, Oakheart?"

The tip of the bracken-colored tom's tail flicked back and forth. "I thought that choice would please you, Bluestar," he meowed, amusement in his tone. "Do you not think she was well mentored?"

"She was excellently mentored." Bluestar's neck fur rose as if he had said something to challenge her, then lay flat again. "Does the rest of StarClan agree?" she asked.

A murmur of assent rose from the watching cats, and the pale gray shape thinned and vanished from the water, leaving it clear and empty again.

Now the black cat stood up and padded to the very edge of the pool. "Here is my choice," he announced. "See and approve it."

This time the shape in the pool was tawny-colored and lean, with strong, well-muscled shoulders. Bluestar gazed down at the image for some moments before nodding. "She has strength and courage," she agreed.

"But Nightstar—does she have loyalty?" called another cat.

The black cat's head whipped around and his claws dug into the ground in front of him. "Are you calling her disloyal?"

"If I do, there's reason for it." The answer was shot back. "She was not born in ShadowClan, was she?"

"Then that could make her a good choice," Bluestar

meowed calmly. "If the Clans cannot work together now, they will all be destroyed. Maybe it will take cats with a paw in two Clans to understand what has to be done." She paused for a moment, but no other objections were forthcoming. "Do StarClan approve?"

There was some hesitation, but it was not too long before soft meows of agreement came from all the assembled cats. The surface of the pool rippled briefly, and when it stilled again the tawny shape had gone.

Another black cat got up and approached the water's edge, limping on one stubby, twisted paw. "My turn, I think," he rasped. "See and approve my choice."

The gray-black shape that formed in the pool was hard to see against the reflection of the night sky, and the cats peered at it for some time before anyone spoke.

"*What?*" the bracken-colored cat exclaimed at last. "That's an apprentice!"

"I had noticed, thank you, Oakheart," the black tom meowed dryly.

"Deadfoot, you can't send an apprentice into danger such as this," another cat called from the back of the crowd.

"Apprentice he may be," Deadfoot retorted, "but he has courage and skill to match many warriors. One day he might make a fine leader of WindClan."

"One day is not now," Bluestar pointed out. "And the qualities of a leader are not necessarily those that the Clans need to save them now. Do you wish to make another choice?"

Deadfoot's tail lashed furiously and his neck fur bristled as he glared at Bluestar. "*This* is my choice," he insisted. "Do you—or any other cat—dare to say he is not worthy?"

"What do you say?" Her gaze went around the circle. "Do StarClan approve? Remember that every Clan will be lost if one of our chosen cats should weaken or fail."

Instead of a murmur of approval, the cats muttered at each other in small groups, casting uneasy glances at the shape in the pool and at the cat beside it. Deadfoot stared back with fury in his eyes, his fur fluffed up so that he looked twice his size. He was obviously ready to take on any cat who challenged him.

At length the muttering died away and Bluestar asked once again, "Does the Clan approve?" The assent came, but it was low and reluctant, and a few cats did not speak at all. Deadfoot let out an ill-tempered growl as he turned and limped back to his place.

When the water was clear again Oakheart meowed, "You have not yet made your choice for ThunderClan, Bluestar."

"No—but I am ready now," she replied. "See and approve my choice." She gazed down proudly as a dark tabby shape formed in the depths of the pool.

Oakheart stared at it, and stretched his jaws wide in a soundless mew of laughter. "*That* one! Bluestar, you never cease to surprise me."

"Why?" Bluestar's tone showed she was nettled. "He is a noble young cat, fit for the challenges this prophecy will bring."

Oakheart's ears twitched. "Did I say he was not?"

Bluestar held his gaze, not looking at the other cats as she demanded, "Does the Clan approve?" When the agreement came, strong and certain, she gave Oakheart a contemptuous flick of her tail and looked away.

"Cats of StarClan," she meowed, raising her voice. "Your choices have been made. Soon the journey must begin, to meet the terrible storm that will be released on the forest. Go to your Clans, and make sure each cat is ready."

She paused, and her eyes blazed with a fierce silver light. "We can choose a warrior to save each Clan, but beyond that we cannot help them. May the spirits of all our warrior ancestors go with these cats, wherever the stars may lead them."

CHAPTER 1

Leaves rustled as the young tabby cat slid through a gap between two bushes, his jaws wide open to drink in the scent of prey. On this warm night in late greenleaf, the forest was full of the scuffles of tiny creatures. Movements twitched endlessly at the edge of his vision, but when he turned his head he could see nothing but thick clumps of fern and bramble, dappled with moonlight.

Suddenly he stepped out into a wide clearing and gazed around in confusion. He could not remember being in this part of the forest before. Smooth-cropped grass, glowing silver in a cold wash of moonlight, stretched in front of him as far as a softly rounded rock where another cat was sitting. Starlight sparkled in her fur, and her eyes were two small moons.

The young tabby's bewilderment increased as he recognized her. "Bluestar?" he meowed, his voice shrill with disbelief.

He had been an apprentice when the great leader of ThunderClan had died, four seasons ago, leaping into the gorge with a pack of blood-hungry dogs after her. Like all her

7

Clan, he had grieved for her and honored her for the way she had given up her life to save them. He had never thought to see her again, and he realized for the first time that he must be dreaming.

"Come closer, young warrior," Bluestar meowed. "I have a message for you."

Shivering with awe, the tabby tom crept across the shining stretch of turf until he crouched below the rock and could look up into Bluestar's eyes.

"I'm listening, Bluestar," he mewed.

"A time of trouble is coming to the forest," she told him. "A new prophecy must be fulfilled if the Clans are to survive. You have been chosen to meet with three other cats at the new moon, and you must listen to what midnight tells you."

"What do you mean?" The young cat felt a prickle of dread, cold as snowmelt, creep down his spine. "What kind of trouble? And how can midnight tell us anything?"

"All will be made clear to you," Bluestar replied.

Her voice faded, echoing strangely as if she were speaking from a cavern far beneath the earth. The moonlight also began to grow dim, leaving thick black shadows to creep out of the trees around them.

"No, wait!" the tabby cat cried out. "Don't go!"

He let out a terrified yowl, thrashing his paws and tail, as darkness rose up and engulfed him. Something poked him in the side and his eyes flew open to see Graystripe, the ThunderClan deputy, standing over him with one paw raised to prod him again. He was scuffling among the moss in the warriors' den, with the golden sunlight leaking through the branches above his head.

"Brambleclaw, you crazy furball!" the deputy meowed. "What's all the noise about? You'll scare off all the prey from here to Fourtrees."

"Sorry." Brambleclaw sat up and began picking scraps of moss from his dark fur. "I was just dreaming."

"Dreaming!" grunted a new voice.

Brambleclaw turned his head to see the white warrior Cloudtail heave himself out of a mossy nest nearby and give a long stretch. "Honestly, you're as bad as Firestar," Cloudtail went on. "When he slept in here he was always muttering and twitching in his sleep. A cat couldn't get a good night's rest for all the prey in the forest."

Brambleclaw twitched his ears to hear how disrespectfully the white warrior spoke about the Clan leader. Then he reminded himself that this was Cloudtail, Firestar's kin and former apprentice, well known for his barbed tongue and ready scorn. His impudent talk didn't stop him from being a loyal warrior to his Clan.

Cloudtail gave his long-furred white coat a shake and slipped out of the den, flicking the end of his tail at Brambleclaw in a friendly way to take the sting out of his words as he went by.

"Come on, you lot," meowed Graystripe. "It's time you were moving." He picked his way through the moss on the floor of the den to prod Ashfur awake. "Hunting patrols will be going out soon. Brackenfur is organizing them."

"Right," Brambleclaw mewed. His vision of Bluestar was

fading, though her ominous message echoed in his ears. Could it really be true that there was a new prophecy from StarClan? It seemed fairly unlikely. For a start, Brambleclaw could not imagine why she would choose to give it to him, of all the cats in ThunderClan. Medicine cats frequently received signs from StarClan, and ThunderClan's leader, Firestar, had often been guided by his dreams. But they were not for ordinary warriors. Trying to blame his wild imaginings on too much fresh-kill the night before, Brambleclaw gave his shoulder one last lick and followed Cloudtail out through the trailing branches.

The sun was barely up above the hedge of thorns that surrounded the camp, but the day was already warm. Sunlight lay like honey on the bare earth in the center of the clearing. Sorrelpaw, the oldest of the apprentices, lay stretched out beside the ferns that sheltered the apprentices' den, sharing tongues with her den mates Spiderpaw and Shrewpaw.

Cloudtail had gone over to the nettle patch where the warriors ate and was already gulping down a starling. Brambleclaw noticed that the pile of fresh-kill was very low; as Graystripe had said, the Clan needed to hunt right away. He was about to go and join the white warrior when Sorrelpaw sprang up and came bounding across the clearing toward him.

"It's today!" she announced excitedly.

Brambleclaw blinked. "What is?"

"My warrior ceremony!" With a little *mrrow* of happiness, the tortoiseshell she-cat hurled herself at Brambleclaw;

the unexpected attack bowled him over and they wrestled together on the dusty ground, just as they used to when they were kits together in the nursery.

Sorrelpaw's hind paws battered Brambleclaw in the belly, and he thanked StarClan that her claws were sheathed. There was no doubt that she would make a strong and dangerous warrior, one that every cat would respect.

"All right, all right, that's enough." Brambleclaw cuffed Sorrelpaw gently over one ear and scrambled up. "If you're going to be a warrior, you'll have to stop behaving like a kit."

"A kit?" Sorrelpaw meowed indignantly. She sat in front of him, her fur sticking up in clumps and covered with dust. "Me? Never! I've waited a long time for this, Brambleclaw."

"I know. You deserve it."

Sorrelpaw had ventured too close to the Thunderpath while she was chasing a squirrel in newleaf. A Twoleg monster had struck her a glancing blow, injuring her shoulder. While she lay in Cinderpelt's den for three long, uncomfortable moons, under the gentle care of the medicine cat, her brothers, Sootfur and Rainwhisker, had become warriors. Sorrelpaw had been determined to follow them as soon as Cinderpelt declared her fit enough to begin training again; Brambleclaw had watched how hard she had worked with her mentor, Sandstorm, until her shoulder was as good as new. She had never shown any bitterness at being forced to train for several moons longer than the usual apprenticeship. She really deserved her warrior ceremony.

"I've just taken fresh-kill to Ferncloud," she meowed to

Brambleclaw. "Her kits are beautiful! Have you seen them yet?"

"No, not yet," Brambleclaw replied. Ferncloud's second litter of kits had been born only the day before.

"Go now," Sorrelpaw urged him. "You've just enough time before we hunt." She sprang up and danced a few steps sideways, as if all her energy had to go somewhere.

Brambleclaw set off for the nursery, which was hidden in the depths of a bramble thicket near the center of the camp. He squeezed through the narrow entrance, wincing as thorns scraped against his broad shoulders. Inside it was warm and quiet. Ferncloud was lying on her side in a deep nest of moss. Her green eyes glowed as she gazed at the three tiny kits curled up snugly in the curve of her body: one was pale gray like her, the other two brown tabbies like their father, Dustpelt. He was in the nursery too, crouched beside Ferncloud with his paws tucked under him, occasionally rasping his tongue affectionately over her ear.

"Hi, there, Brambleclaw," he meowed as the younger warrior appeared. "Come to see the new kits?" He looked ready to burst with pride, quite different from his usual prickly, detached air.

"They're beautiful," Brambleclaw mewed, touching noses with Ferncloud in greeting. "Have you chosen names for them yet?"

Ferncloud shook her head, blinking drowsily up at him. "Not yet."

"There's time enough for that." Goldenflower, the oldest

ThunderClan queen and Brambleclaw's own mother, spoke from her mossy bed. She had no kits of her own to nurse, but she had decided to stay in the nursery and share the care of the new arrivals instead of taking up her warrior duties again; she was nearing the time when she would go to join the elders in their den, and was the first to admit that her hearing and eyesight were no longer sharp enough to keep up with the best hunting patrols. "They're strong, healthy kits, that's what matters, and Ferncloud has plenty of milk."

Brambleclaw respectfully dipped his head to her. "She's lucky to have you to help look after them."

"Well, I didn't do too bad a job with you," Goldenflower purred proudly.

"There's something you could do for me," Dustpelt meowed to Brambleclaw as he was leaving.

"Sure, if I can."

"Keep an eye on Squirrelpaw, would you? I want to spend a day or two with Ferncloud, while the kits are still so small, but Squirrelpaw shouldn't be left without a mentor for too long."

Squirrelpaw! Brambleclaw groaned inwardly. Firestar's daughter, eight moons old, recently apprenticed—and the biggest nuisance in ThunderClan.

"It'll be good practice for when you have an apprentice of your own," Dustpelt added, as if he sensed his Clan mate's reluctance.

Brambleclaw knew that Dustpelt was right. He hoped that Firestar would choose him to be a mentor before much longer, with an apprentice of his own to train in the warrior code, but he also hoped that his apprentice would not be some smart-aleck ginger she-cat who thought she knew it all. He was well aware that Squirrelpaw would not take kindly to orders coming from him.

"Okay, Dustpelt," he meowed. "I'll do my best."

When Brambleclaw emerged from the nursery he saw that more cats had appeared in the clearing. Brightheart, a pretty white she-cat with ginger patches on her fur like fallen leaves, had just chosen a piece of fresh-kill from the remains of the pile and was taking it across to where Cloudtail still sat by the nettle patch. The uninjured side of her face was turned to Brambleclaw, so that he could almost forget the disfiguring wounds she had received when the dog pack roamed the forest. One side of her face was seamed with scars, and her ear had been shredded; there was only a gouge mark where her eye should be. Even though she survived the vicious attack, the Clan had feared that she would never be a warrior. It was Cloudtail who had trained with her and worked out ways of making up for her blindness on that side, even turning it into a strength, so that now she could fight and hunt as well as any cat.

Cloudtail greeted her with a flick of his tail and she sat beside him to eat.

"Brambleclaw! There you are!"

Brambleclaw turned and saw a long-legged ginger warrior heading toward him from the direction of the warriors' den. He padded over to meet him. "Hi, Brackenfur. Graystripe said you're organizing hunting patrols."

"That's right," Brackenfur meowed. "Will you go out with Squirrelpaw this morning, please?"

He angled his ears toward the apprentices' den, and Brambleclaw noticed for the first time that Squirrelpaw was half-concealed in the shade of the ferns. She sat tall, her tail curled around her paws, her green eyes following a bright-winged butterfly. When Brackenfur beckoned her with his tail, she got up and strolled across the clearing, her tail straight up and her dark ginger fur gleaming in the sunlight.

"Hunting patrol," Brackenfur explained briefly. "Dustpelt is busy, so you can go with Brambleclaw. Can you find another cat to go with you?"

Without waiting for an answer, he hurried off toward Sandstorm and Sorrelpaw.

Squirrelpaw yawned and stretched. "Well," she meowed. "Where shall we go?"

"I thought Sunningrocks," Brambleclaw began. "Then we can—"

"Sunningrocks?" Squirrelpaw interrupted, her eyes stretching wide in disbelief. "Are you mouse-brained? On a day as hot as this, all the prey will be hiding down cracks. We won't catch so much as a whisker."

"It's still early," Brambleclaw replied crossly. "The prey will be out for a while yet."

Squirrelpaw let out a heavy sigh. "Honestly, Brambleclaw, you always think you know better than anyone else."

"Well, I *am* a warrior," Brambleclaw pointed out, and knew instantly it was the wrong thing to say.

Squirrelpaw bowed her head in deep and exaggerated respect. "Yes, O Great One," she meowed. "I shall do exactly what you say. And when we come back empty-pawed, maybe you'll admit that I was right."

"Well, then," Brambleclaw mewed, "if you're so clever, where do you think we should hunt?"

"Up toward Fourtrees, by the stream," Squirrelpaw replied promptly. "That's a much better place."

Brambleclaw was even more annoyed when he realized that she might be right. In spite of the endless hot days that had lasted all greenleaf, the stream there still ran cool and deep, with thick clumps of reeds where prey could hide. He hesitated, wondering how he could change his mind without losing face in front of the apprentice.

"Squirrelpaw." A new voice rescued him, and Brambleclaw realized that Sandstorm, Squirrelpaw's mother, had padded over to join them. "Stop ruffling Brambleclaw's fur. You chatter as much as a nest of jackdaws." Her annoyed green gaze turned on Brambleclaw and she added, "And you're just as bad. The pair of you are always squabbling; you can't be trusted to hunt together if you can't even get out of the clearing without scaring half the prey between here and Fourtrees."

"Sorry," Brambleclaw muttered, embarrassment sweeping through his fur from ears to tail-tip.

"You're a warrior; you should know better. Go and ask Cloudtail if you can hunt with him. And as for you," Sandstorm meowed to her daughter, "you can come and hunt with me and Sorrelpaw. Brackenfur won't mind. And you'll do as you're told, or I'll know the reason why."

Without looking back, she headed straight for the gorse tunnel that led out of the camp. Squirrelpaw stood still for a moment, a sulky look in her green eyes, and scuffed the ground with her forepaws.

Sorrelpaw came up and gave her a friendly nudge. "Come on," she urged. "This is my last hunt as an apprentice. Let's make it a good one."

Reluctantly Squirrelpaw nodded, and the two cats set off together after Sandstorm; the dark ginger apprentice shot a last glare at Brambleclaw as she passed him.

Brambleclaw shrugged. Squirrelpaw would get more experienced mentoring from Sandstorm than she would from him, so he wasn't letting Dustpelt down even though the warrior had asked him to keep an eye on her. And he wouldn't have to listen all morning to her annoying chatter, so he wasn't sure why he felt slightly disappointed at being set on a different patrol.

Pushing off the feeling, he bounded over to the nettle patch where Cloudtail and Brightheart were finishing their prey. Their single kit, Whitepaw, had just padded across to join them; as Brambleclaw came up he heard her say, "Are you going hunting? *Please* can I come with you?"

Cloudtail flicked his tail. "No." Whitepaw had begun to look disappointed when he added, "Brackenfur said he'd take you. He is your mentor, after all."

"He told me he's really proud of you," Brightheart purred.

Whitepaw brightened up. "Great! I'll go find him."

Cloudtail gave her an affectionate cuff over the ear with one paw before she dashed off, her tail waving excitedly.

Brambleclaw hoped that didn't mean that Cloudtail and Brightheart wanted to go out alone. "Do you mind if I join you?" he asked.

"Sure, you can come," Cloudtail replied. He jumped up and nodded to Brightheart, then the three cats trotted together across the clearing toward the gorse tunnel.

Just before he headed into the close-growing thorns, Brambleclaw glanced over his shoulder at the quiet activity going on in the camp. Every cat looked well fed, sleek furred, and confident that their territory was safe. Bluestar's message came back to echo in his mind. Could it be true that some great trouble was coming upon the forest? Brambleclaw felt his fur prickle with foreboding. He decided that he would not tell any cat about the dream. That seemed like the only way he could convince himself that it meant nothing, and there was no new prophecy coming to disrupt life in the forest as they knew it.

The sun was setting in a ball of fire, turning the tops of the trees to flame and sending long shadows across the clearing. Brambleclaw stretched and sighed with satisfaction. He was tired after the long day's hunting, but his stomach was comfortably full. All the Clan had fed too, and there was an ample pile of fresh-kill. Greenleaf had been longer and hotter than any cat could remember, but the forest was still full of prey, and there was plenty of water in the stream close to Fourtrees.

A good day, Brambleclaw thought contentedly. *This is how life should be.*

The rest of the Clan was beginning to slip out into the clearing and gather around the Highrock, and Brambleclaw realized it was time for Sorrelpaw's warrior ceremony. He padded closer to the Highrock and sat down close to Ferncloud's brother, Ashfur, who gave him a friendly nod. Graystripe was already sitting at the base of the rock, looking as proud as if his own apprentice were about to be made a warrior. Graystripe had fathered two kits, but they had grown up in RiverClan, where their mother had been born. He had no kits in ThunderClan, but liked to keep an eye on the progress of all the young cats.

As Brambleclaw watched, the deputy was joined by Cinderpelt, the medicine cat, and her apprentice, Leafpaw, Squirrelpaw's sister. She looked nothing like Squirrelpaw; she was smaller and slighter, with pale tabby fur and a white chest and paws. The sisters were not much alike in character either. When Leafpaw sat down and tipped her head to one side to listen to what her mentor and the deputy were saying to each other, Brambleclaw wondered, not for the first time, how she managed to be so quiet and attentive when her sister Squirrelpaw never stopped talking.

At last Firestar, the Clan leader, appeared from his den at the other side of the Highrock. He was a strong, lithe warrior, his pelt blazing like flame in the light of the setting sun. After pausing for a word with Graystripe, he bunched his muscles and leaped to the top of the Highrock, from where he could look down on the Clan.

"Cats of ThunderClan!" he announced. "Let all those cats old enough to catch their own prey join here beneath the Highrock for a Clan meeting."

Most of the cats were there already, but as Firestar's voice echoed around the clearing the last of the Clan members slid out from their dens and trotted over to join the others.

Last of all came Sorrelpaw with her mentor, Sandstorm. Her tortoiseshell fur was freshly groomed, her white chest and paws shining like snow. Her amber eyes gleamed with pride and suppressed excitement as she paced across the clearing. Beside her, Sandstorm looked just as proud; Brambleclaw knew how much the ginger she-cat had suffered when she had seen her apprentice lying injured on the Thunderpath. They had both needed courage and perseverance to reach this cere-mony.

Firestar sprang down from the Highrock to meet the apprentice and her mentor. "Sandstorm," he began, using the formal words that had been handed down through all the Clans, "are you satisfied that this apprentice is ready to become a warrior of ThunderClan?"

Sandstorm inclined her head. "She will be a warrior the Clan can be proud of," she replied.

Firestar raised his eyes to where the first stars of Silverpelt were beginning to appear in the evening sky. "I, Firestar, leader of ThunderClan, call upon my warrior ancestors to look down upon this apprentice." The Clan was hushed as his voice rang out across the clearing. "She has trained hard to understand the ways of your noble code, and I commend her to you as a warrior in her turn." He turned to Sorrelpaw, locking his gaze with hers. "Sorrelpaw, do you promise to uphold the warrior code and to protect and defend this Clan, even at the cost of your life?"

Remembering how he had felt at this moment in his own warrior ceremony, Brambleclaw watched Sorrelpaw's whole body quiver with anticipation as she lifted her chin and replied clearly, "I do."

"Then by the powers of StarClan I give you your warrior name. Sorrelpaw, from this moment you will be known as Sorreltail. StarClan honors your courage and your patience, and we welcome you as a full warrior of ThunderClan."

Stepping forward, Firestar rested his muzzle on top of Sorreltail's head. In return she gave his shoulder a respectful lick before backing away.

The rest of the warriors gathered around her, welcoming her and calling her by her new name. "Sorreltail! Sorreltail!" Her brothers, Sootfur and Rainwhisker, were among the first, their eyes gleaming with pride that their sister had finally joined them as a warrior.

Firestar waited until the noise had died down. "Sorreltail, according to tradition you must keep vigil in silence tonight, and watch over the camp."

"While the rest of us get a good night's sleep," Cloudtail added.

The Clan leader flashed him a warning glance but said nothing as the cats parted to let Sorreltail take up her position in the middle of the clearing. She sat with her tail curled around her paws and her gaze fixed on the darkening sky, where the light of Silverpelt grew steadily stronger.

With the ceremony over, the rest of the cats slipped away into the shadows. Brambleclaw stretched and yawned, looking forward to his comfortable nest in the warriors' den, but content to stay in the clearing for a while to enjoy the warm evening. He could not see any signs that other cats had shared his disturbing dream; and yet Bluestar had suggested that three other cats would be involved in the new prophecy. Brambleclaw felt a purr rising into his throat, half-amused by how quickly he had believed that a cat from StarClan had visited him in his dreams. That would teach him to gulp down fresh-kill just before he went to sleep.

"Brambleclaw." Firestar padded over and settled down beside him. "Cloudtail says you hunted well today."

"Thank you, Firestar."

The leader's gaze was fixed on his daughters, Leafpaw and Squirrelpaw, who were heading toward the pile of fresh-kill.

"Do you miss Tawnypelt?" Firestar meowed unexpectedly.

Brambleclaw blinked in surprise. Tawnypelt was his sister; the former ThunderClan deputy, Tigerstar, had fathered them before he had been banished from the Clan for trying to seize power from Bluestar, who was leader then. Later Tigerstar had made himself leader of ShadowClan, only to be killed by a rogue cat in a failed attempt to extend his power over the whole forest. Tawnypelt had always felt that ThunderClan blamed her for her father's crimes, and she had made the decision to join ShadowClan shortly after he became that Clan's leader.

"Yes," Brambleclaw replied. "Yes, Firestar, I miss her every day."

"I didn't understand how you might feel about her. Not until I saw how close those two are." Firestar nodded toward the two sister apprentices, who were choosing prey from the pile.

"Firestar, you're not being fair to yourself," Brambleclaw insisted uncomfortably. "After all, you miss your sister, don't you?" he dared to add.

Firestar had begun life as a kittypet before he joined ThunderClan, and his sister, Princess, still lived with Twolegs. Firestar visited her from time to time, and Brambleclaw knew very well how important they were to each other. Princess had given Firestar her firstborn kit to raise as a warrior—and that was Cloudtail, Brightheart's loyal friend.

The Clan leader tilted his head to one side, thinking. "Of course I miss Princess," he meowed at last. "But she's a kittypet. She could never live this kind of life. You must wish that Tawnypelt had stayed here in ThunderClan."

"I guess I do," Brambleclaw admitted. "But she's happier where she is."

"That's true." Firestar nodded. "The most important thing is that you've both found a Clan where you can be loyal."

A warm feeling crept through Brambleclaw. Once Firestar had doubted his loyalty because he looked so much like his father, Tigerstar, with the same muscular body and dark tabby pelt, the same amber eyes.

Brambleclaw suddenly wondered if a truly loyal Clan cat would mention the disturbing dream and Bluestar's warning that great trouble was coming to the forest. He was trying to find the words to start when Firestar stood up, dipped his head briefly in farewell, and padded over to where Sandstorm was sitting with Graystripe near the Highrock.

Brambleclaw almost followed him, but then he reminded himself that if StarClan really wanted to send a prophecy of great danger, they would not give it to one of the youngest, least experienced warriors in the Clan. They would tell the medicine cat, or perhaps the Clan leader himself. And obviously Firestar and Cinderpelt had not received an omen, or they would be telling the Clan what to do about it. No, Brambleclaw told himself again, there was nothing whatsoever to worry about.

CHAPTER 2

The sun had not yet risen when Brambleclaw set out with the dawn patrol. Even in the few days since Sorreltail's warrior ceremony, the leaves had begun to turn to gold and the first chill of leaf-fall lay on the forest, though it still hadn't rained for longer than a moon. The young warrior shivered as long grasses, heavy with dew, brushed against his fur. Cobwebs spread a gray film over the bushes, and the air was filled with damp, leafy scents. The twittering of waking birds began to drown out the soft padding of the cats' paws.

Brightheart's brother, Thornclaw, who was in the lead, paused to look back at Brambleclaw and Ashfur. "Firestar wants us to check Snakerocks," he meowed. "Watch out for adders. There are more of them since the weather has been so hot."

Brambleclaw instinctively unsheathed his claws. The adders would be hidden in cracks now, but as soon as the sun came up the warmth would tempt them out again. One bite from those poisoned jaws could kill a warrior before a medicine cat could do anything to help.

Before they had gone very far Brambleclaw began to hear

faint sounds behind him, as if something were moving around in the undergrowth. He paused, glancing back in the hope of an easy bit of prey. At first he could see nothing; then he noticed the fronds of a thick clump of fern waving about, though there was no breeze. He sniffed the air, opening his jaws to drink it in, before letting the breath out again with a sigh.

"Come out, Squirrelpaw," he meowed.

There was a moment's silence. Then the bracken waved again and the stems parted as the dark ginger she-cat came out into the open. Her green eyes glared defiance.

"What's going on?" Thornclaw padded up to Brambleclaw, with Ashfur just behind him.

Brambleclaw indicated the apprentice with a flick of his tail. "I heard something behind us," he explained. "She must have followed us from the camp."

"Don't talk about me as if I weren't here!" Squirrelpaw protested hotly.

"You shouldn't be here!" Brambleclaw retorted; somehow Squirrelpaw had only to open her mouth for him to feel that his fur was being rubbed the wrong way.

"Stop bickering, the pair of you," Thornclaw growled. "You're not kits anymore. Squirrelpaw, tell us what you're doing. Did some cat send you with a message?"

"She wouldn't have been skulking in the bracken if they had," Brambleclaw couldn't resist pointing out.

"No, they didn't," Squirrelpaw meowed with a resentful glance at Brambleclaw. Her paws scuffled in the grass. "I wanted to come with you, that's all. I haven't been on a patrol for *ages*."

"And you weren't told to come on this one," Thornclaw replied. "Does Dustpelt know you're here?"

"No," Squirrelpaw admitted. "He promised last night we'd do some training, but every cat knows he spends all day in the nursery with Ferncloud and their kits."

"Not anymore," Ashfur mewed. "Not since the kits opened their eyes. Squirrelpaw, I think you might be in trouble if Dustpelt goes looking for you."

"You'd better go back to camp right away," Thornclaw decided.

Anger flared up in Squirrelpaw's eyes, and she took a step forward that brought her nose-to-nose with Thornclaw. "You're not my mentor, so don't order me around!"

Thornclaw's nostrils flared minutely as he let out a patient sigh, and Brambleclaw admired his self-control. If Squirrelpaw had spoken to *him* like that, he would have been tempted to rake his claws over her ear.

Even Squirrelpaw seemed to realize she had gone too far. "I'm sorry, Thornclaw," she meowed. "But it's true I *haven't* been on patrol for days. *Please* can I come?"

Thornclaw exchanged a glance with Ashfur and Brambleclaw. "All right," he mewed. "But don't blame me if Dustpelt turns you into crowfood when we get back."

Squirrelpaw gave a little skip of excitement. "Thank you, Thornclaw! Where are we going? Are we looking for anything special? Is there going to be trouble?"

Thornclaw swished his tail across her mouth to silence her. "Snakerocks," he replied. "And it's up to us to make sure there won't be trouble."

"Watch out for adders, though," Brambleclaw added.

"I know that!" Squirrelpaw flashed back at him.

"And we do it *quietly*," Thornclaw ordered her. "I don't want to hear another squeak out of you unless there's something I need to know."

Squirrelpaw opened her mouth to reply, then took in what he had said and nodded vigorously.

The patrol set off again. Brambleclaw had to admit that now she had gotten her own way, Squirrelpaw was behaving sensibly, slipping quietly along behind the leader and staying alert for every sound and movement in the undergrowth.

The sun was well risen by the time the four cats emerged from the trees and saw the smooth, rounded shapes of Snakerocks in front of them. A dark hole gaped at the foot of one of them; it was the cave where the dog pack had hidden. Brambleclaw shuddered, remembering that Tigerstar, his own father, had tried to lead the savage animals to the ThunderClan camp in deadly revenge against his former Clan mates.

Squirrelpaw noticed his expression. "Scared of adders?" she taunted him.

"Yes," Brambleclaw replied. "And so should you be."

"Whatever." She shrugged. "They're probably more scared of us."

Before Brambleclaw could stop her, she bounded forward into the clearing, obviously meaning to poke her nose into the hole.

"Stop!" Thornclaw's voice brought her skidding to a halt. "Hasn't Dustpelt told you that we don't go dashing in anywhere before we're sure of what we're going to find?"

Squirrelpaw looked embarrassed. "Of course he has."

"Well, then, act like you might have listened to him once or twice." Thornclaw padded up beside the apprentice. "Have a good sniff," he suggested. "See if you can scent anything."

The young she-cat stood with her head raised, drawing the morning air into her mouth. "Mouse," she meowed brightly after a moment. "Can we hunt, Thornclaw?"

"Later," the warrior replied. "Now concentrate."

Squirrelpaw tasted the air again. "The Thunderpath, just over there"—she waved her tail—"and a Twoleg with a dog. But that's stale," she added. "I'd guess they were here yesterday."

"Very good." Thornclaw sounded impressed, and Squirrelpaw curled her tail up in delight.

"There's something else," she went on. "A horrible scent . . . I don't think I've smelled it before."

Brambleclaw raised his head and sniffed. He quickly identified the scents Squirrelpaw had mentioned, and the new, unfamiliar one. "Badger," he meowed.

Thornclaw nodded. "That's right. It looks as if it's moved into the cave where the dogs were."

Ashfur groaned. "Just our luck!"

"Why?" Squirrelpaw asked. "What are badgers like? Are they a problem?"

"Are they ever!" Brambleclaw growled. "They're no good to any cat, and they'd kill you as soon as look at you."

Squirrelpaw's eyes widened, though she looked more impressed than frightened.

Ashfur cautiously approached the dark cave mouth, sniffed, and peered inside. "It's dark as a fox's heart in there," he reported, "but I don't think the badger is at home."

While he was speaking Brambleclaw suddenly caught the scent again, much stronger this time, washing over him from somewhere behind them. He leaped around to see a pointed, striped face appear from behind the trunk of a nearby tree, its huge pads crushing the grass, its muzzle snuffling along the ground.

"Look out!" he yowled, every hair on his pelt bristling in fear. He had never been this close to a badger before. Whirling around, he dashed out into the clearing. "Squirrelpaw, *run!*"

As soon as Brambleclaw gave the alarm, Ashfur dived into the undergrowth, while Thornclaw bounded toward the safety of the trees. But Squirrelpaw stayed where she was, her gaze fixed on the huge creature.

"This way, Squirrelpaw!" Thornclaw called, starting to come back.

The apprentice still hesitated; Brambleclaw barreled into her, thrusting her toward the trees. "I said run!"

Her green eyes, blazing with fear and excitement, met his for a heartbeat. The badger was lumbering forward, its small eyes glittering as it scented cats intruding onto its territory. Squirrelpaw pelted toward the edge of the clearing and launched herself up the nearest tree. Reaching a low branch she dug in her claws and crouched there, her ginger fur fluffed out.

Brambleclaw clawed his way up beside her. Down below the badger was blundering back and forth, as if it could not tell where the cats had gone. Its black-and-white head swung threateningly from side to side. Brambleclaw knew that it could not see very well; usually badgers only came out after dark, and this one would be on its way back to the cave after a night's feeding on worms and grubs.

"Would it eat us?" Squirrelpaw asked breathlessly.

"No," Brambleclaw replied, trying to slow his pounding heart. "Even a fox kills to eat, but a badger will kill you just for getting in its way. We're not prey to them, but they won't tolerate any trespassers on their territory. Why did you hang about down there instead of running like we told you?"

"I've never seen a badger before, and I wanted to. Dustpelt says we should get all the experience we can."

"Does that include the experience of having your fur ripped off?" Brambleclaw asked dryly, but for once Squirrelpaw didn't reply.

While he was speaking Brambleclaw hadn't taken his eyes off the creature below. He breathed a sigh of relief as it gave up the search and padded over to the cave mouth, where it squeezed itself inside and was gone.

Thornclaw leaped down from the tree where he had taken refuge. "That was closer than I'd like," he meowed as Brambleclaw and Squirrelpaw scrambled down to join him. "Where's Ashfur?"

"Here." Ashfur's pale gray head popped out of a tangle of briars. "Do you think that badger is the same one that killed

Willowpelt last leaf-bare?"

"Maybe," Thornclaw replied. "Cloudtail and Mousefur drove it away from the camp, but we never found out where it went."

A pang of sadness went through Brambleclaw as he remembered the silver-gray she-cat. Willowpelt was the mother of Sorreltail, Sootfur, and Rainwhisker, but she had not lived to see her kits become warriors.

"So what are we going to do about it?" Squirrelpaw asked eagerly. "Shall we go in there and kill it? There are four of us, and only one badger. How hard could it be?"

Brambleclaw winced, while Thornclaw closed his eyes and waited a moment before speaking. "Squirrelpaw, you *never* go into a badger's den. Or a fox's, for that matter. They'll attack right away, there isn't enough room to maneuver, and you can't see what you're doing."

"But—"

"*No.* We'll head back to camp and report it. Firestar will decide what to do."

Without waiting for Squirrelpaw to argue any more, he set off in the direction they had come. Ashfur fell in behind him, but Squirrelpaw paused at the edge of the clearing. "We could have dealt with it," she grumbled, glancing back longingly at the dark mouth of the cave. "I could have lured it out, and then—"

"And then it would have killed you with one swipe of its paw, and we'd *still* have to go back and report it," Brambleclaw meowed discouragingly. "What do you think we would have said? 'Sorry, Firestar, but we accidentally let a badger get your daughter'? He would have our fur off. Badgers are bad news, and that's that."

"Well, you wouldn't catch Firestar leaving a badger in ThunderClan territory without doing anything." Squirrelpaw swung her tail up defiantly and plunged into the undergrowth to catch up with Thornclaw and Ashfur.

Brambleclaw raised his eyes, murmured, "Great StarClan!" and followed.

When he emerged from the gorse tunnel into the clearing, the first cat he saw was Dustpelt. The brown tabby warrior was pacing up and down outside the apprentices' den, his tail lashing from side to side. Two of the other apprentices, Spiderpaw and Whitepaw, were crouched in the shade of the ferns, watching him apprehensively.

As soon as Dustpelt spotted Squirrelpaw, he marched across the clearing toward her.

"Uh-oh," Squirrelpaw muttered.

"Well?" the tabby warrior's voice was icy. Brambleclaw winced, knowing how short-tempered he was; the only cat who had never felt the rough side of his tongue was Ferncloud. "What have you got to say for yourself?"

Squirrelpaw met his glare bravely, but there was a quaver in her voice as she replied, "I went on patrol, Dustpelt."

"Oh, on patrol! I *see*. And which cat ordered you to go? Graystripe? Firestar?"

"No cat ordered me. But I thought—"

"No, you didn't think." Dustpelt's voice was scathing. "I told you we would train today. Mousefur and Brackenfur took their apprentices to the training hollow to practice their fighting moves. We could have gone with them, but we didn't, because you weren't here. Do you realize that every cat has been searching the camp for you?"

Squirrelpaw shook her head, scuffling the ground with her front paws.

"When no cat could find you, Firestar took out a patrol to try following your scent. Did you see anything of him?"

Another shake of the head. Brambleclaw realized that following a scent in the heavy dew that morning would have been next to impossible.

"Your Clan leader has better things to do than chase after apprentices who can't do as they're told," Dustpelt went on. "Thornclaw, why did you let her go with you?"

"I'm sorry, Dustpelt," Thornclaw apologized. "I thought she'd be safer with us than wandering around the forest by herself."

Dustpelt snorted. "That's true."

"We could still go and do the training," Squirrelpaw suggested.

"Oh, no. No more training for you until you learn what being an apprentice really means." Dustpelt paused for a heartbeat. "You can spend the rest of the day looking after the elders. Make sure they have enough fresh-kill. Change their bedding. Go over their pelts for ticks." He blinked. "I'm sure Cinderpelt has plenty of mouse bile for you."

Squirrelpaw's eyes flew wide in dismay. "Oh, yuck!"

"Well, what are you waiting for?"

The young apprentice stared at him for a moment longer,

as if she couldn't believe he really meant it. When there was no change in her mentor's hard stare, she whisked around and flounced across the clearing toward the elders' den.

"If Firestar's out looking for Squirrelpaw, we'll have to wait for him to get back before we can report the badger," Thornclaw observed.

"Badger? What badger?" asked Dustpelt.

While Thornclaw and Ashfur began to describe what they had seen at Snakerocks, Brambleclaw bounded across the clearing and caught up with Squirrelpaw just outside the elders' den.

"What do you want?" she spat.

"Don't be angry," Brambleclaw mewed. He couldn't help feeling sorry for her, even though she had deserved some sort of punishment for leaving the camp without any cat knowing where she was going. "I'll help you with the elders, if you like."

Squirrelpaw opened her mouth as if she were about to make a rude retort, and then clearly thought better of it. "Okay, thanks," she muttered ungraciously.

"You go and get the mouse bile, and I'll make a start on the bedding."

Squirrelpaw's eyes opened wide in a winning expression. "You wouldn't rather get the mouse bile, would you?"

"No, I wouldn't. Dustpelt especially told you to do that. Don't you think he'll check?"

Squirrelpaw shrugged. "No harm in trying." With a flick of her tail, she stalked off to find Cinderpelt.

Brambleclaw headed for the elders' den, which was in a patch of grass sheltered by a fallen tree. The tree was a burned-out shell; Brambleclaw could still scent the acrid tang from the fire that had swept through the camp more than four seasons ago, when he was only a kit. But the grass had grown up again around the tree trunk, thick and luxuriant, making a comfortable home for the elderly cats whose service to the Clan was done.

When he pushed his way through the grasses he found the elders sunning themselves in the small, flattened clearing. Dappletail, the oldest cat in ThunderClan, was curled up asleep, her patchy tortoiseshell pelt rising and falling with each breath. Frostfur, a still beautiful white queen, was dabbing lazily at a beetle in the grass. Speckletail and Longtail were crouched together as if they were in the middle of a good gossip. Brambleclaw felt the familiar jolt of sympathy when he looked at Longtail; the pale tabby tom was still a young warrior, but his eyesight had begun to fail so that he could no longer fight or hunt for himself.

"Hi, there, Brambleclaw." Longtail's head swung around as Brambleclaw entered the clearing, his jaws parted to take in the newcomer's scent. "What can we do for you?"

"I've come to help Squirrelpaw," Brambleclaw explained. "Dustpelt sent her to look after you today."

Speckletail broke into rasping laughter. "I heard she went missing. The whole camp was in an uproar, looking for her. But I knew she'd just have gone off by herself."

"She tagged onto the dawn patrol," Brambleclaw meowed.

Before he could say any more, there was the sound of another cat pushing through the grasses, and Squirrelpaw appeared. She had a twig clamped in her jaws; hanging from it was a ball of moss soaked in mouse bile. Brambleclaw wrinkled his nose at the bitter scent.

"Right, who's got ticks?" Squirrelpaw mumbled around the twig.

"You're supposed to look for them yourself," Brambleclaw pointed out.

Squirrelpaw shot him a glare.

"You can start with me," Frostfur offered. "I'm sure there's one on my shoulder, just where I can't get at it."

Squirrelpaw padded over to the she-cat, parting her white fur with a forepaw and grunting when she discovered the tick. She dabbed at it with the damp moss until it dropped off; ticks obviously found mouse bile as disgusting as cats did, thought Brambleclaw.

"Don't worry, youngster," Speckletail mewed as Squirrelpaw went on searching Frostfur's pelt. "Your father was punished many a time when he was an apprentice. Even after he became a warrior. I never knew such a cat for getting into trouble, and look at him now!"

Squirrelpaw swung around to look at the elder, her green eyes sparkling, obviously begging for a tale.

"Well, now." Speckletail settled herself more comfortably in her grassy nest. "There was the time when Firestar and Graystripe were caught feeding RiverClan with prey from our own territory. . . ."

Brambleclaw had heard the story before, so he began to collect the elders' used bedding, rolling the moss together until he had gathered it up in a ball. When he took it out into the clearing he spotted Firestar emerging from the gorse tunnel, with

Sandstorm and Cloudtail behind him. Thornclaw was hurrying across to meet them from the other side of the clearing.

"Thank StarClan Squirrelpaw's safe," Firestar was mewing as Brambleclaw came into earshot. "One of these days she'll get into real trouble."

"She's in real trouble now," Sandstorm growled. "Just wait till I get my paws on her!"

"Dustpelt already did." Thornclaw gave a *mrrow* of amusement. "He sent her to help the elders for the rest of the day."

Firestar nodded. "Good."

"And there's something else," Thornclaw went on. "We found a badger up at Snakerocks, living in the cave where the dogs used to be."

"We think it might be the one that killed Willowpelt," Brambleclaw put in, setting his ball of moss down. "We've not seen any trace of a badger anywhere else in the forest."

Cloudtail let out a growl. "Oh, I *hope* it is. I'd give anything to get my claws on that brute."

Firestar swung around to face him. "You'll do nothing of the kind without orders. I don't want to lose more cats." He paused for a moment, then added, "We'll keep watch on it for a while. Pass the word around not to hunt at Snakerocks for the time being. With any luck, it will move on before leaf-bare, when prey gets scarce."

"And hedgehogs might fly," Cloudtail grumbled, stalking past Brambleclaw toward the warriors' den. "Badgers and cats don't mix, and that's the end of it."

CHAPTER 3

"Squirrelpaw is upset," Leafpaw remarked, watching her sister leave the medicine cat's clearing with the twig of mouse bile clenched in her jaws.

"She deserves to be." Cinderpelt glanced up from counting juniper berries. She spoke firmly, though not unsympathetically. "If apprentices think they can go off by themselves, without telling any cat, then where would we be?"

"I know." While Leafpaw prepared the mouse bile, she had listened to her sister raging about how unfair the punishment was. Squirrelpaw's anger churned deep within Leafpaw's belly, as if the air in the camp were water and her sister was sending ripples of cold frustration into the medicine cat's den. Ever since they were tiny kits they had always known what the other was feeling. Leafpaw remembered how her fur had tingled with excitement when Squirrelpaw was made apprentice, and how her sister had been unable to sleep on the night when Leafpaw had been apprenticed as a medicine cat at the Moonstone. Once she had felt an excruciating pain in her paw, and limped around the camp from sunhigh to sunset, until Squirrelpaw returned from a hunting patrol with a thorn driven deep into her pad.

Leafpaw shook her head as if she had a burr clinging to her pelt, trying to push away her sister's emotions and concentrate on her task of sorting yarrow leaves.

"Squirrelpaw will be fine," Cinderpelt reassured her. "It'll all be forgotten tomorrow. Now, did you get any of that mouse bile on your fur? If you did, you'd better go and wash it off."

"No, Cinderpelt, I'm fine." Leafpaw knew her voice was filled with the strain she was feeling, however hard she tried to hide it.

"Cheer up." Cinderpelt limped out of her den to join her apprentice, pressing her muzzle comfortingly against Leafpaw's side. "Do you want to come to the Gathering tonight?"

"May I?" Leafpaw spun to face her mentor. Then she hesitated. "Squirrelpaw won't be allowed to come, will she?"

"After today? Certainly not!" Cinderpelt's blue eyes glowed with understanding. "Leafpaw, you and your sister aren't kits anymore. And you have chosen a very different path from hers, to be a medicine cat. You will always be friends, but you can't do everything together, and the sooner you both accept that, the better."

Leafpaw nodded and bent over the yarrow leaves again. She struggled to calm her feelings of excitement over the Gathering, so that Squirrelpaw would not feel even more upset over being left out. Cinderpelt was right, but all the same she couldn't help wishing that she and Squirrelpaw had been able to attend the Gathering together.

❈   ❈   ❈

The full moon rode high in the sky as Firestar led the cats from ThunderClan up the slope toward Fourtrees. Padding along beside Cinderpelt, Leafpaw shivered with anticipation. This was the place where the territories of all four Clans joined together. At every full moon, the Clan leaders met here with their warriors under the sacred truce of StarClan to exchange news and make decisions that would affect the whole forest.

Firestar paused at the top of the slope and gazed down into the clearing. Leafpaw, near the back of the group, could only just see the tops of the four great oak trees that gave the clearing its name, but she could hear the sounds of many cats, and the breeze brought to her the mingled scents of ShadowClan, RiverClan, and WindClan.

Before her first Gathering, the only other cats Leafpaw had met were the three medicine cats from the other Clans, when she made her journey to Highstones at the half moon to be formally apprenticed. When she had attended a Gathering for the first time, she and Squirrelpaw had been overwhelmed by all the strangers, and had stayed close to their mentors. But this time Leafpaw felt more confident, and she was looking forward to meeting warriors and apprentices from other Clans.

Crouching in the undergrowth, she watched her father for the signal to move down into the clearing. Brambleclaw was standing just in front of her with Mousefur and Sorreltail. Leafpaw could see from the tautness in the young tabby's muscles that he was eagerly waiting for the Gathering to start, while Sorreltail's whole body quivered with excitement at the prospect of her first Gathering as a warrior. Farther ahead, Graystripe and Sandstorm were exchanging a few words, while Cloudtail shifted impatiently from paw to paw. Briefly Leafpaw felt a pang of sadness that Squirrelpaw was not there as well, but to her relief her sister had not minded too much about being left behind, saying that she was looking forward to a good night's sleep after caring for the elders all day.

At last Firestar raised his tail as the sign for his cats to move forward. Leafpaw sprang over the edge of the hollow and found herself racing down the slope just behind Brambleclaw, weaving her way through the bushes until she came out into the clearing.

The shimmering moonlight revealed a mass of cats, some already seated around the Great Rock in the center, others trotting across the clearing to greet cats they had not seen for a moon, or lying in the shelter of the bushes to gossip and share tongues. Brambleclaw slipped into the throng right away, and Cinderpelt went over to speak to Littlecloud, the ShadowClan medicine cat. Leafpaw hesitated, still a little daunted by the number of warriors in front of her, the unfamiliar scents, and the glowing of so many eyes that all seemed to be trained on her.

Then she caught sight of Graystripe with a group of cats who all had the scent of RiverClan. Leafpaw recognized a warrior with dense blue-gray fur whom they had met at the last Gathering, and remembered her name: Mistyfoot, the

RiverClan deputy. The two younger warriors were strangers to her, but Graystripe greeted them affectionately, pressing his muzzle against theirs.

Leafpaw was just wondering if she would be welcome to go and talk to them when Mistyfoot caught her eye and beckoned to her with her tail. "Hi—it's Leafpaw, isn't it? Cinderpelt's apprentice?"

"That's right." Leafpaw padded over. "How are you?"

"We're all well, and the Clan is thriving," Mistyfoot replied. "Have you met Stormfur and Feathertail?"

"My kits," Graystripe added proudly, though it was several moons since these strong cats had left the nursery.

Leafpaw touched noses with the young warriors, realizing that she should have guessed Stormfur was Graystripe's kin. The two cats had the same muscular bodies and long gray pelt. Feathertail's fur was a lighter silver-gray tabby; her blue eyes glowed with warmth and friendliness as she greeted Leafpaw.

"I know Cinderpelt well," she meowed. "She looked after me once when I was ill. You must be proud to be her apprentice."

Leafpaw nodded. "Very proud. But she knows so much, sometimes I wonder if I'll ever learn it all!"

Feathertail purred sympathetically. "I felt the same about becoming a warrior. I'm sure you'll be fine."

"You say the Clan's thriving, Mistyfoot," Graystripe meowed quietly, "but you're looking worried. Is there a problem?"

Now that he mentioned it, Leafpaw could see a glimmer of

uneasiness in the RiverClan deputy's eyes. Mistyfoot hesitated for a couple of heartbeats and then shrugged. "It's probably nothing but . . . Well, you'll hear about it soon enough when the Gathering starts."

As she spoke she glanced toward the Great Rock. Leafpaw saw that two cats were already waiting on the summit. Silhouetted against the shining circle of the full moon was Tallstar, leader of WindClan, easily recognizable by his long tail. Beside him stood Leopardstar, the RiverClan leader, staring around impatiently at the cats below. As Leafpaw watched, she saw Firestar leap up to join them.

"Where is ShadowClan's leader?" Leopardstar called out. "Blackstar, what are you waiting for?"

"Just coming." A heavy white tom with jet black paws shouldered his way through the cats not far from Leafpaw. He crouched at the base of the rock and sprang up to land lightly beside the RiverClan leader.

As soon as his paws touched the rock Leopardstar threw back her head and let out a yowl. At once the noise in the clearing died down and every cat turned to face the Great Rock. Feathertail settled down beside Leafpaw with a friendly glance, and Leafpaw found herself warming to the gentle young warrior.

"Cats of all Clans, welcome." Tallstar, the eldest of all the Clan leaders, moved to the front of the Great Rock, raising his voice to address the assembled cats. Glancing at his fellow leaders, he asked, "Who will speak first?"

"I will." Firestar stepped forward, his flame-colored pelt

turned silver in the moonlight.

Leafpaw listened as her father passed on the news about the badger at Snakerocks. It caused little stir; the creature was unlikely to move from there onto another Clan's territory as long as the forest was full of prey.

"And we have a new warrior," Firestar went on. "The ThunderClan apprentice Sorrelpaw has taken the warrior name of Sorreltail."

A murmur of appreciation rippled around the clearing; Sorreltail was popular and well-known among the other Clans, having been to several more Gatherings than the average apprentice. Leafpaw caught a glimpse of her sitting up very straight and proud beside Sandstorm.

Firestar stepped back and Blackstar took his place. He had taken over the leadership of ShadowClan after the death of Tigerstar. Under his leadership ShadowClan was trusted more than before, though it was still believed that cold winds blew over the hearts of the ShadowClan cats and darkened their thoughts.

"ShadowClan is strong and prey is plentiful," Blackstar announced. "The heat of greenleaf has dried up part of the marshes on our territory, but we still have plenty of water to drink."

His glance raked defiantly around the clearing, and Leafpaw reflected that even if ShadowClan had less than a single raindrop left in their territory, Blackstar was unlikely to admit as much to the Gathering.

Tallstar flicked his tail at Leopardstar, inviting her to

speak, but she drew back, leaving the next place to him. The WindClan leader hesitated for a moment, and Leafpaw saw that his eyes were clouded with worry.

"Blackstar spoke truly of the heat of greenleaf," he began. "It is many days since the forest saw rain, and the moorland streams on WindClan's territory have been scorched away completely this last quarter moon. We have no water at all."

"But the river borders your territory," a cat called out from the shadows beneath the Great Rock; craning her neck to see, Leafpaw recognized Russetfur, the ShadowClan deputy.

"The river runs through a deep, sheer-sided gorge for the whole length of our border," Tallstar replied. "It's too dangerous to go down there. Warriors have tried, and Onewhisker fell, though thank StarClan he was not hurt. Our kits and elders cannot manage the climb. They are suffering badly, and I fear that some of the younger kits might die."

"Can't your kits and elders chew grass for the moisture?" another cat suggested.

Tallstar shook his head. "The grass is parched. I tell you, there is no water anywhere on our territory." Turning with clear reluctance to the RiverClan leader, he meowed, "Leopardstar, in the name of StarClan I must ask that you let us come into your territory to drink from the river there."

Leopardstar came to stand beside the WindClan leader, her dappled golden fur rippling in the moonlight. "The water in the river is low," she warned. "We have not escaped the effects of this drought in my Clan."

"But there is far more than you need," Tallstar responded,

desperation creeping into his tone.

Leopardstar nodded. "That is true." Coming to the very edge of the rock, she looked down into the clearing and asked, "What do my warriors think? Mistyfoot?"

The RiverClan deputy rose to her paws, but before she could speak one of her Clan mates cried out, "We can't trust them! Let WindClan set one paw over our border, and they'll be taking our prey as well as our water."

Leafpaw could see the speaker, a smoky black tom, sitting a few foxlengths away, but she did not recognize him.

"That's Blackclaw," Feathertail murmured into her ear. "He's loyal to the Clan, but . . ." She trailed off, obviously unwilling to say anything bad about her Clan mate.

Mistyfoot turned and fixed Blackclaw with a clear blue stare. "You forget the times when RiverClan has needed help from other Clans," she meowed. "If they had not helped us then, we would not be here today." To Leopardstar she added, "I say we should allow this. We have water to spare."

The clearing fell silent as the cats waited for Leopardstar to make her decision. "Very well, Tallstar," she meowed at last. "Your Clan may enter our territory to drink from the river just below the Twoleg bridge. But you will come no farther, and you do not have leave to take prey."

Tallstar bowed his head, and Leafpaw heard the relief in his voice as he replied, "Leopardstar, RiverClan has our thanks, from the oldest elder to the youngest kit. You have saved our Clan."

"The drought will not last forever, and you will have water

in your territory soon. We will discuss this again at the next Gathering," Leopardstar meowed.

"I'm sure they will," Graystripe muttered darkly. "If I know Leopardstar, she'll make WindClan pay for that water somehow."

"Let us hope that StarClan have sent rain by then," Tallstar meowed, stepping back to let Leopardstar address the Gathering.

Leafpaw's interest quickened as she wondered if they were about to hear what had been troubling Mistyfoot earlier, but at first the RiverClan leader's news was unremarkable: a litter of kits had been born, and Twolegs had left rubbish by the river, attracting rats that had been killed by Blackclaw and Stormfur. Graystripe looked ready to burst with pride when his son was praised, while Stormfur scuffed the ground with his paws, his ears flat with embarrassment.

At last Leopardstar meowed, "Some of you have met our apprentices Hawkpaw and Mothpaw. They are now warriors, and will be known as Hawkfrost and Mothwing."

The cats around Leafpaw craned their necks to see the warriors the RiverClan leader had named; Leafpaw turned to look too, but she could not distinguish them among the throng. The traditional welcoming murmur for all new warriors broke out at the announcement, but to Leafpaw's surprise it was mingled with a few disconcerting growls, which she realized were coming from RiverClan cats.

Leopardstar glared down from the rock and stilled the noise with a flick of her tail. "Do I hear protests?" she spat out angrily. "Very well, I will tell you everything, to stop rumors flying once and for all.

"Six moons ago, at the beginning of newleaf, a rogue cat came to RiverClan, with her two surviving kits. Her name was Sasha, and the birth of her kits had weakened her so much that she needed help with hunting and caring for them. For a time she thought of joining the Clan, and we would have welcomed her as a warrior, but in the end she decided the warrior code was not the way of life for her. She left us, but her kits chose to stay."

A flood of protest surged up from the cats around the rock. One voice rose clear above the yowling. "Rogue cats? Taken into a Clan? Has RiverClan gone mad?"

Graystripe shot a questioning glance at Mistyfoot, who shrugged.

"They are good warriors," she murmured defensively.

Leopardstar made no attempt to quiet the clamor, only staring stonily down until it died away. "They are strong young cats and they have learned their warrior skills well," she meowed when she could make herself heard. "They have sworn to defend their Clan at the cost of their lives, just as all of you have sworn." With a glance at Blackstar, she added, "Were not some of ShadowClan's warriors rogues once?" Before he could reply, her gaze swiveled to Firestar. "And if a kittypet can become Clan leader, why should rogues not be welcome as warriors?"

"She has a point there," Graystripe admitted.

Firestar dipped his head toward Leopardstar. "True," he

mewed. "I will be glad to see these cats fulfill their promise as loyal members of their Clan."

Leopardstar nodded in reply; his words had clearly appeased her.

"Is that what was worrying you, Mistyfoot?" Graystripe asked. "It's no big deal, if they've settled down well."

"I know." Mistyfoot sighed. "And I know I'm the last cat to criticize any warrior for being born outside the Clan, but . . ."

"You do know that Mistyfoot's mother was your old leader, Bluestar?" Feathertail whispered to Leafpaw.

Leafpaw nodded.

"But Leopardstar hasn't told you everything," Mistyfoot went on. The blue-gray warrior broke off as Leopardstar began to speak again.

"Mothwing has chosen a special place within our Clan," she explained. "Mudfur, our medicine cat, is growing old, and the time has come for him to take an apprentice."

This time her voice was drowned completely by the howls of protest. The three other leaders on top of the Great Rock drew together for an anxious conference. Tallstar was clearly unwilling to speak out after Leopardstar had agreed to give him access to the river, and in the end it was Blackstar who replied. "I'm ready to admit that a rogue can learn enough of our code to become a warrior," he rasped. "But a medicine cat? What do rogues know of StarClan? Will StarClan even accept her?"

"*That's* what's bothering me," Mistyfoot muttered to Graystripe.

Leafpaw felt a tingle spread through her fur. She remembered her own conviction, back when she had been little more than a kit, that it was right for her to heal and comfort her Clan mates, and to interpret the signs of StarClan for them. *Had Mothwing felt the same?* Leafpaw wondered. *Could* she have felt the same, if she was not Clan-born? Even Yellowfang, the medicine cat before Cinderpelt, had been forest-born, though ThunderClan had not been the Clan of her birth.

Voices all around the clearing echoed Blackstar's questions. At the base of the rock an old brown tom heaved himself to his paws and waited for quiet; it was Mudfur, the RiverClan medicine cat.

As the noise died down, he raised his voice. "Mothwing is a talented young cat," he meowed. "But because she was born a rogue, I am waiting for a sign from StarClan that she is the right medicine cat for RiverClan. Once I have received that sign, I will take her to Mothermouth at the half-moon time. If I act without the blessing of StarClan, then you can all complain—but not until then." He flopped back down again, his whiskers twitching irritably.

The crowd had parted so that Leafpaw could make out the young cat crouched beside him. She was startlingly beautiful, with glowing amber eyes in a triangular face, and a long golden pelt with rippling tabby stripes.

"Is that Mothwing?" she whispered to Feathertail.

"That's right." Feathertail gave Leafpaw's ear a quick lick. "When the leaders have finished I'll take you to meet her, if you like. She's quite friendly, once you get to know her."

Leafpaw nodded eagerly. She was sure that Mudfur would soon receive the sign that Mothwing could be accepted. There were no other medicine cat apprentices in the forest, and she looked forward to making friends with another one—someone she could talk to about her training and all the mysteries of StarClan that were slowly being revealed to her.

The protests had died down after Mudfur's speech, and as Leopardstar had no more to say Tallstar brought the meeting to an end.

Feathertail leaped to her paws. "Come on, before we all have to leave."

As Leafpaw followed the RiverClan warrior across the clearing, she felt sympathy already for Mothwing. Judging by the response of the other cats tonight, it was easy to imagine the hard path that lay ahead of her before she would be fully accepted by her Clan.

As the Gathering drew to a close and the cats began to separate into their own Clans, Brambleclaw looked around for his sister, Tawnypelt. He had not seen her, and wondered if she had not been chosen to come this time.

He saw Firestar halt in front of a young tabby tom who was sitting near Mudfur, the RiverClan medicine cat.

"Congratulations, Hawkfrost," Firestar meowed. "I'm sure you'll make a fine warrior."

So that's Hawkfrost, Brambleclaw thought with interest, pricking up his ears. *The rogue-born RiverClan cat.*

"Thank you, Firestar," the new warrior replied. "I'll do my

best to serve my Clan."

"I'm sure you will." Firestar touched Hawkfrost on the shoulder with the tip of his tail in a gesture of encouragement. "Pay no attention to all the fuss. It'll all be forgotten in a moon."

He walked on, and Hawkfrost raised his head to look after him. Brambleclaw couldn't quite suppress a shiver when he glimpsed the tom's eyes, an eerie ice blue that seemed to stare through the ThunderClan leader as if he were made of smoke.

"Great StarClan!" he murmured aloud. "I wouldn't like to meet him in battle."

"Meet who?"

Brambleclaw spun around to see Tawnypelt standing behind him. "There you are!" he exclaimed. "I've been looking everywhere for you." Answering her question, he added, "Hawkfrost. He looks dangerous."

Tawnypelt shrugged. "So are you dangerous. I'm dangerous. It's what warriors are for. This whole full-moon thing could be broken by the slash of a claw—and has been before."

Brambleclaw nodded. "True. So how are you, Tawnypelt? How's life in ShadowClan?"

"Pretty good." Tawnypelt hesitated, looking uncharacteristically uncertain. "Look, there's something I wanted to ask you about." Brambleclaw sat down and pricked his ears expectantly. "The other night I had this weird dream. . . ."

"What?" He couldn't bite back the exclamation, and Tawnypelt's green eyes flew wide with alarm. "No, go on," he meowed, forcing himself to be calm. "Tell me about the dream."

"I was in a clearing in the forest," Tawnypelt explained, "but I didn't recognize exactly where it was. There was a cat sitting on a rock—a black cat; I think it was Nightstar. You know, ShadowClan's leader before our father? I . . . I guess if StarClan were going to send a cat to ShadowClan, it wouldn't be Tigerstar."

"What did he say to you?" Brambleclaw asked hoarsely, already knowing what his sister's answer would be.

"He told me that there was some great trouble coming to the forest, and a new prophecy had to be fulfilled. I had been chosen to meet with three other cats at the new moon, and listen to what midnight would tell us."

Brambleclaw stared at her, his fur crawling with ice.

"What's the matter?" Tawnypelt asked. "Why are you looking like that?"

"Because I had exactly the same dream, except that the cat who spoke to me was Bluestar."

Tawnypelt blinked and her brother saw a shiver pass through her tortoiseshell fur. At last she meowed, "Have you told any other cat about your dream?"

Brambleclaw shook his head. "I didn't know what to make of it. To be honest, I thought it was due to something I ate. I mean, why would StarClan send a vision like that to me, instead of to Firestar or Cinderpelt?"

"I thought the same," his sister agreed. "And I expected the other three cats to be from ShadowClan, so when no other cat mentioned it . . ."

"I know, me too. I thought they would be from Thunder-Clan. But it looks as if we were wrong."

Brambleclaw glanced around the clearing. The Gathering was thinning out as cats began to leave, and in spite of the protests over Hawkfrost and Mothwing the general mood was good-humored. No other cats looked as if they had received doom-laden dreams. What possible trouble could be coming—and if it did, what could he and Tawnypelt do about it?

"What do you think we should do now?" Tawnypelt echoed his thoughts.

"If the dream was true, then two other cats should have had it," Brambleclaw replied. "It makes sense that there would be one from each of the other two Clans. We should try to find out who."

"Oh, yes." Tawnypelt sounded scornful. "Are you going to walk into WindClan or RiverClan territory and ask every cat if they had a weird dream? I'm not. They would think we were mad, if they didn't claw our ears off first."

"What do you suggest, then?"

"We're all supposed to meet at the new moon," Tawnypelt mewed thoughtfully. "Nightstar didn't say where, but it must be here at Fourtrees. There isn't anywhere else where cats from four different Clans can get together."

"So you think we should come here at the new moon?"

"Unless you can think of a better idea."

Brambleclaw shook his head. "I only hope the other cats do the same. If . . . if the dream is real, of course."

He broke off as he heard a cat calling his name, and turned to see Firestar standing a short distance away, with the other ThunderClan cats gathered around him. "It's time to go," Firestar said.

"Coming!" Turning back to Tawnypelt he meowed urgently, "At the new moon, then. Say nothing to any cat. And trust StarClan the others will come."

Tawnypelt nodded and slipped into the bushes, following her Clan mates. Brambleclaw hurried over to join Firestar, hoping that his shock and fear did not show on his face. He had tried to forget his dream, but if Tawnypelt had dreamed it as well, he had no choice but to take it seriously. Trouble was coming, and he did not know what to do about it, nor understand how midnight could tell him anything.

Oh, StarClan, he mewed silently. *I hope you know what you're doing!*

CHAPTER 4

☘

Brambleclaw emerged from the warriors' den and glanced around the clearing. Another quarter moon had passed, and still there was no rain. Over all the forest, the air was hot and heavy. The streams near the camp had dried up, so the Clan had to travel to the stream that flowed past Fourtrees when they needed water. Luckily it ran deep through the rocky soil, and flowed even in the driest greenleaf.

Ever since the Gathering Brambleclaw's sleep had been disturbed, and when he woke each morning he struggled with the foreboding that something terrible had happened to the camp during the night. But everything seemed as peaceful as it had been the day before. This morning, Whitepaw and Shrewpaw were practicing their fighting moves outside the apprentices' den. Mousefur emerged from the gorse tunnel with a squirrel clamped in her jaws, followed by her apprentice, Spiderpaw, and Rainwhisker, who also carried fresh-kill. Firestar and Graystripe were talking together at the base of the Highrock, with Squirrelpaw and Dustpelt listening close by.

Firestar beckoned Brambleclaw over with his tail. "Are you up for an extra patrol?" he asked. "I want to check the border with ShadowClan, in case they get the idea of coming across here to find water."

"But Blackstar said that his Clan has all the water they need," Brambleclaw reminded him.

Firestar's ears twitched. "True. But we don't necessarily believe what Clan leaders say at a Gathering. Besides, I've never trusted Blackstar. If he thinks we have richer prey in our territory, he'll send warriors in to help themselves, for sure."

Graystripe growled agreement. "ShadowClan have been quiet for too many moons. If you ask me, it's about time they started making trouble."

"I just thought—" Brambleclaw stopped, embarrassed to be seen objecting to his leader's order, and amazed that he could see a possibility Firestar didn't seem to have considered.

"Go on," Firestar prompted.

Brambleclaw took a deep breath. He couldn't get out of this now, in spite of the green glare that Squirrelpaw was giving him for daring to disagree with her father. "I just think that if there is trouble, it's more likely to come from WindClan," he ventured. "If their territory is as dry as Tallstar said, then they're bound to be short of prey."

"WindClan!" Squirrelpaw burst out. "Brambleclaw, are you completely mouse-brained? RiverClan gave WindClan permission to drink at the river, so if they steal prey from anywhere they'll steal it from RiverClan."

"And that strip of RiverClan territory is really narrow between the river and our border," Brambleclaw retorted. "If

WindClan do hunt, the prey could easily cross into our territory."

"You think you're so clever!" Squirrelpaw sprang to her paws, her fur bristling. "Firestar ordered you to check the ShadowClan border, so you should do what you're told."

"Of course, you've never disobeyed a warrior, have you?" Dustpelt put in dryly.

Squirrelpaw ignored her mentor. "ShadowClan have always caused trouble," she persisted. "But we're friends with WindClan now."

Brambleclaw found himself getting angrier and angrier. Of course he didn't want to question Firestar's authority. Firestar was the hero who had saved the forest from the terrible ambitions of Tigerstar and the rogue cats who followed him. There would never be another cat like him. Yet Brambleclaw really believed that ThunderClan should take a possible threat from WindClan seriously. He would have liked to discuss it properly with Firestar, but that was impossible when Squirrelpaw insisted on arguing with everything he said.

"You're the one who thinks she knows it all," he spat, taking a step toward her. "Will you just listen for one moment?"

He ducked to avoid her paw as she lashed at him, claws unsheathed, and his last scrap of self-control deserted him. Falling into a crouch, he got ready to spring at her, his tail twitching back and forth. If Squirrelpaw wanted a fight, she could have one!

But before either of the young cats could attack, Firestar

pushed in between them. "That's enough!" he snarled.

Brambleclaw froze in dismay. Straightening up, he gave his chest an anxious lick and murmured, "Sorry, Firestar."

Squirrelpaw stayed silent, giving him a mutinous glare, until Dustpelt prompted her. "Well?"

"Sorry," Squirrelpaw muttered, and instantly spoiled her apology by adding, "But he's still a mouse-brain."

"Actually, I think he's got a point, don't you?" Dustpelt meowed to Firestar. "I agree that ShadowClan have always been trouble and always will be, but if WindClan happen to spot a juicy vole or a squirrel on our side of the border, don't you think they might be tempted?"

"You could be right," Firestar conceded. "In that case, Brambleclaw, you'd better take a patrol up the RiverClan border as far as Fourtrees. Dustpelt, you and Squirrelpaw can go as well." His eyes narrowed as he glanced from his daughter to Brambleclaw and back again. "And you *will* get along with each other, or I'll want to know why."

"Yes, Firestar," Brambleclaw replied, relieved that he had gotten off so lightly for nearly flattening Squirrelpaw.

"That's two patrols, then," Graystripe mewed cheerfully. "I'll find some more cats to go with me up the ShadowClan side." He jumped to his paws and vanished into the warriors' den.

Firestar nodded to Dustpelt, giving him authority over the patrol, and padded away to his den on the other side of the Highrock.

"Right, let's go," meowed Dustpelt. He set off toward the

gorse tunnel, only to glance back at Squirrelpaw, who had not moved. "What's the matter now?"

"It's not fair," Squirrelpaw muttered. "I don't want to patrol with *him*."

Brambleclaw rolled his eyes, but had the sense not to start their quarrel again.

"Then you shouldn't have said what you did," Dustpelt told his apprentice. Pacing back, he stood over her and gazed sternly down at her. "Squirrelpaw, sooner or later you must learn there are times to speak, and times to be silent."

Squirrelpaw heaved a noisy sigh. "But it seems like it's *always* time to be silent."

"There, you've got the idea." Dustpelt flicked her ear with his tail, and Brambleclaw caught a glimpse of the affection there was between mentor and apprentice. "Come on, both of you. We'll renew the scent markings, and with any luck we'll come across a mouse or two while we're out."

Squirrelpaw recovered her good temper when she caught a plump vole at Sunningrocks. Brambleclaw had to admit that she was an efficient hunter, patiently stalking her prey and pouncing on it to dispatch it with one blow of her paw.

"Dustpelt, I'm *starving*," she announced. "May I eat it?"

Her mentor hesitated for a heartbeat and then nodded. "The Clan has been fed," he replied. "And this isn't a hunting patrol."

Squirrelpaw shot a glance at Brambleclaw as she crouched over the fresh-kill and took an eager bite. "Mmm . . .

delicious," she mumbled. Then she stopped and nudged the remains of the vole toward Brambleclaw. "Want some?"

Brambleclaw was on the brink of telling her that he could catch his own prey until he realized that Squirrelpaw was trying to make friends again. "Thanks," he meowed, taking a bite.

Dustpelt leaped down from the top of the rock. "When you've quite finished stuffing yourselves . . ." he began. "Squirrelpaw, what can you scent?"

"Apart from vole, you mean?" Squirrelpaw mewed cheekily. Springing to her paws, she tasted the air. The breeze was blowing from RiverClan territory, and she soon replied, "RiverClan cats—strong and fresh."

"Good." Dustpelt looked pleased. "A patrol just went by. Nothing to do with us."

And no sign of WindClan, Brambleclaw commented to himself as they moved off again. Not that this meant his suspicions were wrong—he did not expect to see any of their cats this far downstream, the whole length of ThunderClan territory away from their own border.

As they drew closer to Fourtrees and passed the Twoleg bridge, all three cats paused to scan the slope. The breeze had dropped and the air was still and heavy with the scent of cats.

"WindClan and RiverClan," Brambleclaw mewed quietly to Dustpelt.

The older warrior nodded. "But they're allowed to go down to the river," he reminded him. "There's no sign that they've crossed our border."

"So there!" Squirrelpaw couldn't resist adding.

Brambleclaw shrugged, telling himself that he would rather be proved wrong. He didn't *want* trouble with WindClan.

Dustpelt was just moving off again toward Fourtrees when Brambleclaw caught another scent—WindClan again, but much stronger and fresher than before. Not daring to call out, he signaled frantically to Dustpelt with his tail, angling his ears in the direction where he thought the scent was coming from. Dustpelt crouched down in the long grass and signaled to his companions to do the same.

Please, StarClan, Brambleclaw begged, *don't let Squirrelpaw make a smart remark!*

But the apprentice remained silent, flattening herself to the ground and staring at the clumps of bracken that Brambleclaw had indicated. For a while, the only sound was the slap and murmur of the river nearby. Then there was a dry, rustling sound, and a mottled brown cat peered out of the bracken before creeping into the open a couple of tail-lengths on the ThunderClan side of the border. Brambleclaw recognized Mudclaw, the WindClan deputy. He was followed by Onewhisker and a smallish dark gray cat Brambleclaw had never seen before—an apprentice, he guessed—carrying a vole in his jaws.

Glancing back, Mudclaw murmured, "Head for the border. I can smell ThunderClan."

"I'm not surprised," Dustpelt growled, rising up out of the grass.

Mudclaw recoiled and drew his lips back in a snarl. At

once Brambleclaw leaped up to stand beside his Clan mate, and Squirrelpaw dashed up to her mentor's other side.

"What are you doing on our territory?" Dustpelt demanded. "As if I need to ask."

"We're not stealing prey," Mudclaw retorted.

"Then what's that?" Squirrelpaw asked, flicking her tail toward the vole that the apprentice was carrying.

"It's not a ThunderClan vole," Onewhisker explained. An old friend of Firestar's, he looked thoroughly embarrassed to be caught like this on ThunderClan territory. "It ran across the border from RiverClan."

"Even if that's true, you're stealing it from RiverClan," Brambleclaw pointed out. "You're allowed to drink from the river, not to take prey."

The gray-black apprentice dropped the vole and launched himself across the grass at Brambleclaw. "Mind your own business!" he spat.

He barreled into Brambleclaw and knocked him over; Brambleclaw let out a surprised yowl as the apprentice's teeth closed in the loose skin on his neck. Twisting his body, he managed to score his claws down the other cat's shoulder, and felt strong hind paws scrabbling at his belly. With a screech of fury he tore his neck free and dived for his opponent's throat.

As his teeth found their mark, Brambleclaw caught a glimpse of Onewhisker aiming a blow with his paw. He braced himself to fight both cats at once, before he realized that the WindClan warrior had batted the apprentice away and was standing over him, rage smoldering in his eyes.

"That's enough, Crowpaw!" he snarled. "Attacking a ThunderClan warrior when we're trespassing on their territory? What next?"

Crowpaw shot him a furious look through narrowed eyes. "He called us thieves!"

"And he was right, wasn't he?" Onewhisker turned to Dustpelt, who was standing a few fox-lengths away. As Brambleclaw scrambled to his feet he saw that the Thunder-Clan warrior had thrust himself in front of Squirrelpaw, preventing her from joining in the fight.

"I'm sorry, Dustpelt," Onewhisker went on. "It is a RiverClan vole, and I know we shouldn't have taken it, but there's hardly any prey in our own territory. Our elders and kits are hungry, and—" He stopped as if he thought he had already said too much. "What will you do now?"

"The vole's between you and RiverClan," Dustpelt meowed coldly. "I see no need to tell Firestar about this—unless it happens again. Just get out of our territory, and stay out."

Mudclaw nudged Crowpaw to his paws. The WindClan deputy still looked furious at being found out, and Brambleclaw noticed that he did not add his apology to Onewhisker's. Without a word he headed for the border, with Onewhisker close behind him. Crowpaw hesitated; then with a defiant glance he snatched up the vole and streaked after his Clan mates.

"I suppose we'll never hear the last of *that*!" Squirrelpaw spat at Brambleclaw. Her eyes glittered with annoyance. "Happy now you've been proved right?"

"I didn't say a word!" Brambleclaw protested.

Squirrelpaw didn't reply, but stalked off with her tail in the air. Brambleclaw looked after her with a sigh. He would much rather the incident had never happened. His fur prickled with the sense of impending disaster. Clans were becoming so thirsty and desperate that even decent cats like Onewhisker were prepared to trespass, steal, and lie. Heat lay over the forest with the weight of a huge, choking pelt, and it seemed as if every living thing was waiting for a storm to break. Could this be the trouble that StarClan had foretold?

The next few days and nights, as the moon waned to the merest scratch in the sky, seemed never-ending to Brambleclaw. When he thought of what might happen at Fourtrees when he went to meet Tawnypelt, he felt every hair in his pelt rise up with dread. Would the other Clan cats come? And what exactly would be revealed at midnight? Perhaps StarClan themselves would come down and speak with them.

At last the night came when there was almost no moon at all, but the stars of Silverpelt glittered so brightly that Brambleclaw had no difficulty in finding his way through the gorse tunnel and up the ravine. Leaves rustled as he brushed through the undergrowth from one patch of shade to the next, trying to tread as lightly as if he were creeping up on a mouse. Other ThunderClan warriors might be out late, and Brambleclaw did not want to be seen, nor to explain where he was going. He had not told any cat about his dream, and he knew that Firestar would not approve of his going to meet with cats of other Clans at Fourtrees when he was not protected by the full-moon truce.

The air was cool now, but there was a dusty scent in the air, rising from the parched earth. Plants were drooping or lay withering on the ground. The whole forest cried out for rain like a starving kit, and if it did not come soon, it would not be only WindClan who were short of water.

When Brambleclaw reached Fourtrees the clearing was empty. The sides of the Great Rock glimmered with starshine, and the leaves of the four oak trees rustled gently overhead. Brambleclaw shivered. He was so used to seeing the hollow full of cats that it seemed more daunting than before: so much bigger, with so many unexplained shadows. He could almost imagine that he had stepped into the mystical world of StarClan.

He padded across the clearing and sat at the base of the Great Rock. His ears were pricked to catch the smallest sound, and every nerve from ears to tail-tip was stretched with anticipation. Who would the other cats be? As moments slipped by, his excitement was replaced by anxiety. Not even Tawnypelt had arrived. Perhaps she had changed her mind, or perhaps this was the wrong meeting place after all.

At last he saw movement in the bushes about halfway up the side of the hollow. Brambleclaw tensed. The breeze was blowing away from him, so he could not pick up the scent; from the direction it was coming it could have been either a RiverClan or WindClan cat.

He followed the movement with his eyes as far as a clump of bracken at the bottom of the slope. The fronds waved wildly, and a cat stepped into the clearing.

Brambleclaw stared, frozen for a heartbeat, then sprang to his paws, his neck fur bristling in fury.

"Squirrelpaw!"

CHAPTER 5

❧

Brambleclaw stalked stiff-legged across the clearing until he stood face to face with the apprentice. "Just what do you think you're doing here?" he hissed.

"Hi, Brambleclaw." Squirrelpaw tried to sound calm, but her sparkling eyes betrayed her excitement. "I couldn't sleep, and I saw you leaving, so I've been following you." She gave a little purr of delight. "I was good, wasn't I? You never knew I was there, all the way through the forest."

That was true, though Brambleclaw would have died rather than tell her he was impressed. Instead, he let out a low growl. For two mousetails he felt like springing at the ginger she-cat to claw the smug expression off her face. "Why can't you mind your own business?"

The she-cat narrowed her eyes. "It's any cat's business when a Clan warrior sneaks out of camp at night."

"I wasn't *sneaking*," Brambleclaw protested guiltily.

"Oh, no?" Squirrelpaw sounded scornful. "You leave camp, come straight up here to Fourtrees, and sit waiting for ages, looking like you expect every warrior in the forest to jump out at you. Don't tell me you're just enjoying the beautiful night."

"I don't have to tell you anything." Brambleclaw heard his voice grow desperate; all he wanted was to get rid of this annoying apprentice before any cats from other Clans arrived. She hadn't mentioned the dream, which meant she couldn't have had it as well, so she had no right to be here and find out the next part of the prophecy—if that was what was really going to happen. "This has got nothing to do with you, Squirrelpaw. Why don't you just go home?"

"No." Squirrelpaw sat down and curled her tail around her front paws, glaring at Brambleclaw with wide green eyes. "I'm not leaving until I find out what's going on."

Brambleclaw let out a snarl of sheer frustration, only to jump when a voice growled behind him, "What's *she* doing here?"

It was Tawnypelt, slipping out from behind the Great Rock. She padded across the clearing and narrowed her eyes at Squirrelpaw. "I thought we weren't going to tell any other cats?"

Brambleclaw felt his fur prickle. "I *didn't* tell her. She saw me leaving and followed me."

"And it's a good thing I did." Squirrelpaw stood up and met Tawnypelt's gaze, her ears flat against her head. "You creep out at night and come up here to meet a ShadowClan warrior! What's Firestar going to think about that when I tell him?"

Brambleclaw's belly lurched uncomfortably. Perhaps he ought to have told Firestar about the dream right from the start, but it was too late now.

"Listen," he meowed urgently. "Tawnypelt isn't just a ShadowClan warrior; she's my sister. You know that as well as any cat. We're not plotting anything."

"Then why all the secrecy?" Squirrelpaw demanded.

Brambleclaw was searching for a reply when Tawnypelt interrupted him, flicking her tail toward the slope. "Look."

Brambleclaw caught a glimpse of something gray moving among the bushes, and a heartbeat later Feathertail and Stormfur stepped into the clearing. They glanced around warily, but as soon as Feathertail spotted the other cats she raced across the clearing toward them.

"I was right!" she exclaimed, skidding to a halt in front of Brambleclaw and the two she-cats. Her eyes widened, beginning to look puzzled and a little daunted. "Did you have the dream as well? Is it the four of us?"

"Tawnypelt and I have had it," Brambleclaw replied, at the same moment Squirrelpaw asked, "What dream?"

"The dream from StarClan, telling us that there's trouble ahead." Feathertail sounded more uncertain still, and her gaze flicked tensely from cat to cat.

"Did you both have the dream?" Brambleclaw asked, glancing at Stormfur as the RiverClan warrior caught up with his sister.

Stormfur shook his head. "No, only Feathertail."

"It scared me so much," Feathertail confessed. "I couldn't eat or sleep for thinking about it. Stormfur knew something was wrong, and he pestered me so much that I told him what I'd dreamed. We decided that I should come to Fourtrees tonight, at the new moon, and Stormfur wouldn't let me come by myself." She gave her brother's ear a friendly lick. "He . . . he didn't want me to be in danger. But I'm not, am I?

I mean, we all know each other."

"Don't be so quick to trust every cat," Stormfur growled. "I don't like meeting cats from other Clans in secret like this. It's not what the warrior code tells us."

"But we have each had a message from StarClan, telling us to come," Tawnypelt pointed out. "Bluestar visited Brambleclaw, and Nightstar came to me."

"And I saw Oakheart," Feathertail meowed. "He said great trouble was coming to the forest, and I would have to meet with three other cats at the new moon to hear what midnight tells us."

"I was told that, too," Tawnypelt confirmed. With a twitch of her ears at Stormfur she added, "I don't much like it either, but we should wait and see what StarClan want."

"At midnight, I suppose," Stormfur meowed, glancing up at the stars. "It must be nearly that now."

Brambleclaw's heart sank as he noticed Squirrelpaw's eyes getting wider and wider. "You mean that StarClan told all of you to meet here?" the young she-cat burst out. "And they say there's trouble coming? What kind of trouble?"

"We don't know," Feathertail replied. "At least, Oakheart didn't tell me. . . ." She trailed off, looking flustered, but Brambleclaw and Tawnypelt shook their heads to show that their dream-cats hadn't shared this with them either.

Stormfur's eyes narrowed. "Your Clan mate hasn't had the dream," he mewed to Brambleclaw. "What's she doing here?"

"You didn't have it either." Squirrelpaw wasn't afraid to

stand up to the RiverClan warrior. "I've as much right to be here as you."

"Except I didn't invite you," Brambleclaw growled.

"Chase her off, then," Tawnypelt suggested. "I'll help."

Squirrelpaw took a step toward the ShadowClan warrior, her fur fluffed out and her tail bristling. "Just lay one paw on me . . ."

Brambleclaw sighed. "If we chase her off now she'll go straight to Firestar," he meowed. "She's heard pretty much everything, so she might as well stay."

Squirrelpaw gave a disdainful sniff and sat down again. She drew her tongue down her paw and calmly began to wash her face.

"Honestly, Brambleclaw," Tawnypelt growled. "You should have been more careful. Letting an apprentice track you!"

"What's going on?" A new voice came from behind them, high-pitched and aggressive. "This can't be right—Deadfoot said there were only supposed to be four of us."

Brambleclaw jumped and looked around. His eyes narrowed into a furious glare as he recognized the cat with smoky gray-black fur, lean limbs, and small, neat head. "You!" he spat.

Standing a couple of fox-lengths away was the WindClan apprentice Crowpaw, who had trespassed on ThunderClan territory and stolen a vole.

"Yes, me," he retorted, his fur bristling as if at any moment he might spring and finish off the fight.

Tawnypelt pricked her ears. "This is a WindClan cat, right?" She looked Crowpaw up and down dismissively.

"Undersized specimen, isn't he?"

"He's an apprentice," Brambleclaw explained, as Crowpaw drew his lips back in a snarl. "His name's Crowpaw."

He glanced at Squirrelpaw, willing her to keep silent about the incident with the vole. He wanted WindClan brought to justice over the prey stealing, but properly, at a Gathering, not by provoking a fight here. After all, what they were doing here was already a long way outside the warrior code. Squirrelpaw twitched the tip of her tail, but to Brambleclaw's relief she said nothing.

"You had the dream too?" Feathertail asked; Brambleclaw saw the anxiety beginning to fade from her blue eyes, as if she were drawing courage from a growing certainty that the dreams were true.

Crowpaw gave her a curt nod. "I spoke with our old deputy, Deadfoot," he meowed. "He told me to meet three other cats at the new moon."

"Then that's one cat from each Clan," replied Feathertail. "We're all here."

"Now we just have to wait for midnight," Brambleclaw added.

"Do you know what this is about?" Crowpaw turned his back on Brambleclaw and appealed directly to Feathertail.

"If it were *me*," Squirrelpaw meowed before Feathertail could reply, "I'd be a bit less quick to believe in these dreams. If there was really trouble on its way, do you think StarClan would come to you first, before the Clan leaders or medicine cats?"

"Then how do you explain it?" Brambleclaw asked, all the more defensive because he had felt exactly the same doubts that Squirrelpaw was voicing now. "Why else would we all have had the same dream?"

"Maybe you've all been stuffing yourselves with too much fresh-kill?" Squirrelpaw suggested.

Crowpaw whipped around with an angry hiss. "Who asked you, anyway?" he demanded.

"I can say what I like," Squirrelpaw shot back at him. "I don't need your permission. You're not even a warrior."

"Nor are you," the gray-black cat snapped. "What are you doing here, anyway? You didn't have the dream. No cat wants you here."

Brambleclaw opened his jaws to defend Squirrelpaw. Even though he had been annoyed with her for following him, it was no business of Crowpaw's to tell her what to do. Then he realized that Squirrelpaw wouldn't thank him; with her ready tongue she was quite capable of defending herself.

"I don't see them falling over themselves to welcome you, either," she growled.

Crowpaw spat, his ears flattened and his eyes glaring fury.

"There's no need to get angry," Feathertail began.

The small black cat ignored her. Lashing his tail from side to side, he sprang at Squirrelpaw. An instant later Brambleclaw leaped too, barreling into him and rolling him over before his claws could score down her flank.

"Back off," he hissed, pinning Crowpaw down with a paw on his neck. He could hardly believe that the WindClan apprentice would start a fight now, when they were waiting for a message from StarClan, and linked in the prophecy through their dreams. If StarClan had really chosen them for a mysterious destiny, they would surely not fulfill it by shedding one another's blood.

The light of battle died from Crowpaw's eyes, though he still looked furious. Brambleclaw let him get up; he turned his back and started to groom his ruffled fur.

"Thanks for nothing!" Brambleclaw was hardly surprised to see that Squirrelpaw was glaring at him with just as much hostility as Crowpaw. "I can fight my own battles."

Brambleclaw let out a hiss of exasperation. "You can't start fighting here. There are more important things to think about. And if these dreams are true, then StarClan wants the Clans to work together."

He glanced around the clearing, half hoping that a cat from StarClan would appear to tell them what they were supposed to be doing, before a fight broke out that he couldn't stop. But Silverpelt shone on a clearing empty of any cats but themselves. He could smell nothing but the ordinary night scents of growing plants and distant prey, and hear nothing but the sigh of wind through the branches of the oaks.

"It must be after midnight now," Tawnypelt meowed. "I don't think StarClan are coming."

Feathertail turned to look all around the clearing, her blue eyes once more wide with anxiety. "But they have to come! Why did we all have the same dream, if it wasn't true?"

"Then why is nothing happening?" Tawnypelt challenged her. "Here we are, meeting at the new moon, just as StarClan told us. We can't do any more."

"We were fools to come." Crowpaw gave them all another unfriendly stare. "The dreams meant nothing. There's no prophecy, no danger—and even if there were, the warrior code should be enough to protect the forest." He began to stalk across the clearing to the slope on the WindClan side, and his last words were flung over his shoulder. "I'm going back to camp."

"Good riddance!" Squirrelpaw yowled after him.

He ignored her, and a moment later had disappeared into the bushes.

"Tawnypelt's right. Nothing is going to happen," Stormfur meowed. "We might as well go too. Come on, Feathertail."

"Just a minute," mewed Brambleclaw. "Maybe we got it wrong—maybe StarClan was angry because of the fighting. We can't just pretend that nothing has happened, that none of us had those dreams. We ought to decide what we're going to do next."

"What can we do?" Tawnypelt asked. She flicked her tail toward Squirrelpaw. "Maybe she's right. Why would StarClan choose us and not our leaders?"

"I don't know, but I think they *have* chosen us," Feathertail meowed gently. "But somehow we haven't understood properly. Maybe they'll send us all another dream to explain."

"Maybe." Her brother didn't sound convinced.

"Let's all try to come to the next Gathering," Brambleclaw suggested. "There might be another sign by then."

"Crowpaw won't know to meet us there," Feathertail murmured, glancing at the spot in the bushes where the

WindClan apprentice had vanished.

"No loss," Stormfur remarked, but at his sister's anxious look he added, "We can keep an eye open for him when he comes to the river to drink. If we see him we'll pass the message on."

"All right, that's decided," meowed Tawnypelt. "We meet at the Gathering."

"And what do we tell our Clans?" Stormfur asked. "It's against the warrior code to hide things from them."

"StarClan never said we had to keep the dream secret," Tawnypelt put in.

"I know, but . . ." Feathertail hesitated and then went on, "I just feel it's wrong to talk about it."

Brambleclaw knew Stormfur and Tawnypelt were right; he was already feeling guilty that he had said nothing about his dream to Firestar and Cinderpelt. At the same time he shared Feathertail's instinct to keep silent.

"I'm not sure," he meowed. "Suppose our leaders forbade us to meet again? We could end up having to choose between obeying them or obeying StarClan." Aware of uneasy glances from the others, he went on earnestly; "We don't know *enough* to tell them. Suppose we wait until the next Gathering, at least. We might have other signs by then that will explain it all to us."

Feathertail agreed at once, obviously relieved, and after a pause Stormfur gave a small, reluctant nod.

"But only until the next Gathering," Tawnypelt meowed. "If we haven't found out any more by then, I'll have to tell Blackstar." She gave a huge stretch, her back arched and her forepaws extended. "Right, I'm off."

Brambleclaw touched noses with her in farewell, breathing in her familiar scent. "It must mean something that we were both chosen—brother and sister," he murmured.

"Maybe." Tawnypelt's green eyes were unconvinced. "The other cats aren't kin, though." Her tongue rasped once over Brambleclaw's ear in a rare gesture of affection. "StarClan willing, I'll see you at the Gathering."

Brambleclaw watched her bound across the clearing, before turning to Squirrelpaw. "Come on," he meowed. "I've things I want to say to you."

Squirrelpaw shrugged and padded away from him, toward ThunderClan territory.

Saying good night to Feathertail and Stormfur, Brambleclaw headed up the slope after her. When he emerged from the hollow a hot, clammy breeze was blowing into his face, ruffling his fur and turning back the leaves on the trees. Clouds had begun to mass above his head, cutting off the light of Silverpelt. The forest was silent and the air felt heavier than ever. Brambleclaw guessed that the storm was on its way at last.

As he began trotting down toward the stream, Squirrelpaw paused to wait for him. Her fur was relaxed on her spine now, and her green eyes shone.

"That was *exciting!*" she exclaimed. "Brambleclaw, you have to let me come with you to the next meeting, *please!* I never thought I'd be part of a prophecy from StarClan."

"You're not part of it," Brambleclaw meowed sternly. "StarClan didn't send *you* the dream."

"But I know about it, don't I? If StarClan didn't want me involved, they would have kept me away from Fourtrees somehow." Squirrelpaw faced him, forcing him to halt, and gazed at him with pleading eyes. "I could help. I'd do everything you told me."

Brambleclaw couldn't keep back a puff of laughter. "And hedgehogs might fly."

"No, I will, I promise." Her green eyes narrowed. "And I wouldn't tell any cat. You can trust me on that, at least."

For a few heartbeats Brambleclaw returned her gaze. He knew that if she told Firestar what had happened he would be in deep trouble. Her silence must be worth something.

"Okay," he agreed at last. "I'll let you know if anything else happens, but *only* if you keep your mouth shut."

Squirrelpaw's tail went straight up and her eyes blazed with delight. "Thank you, Brambleclaw!"

Brambleclaw sighed. Somehow he could sense that he would be in even deeper trouble because of the bargain he had just made. He followed Squirrelpaw into the shadows that lay thickly under the trees, feeling a shiver of fear at the thought of what might be watching them, unseen. But the forest around him was no darker or more threatening than the half-offered prophecy. If the trouble that was coming to the forest was as serious as Bluestar had said, then Brambleclaw was in great danger of making a fatal mistake simply because he did not know enough.

CHAPTER 6

All night Leafpaw's sleep had been disturbed by strange, vivid dreams. At first she thought she was following a scent trail toward Fourtrees, running through the forest along the invisible path. Then the dream changed and she felt the fur on her neck and shoulders rise as if she confronted an enemy, with battle only a heartbeat away. The threat of danger faded, but now she grew colder and colder, until she jerked awake to find the clump of ferns where she slept heavy with raindrops, and rain drumming softly on the forest all around her.

Scrambling to her paws, she dashed across the small, fern-enclosed clearing and took shelter just inside Cinderpelt's den. The medicine cat was sleeping soundly in her mossy nest beside the back wall and did not move when Leafpaw came in, shaking water from her pelt.

The young apprentice blinked and yawned as she gazed out into the clearing. Above her head she could just make out the black outlines of trees against a sky that was growing gray with the first light of dawn. Part of her rejoiced that the long, dry spell was coming to an end with this downpour that the forest needed so badly. The rest of her could not help feeling troubled about what her dreams might mean. Was StarClan sending her a sign? Or had she somehow picked up thoughts from Squirrelpaw? This would not be the first time she had known what her sister was doing without being told.

Leafpaw let out a long sigh. Little as she liked the idea, she was almost convinced that Squirrelpaw must have slipped out of camp to hunt by night, sending Leafpaw the images of running through the forest. There was no way she had been on an official patrol. What sort of trouble would Squirrelpaw be in if Firestar found out?

As Leafpaw crouched there, she realized that the rain was easing off and the clouds were turning pale yellow and thinning out. With a last glance at the sleeping Cinderpelt she slipped outside again, ignoring the water that soaked her fur as she pushed through the fern tunnel into the main clearing. Perhaps if she could find Squirrelpaw quickly, she could help her hide whatever she had been up to.

But when she reached the clearing there was no sign of her sister. The other three apprentices had emerged from their den and were lapping eagerly at a shallow puddle that had pooled on the sun-scorched earth. Ferncloud's three kits crept out of the nursery, their eyes huge as they examined this strange new water that had fallen from the sky. Ferncloud looked on with pride in her eyes as they dabbed at it, squealing with excitement as shining drops spun away from their paws.

Leafpaw watched them for a moment, then whirled around when she saw movement at the mouth of the gorse tunnel. *An early hunting patrol,* she wondered, *caught out by the rain? Or could it be Squirrelpaw, returning after her illicit outing?*

Then she realized that the newcomer did not have ThunderClan scent. She drew breath to yowl a warning to the Clan before she recognized the sleek black pelt: it was Ravenpaw, who had once been a ThunderClan apprentice but now lived as a loner in a Twoleg barn on the edge of WindClan territory. Leafpaw had met him once before, on her journey to Highstones with Cinderpelt. Living so close to Twolegs, Ravenpaw hunted mainly by night and was perfectly comfortable with traveling through the forest in pitch dark. He might be just the cat to tell Leafpaw if there had been a ThunderClan apprentice hunting in the forest before dawn.

The visitor crossed the clearing slowly, skirting the deepest puddles and delicately picking up his paws to shake off the water. "Hi—it's Leafpaw, isn't it?" Ravenpaw meowed, pricking his ears toward her. "That was some storm! I'd have been soaked through if I hadn't managed to shelter in a hollow tree. Still, the forest needs the rain."

Leafpaw returned his greeting politely. She was trying to find the right words to ask him if he had seen Squirrelpaw on his way to the camp, when a cheerful yowl interrupted her. "Hey, Ravenpaw!"

Whitepaw and Shrewpaw were bounding across the clearing toward them. Ferncloud's kits abandoned their raindrop games and scuttled after them.

The biggest of the three kits skidded to a halt in front

of Ravenpaw and took an enormous sniff. "New cat," she growled. "New scent."

The loner dipped his head in greeting, the tip of his tail flicking back and forth in amusement.

"Hollykit, this is Ravenpaw," Shrewpaw told her. "He lives on a Twoleg farm, and feasts on more mice than you three have seen in your life."

Hollykit's amber eyes grew huge. "*Every* day?"

"That's right," Whitepaw put in solemnly. "Every day."

"*I* want to go there," the little gray kit mewed. "Can we? Now?"

"When you're bigger, Birchkit," Ferncloud promised, coming up to join them. "Welcome, Ravenpaw. It's good to— Hollykit! Larchkit! Stop that at once!"

The two brown tabby kits had pounced on Ravenpaw's twitching tail, and were batting at it with outstretched paws. Ravenpaw winced. "Don't do that, little kits," he scolded gently. "It's my tail, not a mouse."

"Ravenpaw, I'm sorry," meowed Ferncloud. "They haven't learned how to behave properly yet."

"Don't worry, Ferncloud," Ravenpaw replied, though he drew his tail closely against his side, out of harm's way. "Kits will be kits."

"And these particular kits have been out for long enough." Ferncloud swished her tail around to gather the three kits together and herded them back toward the nursery. "Say good-bye to Ravenpaw now."

The kits mewed good-bye and scampered off.

"Can we do anything for you, Ravenpaw?" Whitepaw asked politely. "Would you like some fresh-kill?"

"No, I ate before I left home, thank you," the black cat replied. "I've come to see Firestar. Is he around?"

"I think he's in his den," Shrewpaw told him. "Shall I take you there?"

"No, I will," meowed Leafpaw. She was getting increasingly anxious to ask the loner if he had seen Squirrelpaw on his journey through the forest. Just then Thornclaw, Shrewpaw's mentor, emerged from the warriors' den. Leafpaw twitched her ears toward him. "Er . . . is your mentor looking for you?" she asked Shrewpaw.

As she spoke, Thornclaw called to Shrewpaw, and the apprentice dashed off with a quick word of farewell. Whitepaw also meowed her good-byes, and went over to join Brackenfur at the fresh-kill pile.

Suddenly the thorny branches that formed the gorse tunnel trembled, and relief flooded over Leafpaw as she watched Squirrelpaw emerge, dragging a rabbit behind her through the mud. Leafpaw had taken a couple of paces toward her before she remembered the Clan's visitor, and turned awkwardly back to him.

"That's your sister, isn't it?" Ravenpaw meowed. "Go and talk to her if you want. I can find my own way to Firestar's den."

Released, Leafpaw bounded toward her sister, who was heading for the fern tunnel. Catching sight of her, Squirrelpaw stopped to wait, dropping the rabbit at her paws; its fur was plastered with mud from being dragged across the clearing, and rain had flattened Squirrelpaw's own pelt against her flanks, but her eyes gleamed with triumph. "Not bad, is it?" she announced, nodding toward her prey. "It's for you and Cinderpelt."

"Where have you *been*?" Leafpaw hissed. "I've been worried sick about you."

"Why?" Squirrelpaw's green eyes looked injured. "Where did you think I had gone? I . . . I only slipped out to hunt when the rain started to ease off. And you might at least say thank-you!"

Snatching up the rabbit, she plunged into the ferns that led to the medicine cats' clearing without waiting for Leafpaw to respond. Leafpaw followed more slowly, not sure whether to be relieved or furious. She had the uneasy feeling that Squirrelpaw was lying to her, for the first time ever. If she had really picked up her sister's thoughts in her dream, then Squirrelpaw had done a lot more than just slip out of camp for a quick chase after a rabbit.

When she emerged into the clearing, she saw that Squirrelpaw had already dumped the rabbit at the mouth of Cinderpelt's den. Her sister gave it an admiring sniff and meowed, "You might at least say I did well to catch it." She still sounded indignant, but she didn't meet Leafpaw's gaze when she spoke.

"You did," Leafpaw admitted. "It's huge! Especially as you had such a disturbed night," she added more sharply.

Squirrelpaw froze; only her green eyes moved, flicking up

to rest on her sister's face. "Who says I did?"

"I know you did. You were awake nearly all night. What was the matter? It was more than a short hunt, I know that."

Squirrelpaw dropped her eyes to the ground. "Oh, I ate a frog late in the evening," she muttered. "It must have disagreed with me, that's all."

Leafpaw unsheathed her claws and dug them into the rain-softened earth. Inwardly she was fighting to stay calm. She *knew* that Squirrelpaw was lying to her, and part of her wanted to start wailing like a kit: *You're my sister! You should trust me!*

"Oh, a frog," she mewed. "You should have come to me for some herbs to chew."

"Yes, well . . ." Squirrelpaw scraped the earth with her one white paw. Leafpaw could see her discomfort in her flattened ears and the guilty look she shot at her, but didn't feel in the least bit sorry. Why was Squirrelpaw lying?

"I'm fine now," Squirrelpaw insisted. "It wasn't anything to make a fuss about."

She glanced around in relief as Cinderpelt appeared from the mouth of her den. Her smoky gray fur was ruffled, and she carried a leaf-wrapped packet in her jaws. "Fresh-kill, I see," she meowed, setting the packet down. "Squirrelpaw, that's a splendid rabbit! Thank you."

Squirrelpaw gave her shoulder a quick lick, her eyes glowing at the medicine cat's praise. But she still avoided her sister's gaze.

Cinderpelt picked up the packet again and padded unevenly across the clearing to set it down in front of Leafpaw.

Many seasons ago, when she was Firestar's apprentice, she had injured her hind leg in an accident on the Thunderpath. She had been unable to finish her warrior training, but while recovering in the care of Yellowfang, the ThunderClan medicine cat, she had found a new path to follow in the service of her Clan.

"Leafpaw, take that to Dappletail, please," Cinderpelt meowed. "It's poppy seed to help her sleep, because her teeth are aching so badly. Mind you tell her to go easy on it."

"Yes, Cinderpelt." Leafpaw picked up the packet and hurried out of the clearing, casting one last glance at her sister as she went. There was no chance to ask Squirrelpaw any more questions, and her sister was still refusing to look at her. Leafpaw felt every hair in her pelt prickle with foreboding as she wondered what could have happened to open up this gulf between them.

"Water! Help! Water everywhere! Swim!" Brambleclaw yowled, then choked as a sharp, salty wave filled his mouth, dragging at his fur and pulling him under. His paws worked frantically as he struggled to keep his head above the surface. He stretched up his neck, straining to find the line of reeds he expected to mark the opposite bank, but all he could see were endless, heaving, blue-green waves. On the horizon, he caught a glimpse of the sun sinking into the waves in a pool of flame, its dying rays tracing a path of blood that stretched toward him. Then his head went under and the cold salt water flooded into his mouth again.

I'm drowning! he wailed silently as he fought for his life. *StarClan help me!*

His head broke the surface and a strong current spun him around with his back legs dangling helplessly beneath him. Choking and gasping for air, he found himself gazing up at a sheer wall of smooth sand-colored rock. Had he been swept into the gorge? No, these cliffs were higher still. At their base, the waves sucked at a dark hole, edged by jagged rocks that made it look like a gaping mouth with teeth. Brambleclaw's terror increased as he realized that the swirling water was carrying him straight toward the stony jaws.

"No! No!" he yowled. "Help me!"

He kicked and thrashed in a panic but he was growing weaker and his sodden fur was dragging him down. The waves drove him onward, crashing against the rocks; now the black mouth loomed over him, spitting salty foam, as if it were about to swallow him alive. . . .

Then his eyes flew open, and there were leaves above him, not sheer cliffs, and he was supported by moss-cushioned sand rather than sinking in bottomless water. Brambleclaw lay shuddering with relief as he realized that he was lying in his nest in the warriors' den. The thunder of the waves became the rushing of wind in the branches above his head; water had dripped through the thick canopy of leaves and formed an icy trickle in his neck fur, and he knew the rain must have come at last. His throat was as sore as if he had swallowed a riverful of salty water, and his mouth was parched.

Brambleclaw sat up restlessly. Dustpelt lifted his head and muttered, "What's wrong with you? Can't you keep quiet and let the rest of us sleep?"

"Sorry," Brambleclaw meowed. He began grooming the moss out of his fur, his heart still thudding as if it were going to break out of his chest. He felt as limp and exhausted as if he had really been struggling to save himself in that strange salt water.

Gradually the strengthening of the light in the den told him that the sun had come out. He heaved himself to his paws and poked his head out between the branches, blinking as he looked for a puddle where he could quench his thirst.

A fresh breeze was driving the clouds away. In front of Brambleclaw the clearing was filled with pale yellow light from the rising sun, reflecting from puddles on the ground and water droplets hanging on every branch and frond of fern. The whole forest seemed to be drinking in the life-giving water, the trees lifting their dusty leaves to catch each sparkling drop.

"Thank StarClan!" Mousefur meowed as she pushed her way out of the den beside Brambleclaw. "I'd almost forgotten what rain smells like."

Brambleclaw staggered across the clearing to a puddle near the base of the Highrock, where he lowered his head and lapped, trying to wash the taste of salt from his mouth. He had never imagined that water could taste like that; like the other cats, he would sometimes lick salt from the surface of rocks, or taste it in the blood of prey, but the memory of drinking that salt-laden water made every hair on his pelt prickle.

A final gust of rain ruffled the pools of water and rinsed the sticky feel of salt from Brambleclaw's fur. Raising his head to enjoy the sharp, cold shower, he spotted Firestar emerging from his den under the Highrock and turning to speak to the cat who followed him out. Brambleclaw was surprised to see that the second cat was Ravenpaw.

"Twolegs are always doing strange things," Firestar was saying as they came into earshot. "I'm grateful that you came all this way to tell us, but I really don't think it's got anything to do with us."

Ravenpaw looked uneasy. "I know Twolegs often act without reason, but I've never seen anything like this. There are far more of them on the Thunderpath than before, walking along the edge with shiny, bright-colored pelts. And they have new kinds of monsters—huge ones!"

"Yes, Ravenpaw, so you said." Firestar sounded faintly impatient with his old friend. "But we haven't seen any of them in our territory. I'll tell you what. . . ." He paused to press his muzzle affectionately against Ravenpaw's side. "I'll tell the patrols to keep their eyes open for anything unusual."

Ravenpaw twitched the fur on his shoulders. "I suppose that's all you can do."

"And you could drop in on WindClan on your way home," Firestar suggested. "They're closer than we are to that part of the Thunderpath, so Tallstar ought to know if something strange is going on."

"Yes, Firestar, I'll do that."

"Wait a moment, I've got a better idea," meowed Firestar. "Why don't I come with you part of the way? I could take a patrol up to Fourtrees at the same time. Stay there, and I'll fetch Graystripe and Sandstorm." He bounded off into the warriors' den without waiting for Ravenpaw to reply.

When the Clan leader had gone, Ravenpaw caught sight of Brambleclaw and gave him a friendly nod. "Hi, how are you?" he meowed. "How's the prey running?"

"Fine. Everything's fine." Brambleclaw was aware that his voice still sounded shaky, and he wasn't surprised when Ravenpaw peered at him more closely.

"You look like you've been chased all night by a horde of badgers," the loner meowed. "Is anything the matter?"

"Nothing really . . ." Brambleclaw scuffled his paws on the ground. "I had a dream, that's all."

Ravenpaw's eyes were sympathetic. "Do you want to tell me about it?"

"It was nonsense really," Brambleclaw murmured. His ears filled again with the sound of the saltwater waves crashing and bellowing against the cliffs, and he suddenly found himself spilling everything to Ravenpaw: the vast expanse of water, the salt taste of it when it filled his mouth, the gaping black jaws in the cliff that had threatened to swallow him, and, most alarmingly of all, the sun sinking in a pool of bloodred fire. "That place can't be real," he finished. "I don't know why it's gotten to me like this. It's not like I don't have anything else to think about," he added grimly.

To his surprise, Ravenpaw did not leap in to agree that Brambleclaw had had a meaningless dream about a place that existed only in his troubled imagination. Instead, the black cat was silent for a long time, his eyes clouded with thought.

"Salt water, cliffs," he murmured. Then, "The place is real," he meowed. "I've heard of it before, though I've never seen it for myself."

"Real? Wh-what do you mean?" Brambleclaw stared at him, his fur standing on end.

"Rogue cats come to the Twoleg farm sometimes, when they have traveled far and are in need of shelter for the night and a spare mouse or two," Ravenpaw explained. "Cats who live toward the place where the sun sets. They have told Barley and me about a place where there is more water than you could possibly imagine, like a river that has only one bank, and it's too salty to drink. Every night it swallows the sun in a flash of fire, bleeding into the waves without a sound."

Brambleclaw shivered; the loner's words brought his dream back far too vividly for comfort. "Yes, I saw the place where the sun drowns. And the dark cave with teeth?"

"I can't tell you about that," Ravenpaw admitted. "But this dream must have been sent to you for a reason. Be patient, and perhaps StarClan will show you more."

"StarClan?" Brambleclaw felt his belly flip over.

"How could you dream of a place you have never seen unless StarClan willed it?" Ravenpaw pointed out.

Brambleclaw had to admit the logic in what the loner said.

"Say it was StarClan who sent me this dream about the sun-drown place," he began. "Do you think they could possibly be telling me to *go* there?"

Ravenpaw's eyes widened in surprise. "Go there? Why?"

"Well, I had another dream first," Brambleclaw explained uncomfortably. "I . . . I thought I met Bluestar in the forest. She told me about a new prophecy, that great trouble is com-ing to the forest. She said that I'd been chosen. . . ." He said nothing about the cats from the other Clans. Even though Ravenpaw lived outside the warrior code, he would not approve of meeting with the others in secret, as Brambleclaw had done. "Why me?" he finished in confusion. "Why not Firestar? He would know what to do."

The loner gazed at him solemnly for a long moment. "There was a prophecy once about Firestar, too," he meowed at last. "StarClan promised that fire would save the Clan, though they didn't say exactly how. Firestar never understood it, never knew the prophecy was about him, until Bluestar told him just before she died."

Brambleclaw met his gaze and could find nothing to say. He had heard about the fire prophecy—every Clan cat had, as part of the stories told about their leader—but it had never occurred to him that Firestar might once have felt as con-fused as he felt now.

"There was a time when Firestar was a young warrior just like you," Ravenpaw went on as if he could read Brambleclaw's thoughts. "He often wondered if he was making the right decisions. Oh, yes, he's a hero now, he saved the forest, but to begin with, his task looked as impossible as yours—whatever it might be. His prophecy has been fulfilled," he added. "Maybe it's your time now. Remember that StarClan don't like to make things obvious. They send us prophecies, but they never tell us exactly what we should do. They expect us to show courage and loyalty to achieve what has to be done, just as Firestar did."

Brambleclaw was puzzled by the reverence with which Ravenpaw, a loner who chose not to dwell in a Clan, spoke of StarClan. Disconcertingly, the black cat murmured, "Just because I live outside the forest doesn't mean that I reject the warrior code. It is a noble path for cats to walk, and I would defend it as willingly as any warrior."

He gave Brambleclaw a friendly nod as Firestar returned with Graystripe and Sandstorm. Brambleclaw murmured farewell and watched the four cats pad across the clearing and vanish into the gorse tunnel.

If the dreams were true—both of them—then an enormous task lay in front of him. He had no idea how he could find the salt water, except that he would need to follow the setting sun. And he did not know how far away it was: farther than any forest cat had ever gone before, that was for sure.

Ravenpaw's words echoed in his ears. *Maybe it's your time now.*

Had the other three cats dreamed of the sun-drown place too? *What if he's right?* Brambleclaw asked himself. *What should I do next?*

CHAPTER 7

Brambleclaw emerged warily from the undergrowth at the edge of the trees above the riverbank, tasting the air for the scent of cats. The traces of ThunderClan were all stale, though fresher RiverClan scents drifted across from the other side of the river. Hoping that no cat from either Clan would see him, Brambleclaw slipped swiftly down the bank to the water's edge.

Brown water churned along past his paws. More rain had fallen during the day, though the clouds were thinning now to let pale sunshine through, so that the forest steamed. The river was swollen, half submerging the stepping-stones, and Brambleclaw had to brace himself before he dared leap out onto the first of them.

He was on his way to visit Feathertail and Stormfur. All day he had been thinking about the second dream, becoming more and more convinced that they had to travel to the sun-drown place before they could learn what StarClan had to tell them. The dream had been too real to ignore—he could still taste salt in his mouth, and he flinched as droplets splashed against his nose from the stepping-stone, expecting the same sharp tang. And they ought to leave at once; his fur prickled with a strange sense of urgency, warning him that there was no time to wait until the next Gathering. If the other chosen cats had also had the dream, they shouldn't be hard to persuade.

He still had not told Squirrelpaw about the second dream. Although he felt guilty that he was not keeping his promise, he was well aware that if she knew about the journey he was planning she would want to come too. And what would Firestar think if Brambleclaw dragged his daughter off into the unknown?

Water lapped cold around his paws as Brambleclaw landed on the first stone and crouched, ready for his leap to the next. Before he pushed off, he scanned the far bank again. Although there was friendship now between ThunderClan and RiverClan, he was not sure of his welcome if he trespassed uninvited on their territory. He would prefer to find Feathertail and Stormfur before any other cats knew he was there.

He managed to reach the next stone, and the one after that, shivering as cold water splashed up onto his fur. The next stepping-stone had vanished completely, with only a ripple of water flowing over it to tell him where it was. Keeping his gaze fixed on the spot, he leaped, but as he landed his paws slipped off the edge, and he found himself splashing into the river. He let out a yowl of alarm as his head went under.

Terror surged over him as he was plunged into bottomless,

blue-green waves like those of his dream. Clawing his way upward, he surfaced to see reeds instead of sand-colored cliffs, and gray-brown water running in ripples, not waves. The current was carrying him close to the opposite bank, and Brambleclaw struck out, kicking strongly across the flow of water. To his relief, his paws scraped on pebbles; a heartbeat later he managed to stand and flounder into the shallows. Panting, he hauled himself onto the bank and shook himself vigorously.

Suddenly fresh RiverClan scent wafted into his nostrils; he dived into a clump of bracken and peered out between the fronds. A moment later he murmured thanks to StarClan as Feathertail and Stormfur—the two cats he wanted to see— appeared farther along the riverbank.

Brambleclaw plunged out of the bracken and stood shivering in front of them. "Hi," he mewed.

"Great StarClan!" Stormfur looked him up and down. "Have you been for a swim?"

"I fell off the stepping-stones. Feathertail, can I have a word with you?"

"Of course. Are you sure you're all right?"

"Yes, I'm fine. Feathertail, have you had another dream?"

The gray she-cat looked puzzled. "No. Why, have you?"

"Yes." Settling into the grass so they could talk more comfortably, Brambleclaw told them quickly about the sun-drown place and the cave with teeth, feeling his fur bristle with fear again. "I spoke to Ravenpaw this morning—you know, the loner who lives near Highstones? He says the sun-drown place is real. And he told me that StarClan's prophecies are always vague. We need the faith and courage of warriors to understand them, and to trust that what StarClan wants us to do is right."

"Which is what?" Stormfur queried.

"I . . . I think we should go to the sun-drown place," Brambleclaw replied, his belly churning with tension. *"That's where StarClan will tell us what we need to know."*

Feathertail had listened in silence, her blue gaze fixed on his face. When he stopped speaking, she nodded slowly. "I think you're right."

"What?" Stormfur sprang to his paws. "Are you mad? You don't even know where this place is."

Feathertail flicked him with her tail. "No, but StarClan will guide us."

Brambleclaw waited tensely. If Stormfur refused to agree, he might tell Leopardstar what was going on, and the Clan could stop Feathertail from leaving with him.

The gray warrior paced along the bank and back again, his tail fluffed up in agitation. "Faith and courage—we'd certainly need those if we went to this place," he muttered. "I'm still not convinced that you're right, mind you," he added wryly to Brambleclaw. "But if you're not, maybe StarClan will send another sign to turn us back."

Feathertail's blue eyes glowed. "Does that mean you'll come with us?"

"Try to stop me," her brother meowed grimly. He swung around to face Brambleclaw. "I know I've not had any dreams, but an extra warrior could be useful."

"You're right." Brambleclaw was so relieved to have won their agreement that he did not try to argue. "Thanks, both of you."

"So when do we leave?" Stormfur mewed.

"I thought the day before half-moon," Brambleclaw suggested. "That should give us enough time to talk to the others."

Rising to his paws, he padded down to the water's edge. The sun was going down, red behind bars of dark cloud. A breeze ruffled his drying fur and he shivered again, less from cold than from the thought of the path they had to travel.

"I know Tawnypelt will come if I ask her," he meowed, "but what about Crowpaw? He'd rather eat fox dung than go on a journey with us. But if all the cats StarClan have chosen don't go together, we might fail the prophecy."

"Crowpaw will understand," Feathertail tried to reassure him, though Brambleclaw wished he had her confidence.

"We'll help you persuade him," Stormfur offered. "He comes to the river to drink every day about sunset. It's too late now, so why don't we meet there tomorrow and talk to him together?"

"Okay." Brambleclaw blinked his gratitude. Somehow, the prophecy seemed to weigh less heavily when he was sharing it with friends. "Provided he comes, after this rain. WindClan should have water of their own now, remember."

"If he doesn't come," mewed Feathertail, sounding determined, "we'll just have to think of something else."

※   ※   ※

More rain fell during the night. WindClan's moorland streams would be flowing again without a doubt, making Brambleclaw more anxious than ever that the WindClan apprentice would not come into RiverClan territory to drink. He was restless all day; Cloudtail, on hunting patrol with him and Dustpelt, kept asking if he had ants in his fur.

When the fresh-kill pile had been restocked, Brambleclaw managed to slip out of camp again on his own. He especially wanted to avoid Squirrelpaw, who was bound to ask him where he was going.

The sun was sinking by the time he reached the border with RiverClan, in sight of the Twoleg bridge. It wasn't long before he saw the two RiverClan warriors climbing the river-bank and scooting across the bridge with their heads low. Stormfur beckoned with his tail, and Brambleclaw raced across the border to meet him and Feathertail at the near end of the bridge.

"Better hide," Stormfur meowed. "We don't know how many WindClan cats will come, and you're not supposed to be here."

Brambleclaw nodded. The three cats crept into the shelter of a thornbush near the place where the WindClan cats came to drink. Just below their hiding place the river raced noisily past, its brown water flecked with foam as it poured out of the gorge.

They did not have long to wait before Brambleclaw caught a strong WindClan scent and a group of cats appeared from the direction of Fourtrees. The Clan leader, Tallstar, came first, followed by Onewhisker and a ginger warrior Brambleclaw didn't recognize. Other cats came after them and Brambleclaw's heart began to race uncomfortably when he spotted Crowpaw among them with his mentor, Mudclaw.

The WindClan cats padded down the slope to the riverbank and crouched at the water's edge to drink. Frustrated, Brambleclaw saw that Crowpaw stayed in the middle of the group, too far away to call to him without other cats hearing.

"I'll have to go and fetch him," Feathertail murmured. She slipped out from underneath the bush and headed for the river.

Brambleclaw watched her greet the WindClan cats, stopping to speak briefly with Morningflower, one of the WindClan elders. Their exchange was polite, though not friendly; Brambleclaw wondered how long the Clans' uneasy alliance over the water would last if WindClan went on coming to drink now that the drought was over.

Soon Feathertail went to crouch beside Crowpaw at the water's edge. Brambleclaw dug his claws into the ground as he watched her straighten up again, shake water from her whiskers, and set off back to the thornbush. Crowpaw was not following her; had the WindClan apprentice decided he wanted no more to do with the mission, or had Feathertail been unable to tell him about the meeting?

"What's the matter?" he hissed as Feathertail crawled back into the shelter of the branches. "Did you talk to him?"

"It's okay." Feathertail pushed her muzzle into his side. "He's coming. He just doesn't want WindClan to see."

While she was speaking, Crowpaw backed away from the river and began to pad up the bank toward the bush. His Clan mates were still drinking. A couple of foxlengths away he glanced around casually and then dived for the bush before any cat could notice him go.

As the leaves rustled into place around him he glared at Brambleclaw with hostility in his green eyes. "I thought I could smell ThunderClan," he growled. "What do you want now?"

Brambleclaw exchanged an apprehensive glance with Feathertail. This wasn't a good start. "I've had another dream," he began, swallowing nervously.

"What sort of dream?" Crowpaw's voice was cold. "I haven't had one. Why would StarClan send you a dream and not me?"

Stormfur raised his hackles and Brambleclaw bit back a sharp response. "I don't know," he admitted.

A grunt was Crowpaw's only reply, but he listened in silence as Brambleclaw described what he had seen. "Ravenpaw, the loner who lives on the far side of your territory, visited the camp yesterday," he finished. "He told me that the sun-drown place is real. I . . . I think StarClan are telling us to go there. And we should go soon, all of us, in case the rest of the prophecy comes true and the Clans are in too much trouble to be saved."

Crowpaw's eyes stretched wide. "I can't believe I'm hearing

this," he meowed. "You're asking us to leave our Clans and go trekking off into the unknown—StarClan knows how far!—just because you've had a dream that none of us have had? Who died and made you leader?"

Brambleclaw found it hard to meet his eyes; Crowpaw was only echoing his own doubts. "I'm not trying to be leader," he stammered. "I'm just telling you what I think StarClan want."

"I'm willing to go," Feathertail added. "Even though I haven't had another dream."

"Then you're more mouse-brained than he is," Crowpaw retorted. "Well, I won't go. I'll be made a warrior soon. I've worked hard for it, and I'm not leaving the Clan so close to the end of my training."

"But Crowpaw—" Brambleclaw started to protest.

"No!" The apprentice showed his teeth in a snarl. "I'm not coming. What would my Clan think?"

"Maybe they'll honor you," Stormfur meowed. The gray warrior's eyes were serious. "Think, Crowpaw! If trouble is really coming, worse than anything we've seen before, what will the Clans think of the cats who help them? They'll understand how much faith we had to place in StarClan, that they were leading us on a genuine mission, and they'll know how much courage it took to do this."

"But you weren't chosen!" Crowpaw pointed out. "It doesn't matter to you one way or the other."

"Maybe not, but I'm coming anyway," Stormfur told him.

"And the reason StarClan aren't giving us clear instructions is because they want us to show faith and courage,"

Brambleclaw added. "Those are the qualities that a true warrior needs."

"Please, Crowpaw!" Feathertail's eyes shone. "The mission might fail without you. Remember that you *were* chosen—the only apprentice singled out by StarClan. They must believe that you can do this."

Crowpaw hesitated, looking at her. The red light of sunset had faded, leaving them in twilight, and Brambleclaw could hear and scent the WindClan cats as they passed the bush on their way back to their own territory. Crowpaw would have to leave with them before they noticed he was missing; there was no more time to plead or reason with him.

"All right," Crowpaw meowed at last. "I'll come." His eyes narrowed as he gazed at Brambleclaw. "Just don't start telling me what to do. Dreams or no dreams, I'm not going to take orders from you!"

Brambleclaw picked his way along the stone-lined tunnel under the Thunderpath, skirting the puddles that had formed there since the rain. Darkness lay all around, along with the reek of ShadowClan.

He had come here straight from the encounter with Crowpaw. The RiverClan warriors had offered to come with him, but Brambleclaw thought it was too risky. Alone, he would be less of a threat if ShadowClan warriors found him on their territory. Emerging on the other side of the Thunderpath, he tasted the air for fresh scents of ShadowClan warriors, but detected nothing except the damp odors of the marshy ground.

His belly skimming the earth, he darted across an open space and into the shelter of some bushes.

There were few tall trees in ShadowClan territory. Most of the ground was choked with brambles and nettles, separated by shallow pools of water. Brambleclaw's paws sank into the peaty earth at every step, and he shivered as his belly fur grew soaked.

"How do ShadowClan stand it?" he muttered. "It's so wet, I'm surprised they haven't all got webbed paws!"

He had a pretty good idea of where he might find Tawnypelt. She had once told him about a huge chestnut tree beside the stream that led down into ThunderClan territory. Her eyes had glowed as she described this favorite spot for sunning herself and catching squirrels, making Brambleclaw wonder if she was secretly missing the trees of ThunderClan. With any luck, she might be there now.

Brambleclaw located the stream and began to follow it, sometimes gritting his teeth and splashing through the shallows in the hope of hiding his scent from ShadowClan warriors. He saw a patrol crossing the stream a short way ahead, and crouched down behind a clump of sedge until they had vanished into the undergrowth and their scent faded away.

Not long after that he came to the chestnut tree. Its roots twisted around him, stretching down into the stream. Brambleclaw thought he could detect his sister's scent, but under the thick canopy of leaves it was too dark to see her.

"Tawnypelt!" he called softly. "Are you there?"

The answer came as a weight that crashed down on him,

bowling him over. He let out a startled yowl that broke off as his muzzle was pressed into the damp earth. A paw landed on his neck, pinning him with barely sheathed claws, and a voice growled close to his ear, "What are you doing here, you stupid furball?"

Brambleclaw let out a gasp of relief. The claws retracted and the weight lifted off him, letting him scramble to his paws. Tawnypelt was perched on a tree root, looking down at him.

"If you're found here, you'll be crowfood," she hissed. "What's gotten into you?"

"Something's happened. I've had another dream." Brambleclaw quickly told her about it.

Tawnypelt settled herself on the root to listen. "So Ravenpaw reckons it's a real place," she mused when he had finished. "And you think StarClan wants us to go there. They don't ask much, do they?"

Brambleclaw felt his ears droop. "You mean you won't come?"

His sister's tail twitched irritably. "Did I say that? Of course I'm coming. But no cat says I have to like it. And what about Stormfur? Why does he have to get involved? StarClan haven't chosen him."

Brambleclaw sighed. "I know. But try stopping him. Besides, he's a good warrior, and we might be glad of his support. We don't know what we're going to meet out there. And another thing," he added. "He and Feathertail do everything together. I think it comes of having their father in another Clan."

"I can understand that." Tawnypelt's tone was dry, and her brother realized how much sympathy she might have for the two RiverClan warriors. Her father was dead and both her brother and her mother, Goldenflower, remained in ThunderClan. Tawnypelt might well feel like a stranger in the Clan she had chosen. But Brambleclaw recognized the pride that would not let her voice her loneliness, and her determination to be a loyal ShadowClan warrior. Regret surged through him, not for the first time, as he thought what a loss she was to ThunderClan.

"You will serve your Clan well by coming on this journey," he reminded her.

"That's true." A trace of eagerness crept into Tawnypelt's voice, and grew stronger as she went on. "StarClan must have chosen us because they think we're the right cats. We must have something to offer that no other cats can give." She sprang down from the root and landed with a soft thud at Brambleclaw's side. "ShadowClan has many strong warriors to keep up the patrols. They can do without me for a while. When do we leave?"

Brambleclaw let out an affectionate purr. "Not right now! I told the others the night before the half-moon. We'll meet at Fourtrees."

Tawnypelt's tail lashed with enthusiasm. "I'll be ready. And now," she added, "I'd better show you to the border. Even one of StarClan's chosen can get his fur ripped off for trespassing."

CHAPTER 8

❧

"Snakerocks is the best place in the forest to find chervil," Cinderpelt explained over her shoulder as she limped along the fern-shaded path. "But we can't go there just now, thanks to that wretched badger."

"It's still there, then?" Leafpaw asked. She and the medicine cat were on an herb-gathering expedition. The sun shone brilliantly from a sky that was clear again, but the rain had revived the forest plants, and Leafpaw was enjoying the delicious coolness on her paws as she followed her mentor along the narrow track.

"So the dawn patrol said," Cinderpelt replied. "Keep your eyes open for—Ah!"

She swerved into the ferns and up a sandy slope, where several clumps of a strongly scented herb were growing; the flowers were gone but Leafpaw recognized the large, spreading leaves, and as she drew closer she smelled the sweetish scent of chervil.

"Tell me what we use it for," Cinderpelt prompted, beginning to gnaw one of the stems at its base.

Leafpaw narrowed her eyes and tried to remember. "The

juice of the leaves for infected wounds," she mewed. "And if you chew the root it's good for bellyache."

"Well done," Cinderpelt purred. "Now you can dig up a few roots—not too many, though, or there'll be no more in seasons to come."

She went on biting the stems while Leafpaw obediently began to scrape at the ground to uncover the roots. The chervil scent was all around them, making her feel light-headed, but after a few moments she began to scent something else—something that reminded her of the acrid tang of the Thunderpath, though it was not quite the same.

She glanced up and spotted a thin thread of smoke rising from a clump of dead bracken a little way down the slope. "Cinderpelt, look," she mewed uneasily, pointing with her tail.

The medicine cat looked around and froze, her neck fur bristling and her blue eyes blazing. "Great StarClan, no!" She gasped. Awkwardly, because of her injured leg, she began scrambling down toward the burning bracken.

Leafpaw leaped after her and passed the medicine cat in a couple of bounds. As she drew closer to the clump of bracken, a searing light flashed, dazzling her eyes. Blinking, she made out something shiny and clear sticking out of the ground, some spiky scrap of Twoleg rubbish. The sun was falling straight onto it and the bracken behind was slowly blackening and sending the wisp of smoke into the sky.

"Fire!" Cinderpelt yowled, coming up behind her. "Quick!"

Suddenly the bracken burst into flame. Leafpaw sprang back from the wave of heat. Turning to flee, she saw that

Cinderpelt stood still, gazing into the scarlet and orange blaze that leaped hungrily at the brittle stalks.

Was she frozen in panic? Leafpaw wondered. Sandstorm had told her about the terrible fire that once swept through the ThunderClan camp. Cinderpelt had survived, but several cats had not, and fire must be especially frightening to the medicine cat when her injured leg made it hard for her to run away.

Then Leafpaw saw that Cinderpelt's eyes were not wide with fear, but something else. Her gaze was fixed and remote, and Leafpaw realized with a shiver from her ears to her tail tip that her mentor was receiving a message from StarClan.

As quickly as it had blazed up, the fire began to die, and Leafpaw let out a sigh of relief. The flames sank into bright embers and began to wink out, the fronds of bracken disintegrating into flecks of ash. Cinderpelt took a step backward. She was even more unsteady than usual; Leafpaw darted forward to press up against her side, supporting her and helping her to sit down.

"Did you see it?" Cinderpelt whispered.

"See what, Cinderpelt?"

"In the flames . . . a leaping tiger. I saw it clearly, its huge head, the leaping paws, stripes as black as night along its body. . . ." The medicine cat's voice was hoarse. "An omen from StarClan, fire and tiger together. It must mean something, but what?"

Leafpaw shook her head. "I don't know," she confessed, feeling scared and helpless.

Cinderpelt got shakily to her paws, shrugging off Leafpaw's

attempt to help her up. "We must go straight back to camp," she mewed. "Firestar should hear about this at once."

The ThunderClan leader was alone in his den under the Highrock when Cinderpelt and Leafpaw returned. Cinderpelt paused outside the curtain of lichen that covered the entrance and called out, "Firestar? I need to talk to you."

"Come in," Firestar's voice replied.

Leafpaw followed her mentor into the den to see her father curled up on the bed of moss by the far wall. His head was raised as if Cinderpelt had roused him from sleep, and when the medicine cat and her apprentice entered he rose and stretched, arching his back so that the muscles rippled under his flame-colored pelt.

"What can I do for you?"

Cinderpelt padded across the den toward him, while Leafpaw sat quietly beside the entrance, wrapping her tail around her paws as she tried to push down her sense of approaching danger. She had never seen Cinderpelt receive a message from their warrior ancestors before, and she was unsettled by the fear she had seen in her mentor's eyes on the journey back through the damp green forest.

"StarClan have sent me an omen," the medicine cat began. She described how the Twoleg rubbish had caught the sun's rays and set fire to the bracken. "In the flames I saw a leaping tiger. Fire and tiger together, devouring the bracken. Such power, unleashed, could destroy the forest."

Firestar was crouched in front of her, with his paws tucked in and his green gaze fixed on her face so intently that

Leafpaw almost expected her mentor's gray fur to start smoking like the bracken burning under the hot sunlight. "What do you think it means?"

"I've been trying to work it out," Cinderpelt meowed. "I'm not sure I'm right, but . . . in the old prophecy, 'fire will save the clan,' 'fire' meant you, Firestar."

The ThunderClan leader gave a start of surprise. "You think it refers to me now? Well . . . perhaps, but what about 'tiger'? Tigerstar is dead."

Leafpaw felt uneasiness stir inside her as her father calmly named the fearsome cat who had shed so much blood in his quest for power.

"He is dead—but his son still lives," Cinderpelt pointed out quietly. She glanced at Leafpaw sitting in the shadows, as if she were uncertain her apprentice should be hearing this. Leafpaw stayed absolutely still, determined to listen to the rest.

"Brambleclaw?" Firestar exclaimed. "Are you saying he's going to destroy the forest? Come on, Cinderpelt. He's as loyal as any warrior in the Clan. Look at the way he fought for us in the battle against BloodClan."

Leafpaw felt a sudden urge to say something in Brambleclaw's defense, though it was not her place to speak here. She did not know the young warrior particularly well, but some instinct inside her cried out, *No! He would never harm his Clan, or the forest.*

"Firestar, use your head." Cinderpelt sounded irritable. "I haven't said that Brambleclaw will destroy the forest. But if 'tiger' doesn't mean him, then which cat does it mean? And something else . . . if 'tiger' is Tigerstar's son, then maybe 'fire' is Firestar's daughter."

Leafpaw flinched as if a badger had sunk its teeth into her fur.

"Oh, I don't mean you." Cinderpelt turned to her apprentice with amusement gleaming faintly in her blue eyes. "I'll keep an eye on you, don't worry." Glancing back at Firestar, she added, "No, I think it more likely means Squirrelpaw. She has a flame-colored pelt like you, after all."

Leafpaw's brief sense of relief was swallowed up in fear and dismay as she realized where the medicine cat's logic was leading. Her own sister, the cat who was dearer to her than all others—was she prophesied to do something so terrible that her name would be cursed by all the Clans, just as queens told their kits now that if they were naughty the terrible Tigerstar would come and get them?

"My own daughter . . . she's headstrong, yes, but not dangerous . . ." Firestar's eyes were deeply troubled; Leafpaw saw that he had too much respect for Cinderpelt's wisdom to argue with her interpretation, though it was bitter as mouse bile to hear. "What do you think I should do?" he asked helplessly.

Cinderpelt shook her head. "That's your decision, Firestar. I can only tell you what StarClan have shown me. Fire and tiger together, and danger to the forest. But I'd advise you not to tell the Clan yet, not until I receive another sign. They'll only panic, and that will make things worse." Her head swiveled to fix an icy stare on Leafpaw. "Say nothing about this, on your loyalty to StarClan."

"Not even to Squirrelpaw?" Leafpaw asked nervously.

"Especially not to Squirrelpaw."

"I must tell Graystripe," Firestar mewed. "And Sand-storm—StarClan know what Sandstorm will think about this!"

Cinderpelt nodded. "That is wise, I think."

"And it might be as well to keep the two of them apart." Firestar spoke half to himself. Leafpaw could see how he was torn between doing his best for his Clan, and his deep feelings for his daughter and the warrior who had once been his apprentice. "She's an apprentice, he's a warrior; it shouldn't be hard," Firestar went on. "We'll make sure they have enough to do, and not in each other's company. Maybe StarClan will send another omen to tell us when the danger is past?" he suggested, glancing hopefully at Cinderpelt.

"Maybe." But the medicine cat's tone was not reassuring. She rose and flicked her tail for Leafpaw to follow her. "If they do, you'll be the first to know."

She dipped her head and backed out of the den. Leafpaw moved to follow her, hesitated, then rushed across to her father and buried her muzzle in his pelt, wanting to be comforted as much as to comfort him. Whatever this omen might mean, she was scared by it. She felt Firestar's tongue rasp warmly over her ear. Her eyes met his and she saw her own sorrow and fear reflected there.

Then Cinderpelt called "Leafpaw!" from outside, and the moment was over. Leafpaw bowed her head to her leader and left him alone, to wait for further news from StarClan about the destiny of his cats.

CHAPTER 9

❧

Brambleclaw chose a plump starling from the fresh-kill pile, carrying it a few paces away before he began to gulp it down. Sunhigh was just past, and the clearing was full of cats enjoying the warmth. Brambleclaw caught a glimpse of Leafpaw padding over to the elders' den, a wad of herbs in her jaws. He was surprised to see how unhappy she looked; perhaps she was in trouble with her mentor, though he found it hard to imagine that Cinderpelt would drive any cat to look so worried.

Closer to the nettle patch, Firestar was eating with Graystripe and Sandstorm. As Brambleclaw bit into his prey he saw his leader raise his head and give him a hard stare, as if he might be in trouble. Brambleclaw couldn't remember anything he had done wrong that his leader knew about, but his fur prickled uneasily; surely Firestar hadn't found out about the dreams?

He braced himself for his leader to call him over and tell him what was on his mind, but when he heard a cat speak his name it was Squirrelpaw. She snatched a mouse from the heap of fresh-kill and bounced across to sit by his side.

"Whew!" she exclaimed, dropping the mouse. "I thought

I'd never finish feeding the elders. Longtail has the appetite of a starving fox!" She took a bite from her piece of prey and gulped it down. "So what's happening?" she asked. "Have you had any more messages from StarClan?"

Brambleclaw swallowed his mouthful of starling. "Ssshhh, not so loud," he hissed.

It was the day after his encounter with Crowpaw and his visit to ShadowClan territory, and he had still not decided how much to tell Squirrelpaw about the second dream. If he vanished on the day before the half-moon without confiding in her, he would have broken his part of their bargain, but he did not know what he would say if she demanded to come with them.

"Well, have you?" Squirrelpaw persisted, lowering her voice.

Brambleclaw chewed slowly, playing for time. He had just decided that he would have to tell the nosy she-cat something, if only to stop all her questions, when he realized that Firestar had padded over from the nettle patch and was standing over them. He stiffened, instinctively unsheathing his claws so that they sank into the breast of the starling.

"Squirrelpaw, I want you to go out with Thornclaw," Firestar ordered. "He's going to show Shrewpaw the best hunting places near Fourtrees."

Squirrelpaw took another gulp of mouse and swiped her tongue over her whiskers. "Do I have to? I've been up there with Dustpelt loads of times."

The tip of Firestar's tail twitched back and forth. "Yes, you do. When your leader gives you an order, you obey it."

Squirrelpaw rolled her eyes at Brambleclaw before picking up the last of the mouse and swallowing it.

"*Now*, Squirrelpaw." Firestar's tail twitched again. "Thornclaw's waiting." He nodded toward the tabby warrior, who was padding across the clearing with Shrewpaw.

"You could at least let me finish my mouse in peace," Squirrelpaw argued. "I've been on my paws all morning, chasing after the elders."

"And so you should be!" Firestar's voice was sharp. "That's what being an apprentice is all about. I don't want to hear you complaining."

"I'm *not* complaining!" Squirrelpaw leaped to her paws, her fur bristling. "I only said I wanted a bit of peace and quiet to eat. Why are you always nagging at me? You're not my *mentor*, so stop acting like you are. Or are you just afraid that I'll let you down, and not live up to our great leader's shining example?"

Without waiting for a response, she spun around and flounced off to meet Thornclaw and Shrewpaw near the entrance to the camp. Brambleclaw noticed that the tabby warrior looked surprised when Squirrelpaw spoke to him, though he was too far off to hear what she said, and it crossed his mind that Thornclaw hadn't been expecting her to join the patrol at all. Then the warrior nodded, and all three cats vanished into the gorse tunnel.

Firestar watched Squirrelpaw go with a grim look. He didn't say a word to Brambleclaw, but turned and padded back to Sandstorm and Graystripe.

Brambleclaw heard Sandstorm growl, "You know that's the wrong way to handle her. If you order her about, she'll just get more stubborn."

Firestar replied in a low voice that Brambleclaw couldn't catch; then the cats got up and headed toward Firestar's den.

What was all that about? Brambleclaw wondered. *Firestar was annoyed with Squirrelpaw, so he made up an excuse to get her out of the camp.* His blood ran chill. *To get her away from me, maybe?*

If he was right, there could only be one reason. Squirrelpaw must have told her father about the first dream, and the meeting with the other cats at Fourtrees. She might have done it deliberately, or she might have let something slip because she wasn't thinking. Whatever had happened, Brambleclaw knew there would be more trouble to come, but at least it meant he didn't have to tell her about the second dream; she had obviously broken the agreement they had made at Fourtrees.

Trying to put his fears about what Firestar might do next out of his mind, he went back to the fresh-kill pile. If he was going to set off on a long journey in a few days' time, it would be a good idea to eat more and build up his strength. He would also ask Cinderpelt about the traveling herbs that cats ate to give them strength for the journey to Highstones, as long as he could think of a way to do it without arousing the medicine cat's suspicions.

He was just reaching down to pick up a juicy-looking vole when he heard a voice behind him. "Hey—what do you think you're doing?"

It was Mousefur. Brambleclaw looked around to see the brown she-cat glaring at him from a few foxlengths away.

"I've been watching you," she went on. "You've already eaten. You haven't hunted enough today to take any more prey."

Embarrassment flooded over Brambleclaw. "Sorry," he mumbled.

"So I should think," Mousefur snapped.

Cloudtail, who was standing beside her, let out an amused purr. "He's trying to compete with Graystripe," he teased. "Looks like one big eater isn't enough for ThunderClan. Never mind, Brambleclaw. Do you want to hunt with me and Brightheart? We'll catch as many voles as you can eat, and double the fresh-kill pile."

"Er, thanks," Brambleclaw stammered.

"Hang on, I'll just fetch Brightheart." Cloudtail raced over to the warriors' den, and Mousefur, with a last glare at Brambleclaw, followed him.

While Brambleclaw waited for his friends to reappear, he decided to suggest going up to Fourtrees, where they might come across Thornclaw's patrol. He needed to get hold of Squirrelpaw and find out exactly what she had told her father. If Firestar knew that StarClan had chosen four cats, each from a different Clan, would he try to warn the other leaders, and put a stop to their journey before it even started?

But Brambleclaw's patrol saw nothing of Squirrelpaw and the others while they were out, and by the time he returned to camp with Cloudtail and Brightheart, with plenty of prey to add to the pile, night was falling. Most of the cats were already heading for their dens. Brambleclaw kept watch until the evening patrol had left and the moon had appeared above the trees, but he still did not see Squirrelpaw. He slept badly that night, worried about the prophecy and Squirrelpaw's unwanted involvement.

The next morning he pushed his way out of the warriors' den as soon as he woke, determined to find the ginger apprentice and get some answers to his questions. But it seemed as if StarClan itself were against him, making him hiss out loud with frustration. No sooner had he set paw in the clearing than Graystripe called him to join the dawn patrol with Sorreltail and Rainwhisker. By the time they returned, after a circuit of the whole territory, it was almost sunhigh. When Brambleclaw checked the apprentices' den it was empty, and as he could not see Dustpelt in the camp either, he assumed that Squirrelpaw had gone out training with her mentor.

He took a nap in the heat of the day, his worries soothed for a short while by the quiet murmur of bees and the sigh of wind in the branches, and woke to catch sight of Squirrelpaw disappearing into the gorse tunnel, a wad of old bedding clamped in her jaws. Springing to his paws, he was about to follow her when a cat called his name.

Brackenfur was padding toward him with his apprentice, Whitepaw. For some reason the golden brown tom looked uneasy. "Hi, Brambleclaw. I . . . I thought you might like to come and watch a training session," he meowed.

Brambleclaw stared at him in surprise. Warriors hardly ever watched the apprentices training, unless they were mentors themselves. With a swift glance at the tunnel where Squirrelpaw was now out of sight, he replied, "Er . . . thanks, Brackenfur, but some other time, okay?"

He headed quickly toward the camp entrance, but realized after a couple of heartbeats that Brackenfur was keeping pace with him.

"It's just that Firestar thought it might be good practice for you," the older warrior explained. "For when you have an apprentice of your own."

Brambleclaw halted. "Let me get this straight," he meowed. "*Firestar* asked you to tell me to watch you and Whitepaw training?"

Brackenfur's gaze slid past him and he looked acutely embarrassed. "That's right," he mewed.

"But we *never* do that," Brambleclaw protested. "Anyway, it'll be moons before Ferncloud's kits are ready for mentors."

Brackenfur shrugged. "An order's an order, Brambleclaw."

Brambleclaw blinked. "It's an *order?*" He shook his head crossly. It wasn't StarClan that was against him—it was his own leader. And it was hardly surprising, if Squirrelpaw had told Firestar that one of his warriors had been having prophetic dreams without telling the rest of the Clan.

Fuming, he followed Brackenfur and his apprentice out of the camp and along the ravine to the sandy hollow where the training sessions took place. He sat on the edge, watching

Brackenfur put Whitepaw through her fighting moves. A little later, Mousefur arrived with Spiderpaw, and the two apprentices started a mock battle. Brambleclaw watched as Whitepaw darted in to give Spiderpaw a quick nip in the neck; Spiderpaw spun around at once, his long black limbs whirling as he leaped on her and pinned her to the ground. They were both making good progress, Brambleclaw noticed idly, yawning with boredom.

I could be doing something useful, he thought miserably. There were only two days to go before he was due to meet the other cats at Fourtrees and set out on their journey. He needed to talk to Squirrelpaw soon.

When Mousefur called a halt and the two apprentices climbed out of the hollow, shaking sand from their fur, Brambleclaw returned to camp even more determined to find Squirrelpaw and get some answers. To his relief, when he emerged from the gorse tunnel he spotted her with Shrewpaw beside the apprentices' den.

Racing across the clearing, he halted in front of her and demanded, "I want to talk to you."

He knew that issuing orders was not the way to handle Squirrelpaw. Ready for her to snarl or spit, he was surprised when she mewed in a hurried, low voice, with an uneasy glance at Shrewpaw, "Okay, but not here. Meet me behind the nursery."

Brambleclaw nodded and padded away to greet Sootfur and Ashfur, who were returning with fresh-kill. He paused at the entrance to the nursery where Ferncloud was watching her kits play, forcing himself to sound normal as he commented on how strong and healthy they were growing. Finally he made his way behind the nursery, a sandy area bounded by nettles where the cats went to make their dirt.

Squirrelpaw was already waiting for him, her dark ginger fur almost hidden in the shadows. "Brambleclaw, I—"

"You've told your father something, haven't you?" Brambleclaw interrupted. "After you promised to keep your mouth shut."

Squirrelpaw straightened up to face him, her neck fur bristling furiously. "I have *not*! I haven't said a word to any cat."

"Then why is Firestar so determined to keep us apart?"

"Oh, you've noticed too, have you?" Squirrelpaw tried to sound calm, but her voice rose to a wail as she went on, "I don't *know*! I promise I didn't tell him anything. But he looks at me like I've done something bad, and I *haven't*."

Suddenly feeling sorry for the confused, unhappy she-cat, Brambleclaw padded up to her to press his muzzle against her side, but she whisked away from him, her teeth bared in the beginnings of a snarl.

"It's nothing I can't handle. Leafpaw's upset, too," she added. "She hasn't said anything, but I can tell."

Brambleclaw sat down and stared across the nettles to the thorn hedge around the camp, without really seeing it. He couldn't make any sense of Firestar's behavior if Squirrelpaw was telling the truth about keeping quiet. Brambleclaw couldn't bring himself to think that she was lying to him, which meant there had to be another reason Firestar was angry with them both. But what on earth could it be?

"Perhaps we should ask him?" he suggested. "If he told us what the matter is, we might be able to put it right."

Squirrelpaw looked doubtful, but before she could reply Brambleclaw heard the sound of more cats pushing their way through the nettles. Springing to his paws, he whipped around to see Firestar himself, with Graystripe just behind.

"So." The ThunderClan leader stepped forward until he stood between his daughter and Brambleclaw. "Shrewpaw said I'd find you here."

"We weren't doing anything wrong!" Squirrelpaw blurted out.

"But I wonder what you think you *are* doing." Firestar gave his daughter a hard stare and then transferred it to Brambleclaw. "Wasting your time, for one thing, when there's work to be done."

"We've worked hard all day, Firestar," Brambleclaw meowed, ducking his head respectfully.

"That's true, Firestar, they have," Graystripe put in.

Firestar shot him a quick glance, but did not respond. "Does that mean you think there's nothing more to do?" he asked Brambleclaw. The younger warrior opened his mouth to protest, but his leader did not give him the chance. "If you're so sure," he went on, "then take a look at the elders. Frostfur got burrs tangled in her pelt today. You can help her get them out."

Anger flared inside Brambleclaw. That was an apprentice task! But he could see from Firestar's cold green gaze that there was no point in arguing. He mumbled, "Yes, Firestar," and padded away toward the main clearing.

Once the nettles had rustled back into place, screening him from the little group of cats, he paused to hear Firestar speaking to Squirrelpaw, still in that same hard, displeased tone. "Squirrelpaw, you must have better things to do than hang about with an inexperienced warrior like Brambleclaw. Stay with your own mentor in the future."

Brambleclaw couldn't hear Squirrelpaw's response, and it wasn't safe to stay there listening any longer. Sadness flooded over him as he made his way to the elders' den. Somehow he had lost his leader's respect, and if Squirrelpaw really hadn't told her father about the dream and the meeting with the other cats at Fourtrees, he couldn't imagine why.

In two nights' time he was supposed to leave on his journey with the cats from the other Clans to find the sun-drown place, and see what midnight told them. How could he possibly go, Brambleclaw wondered despairingly, when Firestar was watching him so closely? A chill ran through him from ears to tail-tip as he realized that to be loyal to the prophecy and to StarClan, he might have to be disloyal to his leader.

CHAPTER 10

Brambleclaw scarcely slept that night, and when he did, his dreams were full of Firestar's anger, and images of his leader driving him away from the camp. When he pushed his way out of the warriors' den the next morning, he still felt exhausted—even more so when he reflected that this was his last day in camp before his journey would begin.

A gray dawn light was filtering through the camp, and the wind was chilly. Tasting the air, Brambleclaw thought he could make out the first scent of approaching leaf-fall. Change was on the way, he realized, whatever he and the other chosen cats tried to do.

Throughout the day he did not even bother trying to speak to Squirrelpaw. Though Firestar had not ordered them to stay apart, he obviously didn't like them to be together. There was no point in deliberately looking for trouble. Brambleclaw caught a glimpse of the young apprentice leaving the camp with Dustpelt; she looked oddly subdued, with her tail trailing against the earth and her ears flat.

"You look as if you've lost a rabbit and found a shrew," a brisk voice spoke beside him.

Brambleclaw looked up; it was Mousefur.

"Do you want to come hunting with me and Spiderpaw?" the she-cat meowed.

For once Brambleclaw felt he hardly had the energy for hunting or anything else. With his journey due to start the next day, worries were crowding around him like cats at a Gathering. Was he really meant to lead four other cats out into the unknown, to face dangers they could not even imagine?

Mousefur was still waiting for Brambleclaw to answer. He couldn't help wondering if her suggestion of hunting together was another of Firestar's orders to keep him busy. But the brown she-cat blinked at him in a friendly way, and he realized that he would be better off hunting than hanging about the camp worrying. Perhaps if he brought back plenty of prey he would start to regain Firestar's good opinion.

But the hunt didn't go well. Spiderpaw was too easily distracted, as playful as a kit on its first outing. Once, as he was creeping up on a mouse, a leaf spiraled down past his nose, and he lifted one paw to bat at it. Startled by the clumsy movement, the mouse vanished under a root.

"Honestly!" Mousefur sighed. "Do you expect the prey to come and jump into your mouth?"

"Sorry," Spiderpaw mewed, looking abashed.

He made more of an effort after that. When the patrol came upon a squirrel nibbling an acorn in the middle of a clearing, Spiderpaw began stalking it, moving each long black leg stealthily. He was almost ready to pounce when the wind changed and carried his scent to his prey. The squirrel started, tail flicking up, and bounded toward the edge of the clearing.

"Bad luck!" Brambleclaw called.

Instead of answering, Spiderpaw raced after the squirrel and disappeared into the undergrowth.

"Hey!" Mousefur shouted after him. "You'll never catch a squirrel like that." Spiderpaw did not reappear, and his mentor bared her teeth in a resigned growl. "One day he'll learn." She padded off into the undergrowth to find him.

Left to himself, Brambleclaw stood still, listening for the sound of prey. There was a faint rustling in the leaves under the nearest tree. A mouse appeared, scuffling after seeds. Brambleclaw dropped into a hunting crouch and crept up on it, trying to make his paws float over the ground. Then he sprang, and killed his prey with one swift snap.

He scraped earth over it so that he could collect it later, half wishing that Mousefur had been there to see his success. At least she could have told Firestar that he was still hunting well for his Clan—whatever the leader's complaint was, it couldn't be about that. Listening for more prey, promising himself one last good hunt before he left, he pricked up his ears instead at the sound of something bigger rustling among the bushes a little way off, in the opposite direction from where Spiderpaw and Mousefur had disappeared. Brambleclaw drew the air into his mouth, but could scent nothing except ThunderClan cats. He began to pad forward, only to quicken his pace as the rustling grew louder and was followed by a furious yowl. He ran around the edge of a bramble thicket and stopped dead.

There was a gorse bush in front of him, and Squirrelpaw

was struggling madly among its thick, spiky branches. Her front paws were off the ground and her fur was tangled in the thorns. Brambleclaw couldn't suppress a *mrrow* of laughter. "Having fun?"

Instantly Squirrelpaw's head whipped around and her green eyes flashed fury at him. "That's right, have a good laugh, you stupid furball!" she snapped. "Then maybe you'll have time to get me out of here!"

She sounded so much like the old Squirrelpaw rather than the dejected creature that had left the camp that morning that Brambleclaw felt better at once. Tail waving, he strolled toward her. "How did you manage to get so stuck?"

"I was chasing a vole." Squirrelpaw sounded exasperated. "Dappletail said she fancied one, so I thought I'd better oblige, seeing that Firestar seems to want me to feed the elders, like, forever. It ran under here, and I thought there was room for me to run after it."

"There isn't," Brambleclaw pointed out helpfully.

"I know that now, mouse-brain! Do something!"

"Keep still, then." Approaching the bush, Brambleclaw saw where the worst tangles were, and began to tease out her fur, carefully using his teeth and claws. Some of the thorns pierced his nose, making his eyes water, but he kept on without complaining.

"Hang on," Squirrelpaw muttered after a while. "I think I'm loose."

Brambleclaw jumped out of the way as the apprentice plunged forward, forepaws scrabbling the earth as she dragged her hindquarters clear of the branches. A moment later she was free, shaking herself irritably while she stared at the tufts of ginger fur she had left behind.

"Thanks, Brambleclaw," she meowed.

"Are you hurt at all?" he asked. "Maybe you ought to let Cinderpelt have a look at—"

"Squirrelpaw!"

Brambleclaw froze and his heart sank. He slowly turned around to see Firestar stalking toward them.

The Clan leader had an expression like ice in his eyes as he looked from Brambleclaw to his daughter and back again. "Is this how you obey orders?" he growled.

The unfairness of Firestar's attitude took Brambleclaw's breath away. For a couple of heartbeats he couldn't find words to answer, and when he did he knew he sounded guilty. "I'm not disobeying orders, Firestar."

"Oh? I'm sorry." Firestar's voice was as dry as a sun-scorched rock. "I thought you were supposed to be on a hunting patrol, but I must have heard wrong."

"I *am* on a hunting patrol," Brambleclaw mewed desperately.

Firestar made a great show of looking around. "I don't see Mousefur or Spiderpaw."

"Spiderpaw went off after a squirrel." Brambleclaw pointed with his tail. "Mousefur went after him."

"Why are you being so horrible?" Squirrelpaw interrupted, glaring at her father. "Brambleclaw isn't doing anything wrong."

"Brambleclaw isn't doing what he was told," Firestar growled. "That isn't the warrior code as I was taught it."

Squirrelpaw sprang forward to stand nose-to-nose with her father and lifted her voice in a yowl of pure fury. "I was stuck in the bush! Brambleclaw helped me! It's not his fault!"

"Be quiet," Firestar rasped. Brambleclaw was struck by how much alike father and daughter looked: green eyes flashing, ginger pelts bristling angrily. "This has nothing to do with you."

"It looks like it has," Squirrelpaw argued. "You growl at Brambleclaw every time he so much as glances at me—"

"*Silence!*" Firestar hissed.

Brambleclaw stared in alarm. Just at that moment, Graystripe thrust his way into the clearing, a vole clamped in his jaws.

"Firestar?" he meowed, dropping his prey. "What's going on?"

Firestar lashed his tail, then straightened up with an impatient shake of his head. Brambleclaw forced himself to relax the fur on his neck.

"Oh, right." Graystripe's amber eyes glowed with understanding as he looked at the other cats in the clearing, and Brambleclaw realized that whatever was making Firestar act like this, his deputy knew all about it. "Come on, Firestar," he went on, padding up to the Clan leader and giving him a nudge. "These two aren't doing any harm."

"And not much good, either," Firestar retorted. He faced the two younger cats. "My decisions, and the orders I give, are for the good of the whole Clan," he reminded them. "If you can't understand that, then maybe you aren't fit to be warriors."

"What?" Squirrelpaw's jaws opened on a howl of outrage, but a furious hiss from her father silenced her.

Brambleclaw was too bewildered even to try protesting. Something—some knowledge Firestar and Graystripe shared—had turned Firestar against him. If Squirrelpaw hadn't told her father about the dream, then it had to be something else. But he had no idea what it could be, or what he could do about it.

"You," Firestar went on crisply, flicking his tail at Squirrelpaw, "take that vole of Graystripe's to the elders, and then carry on hunting for them. You"—with a flick at Brambleclaw—"find Mousefur and see if you can possibly bring back some fresh-kill before dark. Do it now."

Without waiting to see if his orders were obeyed, he whipped around and stalked off through the bushes.

Graystripe paused before following him. "He's got a lot on his mind," he murmured apologetically. "Don't take it too much to heart. Everything will work out okay; you'll see."

A yowl of "Graystripe!" came from the direction where Firestar had disappeared. Graystripe twitched his ears, nodded farewell to the two younger cats, and hurried after his leader.

Squirrelpaw stared after them. Now that Firestar had gone and she no longer had to go on defying him, her tail drooped, and the gaze she turned on Brambleclaw was full of distress.

"I can't do anything right," she meowed. "You heard what he said. He thinks I'm not fit to be a warrior. He'll never give me my warrior name."

Brambleclaw did not know what to say. His bewilderment was melting into a slow, furious anger. He *knew* he hadn't done anything wrong. Whatever was making Firestar behave like this, it wasn't his fault. It wasn't Squirrelpaw's, either. She could be annoying, but she was a loyal and hardworking apprentice. Any leader worth a couple of mousetails could see what a great warrior she would make.

He glared down at the ground, and when Squirrelpaw spoke his name he scarcely heard her. He felt his mind clearing, like a gray sky when the wind tore the clouds away and the sun shone through. The day before, after the confrontation behind the nursery, he had felt torn between the demands of the prophecy and loyalty to Firestar. Now he looked ahead to see day after day of struggling to please his leader with no chance of success, because he did not know why Firestar was angry with him in the first place. There was only one solution. He must leave on the journey with only the word of StarClan to guide him, and not come back until he had discovered answers that would prove to Firestar how loyal he had been all along. Or else he would not come back at all.

"Go on," Brambleclaw meowed roughly, nodding toward the dropped vole. "Take that back, or he'll have another go at you."

"What about you?" Squirrelpaw, usually so bright and confident, sounded nervous.

"I . . ." He had been about to lie to her, and tell her that he was going to look for Mousefur. Then he realized how deeply betrayed she would feel when he didn't come back. After all, they were in this together, at least as far as Firestar's hostility was concerned. "I'm leaving," he told her.

"Leaving?" Squirrelpaw echoed in dismay. "Leaving ThunderClan?"

"Not leaving for good," Brambleclaw put in quickly. "Squirrelpaw, listen. . . ."

She sat in front of him, and her wide green eyes never left his face as he told her about the second dream, of drowning in endless salty water and being swept toward the cave with teeth.

"Ravenpaw says it's a real place," he explained. "I think StarClan are telling me to go there, and the other cats agree. We're starting at sunrise tomorrow."

The hurt in Squirrelpaw's eyes was clear. "You told them and not me?" she wailed. "Brambleclaw, you *promised!*"

"I know." Brambleclaw felt guilt gnawing at him. "I was going to, and then all this trouble with Firestar started— StarClan know why, and if they do, they're telling me even less about it than they've told me about the prophecy."

"And you're really going all that way? But you don't even know how far it is."

"None of us do," Brambleclaw admitted. "But Ravenpaw has spoken to cats who have seen the place, so it must be possible to get there. I'm not coming back to the camp," he added. "I'll spend the night somewhere in the forest, and meet the others at Fourtrees in the morning. Please, Squirrelpaw, don't give us away. Don't tell any cat where we've gone."

As he spoke, Squirrelpaw's eyes brightened until they were gleaming with excitement. Brambleclaw knew what she was going to say a heartbeat before she said it.

"I won't breathe a word to any cat," she promised. "I can't, because I'm coming with you."

"Oh, no, you're not!" Brambleclaw retorted. "You're not one of the chosen cats. You're not even a warrior yet."

"Crowpaw isn't a warrior," Squirrelpaw flashed back at him. "And I'd bet a moon of dawn patrols Stormfur is coming. He'd never let Feathertail go without him. So why do I have to be left out?" She hesitated, and then added, "I didn't tell any cat about the first dream, Brambleclaw. I never said a word. Not even to Leafpaw."

Brambleclaw knew that was true. If Squirrelpaw had dropped even a hint, it would have been all around the camp by now.

"I didn't promise you could come," he reminded her. "I promised to tell you, and I've done that."

"But you *can't* leave me behind," Squirrelpaw cried. "If I don't know what happens next, my fur will fall out from wondering!"

"It's just too dangerous, Squirrelpaw; can't you see that? The prophecy is a heavy enough weight for me to bear, without having to look after you as well."

"Look after me!" Squirrelpaw's eyes blazed indignantly. "I

can look after myself, thank you. I'm coming, whether you like it or not. If you won't let me come with you, I'll follow you. Think about what happened today. I don't want to go back to camp and be told off for nothing, over and over again, any more than you do!"

Brambleclaw stared at her, indecisive. He did not want the responsibility of taking a young apprentice into danger . . . but she would be in much more danger if she tried to follow him alone through unknown territory. And if she returned to the camp, once Firestar realized that Brambleclaw had gone missing, he would badger Squirrelpaw until she told him what she knew, and maybe even send an expedition to bring him back. For a couple of heartbeats Brambleclaw understood what it meant to be a leader, his fur weighed down with doubts and questions heavier than a whole riverful of floodwater.

He heaved a sigh that seemed to go down to the tips of his paws. "All right, Squirrelpaw," he meowed. "You can come."

CHAPTER 11

❧

"Where are we going to sleep?" Squirrelpaw asked.

As soon as Brambleclaw agreed to take her with him on the journey, her hurt and anger had vanished like dawn mist under a hot sun. He did not think she had stopped talking for a moment since they left the clearing where Firestar had found them.

"Quiet!" he hissed. "If any cat is looking for us, they'll be able to hear you right across the forest."

"But where?" Squirrelpaw persisted, though she did lower her voice.

"Somewhere not too far from Fourtrees," Brambleclaw replied. "Then we'll be ready to meet the others at sunrise."

Darkness had fallen as he led the way through the undergrowth. Clouds had massed to cover the sky, so that no gleam of star or moon broke through. A cold breeze whispered in the grass, and once again Brambleclaw tasted the scents of approaching leaf-fall.

With possible pursuit in mind, he had considered finding shelter near Snakerocks, which the Clan had been ordered to avoid, but the risk of encountering the night-hunting badger was too great. Instead he decided to make for the Thunder-path, hoping that the acrid smells of Twoleg monsters would mask his own scent and Squirrelpaw's.

"I know a good tree by the Thunderpath," Squirrelpaw suggested. "You can get right inside. We could hide there."

"And have spiders and beetles crawling through our fur all night?" Brambleclaw mewed discouragingly. "No, thanks."

Squirrelpaw sniffed. "Why do you always know better?"

"Maybe because I'm a warrior?"

Distracted by a rustling in the undergrowth, the apprentice made no reply. Barely pausing to track her prey, she dived into a clump of bracken and came back a couple of heartbeats later with a mouse dangling from her jaws.

"Well done," meowed Brambleclaw.

The sight of the fresh-kill made him realize how hungry he was. Not long after, he managed to catch a mouse for himself, and the two cats paused to eat in quick, wary gulps, their ears pricked to catch the faintest traces of a ThunderClan patrol. But Brambleclaw could hear nothing except the ordinary night sounds of the forest and the nearby roar of monsters on the Thunderpath. Their stench was so strong here that it masked most others, as Brambleclaw had hoped, though he shrank from the thought of spending the night with that in his nostrils.

While they ate, a thin, cold rain began to fall, growing steadily heavier until Brambleclaw's fur was soaked and he was colder than he could remember feeling in moons.

"We need shelter," Squirrelpaw mewed, shivering. She

looked small and vulnerable, with her fur plastered darkly to her body. "What about finding that tree?"

Brambleclaw was about to agree when they emerged from the undergrowth at the top of a grassy bank, and he found himself looking down at the Thunderpath. A Twoleg monster roared past, its glaring eyes cutting shafts of yellow brightness through the night. Before it swept by, the light showed Brambleclaw a looming dark shape, the biggest monster he had ever seen, squatting on the verge of the Thunderpath. The reek of it flooded his senses.

"What's *that*?" exclaimed Squirrelpaw, brushing close beside him.

"I don't know," Brambleclaw admitted. "I've never seen anything like it before. Stay here while I take a look."

Cautiously he padded forward until he stood a couple of foxlengths away from the monster. Was it dead, he wondered, and was that why its Twolegs had abandoned it here? Or was it crouching, watching, waiting to spring as he would spring on a helpless mouse?

"Look, we could get underneath it," Squirrelpaw pointed out, trotting up to join him; of course she had not obeyed his order to wait at the top of the bank. "We could shelter from the rain."

There was just enough light for Brambleclaw to make out a darker gap between the monster's belly and the ground. His fur bristled at the thought of crawling into the narrow space, but he didn't want to seem a coward in front of Squirrelpaw, and her suggestion was a good one. The overwhelming scent would certainly hide them from any pursuers.

"Okay," he meowed. "But let me—" He broke off as Squirrelpaw bounded forward, flattened herself to the ground, and wriggled underneath the monster.

"—go first," Brambleclaw finished resignedly, following her.

A faint dawn light seeping under the monster's belly roused Brambleclaw the next morning. Squirrelpaw was curled beside him. For a heartbeat he couldn't remember why she was sleeping in his den instead of her own. Then the acrid reek of the monster, and a continuous roar from the Thunderpath close by, reminded him where he was and why. This was the morning when the journey would really begin! But instead of excitement, he felt only uncertainty dragging at his paws, along with the dismal thought that he had as good as exiled himself from his Clan by disappearing without his leader's permission.

Brambleclaw crept out from beneath the monster and lifted his head to taste the air. The grass was still wet from the previous night's rain, and the bushes at the top of the bank were heavy with drops of water. Mist curled through the trees in the gray dawn. There was no sound or scent of other cats.

Turning back to the monster, he called to Squirrelpaw, "Wake up! It's time we were on our way to Fourtrees."

He was beginning to think he would have to slide back under the monster's belly to rouse the apprentice when she crawled out, blinking. "I'm starving," she complained.

"We'll have time to catch prey on the way," Brambleclaw told her. "But we *must* get moving. The others will be waiting."

"Okay." Squirrelpaw raced up the bank and headed toward Fourtrees, following the line of the Thunderpath. Brambleclaw caught up to her, and for a time the two cats loped along side by side. The mist cleared and a golden light gathered on the horizon where the sun would rise. Birds began to sing in the branches overhead.

Once she was properly awake, Squirrelpaw seemed to forget about stopping to hunt. She hurried on, paying no attention to anything around her. Brambleclaw was torn between wanting to get to Fourtrees as soon as possible, and staying alert for possible trouble. When he heard rustling in the bushes behind them he halted, ears flicking up and jaws parted to detect the scent of their pursuer.

"Squirrelpaw!" he hissed. "Get out of sight!"

But Squirrelpaw whirled around a heartbeat before he spoke, and stood staring in the direction of the sound, her green eyes wide. At the same moment, Brambleclaw picked up the strong, familiar scent of a ThunderClan cat. Then the branches of a nearby bush quivered and parted to reveal Leafpaw.

The two sisters stood rigid for a moment, their gazes locked together. Then Leafpaw padded forward and set down the packet of herbs she was carrying at Squirrelpaw's feet.

"I brought you some traveling herbs," she murmured. "You're going to need them."

Brambleclaw stared from her to Squirrelpaw. "I thought you said you hadn't told any cat!" His voice was loud with outrage. "How does she know? You've been lying to me!"

"I have not!" Squirrelpaw spat.

"No, she hasn't," Leafpaw's gentler voice added. "But she didn't need to tell me anything. I just knew, that's all."

Brambleclaw shook himself. "You mean, you know everything?" he asked. "About the dreams, and the journey to the sun-drown place?"

Leafpaw turned her serious gaze on him, and he saw unhappiness and bewilderment in the depths of her eyes. "No," she mewed. "Only that Squirrelpaw is going away." She hesitated, closing her eyes briefly. "And there will be great danger."

A pang of pity for her stabbed through Brambleclaw, sharp as a thorn, but he could not afford to give in to it. He had to know what Leafpaw had done with her knowledge.

"Who else knows?" he demanded roughly. "Have you told your father?"

"No!" The flash of anger in Leafpaw's eyes suddenly made her look very much like her sister. "I wouldn't tell on Squirrelpaw, not even to Firestar."

"She wouldn't, Brambleclaw," Squirrelpaw added.

Brambleclaw nodded slowly.

"I almost wish I had," Leafpaw went on, bitterness in her voice. "Perhaps I could have stopped it all, and kept you here. Squirrelpaw, do you really have to go?"

"I must! This is the most exciting thing that has ever happened to me. Don't you see? It's a command from *StarClan*, so it's not like we're going against the warrior code."

She began pouring out to Leafpaw the whole story of Brambleclaw's dreams, and the meeting with the cats from other Clans. Leafpaw listened, her eyes widening in dismay. Brambleclaw fidgeted from paw to paw, acutely aware of the passing of time as the daylight strengthened.

"But *you* don't need to go!" Leafpaw wailed when Squirrelpaw had finished. "You haven't been chosen."

"Well, I'm not going back. I can't do anything right, as far as Firestar is concerned. Do you know he even told me I might not be fit to be a warrior? I'll show him whether I'm fit or not!"

Brambleclaw glanced at Leafpaw. She knew as well as he did how useless it was to argue with Squirrelpaw when she had made up her mind. There was something else, too, in Leafpaw's amber eyes: a hint of trouble, as if she knew more than she was telling.

"But you might not come back." Leafpaw's voice shook, and Brambleclaw was reminded even more forcibly that as well as a medicine cat, Leafpaw was Squirrelpaw's sister. "What will I do without you?"

"I'll be okay, Leafpaw." Brambleclaw was amazed at the gentleness of Squirrelpaw's voice, and the way that she pressed her muzzle comfortingly against her sister's side. "I've *got* to go. You do see that, don't you?"

Leafpaw nodded.

"And you won't tell anyone where we've gone?" Squirrelpaw pressed.

"I don't know where you're going—and neither do you," Leafpaw pointed out. "But no, I won't say anything. Just remember that Firestar does love you. He has things on his mind that you know nothing about." She drew in a shaky breath. "Now take the herbs and go."

Squirrelpaw dabbed at the packet of herbs, dividing them between herself and Brambleclaw. As they gulped down the bitter-tasting leaves, Leafpaw looked on, her eyes huge and somber.

"Even if you don't have a medicine cat with you, you can still find herbs as you go along. Don't forget marigold for wounds," she meowed rapidly. "And tansy for coughs—oh, and juniper berries for bellyache. And borage leaves are best for fever, if you can find any." She sounded as if she were trying to pass on the whole of her training in the few moments she had left.

"We won't forget," Squirrelpaw promised. She finished the last mouthful of herbs and swiped her tongue around her mouth. "Come on, Brambleclaw."

"Good-bye, Leafpaw," Brambleclaw mewed. "You—and the rest of the Clan—take care. If trouble is really coming to the forest, we . . . we might not be back in time to help you fight it."

"That is in the paws of StarClan," Leafpaw agreed sadly. "I will do my best to be ready, I promise."

"And don't worry about Squirrelpaw," Brambleclaw added. "I'll look after her."

"And I'll look after him." Squirrelpaw flashed him a

challenging look before padding up to her sister and touching noses with her. "We *will* come back," she murmured.

Leafpaw dipped her head, sadness clouding her eyes. As Brambleclaw headed once again for Fourtrees, he glanced back to see her watching them, a motionless light brown figure against the ferns. As he raised his tail in a gesture of farewell she turned swiftly, and the undergrowth swallowed her up.

CHAPTER 12

❧

Leafpaw caught a vole on her way back to the camp, and slipped
down the ravine with it clamped in her jaws, hoping that any
cat who saw her would think that she had been out on an early
hunting expedition. Her mind was still whirling with her sister's departure, and how the prophecies of StarClan seemed
to be gathering around Squirrelpaw and Brambleclaw like
mist clinging to the branches of a gorse bush.

As she emerged into the clearing she heard Mousefur's
voice raised loudly. "That Brambleclaw is a lazy lump! It's
well past sunrise, and he isn't up yet. I want him for a
hunting patrol."

"I'll wake him." Brightheart, who was sitting with Mousefur
near the nettle patch, got up and went into the warriors' den.

Leafpaw felt a cold knot in her belly at the thought of what
would happen when the rest of ThunderClan discovered
that Brambleclaw and Squirrelpaw had vanished. At that
moment, Dustpelt appeared from the nursery and padded
over to the apprentices' den, where Whitepaw and Shrewpaw
were sunning themselves.

"Hi," the brown warrior greeted them. "Have you seen

Squirrelpaw? She's not ill, is she? She's usually raring to go by now—before I've even had time for a piece of fresh-kill."

Whitepaw and Shrewpaw exchanged a glance. "We haven't seen her," Whitepaw mewed. "She didn't sleep in the den last night."

Leafpaw saw Dustpelt roll his eyes. "What is she up to now?"

Brightheart pushed her way out of the warriors' den and bounded across to Mousefur. Leafpaw trotted across to the fresh-kill pile with her vole so that she could hear what they were saying.

"Brambleclaw's not there," Brightheart reported.

"What?" Mousefur's tail twitched in surprise. "Where is he, then?"

Brightheart shrugged. "He must have gone hunting on his own. Never mind, Mousefur. Cloudtail and I will come with you."

"Fine." Mousefur shrugged, and as soon as Cloudtail emerged from the den, blinking sleep out of his eyes, she roused Spiderpaw and all four cats left the camp.

Meanwhile, Dustpelt was heading for the fresh-kill pile, irritably calling on StarClan to tell him how he was supposed to mentor an apprentice if she was never where she was meant to be.

"If you see your sister," he growled to Leafpaw, "tell her I'm in the nursery. And she'd better have a good excuse for going off on her own again." He snatched up a starling and headed back to Ferncloud.

Leafpaw watched him go before heading for the fern tunnel that led to the medicine cat's den. She was relieved that
Dustpelt had not stopped to question her about Squirrelpaw,
but she knew that as time went on and the two cats did not
return, there would certainly be questions—lots of them.
And she had no idea at all how to answer.

By midday, gossip was beginning to fly around the camp.
On her way through the main clearing to fetch fresh-kill for
Cinderpelt, Leafpaw overheard Firestar ordering the patrols
to keep an eye open for the two missing cats.

"So Brambleclaw is padding after Squirrelpaw, is he?"
Cloudtail remarked, his eyes gleaming with amusement. "Well,
she's a very attractive young cat; I'll say that for her."

"I can't think what they're up to." Firestar sounded more
annoyed than worried. "I'll have something to say to both of
them when they come back."

Leafpaw crouched down, pretending to be choosing the
best piece of prey, while the warriors dispersed, leaving her
father and mother alone together.

"You know," Sandstorm meowed to Firestar, "Graystripe
told me what happened last night, when you found them
hunting alone. It sounds as if Squirrelpaw and Brambleclaw
haven't been back since. From what Graystripe said about the
way you spoke to them, I'm not surprised they want to get
away for a while."

"Surely I didn't upset them that much?" Firestar sounded
anxious. "Not enough to leave the camp?"

Sandstorm gave him a direct look from wide green eyes just like Squirrelpaw's. "I've told you over and over again that you don't get anywhere with Squirrelpaw by criticizing her and ordering her around. She'll do the opposite just to be difficult."

"I know." Firestar let out a heavy sigh. "It's just this prophecy . . . fire and tiger together, and trouble for the forest. I thought after we dealt with BloodClan the Clans would be at peace."

"We've had many moons of peace." Sandstorm padded up to Firestar and pressed her muzzle against his cheek. "All thanks to you. If there is more trouble to come, it's not your fault. I've been thinking about that omen," she went on, sitting down with a quick glance around to make sure none of the warriors were in earshot.

Leafpaw gave a guilty start, wondering if she should creep out of the shadows on the far side of the pile of fresh-kill, but if her mother knew she was there, she paid no attention to her; after all, Leafpaw already knew about the StarClan message.

"It mentions fire and tiger, and trouble," Sandstorm continued, "but it doesn't say that fire and tiger will *cause* the trouble, does it?"

Leafpaw saw a shiver run right through Firestar's body, rippling his flame-colored fur.

"You're right!" he murmured. "The prophecy might mean they'll *save* us from the trouble."

"It might."

Firestar straightened up, suddenly looking very young. "Then it's even more important to get them back!" he burst out. "I'll lead a patrol myself."

"I'll come with you," mewed Sandstorm. Raising her voice, she added, "Leafpaw, you've had time to sniff every piece of fresh-kill on that pile. Cinderpelt will be waiting—and remember that you've promised not to say anything to any cat about this message from StarClan."

"Yes, Sandstorm." Leafpaw grabbed a vole and headed back to the medicine cat's den. She wondered if she ought to confess what her sister had told her about the journey—but she had promised Squirrelpaw to keep silent, too. The weight of the two secret prophecies weighed on her fur like raindrops. She did not know how she would manage to keep both her promises, and stay faithful to her vows as a medicine cat to act only for the good of the Clan, all at the same time.

For the rest of that day, Cinderpelt kept Leafpaw busy going over their stocks of herbs, sorting out what needed to be replenished before leaf-fall set in for good. The sun was going down and the air growing cold with the scent of damp leaves when they heard the noise of a cat brushing through the fern tunnel.

"It's Firestar," Cinderpelt meowed, glancing out of the mouth of the den. "You carry on with that, and I'll see what he wants."

Leafpaw was thankful to stay hidden in the hollow rock and count juniper berries. She caught a glimpse of her father in the clearing outside, the sun turning his pelt to brilliant flame, and shrank farther back so that he would not see her.

"There's no sign of them anywhere." Firestar sounded weary. "I tried to follow their scent, but the rain last night must have washed it away. They could be anywhere. Cinderpelt, what do you think I should do?"

"I don't see what else you can do, except stop worrying." Cinderpelt's voice was brisk but sympathetic. "I remember a couple of apprentices who were always sneaking off for one reason or another. No harm ever came to them."

"Me and Graystripe? That was different. Squirrelpaw—"

"Squirrelpaw has a strong young warrior with her. Brambleclaw will look after her."

There was a short silence. Leafpaw risked another glance out of the opening in the rock to see her father sitting with his head bowed. He looked utterly defeated, and Leafpaw's heart twisted in pity. She wanted to go and comfort him, but there was no comfort she could give without breaking her word.

"It's my fault," Firestar went on in a low, shaken voice. "I should never have said what I did. If they don't come back, I'll never forgive myself."

"Of course they'll come back. The forest is safe at the moment. Wherever they are, they will be well fed and sheltered."

"Maybe." Firestar didn't sound convinced. Without saying any more, he got up and disappeared into the fern tunnel.

When he had gone, Cinderpelt came back into the cave.

"Leafpaw," she meowed, "do *you* know where your sister is now?"

Leafpaw chased with her paw after a juniper berry that had rolled across the floor, not wanting to meet her mentor's gaze. When she thought about Squirrelpaw, she had a sensation of warmth and safety, and the presence of other cats. She guessed they were at Ravenpaw's barn, but she couldn't be sure. She answered truthfully, "No, Cinderpelt, I don't know where she is."

"Hmm . . ." Leafpaw was aware of Cinderpelt's gaze, and she looked up into her mentor's blue eyes to see no anger there, only deep pools of wisdom and understanding. "If you did know, you would tell me, wouldn't you? A medicine cat's loyalties are not the same as other cats', but in the end we are all loyal to StarClan and the four Clans in the forest."

Leafpaw nodded, and to her relief her mentor turned away and started to examine their stocks of marigold leaves.

I didn't lie to her, Leafpaw told herself miserably. But it didn't help. StarClan prophecy or not, she knew the warrior code as well as any Clan cat. One of the worst things an apprentice could do was lie to her mentor, and even though the words she had spoken had been the exact truth, Leafpaw felt desperately guilty.

Oh, Squirrelpaw, she protested. *Why did you have to go?*

CHAPTER 13

This isn't the quickest way to Fourtrees," Squirrelpaw protested when Brambleclaw paused on the edge of a bramble thicket. She flicked her tail. "We should be going that way."

"Fine." Brambleclaw sighed. Squirrelpaw had been unusually quiet after saying good-bye to her sister, but unfortunately the silence hadn't lasted. "Go that way, if you feel like a swim. This way the stream is narrower, and there's a rock we can use to jump across."

"Oh—okay." Squirrelpaw seemed disconcerted for a moment, but then she shrugged and raced through the trees at Brambleclaw's side; they crossed the stream in a couple of bounds and headed up the last slope that led to Fourtrees. Brambleclaw realized that the whole disk of the sun had risen above the horizon by the time they reached the edge of the hollow.

He paused, sweeping his tail to hold back Squirrelpaw so that she wouldn't go dashing into the clearing before they knew what they would find there. Drinking in the air, he could taste the mingled scents of the three other Clans, and when he looked down the slope he saw Tawnypelt, Feathertail, and

Stormfur sitting at the base of the Great Rock, while Crowpaw paced restlessly up and down in front of them.

"At last!" Tawnypelt sprang to her paws as Brambleclaw and Squirrelpaw burst out of the bushes at the foot of the slope. "We thought you weren't coming."

"What's *she* doing here?" Crowpaw demanded, glaring at Squirrelpaw.

Squirrelpaw returned the glare, her neck fur bristling angrily. "I can speak for myself, thanks. I'm coming with you."

"What?" Tawnypelt padded up to her brother's side. "Brambleclaw, have you lost your mind? You can't bring an apprentice. This is going to be dangerous."

Before Brambleclaw could reply, Squirrelpaw hissed, "*He's* an apprentice!" and flicked her tail at Crowpaw.

"I was chosen by StarClan," Crowpaw pointed out immediately. "You weren't." Seeming to think that settled it, he sat down and started to wash his ears.

"He's not chosen either," Squirrelpaw protested, transferring the glare to Stormfur. "Don't tell me he's here just to say good-bye to his sister!"

The two RiverClan cats said nothing, just exchanged a worried glance.

"She's coming, and that's that." Brambleclaw's patience was rapidly running out. At this rate the mission would fall apart in bickering and bad temper before it had even started. "Now let's get going."

"Don't order me around!" Crowpaw snapped.

"No, he's right," Tawnypelt sighed. "If we can't stop

Squirrelpaw coming—"

"You can't," Squirrelpaw put in.

"—then we might as well get moving and make the best of it."

To Brambleclaw's relief, even Crowpaw seemed to see the sense in that. He got to his paws, turning his back on Squirrelpaw as if she didn't exist. "Pity you can't leave your Clan without dragging along a burr in your pelt," he jeered at Brambleclaw.

The two RiverClan cats rose too, and padded up to join the group. "Don't worry," Feathertail murmured, touching Squirrelpaw's shoulder briefly with her muzzle. "We're all feeling a bit nervous. It'll be better once we're on our way."

Squirrelpaw's eyes flashed as if she were about to make a sharp reply, but meeting Feathertail's gentle gaze she clearly thought better of it, and dipped her head, her neck fur beginning to lie flat again.

As if obeying an unspoken command, all six cats padded through the bushes to the top of the slope, emerging at the edge of WindClan territory. When Brambleclaw looked out on the moorland slopes, the tough, springy grass ruffled by the wind like the fur of a huge animal, his heart pounded until he thought it would burst right out of his chest. This was the moment he had been waiting for, ever since Bluestar had spoken to him in his dream. The time of the new prophecy was here. The journey had begun!

But as he took his first steps across the moor, he was pierced by a sharp pang of regret for everything he was leaving behind—the familiar forest, his place in the Clan, his friends. From now on, everything would be different.

Can we really live by the warrior code outside the forest? Bramble-claw wondered. Glancing back to the dark line of the trees, he added silently, *Will any of us ever see our Clans again?*

Brambleclaw crouched in the shelter of a hedge and looked down at the clustered buildings of a Twoleg farm. Behind him, the other cats shifted restlessly.

"What are we waiting for?" Crowpaw demanded.

"That's the barn where Ravenpaw and Barley live," Brambleclaw replied, indicating it with his tail.

"Yes, I know," meowed the WindClan apprentice. "Mud-claw took me there when I made my apprentice journey to Highstones. We're not stopping there now, are we?"

"I think perhaps we should." Brambleclaw was careful not to sound as if he were giving the touchy apprentice an order. "Ravenpaw knows about the sun-drown place. He might be able to tell us something useful."

"And his barn is crawling with mice." Tawnypelt swiped her tongue around her whiskers.

"We could do worse than spend the night there," Bramble-claw agreed. "A couple of good meals will help to build up our strength."

"But we could easily make Highstones before dark if we keep going," Crowpaw pointed out.

Brambleclaw suspected uncharitably that the WindClan apprentice was arguing just for the sake of it. "I still think it might be best if we stay here for tonight," he meowed. "This way we'll get to Highstones early next morning, with most of the day to get a good start in unknown territory."

"Would you rather sleep on bare stone with no prey," Stormfur murmured, "or warm and comfortable with a full stomach? I vote for Barley's barn."

"Me too!" Squirrelpaw mewed.

"You don't get a vote," Crowpaw retorted.

Squirrelpaw refused to be crushed. Green eyes gleaming with anticipation, she sprang to her paws. "Let's go!"

"No, wait." Feathertail pushed in front of the eager apprentice a heartbeat before Brambleclaw. "There are rats around here. We have to be careful."

"Dogs, too," Tawnypelt added.

"Oh—okay."

Brambleclaw remembered that Squirrelpaw hadn't yet made the journey that all the apprentices took to Highstones before they could be made into warriors. In fact, this must be the first time she had left ThunderClan territory beyond Fourtrees. Privately, he admitted that she had done well so far, crossing WindClan territory without fuss and being sensible about avoiding WindClan patrols so that Crowpaw's departure could remain secret. Perhaps she would cope better than he first feared with the longer path that lay ahead of them.

Brambleclaw emerged from the hedge and led the way past the farm buildings toward the barn. He froze briefly when he heard the barking of a dog, but it sounded distant, and the scent that came to him was faint.

"Get on, if we're going," Crowpaw muttered at his shoulder.

The barn was some way away from the main Twoleg nest. There were holes in the roof, and the door sagged on its supports. Brambleclaw approached warily and sniffed at a gap at the bottom of the door. The scent of mouse flooded his senses; his mouth started to water and he had to concentrate hard to distinguish the cat scent that was almost drowned out.

A familiar voice spoke from just inside. "I smell Thunder-Clan. Come in, and welcome."

It was Ravenpaw. Brambleclaw slid through the gap to see the sleek black loner standing just in front of him. Barley, the black-and-white cat who shared the barn with him, was crouched a pace or two behind, his eyes widening uneasily as Brambleclaw's companions slipped in as well. Brambleclaw realized that Barley had probably not seen so many cats since he came to the forest to help the Clans fight against Blood-Clan, four seasons ago.

"I took your advice, Ravenpaw," Brambleclaw meowed. "I think StarClan sent me the dream because they want me to travel to the sun-drown place. These are the cats StarClan has chosen to go as well."

"Or some of us are," Crowpaw muttered disagreeably.

Brambleclaw ignored him, and introduced the rest of the cats to Ravenpaw and Barley. The older loner merely dipped his head in greeting and slid away into the shadowy depths of the barn.

"Don't mind Barley," Ravenpaw meowed. "It's not often we have so many visitors all at once. So this is Squirrelpaw," he went on, touching noses to greet the young apprentice.

"Firestar's daughter! I've seen you before, when you were a kit in the nursery with Sandstorm, but you won't remember that. I said then that you would look just like your father, and now I see I was right."

Squirrelpaw scuffled her paws in embarrassment; Brambleclaw guessed she was for once lost for words to meet this cat who had played such a large part in the history of her Clan.

"What does Firestar think about the journey?" Ravenpaw asked Brambleclaw. "I'm surprised he let Squirrelpaw go so far when she isn't a warrior yet."

Brambleclaw and Squirrelpaw exchanged an uneasy glance. "It wasn't quite like that," Brambleclaw admitted. "We left without telling him."

Ravenpaw's eyes widened with shock, and for a heartbeat Brambleclaw wondered if he would send them away again.

But Ravenpaw only shook his head. "I'm sorry to hear that you couldn't tell him what's going on," he meowed. "Perhaps you'll tell me more when you've eaten. Are you all hungry?"

"Starving!" Squirrelpaw exclaimed.

A *mrrow* of laughter escaped Ravenpaw. "Feel free to hunt," he invited them. "There are plenty of mice."

A short time later, Brambleclaw was curled up comfortably in the straw, his stomach stuffed full of mice that had almost lined up to leap into his mouth. If Ravenpaw and Barley ate like this every day, it was no wonder they looked so strong and healthy.

His companions were sprawled around him, equally full and growing sleepy as the sun went down, sending shafts of red light through the holes in the barn roof. All around they could hear scuffling noises and faint squeaking in the straw, as if their hunt had made no difference at all to the number of prey.

"If you don't mind, we'll sleep here tonight and leave first thing in the morning," Brambleclaw meowed.

Ravenpaw nodded. "I'll come with you as far as Highstones." Before Brambleclaw could protest that there was no need, he went on, "There are even more Twolegs than before around the Thunderpath. I've been keeping an eye on them, so I know the safest ways to go."

Brambleclaw thanked him, only to feel Crowpaw shift closer to him and mutter into his ear, "Can we trust him?"

Ravenpaw's ear twitched; he had obviously heard the remark. Brambleclaw thought he was going to sink through the floor with embarrassment, and Squirrelpaw lifted her head to aim a furious hiss at Crowpaw.

"Don't be angry with him," Ravenpaw meowed. "That's good thinking, Crowpaw. Thinking like a warrior, in fact. Where you're going, you must trust nothing and no cat without very good reason."

Crowpaw ducked his head, looking pleased at the loner's praise.

"But you can trust me," Ravenpaw continued. "I may not be able to do much to help with the rest of your journey, but at least I can see that you get to Highstones safely."

Wind struck Brambleclaw squarely in the face, flattening his pelt to his sides and almost carrying him off his paws.

When he unsheathed his claws to steady himself, they scraped against bare rock. He and his companions were standing on the summit of Highstones, gazing out over endless, unknown territories.

They had set out in the first faint light of dawn and reached the stony slopes well before sunhigh, led swiftly by Ravenpaw. He stood beside Brambleclaw now, his ears pricked into the distance.

"You'll avoid that tangle of Thunderpaths," he meowed, pointing with his tail to the thick gray smudge in the landscape. "Just as well. That's the place where WindClan took refuge when Brokenstar drove them out. It's full of rats and carrion."

"I know about that!" Squirrelpaw put in. "Graystripe told me how he and Firestar went to fetch WindClan back."

"There are many smaller Thunderpaths to cross," Ravenpaw went on. "And Twoleg nests to avoid. I've traveled that way now and again—not far, but far enough to know that it's not a place for warriors."

Squirrelpaw shot a nervous glance at Ravenpaw. "Is there no more forest at all?" she asked.

"Not that I saw."

"Don't worry," Brambleclaw meowed reassuringly. "I'll look after you."

To his surprise she whirled on him, the light of fury in her green eyes. "How many times do I have to tell you, I don't *need* looking after!" she spat. "If you're going to behave like Firestar all the way to the sun-drown place, I might as well have stayed at home."

"Oh, don't we wish," Crowpaw murmured, rolling his eyes.

Tawnypelt gave Squirrelpaw a curious glance. "Are you going to let an apprentice talk to you like that?" she asked her brother.

Brambleclaw shrugged. "You try stopping her."

His sister's ears twitched. "ThunderClan!"

Feathertail exchanged a glance with Stormfur, and then padded up to Squirrelpaw's side. "I'm nervous, too," she admitted. "I get shivers all along my spine when I think of being so close to all those Twolegs. But StarClan will bring us through."

Squirrelpaw nodded, though her eyes were still troubled.

"If you've all quite finished," Crowpaw mewed loudly, "it's time we were moving."

"Okay." Brambleclaw turned to Ravenpaw. "Thank you for everything," he meowed. "It makes a difference that you understand why we are doing this."

The loner dipped his head. "Think nothing of it. Good luck, all of you, and may StarClan light your path."

He stood aside, and one by one the six cats began to pick their way down the far slope of the hill. The rising sun cast long blue shadows in front of them as they took the first steps on the longest journey of their lives.

CHAPTER 14

Brambleclaw heaved a sigh of relief to come down from Highstones
and feel grass under his paws again. They were alone now,
a tiny band of cats in a vast, unknown territory. Ravenpaw
had pointed out a path across fields divided by sharp, shiny
Twoleg fences, and there were many scents of Twolegs and
dogs, though none of them were fresh. Wooly faced sheep
stared at the traveling cats as they slipped past, their heads
low and their ears flat, uncomfortable at being out in the
open.

"You'd think they'd never seen a cat before," Stormfur
grunted.

"Maybe they haven't," Tawnypelt replied. "There's no reason for cats to come here. I haven't had so much as a sniff of
prey since we left the barn."

"Well, I've never seen a sheep before," Squirrelpaw
pointed out. She padded a little closer to the nearest one, and
Brambleclaw unobtrusively moved up behind her; as far as
he knew sheep were not dangerous, but he was taking no
chances. Squirrelpaw paused a tail-length away, took a good
sniff, and wrinkled her nose. "Yuck! They might look like

fluffy clouds on legs, but they smell horrible!"

Tawnypelt yawned. "Can we get *on*, for the love of StarClan?"

"I wonder why StarClan are sending us to the sun-drown place," Feathertail meowed, swerving to avoid a grass-cropping sheep that was too close for comfort. "Why couldn't they have told us what we need to know back in the forest? And why do we have to hear the message at midnight?"

Crowpaw snorted. "Who knows?" He narrowed his eyes and stared at Brambleclaw. "Maybe the ThunderClan warrior can tell us. After all, he's the only one of us who has seen this place—or so he says."

Brambleclaw gritted his teeth. "You know as much as I do," he meowed. "We just have to trust StarClan that it will all come clear in the end."

"Easy enough for you to say," Crowpaw retorted.

"Leave him alone!" To Brambleclaw's amazement, Squirrel-paw darted forward and planted herself in front of the WindClan apprentice. "Brambleclaw didn't ask for the second dream. It's not his fault that StarClan chose him."

"And what do you know about it?" Crowpaw growled. "In WindClan, apprentices know when to keep their mouths shut."

"Oh, so you'll be quiet from now on?" Squirrelpaw mewed cheekily. "Good."

With his top lip drawn back in a snarl, Crowpaw stalked around her and went on.

Brambleclaw padded across to his Clan mate. "Thanks for backing me up there," he murmured.

Squirrelpaw's eyes flashed angrily at him. "I'm not doing it for you!" she snapped. "I'm just not letting that stupid furball think WindClan is so much better than ThunderClan." She dashed off with an annoyed hiss, past Feathertail and Stormfur, who had stopped to watch.

"Don't get too far ahead!" Brambleclaw called after her, but she ignored him.

As he set off in pursuit, Brambleclaw was uncomfortably aware that none of the other cats had tried to defend him, not even Tawnypelt. They must all be full of doubts about his vision of the sun-drown place, and why they had to go there, just like Feathertail. A sense of responsibility was settling more heavily on Brambleclaw with every step he took, and he knew that if any of his companions were injured or even killed on the journey, it would be his fault. Perhaps StarClan had gotten it wrong this time. Perhaps in the end, not even the faith and courage of warriors would be enough to bring them through safely.

Not long after sunhigh, they came to their first Thunderpath. It was narrower than the one they were used to, and curved so that they could not see monsters approaching until the last moment. On the opposite side, a tall hedge stretched as far as they could see in both directions.

Crowpaw approached cautiously and sniffed the hard black edge of the Thunderpath. "Ugh!" he exclaimed, wrinkling his nose. "It's foul stuff. Why do Twolegs spread it all over the place?"

"Their monsters travel on it," Stormfur told him.

"I know that!" Crowpaw snapped. "Their monsters stink, too."

Stormfur shrugged. "That's Twolegs for you."

"Are we going to sit here until sunset discussing the habits of Twolegs?" Tawnypelt interrupted. "Or are we going to cross this Thunderpath?"

Brambleclaw crouched on the grass verge, ears pricked to catch the sound of approaching monsters. "When I say 'now,' run," he told Squirrelpaw, who was crouching beside him. "You'll be fine."

Squirrelpaw didn't look at him. She had been in a bad mood ever since her earlier quarrel with Crowpaw. "I'm not scared, you know," she hissed.

"Then you should be," Tawnypelt grunted from her other side. "Didn't you listen to what we told you when we crossed the Thunderpath near Highstones? Get this straight: they're dangerous even for experienced warriors. Cats have died on them."

Squirrelpaw glanced up at her and nodded, her green eyes huge.

"Good," mewed the ShadowClan warrior. "So listen to Brambleclaw, and when he tells you to go, run like you've never run before."

"Before we cross"—Brambleclaw raised his voice so all the cats could hear him—"I think we should decide what we are going to do on the other side. We can't see beyond that hedge, and I can't pick up any scents for the reek of the Thunderpath."

Stormfur raised his head and opened his jaws to taste the air. "Nor can I," he agreed. "I suggest we cross, go straight through the hedge, and meet up again on the other side. If there is anything dangerous through there, the six of us together should be able to deal with it."

Brambleclaw was impressed by Stormfur's sensible thinking. "Okay," he meowed, and the rest of the cats, even Crowpaw, murmured their assent.

"Brambleclaw, you give the word," Stormfur mewed.

Once more Brambleclaw strained to listen. A low growling in the distance quickly grew into a roar, and a monster leaped around the bend, its unnatural, shiny pelt gleaming as it swept past. It buffeted the cats with a hot, gritty wind and left them choking in the reek it left behind.

Almost at once another monster passed, going in the other direction. Then quiet fell again, heavy like a blanket of snow; when Brambleclaw pricked his ears he could hear nothing but the distant barking of a dog.

"Now!" he yowled.

He sprang forward, aware of Squirrelpaw keeping pace with him on one side and Feathertail on the other. His paws pattered on the hard surface of the Thunderpath; then he reached the narrow strip of grass on the other side and was thrusting through the hedge, spiky branches snagging in his fur.

Pushing hard, he burst through into the open. For a moment he could not make sense of what he saw, and almost froze in panic. He caught a glimpse of leaping flame, and the acrid tang of smoke filled his throat. There was a high-pitched shout and a Twoleg kit came running toward him, not much taller than a fox, with thick, unsteady legs. The barking of the dog was suddenly much louder.

"Squirrelpaw, stay with me!" He gasped, but when he turned to look for her the ginger apprentice had disappeared.

He heard Stormfur yowling, "Stay together! Over here!"

Brambleclaw glanced around, but he could not see any of his companions, and his paws were carrying him into the depths of a holly bush, the closest refuge he could see. His belly brushing the earth, he crawled into shelter, and felt himself pressing up against fur. He heard a frightened whimper; in the dim light he made out a flecked gray pelt and recognized Feathertail.

"It's only me," he murmured.

"Brambleclaw!" Feathertail's voice was shaking. "For a moment I thought it was that dog."

"Have you seen the others?" Brambleclaw asked her. "Did you see where Squirrelpaw went?"

Feathertail shook her head, her blue eyes wide with fear.

"Don't worry, I'm sure they're fine," he mewed, giving her ear a comforting lick. "I'll see what's happening out there."

He crept forward a couple of tail-lengths until he could peer out. The fire, he realized thankfully, was only a heap of burning branches, confined to a small area not far from where he had broken in; a fully-grown Twoleg was feeding more branches to it. The Twoleg kit had joined him. Brambleclaw could still hear the dog barking, but he could not see it, and the smoke prevented him from scenting it. More important, he could not see any of his missing companions.

Wriggling back to Feathertail, he whispered, "Come on, follow me. The Twolegs aren't paying any attention."

"What about the dog?"

"I don't know where it is, but it isn't here. Listen, this is what we'll do." Brambleclaw knew that he had to come up with a plan right away, to get Feathertail out of there before panic froze her completely. Their holly bush was growing close to a wooden fence, and a little farther along a small tree stretched its branches into the next garden. "Over there," he meowed, twitching his ears toward it. "Climb the tree; then we can get on top of the fence. We can go anywhere from there."

He wondered briefly what he would do if Feathertail was so spooked that she refused to move, but the gray she-cat nodded determinedly.

"Now?" she asked.

"Yes—I'll be right behind you."

At once Feathertail dived out of their refuge, raced along the bottom of the fence, and took a flying leap into the tree. Brambleclaw, hard on her paws, heard the Twoleg kit shout again. Then he was clawing at the trunk, scrabbling hard until he reached the safety of a branch and the shelter of thick leaves. He caught Feathertail's scent and saw her blue eyes peering worriedly at him.

"Brambleclaw," she mewed, "I think we've found the dog."

She twitched her whiskers to point down into the next garden. Brambleclaw peered out of the leaves and saw the dog—a huge brown brute—leaping up and scraping the fence with blunt claws in its efforts to climb up and attack them. As Brambleclaw peered down it let out a flurry of hysterical barking.

"Fox dung!" Brambleclaw spat at it.

He wondered what their chances would be of escaping along the top of the fence, but it was flimsier than the ones he had scaled at the edge of ThunderClan territory, and the dog was shaking it so much that any cat trying to balance there was likely to be flung off into the garden. Brambleclaw imagined those teeth meeting in his leg or neck and decided they were better off staying put.

"We'll never find the others at this rate," Feathertail whimpered.

Then Brambleclaw heard the door of the Twoleg nest open. A full-grown Twoleg stood there, shouting at the dog. Still barking wildly, the creature kept up its attack on the fence. The Twoleg shouted again and strode into the garden, grabbed the dog by its collar, and dragged it, protesting, into the nest. The door slammed shut; the barking continued for a moment longer and then stopped.

"See?" Brambleclaw meowed to Feathertail. "Even Twolegs have their uses."

Feathertail nodded, her eyes filled with relief. Brambleclaw slipped out of the tree to the top of the fence and, balancing carefully, padded along it until he reached the hedge that bordered the Thunderpath. From here he had a good view of the gardens on either side. Everything seemed quiet.

"I can't see or hear the others," Feathertail mewed as she joined him.

"No, but that could be a good sign," Brambleclaw pointed out. "If the Twolegs had caught them, they would make such a racket we'd be bound to hear."

He wasn't sure that was quite true, but it seemed to reassure Feathertail.

"What do you think we should do?" she asked.

"The danger is inside these gardens," Brambleclaw decided. "We'll be safer on the other side of the hedge, beside the Thunderpath. The monsters won't bother us if we stick to the verge, and once we get to the end of these Twoleg nests there won't be any more problems."

"But what about the others?"

That was the question Brambleclaw couldn't answer. It was impossible to look for their companions with dogs and Twolegs all around. Anxiety stabbed deep in his belly when he thought of Squirrelpaw alone and bewildered in this strange and frightening place.

"They'll probably do the same," he meowed, hoping he sounded convincing. "They might even be waiting for us. If not, I'll come back and have a look after dark, when the Twolegs will be in their nests."

Feathertail nodded tensely and both cats jumped down from the fence, landing lightly on their forepaws on short, bright green grass. They slipped back through the hedge and along the Thunderpath, keeping well away from its smooth black surface. Monsters passed from time to time, but Brambleclaw was so worried about the missing cats that he hardly noticed the guttural roar and the rush of wind that rocked him on his paws.

Eventually they came to the end of the hedge. The Thunderpath curved away to join another one a little way ahead. Between the two was a wedge of open ground, almost covered by a tangle of hawthorn bushes. On the other side of the Thunderpath, fields stretched away into the distance. A cold breeze ruffled the fur on Brambleclaw's flank as he gazed across the fields to where the sun was beginning to sink.

"Thank StarClan!" Feathertail breathed.

Brambleclaw led the way into the bushes. They would be safer there, and some of their friends might already be waiting. Leaving Feathertail to keep a lookout, he plunged deeper, searching and calling out their names in a low voice. There was no reply, and he could not pick up any familiar scents.

When he returned to Feathertail, she was sitting with her tail wrapped around her paws. A dead mouse lay beside her.

"Do you want to share?" she mewed. "I caught it, but I don't really feel like eating right now."

The sight of prey reminded Brambleclaw how hungry he was. He had eaten well that morning in Ravenpaw's barn, but they had traveled a long way since then.

"Are you sure? I can catch one for myself."

"No, go on." She shoved the mouse toward him with one paw.

"Thanks." Brambleclaw crouched beside her and took a bite, the warm flavors flooding his mouth. "Try not to worry," he mewed as Feathertail bent her head to take a halfhearted mouthful. "I'm sure we'll meet up with the others soon."

Feathertail stopped eating to give him an anxious look. "I hope so. It feels weird being without Stormfur. We've always been closer than most littermates. I suppose it comes from having a father in a different Clan."

Brambleclaw nodded, remembering how close he had felt to Tawnypelt when they were kits, as they struggled to make sense of their bloodstained heritage from their father, Tigerstar.

"Of course, you'll understand that." Feathertail invited him with a twitch of her ears to take more of the mouse.

"Yes," Brambleclaw replied. He shrugged. "But I don't miss my father as much as you must miss Graystripe. I wish I could honor his memory, but I can't."

"That must be very hard." Feathertail pressed her muzzle against his shoulder. "At least we see Graystripe at Gatherings. And we were so proud when he was made Clan deputy."

"He's proud of you, too," mewed Brambleclaw, glad to leave the subject of his father behind.

He took his remaining share of the mouse, and while Feathertail forced herself to finish hers he began to plan what they should do next. Venturing out of the bushes he could see the sun setting in rays of fire, blazing out the path that they must take. But there was no hope of continuing until they had found the others.

"They're not here," Feathertail murmured, padding up to join him so that her breath was soft against his ear.

"No, I'll have to go back. You stay here in case—"

A furious yowling interrupted him: the voices of angry, frightened cats, coming from the last garden in the row. Springing to his paws, he met Feathertail's startled glance.

"There they are!" He gasped. "And they're in trouble!"

CHAPTER 15

Leafpaw opened her eyes to see fronds of fern above her head, outlined against a paling sky. At once she remembered that this was the day of the half-moon, when all the medicine cats and their apprentices made the journey to Highstones to meet with StarClan at the mysterious Moonstone. A shiver of excitement ran through her; she had traveled there only once before, when StarClan had received her as a medicine cat apprentice, and the experience would stay with her for the rest of her life.

Leaping up from her comfortable mossy nest, she stretched and yawned, blinking away the last traces of sleep. She could hear Cinderpelt moving around inside her den, and a few moments later the medicine cat poked her head out and scented the air.

"No smell of rain," she meowed. "We should have a good journey."

Without any more delay she led the way out of camp. Leafpaw cast a regretful look at the pile of fresh-kill as they passed it; no cat who wanted to share tongues with StarClan was allowed to eat beforehand.

Ashfur, who was on guard beside the entrance to the gorse tunnel, dipped his head as Leafpaw and her mentor went by. Leafpaw felt faintly embarrassed. She was conscious that she was still only an apprentice, and was not yet used to the honor with which warriors treated all medicine cats.

Shadows still lay in the ravine and under the trees as Cinderpelt limped toward Fourtrees, where she and Leafpaw would cross into WindClan territory. Faint rustlings in the undergrowth told them where prey was stirring, but the tiny creatures were safe from hunting for now. From time to time a bird uttered an alarm call as the two cats passed by, no more than shadows themselves in the gray light.

"Practice your scenting skills," Cinderpelt instructed Leafpaw after a while. "If you can find any useful herbs, we'll collect them on the way back."

Leafpaw obeyed, concentrating as hard as she could, until they reached the stream. She and Cinderpelt crouched to lap at the water, then padded along the bank until they reached the place where a rock midstream made it easier to cross. Leafpaw kept an eye on her mentor, worried that her injured leg would give her trouble, but Cinderpelt managed the jump with the ease of long practice.

As they climbed the slope that led to Fourtrees, Leafpaw began to pick up the scent of other cats. "ShadowClan," she murmured. "That must be Littlecloud."

Cinderpelt nodded. "He usually waits for me."

Leafpaw knew that Cinderpelt had saved Littlecloud's life when sickness raged through ShadowClan; because of that,

Littlecloud had chosen to follow the path of a medicine cat, and ever since there had been a bond of friendship between him and Cinderpelt, beyond even the common loyalty shared by all medicine cats.

When they reached the top of the hollow, Leafpaw spotted the ShadowClan medicine cat sitting at the base of the Great Rock. The small but dignified tabby figure was alone, as he had no apprentice. He leaped to his paws as soon as he saw them, calling out a greeting. At the same moment the bushes farther around the hollow rustled, and Mudfur from RiverClan stepped into the clearing with his apprentice, Mothwing.

Leafpaw was pleased to see the RiverClan apprentice. She bounded down the slope to join her as Cinderpelt and the other two medicine cats met in the center of the clearing and began to exchange their news.

"Mothwing!" she meowed. "It's good to see you."

The sun had risen fully above the trees, and Mothwing's golden fur glowed amber. Leafpaw thought again how beautiful she was, but she was disconcerted when her friendly greeting was not returned.

Instead, Mothwing nodded coolly. "Greetings. I wondered if Cinderpelt would bring her apprentice."

Something about the way she spoke made Leafpaw feel small, as if Mothwing were trying to put her in her place. Of course, Mothwing was already a warrior, so perhaps she expected respect and not friendship from an apprentice. Disappointment stabbed Leafpaw like a thorn; she dipped her head and fell back a pace to follow the other cats as they made their way up the side of the hollow and across the border into WindClan territory.

Her spirits rose again as they began to cross the moorland; the bright, early leaf-fall sunlight, the breeze ruffling the grass that felt springy under her paws, the scents of gorse and heather were all so different from the lush, shady forest of ThunderClan. Seeing that Mothwing was padding behind her mentor without joining in the talk of the medicine cats, Leafpaw went over to join her.

"I didn't think you would be here," she mewed. "I thought that Mudfur would have taken you to Mothermouth already."

Mothwing swung around to look her full in the face, her amber eyes smoldering as if Leafpaw had said something to offend her. Leafpaw flinched. "I'm sorry . . ." she began.

Suddenly Mothwing relaxed and the hostile light died out of her eyes. "No, I'm sorry," she meowed. "It's not your fault. You heard what Mudfur said at the last Gathering, about waiting for a sign from StarClan that I would be the right medicine cat for the Clan?"

Leafpaw nodded.

"The sign didn't come." Mothwing paused and began to tug at the tough moorland grass with the claws of one forepaw. "There was nothing! I thought that meant StarClan had rejected me—and the other cats were quick enough to start talking about it! Just because my mother was a rogue, and I'm not Clan-born." The fierce light shone briefly in her eyes again, and then faded.

"Oh, no—I'm so sorry!" Leafpaw exclaimed, eyes wide with sympathy.

"Mudfur just told me to be patient." Mothwing's lips twisted wryly. "He may be good at that, but I'm not. I tried, but still the sign didn't come. I was ready to leave the Clan, but Hawkfrost—you remember my brother, Hawkfrost?—told me not to listen. He said I didn't have to prove my loyalty to jealous cats, only to StarClan, and he was sure they would send the sign eventually."

"And he was right," mewed Leafpaw, "or you wouldn't be here now."

"Yes, he was right." Relief sparkled in Mothwing's eyes. "It was only two dawns ago. Mudfur came out of his den and found a moth's wing at the entrance. He showed it to Leopardstar and all the other Clan cats. He said you couldn't have a clearer sign than that."

"And did Leopardstar—" Leafpaw was interrupted by a distant yowling and looked up. The three medicine cats had paused at the top of a distant rise and were looking back toward the two of them.

"Are you coming with us or not?" Mudfur's voice came faintly on the wind.

Leafpaw exchanged a startled glance with Mothwing and let out a *mrrow* of laughter. The sign had been sent from StarClan, so Mothwing could have nothing to worry about. The Moonstone awaited them both, ready to let them into the mysteries of their warrior ancestors. At that moment,

Leafpaw couldn't imagine anything better than being an apprentice medicine cat. "Come on," she mewed excitedly to her companion. "We're being left behind!"

At sunhigh, they met up with Barkface, the WindClan medicine cat, beside the source of one of the moorland streams. Leafpaw watched Barkface and Mudfur greet each other with friendly meows, in spite of the tension between their Clans over WindClan's determination to drink at the river until the next Gathering. Usual Clan rivalries did not exist between medicine cats—their loyalty was to StarClan, which stretched across all forest boundaries.

After a while, Leafpaw noticed that Cinderpelt was beginning to limp badly, and guessed that her old injury was bothering her. But the ThunderClan medicine cat would never admit that the pace was too much for her, so Leafpaw decided to slow the cats down herself. "Can't we have a rest?" she begged, flopping down on a patch of soft heather. "I'm really tired!"

Cinderpelt gave her a keen glance, as if she guessed what Leafpaw was thinking, and then meowed agreement.

"Apprentices," Barkface muttered. "No stamina."

"*He* hasn't traveled as far as us," Mothwing whispered as she settled down beside Leafpaw. "And he doesn't have an apprentice, so what does he know?"

"He's not really unkind," Leafpaw murmured back. "I think he just likes to sound grumpy." She lay on one side and began to give herself a thorough wash, wanting to look her best when she stood before StarClan.

Mothwing started to do the same, and then paused. "Leafpaw, will you test me?" she begged.

"Test you—on what?"

"Herbs." Mothwing's eyes were wide and anxious. "In case Mudfur expects me to know all of them. I don't want to let him down. We use marigold to stop infection, and yarrow leaves to expel poison, but what's best for bellyache? I can never remember."

"Juniper berries, or chervil root," Leafpaw replied, mystified. "But why are you getting so worked up? You can always ask your mentor. He won't expect you to know everything already."

"Not when I meet StarClan!" Mothwing was almost wailing in distress. "I have to show them that I'm fit to be a medicine cat. They might not accept me if I can't remember the things I ought to know."

Leafpaw almost burst out laughing. "It's not like that," she meowed patiently. "StarClan won't ask you questions. They . . . Well, it's difficult to explain, but I'm sure you don't have anything to worry about."

"It's easy enough for you." To Leafpaw's surprise, there was a hint of bitterness in Mothwing's tone. "You were born a forest cat. I have to be better than any other cat, just to be accepted in the Clan."

Her eyes were huge, shining with a mixture of anger and determination. Pity for her squeezed Leafpaw's heart, and she swept her tail around to touch Mothwing's shoulder.

"That might be true of RiverClan," she meowed, "but it isn't true of StarClan. You don't *earn* StarClan's approval—they give it as a gift."

"Well, they might not give it to me," Mothwing muttered.

Leafpaw stared at her friend in amazement. She was so strong and beautiful, she had all of a warrior's skills as well as the chance to learn those of a medicine cat, but she was still afraid that she would never belong in the forest.

Moving closer to her, Leafpaw pressed her muzzle comfortingly into Mothwing's side. "You'll be fine," she murmured. "Look at Firestar. He's not Clan-born, but now he's ThunderClan leader." When Mothwing still looked uncertain, she added, "Trust me. When you stand in front of the Moonstone, you'll understand everything."

The sun was beginning to sink as the medicine cats approached Highstones. The rough moorland grass gave way to a steep slope of bare soil, with here and there a clump of heather. Outcrops of rock poked through it, blotched with yellow lichen.

Barkface, who had taken the lead, paused on a flat rock and gazed upward. Just below the peak a dark hole gaped in the hillside beneath a stone archway.

"There's Mothermouth," Leafpaw explained to Mothwing, and then remembered that her friend would have seen it before, when she made her apprentice journey during her warrior training. "Sorry," she added. "I know this isn't your first time."

Mothwing's eyes widened as she gazed up at the yawning gap. "This is as far as I went," she replied. "I wasn't chosen to go inside."

"It is frightening, I know—but it's wonderful, too," Leaf-paw reassured her.

Mothwing drew herself up. "I'm not afraid," she insisted. "I'm a warrior. I'm not afraid of anything."

Not even rejection by StarClan? Leafpaw didn't dare put words to her thought, but as she settled down beside her friend to wait for nightfall she couldn't help noticing that Mothwing was trembling.

At last the half-moon floated above the peak and Mudfur rose to his paws. "It's time," he rasped.

Leafpaw felt tension in her belly as she followed her mentor up the slope and underneath the stone archway. Cold, damp air flowed toward them, and it almost seemed as if a river of darkness flowed out too, blacker than the night that surrounded them. Leafpaw took her place at the back of the line of cats, just behind Mothwing.

The tunnel sloped down, winding back and forth until Leafpaw lost all sense of direction. The air seemed thick, as if they were underwater as well as underground. She could see nothing, not even Mothwing padding no more than a rabbit-hop in front of her, though she could hear the RiverClan cat's shallow breathing and smell the fear-scent that came from her.

At last Leafpaw felt a cool ripple in the air around them, and her fur tingled with excitement as she recognized the first sign that they were coming to the heart of the hill. Fresh scents of the world above came faintly to her as she stepped into a large cavern; a glitter of starshine through a hole in the roof showed her soaring walls of stone, and underneath her paws the floor was smooth, well-worn stone. In the center of the cave stood a rock three tail-lengths high. Leafpaw's eyes widened in awe as she gazed at it, though as yet it was dark, a formidable sleeping presence.

Mothwing's fur brushed her lightly. "Where are we?" she whispered. "What's happening?"

"Mothwing, come before the Moonstone," Barkface announced from farther in the cavern. "We must all wait until the time comes to share tongues with StarClan." He and the other medicine cats sat around the stone, about a foxlength from it.

Leafpaw heard a shuddering sigh from her friend, and pressed reassuringly against the RiverClan apprentice's shoulder. "It's okay for us to sit, too," she breathed into Mothwing's ear. As she took her place a tail-length behind Cinderpelt, she felt Mothwing hesitantly sit down beside her.

In the darkness, time stretched out until Leafpaw almost believed that they had been waiting there for seasons. Then, within a heartbeat, brilliant white light flashed into the cave as the moon appeared through the hole in the roof. She heard Mothwing gasp. The Moonstone woke into dazzling life in front of them, glittering in moonlight as if the whole of Silverpelt had swirled down into its crystal surface.

As Leafpaw's eyes became used to the brilliant light she saw Mudfur rise to his paws, turn, and pace slowly across the cavern floor to stand in front of his apprentice. The white light flooded over his fur so that he looked as if he were covered in ice.

"Mothwing," he meowed solemnly, "is it your wish to enter into the mysteries of StarClan as a medicine cat?"

Mothwing hesitated. Leafpaw saw her swallow before she replied, "It is."

"Then come forward."

Mothwing rose and followed her mentor back across the cavern until both cats stood close to the stone. In its light Mothwing looked unearthly, her golden fur pale as ash and a glint of silver in her eyes—almost as if she had already joined the ranks of StarClan. Leafpaw shivered. That could not be a good thought; she pushed it out of her mind, reluctant to believe that it might be an omen.

"Warriors of StarClan," Mudfur continued, "I present to you this apprentice. She has chosen the path of a medicine cat. Grant her your wisdom and insight so that she may understand your ways and heal her Clan in accordance with your will."

He waved his tail and spoke to Mothwing. "Lie down here, and press your nose against the stone."

As if she moved in a dream, Mothwing obeyed. Once she was settled, all the medicine cats moved forward to lie in the same position around the Moonstone, and Cinderpelt gestured to Leafpaw to join them. Her fur crawled with anticipation; she knew what was about to happen.

"It is time to share tongues with StarClan," Barkface murmured.

"Speak with us, warrior ancestors," Littlecloud meowed. "Show us the destiny of our Clans."

Leafpaw closed her eyes and pressed her nose against the surface of the stone. At once the cold gripped her body like the talon of a hawk, or as if she had fallen headlong into dark water. She couldn't see or hear anything, or feel the stone floor of the cavern underneath her; she was floating in a dark night without even the light of Silverpelt.

Then a series of rapid scenes began to flash across her vision. She saw Fourtrees, but the great trees were bare, with only a few ragged leaves still clinging to the branches. One of the trees was shaking back and forth, more violently than in the strongest wind, while the others stood still around it. Almost at once, the picture was replaced with a view of monsters speeding by on the Thunderpath, and a long line of cats trekking through snow, a dark line against the endless white landscape. There were no trees here, and nothing to suggest that it was anywhere in the four territories.

The last scene of all showed her Squirrelpaw, and though Leafpaw knew she was forbidden to speak, she could barely hold back a cry of relief and delight. Her sister was trotting over a broad green field, and Leafpaw had the impression of several other cats with her before the vision was gone, and she was left in darkness once more.

Gradually the cold stone beneath her seeped back into her fur, and the endless space inside the dreams of StarClan dwindled to the ordinary freshness of a night in leaf-fall. Leafpaw opened her eyes, blinking, and drew away from the

Moonstone, before shakily rising to her paws. She felt oddly comforted, as though she were a kit again, protected by her mother while she slept. StarClan had preserved her link with Squirrelpaw, even though they were so far apart.

The other medicine cats were getting to their paws around her, ready to return to the surface. Mothwing stood among them, her eyes blazing with a mixture of triumph and wonder at the things StarClan had shown her. Leafpaw felt a sharp pang of relief as she realized that their warrior ancestors must have accepted Mothwing. Whatever she felt about her Clan mates, the RiverClan cat didn't have to doubt StarClan's approval anymore.

Mudfur touched Mothwing's mouth with his tail-tip, a sign for silence, and led the way out of the cavern. Once again Leafpaw brought up the rear, padding along the twisting underground tunnel, back toward the everyday world.

As soon as they reached the entrance, Mothwing leaped to the top of a jutting spur of rock. She flung back her head and let out a yowl of pure triumph.

Mudfur watched her, shaking his head indulgently. "Not so bad after all, then, was it? Well," he went on as Mothwing sprang down to his side again, "you're a true medicine cat apprentice now. How does it feel?"

"Wonderful!" Mothwing replied. "I saw Hawkfrost leading a patrol, and—" She broke off as Leafpaw widened her eyes at her, trying to signal that medicine cats did not share their dreams until they had some idea of what they meant.

Leafpaw padded over and touched noses with the

RiverClan apprentice. "Congratulations," she murmured. "I told you it would be all right."

"Yes, you did." Mothwing's eyes shone. "Everything will be all right now. RiverClan will hear that StarClan approve of me. They'll have to accept me now!"

She bounded off down the slope, leaving the others to follow more slowly. Leafpaw watched her with her heart full of questions. What had Mothwing seen? And what visions had StarClan sent to Cinderpelt? The ThunderClan medicine cat was looking thoughtful, but her expression gave nothing away.

Suppressing a shiver, Leafpaw remembered her own visions. What was powerful enough to shake one of the great oaks at Fourtrees? And why were cats traveling in the bitter cold of leaf-bare? If StarClan had sent her signs of what the future would bring, how was she supposed to interpret them?

Yet for all her uncertainty, Leafpaw was full of hope. Even though Squirrelpaw was a long way from the forest, StarClan had shown her that she was safe.

Send her back soon, Leafpaw prayed as she followed the other cats down the hill. *Wherever this journey leads them, please bring them safely home.*

CHAPTER 16

Brambleclaw raced back to the hedge with Feathertail right behind him. All his instincts told him to dash into the garden and rescue the other cats, but the memory of what happened when they had first crossed the Thunderpath warned him to be more careful. Instead, he pushed his way through the branches until he could peer out while still remaining hidden.

What he saw made his belly flip over. Near the Twoleg nest, two huge kittypets had cornered Stormfur and Crowpaw. The WindClan apprentice was crouched close to the ground, his ears flattened and his lips drawn back in a snarl. Stormfur had one paw stretched out in front of him, threatening the kittypets with unsheathed claws. Brambleclaw could see that they wouldn't get away without a fight, and there was nowhere for them to retreat except through the half-open door of the Twoleg nest.

"Great StarClan!" Feathertail gasped in his ear. "Those kittypets are bigger than most warriors!"

Brambleclaw wasn't sure that mattered. Size and a glossy pelt didn't make a warrior. He didn't have any doubts that he and his friends would win the battle, but the two kittypets were defending their territory, and they looked capable of inflicting nasty wounds—wounds the Clan cats could not afford if they were to keep on with their journey.

He tensed his muscles, preparing to leap on the kittypets from behind, but before he could move, a flame-colored streak flashed down from the fence and across the garden.

"Squirrelpaw, no!" Brambleclaw yowled.

The apprentice took no notice; he was not even sure she had heard. Hurling herself into the midst of the bristling cats, she clawed at the nearest kittypet. Both of them swung around, snarling.

At once Brambleclaw called out, "Stormfur, Crowpaw! Over here!"

Crowpaw shot across the grass and crashed into Feather-tail's flank as he charged under the hedge, but Stormfur stayed where he was, screeching at the advancing kittypets with Squirrelpaw beside him. At the same moment Tawnypelt appeared on top of the fence from the next garden and leaped down to join them.

"Back off, fox dung!" Squirrelpaw spat as the two kittypets closed in.

The nearest of them lashed at her with one paw, missing her by a whisker. Then the door to the Twoleg nest was flung open and a female Twoleg appeared, shouting and waving her arms. The kittypets fled around the side of the nest, while the Clan cats dashed for the refuge of the hedge. The Twoleg glared after them for a moment and then retreated into her nest, banging the door behind her.

"Squirrelpaw!" Brambleclaw hissed as the apprentice skidded to a halt. "What were you thinking of out there? Those two could have clawed your fur off."

Squirrelpaw shrugged, quite unrepentant. "No, they couldn't. All kittypets are soft," she meowed. "Anyway, Stormfur and Crowpaw were there."

"Brambleclaw, don't scold her." Stormfur's amber eyes glowed as he gazed at Squirrelpaw. "That was the bravest thing I've ever seen."

Feathertail murmured agreement, and Brambleclaw began to feel uncomfortable. Tawnypelt gave the young cat a nod of approval, too; only Crowpaw looked cross, perhaps aware that Squirrelpaw had come off better than him, perhaps regretting that in the moment of crisis he had obeyed an order from Brambleclaw.

"I never said she wasn't brave," Brambleclaw defended himself hotly. "Just that she needs to think first. We've still got a long way to go, and if any of us is injured it's going to hold us back."

"Well, we're all here now," Tawnypelt pointed out. "Let's get going."

Brambleclaw led the way back to the patch of rough ground where he had waited with Feathertail. By now the sun had gone, but red streaks stained the sky, showing them the path they must follow.

"We could spend the night here," Feathertail suggested. "There's shelter, and prey."

"It's too close to the Twoleg nests," Stormfur argued. "If

we cross the Thunderpath into those fields, we'll be able to find a safer place."

No cat disagreed with that. StarClan sent them an easy crossing of the second Thunderpath, and as twilight gathered they began the trek across the fields. The surface was rough, with boggy patches and heaps of stone, as if once there had been Twoleg nests here that had been allowed to fall into ruin.

It was almost dark when they came to a stretch of broken-down wall. Ferns and grasses had rooted in the cracks, giving some shelter, and moss covered the fallen stones.

"This doesn't look too bad," Stormfur meowed. "We could stop here."

"Oh, yes, please!" Squirrelpaw agreed. "I'm so tired I think my paws will drop off!"

"Well, I think we should go on a bit farther," Crowpaw objected stubbornly. Brambleclaw suspected he was just trying to be difficult. "There's no prey-scent here."

"We've traveled a long way today," Brambleclaw meowed. "If we go any farther we could run into more trouble, or have to spend the night in the open. Let's look around first, though, and make sure there aren't any nasty surprises. No badgers or foxes holed up nearby."

The rest of the cats agreed, all except Crowpaw, who grunted disagreeably. Squirrelpaw went to investigate on the other side of the wall. When she had been gone for a while, Brambleclaw set off after her, bracing himself to find that she had run into trouble again, only to meet her bouncing back around the line of stones.

"This is a great place!" she announced, shaking droplets of water from her whiskers, while Brambleclaw wondered where all her energy came from. "There's a puddle on the other side, with plenty of water."

"Water? Lead me to it," Tawnypelt mewed, trotting in the direction Squirrelpaw indicated. "My mouth's as dry as last season's leaves."

A moment later she came back, and stalked threateningly across to Squirrelpaw with her tail bristling. "That was a dirty trick," she growled.

Squirrelpaw looked bewildered. "Trick? I don't know what you mean."

Tawnypelt spat. "The water tastes disgusting. Full of salt or something."

"No, it doesn't!" Squirrelpaw protested. "I had a good long drink, and it was as fresh as anything."

Tawnypelt turned away and snatched angrily at some juicy stalks of grass. Stormfur shot Squirrelpaw a worried glance. "Wait there," he ordered. A moment later he reappeared with drops gleaming on his whiskers. "No, it's fine," he reported.

"Then why did I get a mouthful of salt?" Tawnypelt mewed.

A shiver ran down Brambleclaw's spine. "What if . . ." he began, his gaze darting from one cat to another. He swallowed. "What if it's a sign from StarClan that we're doing the right thing, trying to find the sun-drown place? My dream was about salt water, remember."

The four chosen cats looked at each other, eyes stretched wide with awe and, Brambleclaw thought, apprehension.

"If you're right," Feathertail murmured, "it would mean that StarClan are watching us, all the time." She glanced around as if she expected to see starry shapes stalking toward them across the darkening field.

Brambleclaw dug his claws into the earth, feeling the need to anchor himself in something real and solid. "Then that's a good thing," he meowed.

"So why haven't we all had a sign?" Crowpaw asked challengingly. "Why just the two of you?"

"Perhaps we'll have one later," Feathertail suggested, brushing her tail against Crowpaw's flank. "Maybe they're spread out to let us know we're staying on the right path."

"Perhaps." Crowpaw shrugged angrily and went off to curl up by himself at one end of the wall.

The rest of the party settled down too. Brambleclaw thought longingly of the mice in Ravenpaw's barn; there was no prey-scent here, and they would have to go to sleep hungry. The next day they would have to spend some time hunting before they went much farther.

The first stars of Silverpelt were beginning to appear above his head. *Warriors of StarClan,* Brambleclaw thought drowsily, *watching us and guiding us on our journey.*

If only I could speak to you right now, he thought. *I wish I could ask you if we're really doing the right thing, and why we have to travel so far. I wish I could ask you what trouble you have foreseen for the forest.*

The stars glittered more brightly still, but no answers came.

CHAPTER 17

Brambleclaw jumped awake when a paw prodded him in the side.

Squirrelpaw's voice meowed urgently, "Wake up, Bramble-claw! Feathertail and Crowpaw—are gone!"

Brambleclaw sat up, blinking. Tawnypelt was on her paws, and Stormfur was just emerging from the nest he had made for himself under a clump of ferns. But Squirrelpaw was right. There was no sign of Feathertail and Crowpaw.

His head whirling, he staggered to his paws. The sun had already climbed above the horizon in a bright blue sky dotted with puffs of white cloud. A stiff breeze was blowing, rippling the grass in the field, but it brought no scent of the missing cats. For a couple of heartbeats Brambleclaw wondered if they had gone home. They had not received the saltwater sign from StarClan; had that made them feel like giving up, as if they had been judged and found lacking? And if Feathertail and Crowpaw had turned back, could he and Tawnypelt succeed if they went on alone?

Then he realized he was being stupid. Crowpaw might think like that, but Feathertail never would, and wherever the two cats had gone they must be together. And it was unlikely that a predator had taken them; there were no scents of danger here, and in any case the noise would have woken the rest of them.

"See if they've gone for a drink at the pool," he suggested to Squirrelpaw, who was still gazing at him with panic in her green eyes.

"I already have," she mewed. "I'm not mouse-brained."

"No, okay, then . . ." Brambleclaw glanced around wildly, desperate to come up with a plan, and caught sight of two small figures, pale gray and black, approaching across the field. The wind, blowing toward the broken-down wall, had carried their scent away. "There they are!" he exclaimed.

Feathertail and Crowpaw trotted briskly up to the stones. Their mouths were full of fresh-kill, and their eyes gleamed with satisfaction.

"Where have you been?" Brambleclaw demanded. "We were worried about you."

"You shouldn't wander off like that," Stormfur added to his sister.

"What does it look like?" Crowpaw snapped, dropping the two mice he was carrying. "You were all snoring like hedgehogs in winter, so we thought we'd go and hunt."

"There's lots of prey over there." Feathertail gestured with her tail toward a thicket in the next field. "We caught a whole pile, but we'll have to go back and fetch the rest."

"Let these lazy lumps do it themselves," Crowpaw muttered.

"Of course we'll help," meowed Brambleclaw, his mouth

already starting to water at the smell of the fresh-kill. "You've done brilliantly. You stay and eat, and we'll fetch the rest of the prey."

Crowpaw had already crouched down, ready to take a bite from one of the mice. "Don't talk to us as if you're our mentor," he growled.

He was obviously determined to be difficult, so Brambleclaw left him to it. In spite of the younger cat's bad temper, he couldn't help feeling optimistic. They had survived the trouble in the Twoleg gardens, Tawnypelt's sign meant that they were still following the will of StarClan, and now they had a good meal to look forward to. As he led the way toward the thicket he decided that things could be a good deal worse.

"What are *those*?" Brambleclaw asked.

Three days had passed since the trouble in the Twoleg gardens, and the journeying cats had traveled on across farmland, avoiding the Twoleg nests dotted here and there, and meeting nothing more threatening than sheep. Now they were crouched in a ditch that ran along the line of a hedge between two fields. They were peering out at two of the biggest animals Brambleclaw had ever seen, which were running back and forth across the field, snorting and tossing up their heads. The impact of their huge feet made the ground shudder.

"Horses," Crowpaw replied loftily; his eyes gleamed as if he was delighted to know something that Brambleclaw didn't. "They run across our territory sometimes with Twolegs on their backs."

Brambleclaw thought he had never heard anything so mad in his life. "I guess even Twolegs want four legs sometimes," he joked.

Crowpaw shrugged.

"Can we please get going?" Squirrelpaw mewed plaintively. "There's water in this ditch, and my tail is getting wet."

"Fine, go," Brambleclaw muttered. "But I don't fancy getting crushed."

"I don't think horses are dangerous," Stormfur meowed. "We've seen them at the farm on the edge of RiverClan territory. They never pay much attention to us."

"If they did tread on us, they wouldn't mean to," Feathertail added.

Brambleclaw felt that wouldn't be much consolation; a blow from one of those feet, which looked like chunks of weathered stone, could break a cat's spine.

"We just need to run across while they're down at the other end," Tawnypelt pointed out. "I doubt they'd follow us. They must be quite stupid, or they wouldn't let Twolegs on their backs."

"Okay." That sounded like good sense to Brambleclaw. "Straight across this field and through that hedge opposite. And for StarClan's sake, let's stay together this time."

They waited until the horses had cantered off to the other end of the field.

"Now!" mewed Brambleclaw.

He launched himself into the open, wind streaming through his fur, aware of his companions racing beside him. He thought he could hear the pounding of the horses' massive feet, but he did not dare slow down to take a look. Then he was leaping the ditch that bordered the hedge on the far side, and plunging into the shelter of low-growing bushes.

Peering out cautiously, he saw that the others had reached safety with him. "Great!" he meowed. "I think we're starting to get the hang of this."

"It's about time." Crowpaw sniffed.

There were large animals in the next field too, this time standing together in the shade of a couple of trees, swishing their tails and munching grass. These were cows: Brambleclaw had seen them near Ravenpaw's barn on his apprentice journey to Highstones. They had smooth black-and-white pelts and enormous eyes like giant peaty pools.

The cows seemed to take no notice of the group of cats, and so they crossed this field more slowly, keeping an eye on the animals as they brushed through the long, cool grass. It was almost sunhigh, and Brambleclaw would have been happy to settle down for a nap, but he knew that they had to go on. He kept checking the position of the sun in the sky, impatient for it to start going down so that he could be sure they were still traveling in the right direction. Where the sun touched the horizon, that was the sun-drown place. Brambleclaw pushed away his nagging worry that they would have nothing to guide them if clouds came to hide the sun, and he hoped the good weather would hold.

Leaving the cows behind, they came to a field so huge they could not see the other side. Instead of grass, it was covered by thicker stems, yellow and stiff like the straw in Ravenpaw's barn, cut short so they were hard and spiky to walk on. In the distance they could hear the roar of a monster.

"It's over there." Squirrelpaw had leaped onto a low branch of an elder tree that was growing in the hedge. "A huge monster, in the *field*! This far from any Thunderpath!"

"What? It can't be!" Brambleclaw leaped up to the branch beside her. To his amazement, Squirrelpaw was right. A monster far bigger than most of the ones that traveled along the Thunderpath was roaring slowly across the field. Some sort of cloud surrounded it, filling the air with churning yellow dust.

"Satisfied?" Squirrelpaw meowed sarcastically.

"Sorry." Brambleclaw jumped down to rejoin the others. "Squirrelpaw's right. There is a monster in the field."

"Then we'd better get on as quickly as we can, before it sees us," Stormfur meowed.

"They're supposed to stay on the Thunderpath," Feathertail complained. "It's not *fair*!"

Crowpaw dabbed warily at the thick, spiky stems in the field. "This is no good," he spat. "We'll all have scratched pads if we try walking across that. We'll have to go around the edge."

He glared at the other cats as he spoke, as if he were expecting one of them to contradict him, but there was no reply except a murmur of agreement from Feathertail. Crowpaw had good ideas, Brambleclaw decided, if only he'd be less aggressive about sharing them.

The WindClan apprentice led the way and the rest followed, keeping close to the hedge so that they would be able to hide if the monster came after them. There was a narrow grassy space between the hedge and the rough yellow stems, just wide enough for the cats to walk in single file.

"Look at that!" Tawnypelt exclaimed.

She twitched her ears toward a mouse crouched among the spikes, nibbling at seeds that were strewn on the ground. Before any other cat could move, Squirrelpaw pounced, rolled over among the crackling stems, and scrambled to her paws again with the mouse in her jaws.

"Here," she meowed, dropping it in front of Tawnypelt. "You saw it first."

"I can catch my own, thanks," Tawnypelt mewed dryly.

Now that Brambleclaw knew what to look for, he realized there were more mice scuffling among the stems, stuffing themselves on the scattered seeds. It was almost as if StarClan had sent them the chance to hunt and feed well. Once Squirrelpaw had eaten he sent her to keep watch in another tree, to report if the monster changed direction and came toward them.

But the monster kept its distance. Brambleclaw felt more hopeful and stronger from the food when they went on, especially as the sun started to sink and he could check their direction. Before long they were able to leave the strange, spiky field, and the going became easier. The air was heavy with the heat of the day; bees hummed in the grasses and a butterfly flew past. Squirrelpaw dabbed a paw at it, but she looked too drowsy to chase it.

Tawnypelt had taken the lead as they approached the edge of the meadow, with Stormfur and Squirrelpaw just behind her and Crowpaw with Feathertail. Brambleclaw, bringing up the rear, kept a lookout behind for possible danger.

This time there was no hedge, but a Twoleg fence, made of some thin, shiny material. It was a kind of mesh, like interlaced twigs, except that the spaces were regular. They were too small to climb through, but there was a gap at the bottom where a cat could flatten itself against the ground and squeeze underneath.

Brambleclaw scrabbled his way under, feeling the fence stuff scrape against his back. Beside him, Stormfur was doing the same. As Brambleclaw straightened up again, he heard a furious wail from farther down the fence.

"I'm stuck!"

The voice was Squirrelpaw's. Heaving a sigh, Brambleclaw padded along the fence toward her, with Stormfur beside him. Crowpaw and Feathertail were already standing beside the young apprentice, and Tawnypelt came up a moment later.

"Well, what are you all staring at?" Squirrelpaw meowed. "Get me out!"

The ginger apprentice was flat on her belly, halfway beneath the fence. Just where she had tried to slide through, the fence stuff had started to come unraveled, and the ends were tangled in her fur. Every time she wriggled, the sharp ends of fence stuff dug into her skin and made her squeak with pain.

"Keep still," Brambleclaw ordered. He turned and studied the sturdy wooden post. "Then we can see what to do. Maybe if we dig up the fence post the stuff will come loose." The post looked pretty solidly set in the ground, but if they all helped . . .

"It would be quicker to bite through the fence," Stormfur argued. He tugged at the shiny strands with his front teeth, but they did not give way. He straightened up, spitting. "No, it's too tough."

"I could have told you that," Crowpaw meowed. "Far better to bite through her fur and free her that way."

"You leave my fur alone, mouse-brain!" Squirrelpaw snapped.

The WindClan apprentice bared his teeth with the hint of a snarl. "If you'd been more careful, this wouldn't have happened. If we can't get you out, you'll have to stay here."

"No, she won't!" Stormfur rounded on the other cat. "I'll stay with her, if no one else will."

"Fine." Crowpaw shrugged. "You stay here, and the four of us who are actually *chosen* will go on without you."

Stormfur's neck fur bristled and he sank his weight onto his haunches so that his leg muscles bulged under the dark gray fur; the two cats were heartbeats away from a fight. With a stab of panic Brambleclaw realized that two or three sheep had wandered up and were staring at the group of cats, while from farther away came the sharp barking of a dog. They would have to move quickly.

"That's enough," he meowed, thrusting himself between

the two hostile toms. "No cat is being left behind. There must be a way to get Squirrelpaw out of there."

He turned back to the apprentice to see Tawnypelt and Feathertail crouched beside her. Feathertail was chewing up dock leaves. "Honestly!" she exclaimed as she spat out the last of them and shot an exasperated glance at Brambleclaw. "Do you toms never do anything but argue?"

"It's what they do best," Tawnypelt mewed, a gleam of amusement in her eyes. "That's right, spread the dock leaves on her fur. They should make it good and slippery. Breathe in, Squirrelpaw. You've been eating too many mice."

Brambleclaw watched as Feathertail worked the chewed-up dock into Squirrelpaw's pelt, rubbing it with one forepaw into the tangle of fur around the fence stuff.

"Now try again," Tawnypelt directed.

Squirrelpaw scrabbled at the ground with her forepaws and tried to use her hind legs to push herself forward. "It's not working!" She gasped.

"Yes, it is." Feathertail's voice was tense, and she pressed her paw against Squirrelpaw's shoulder, which was slippery with green slime. "Keep going."

"And hurry!" Brambleclaw added.

The dog barked again and the watching sheep scattered. Dog-scent drifted toward them on the breeze, getting stronger. Stormfur and Crowpaw braced themselves to flee.

Squirrelpaw gave one last enormous heave and shot through into the field. A knot of ginger fur slid off the fence stuff; a few strands of it were left behind, but Squirrelpaw was free. She stood up and shook herself. "Thanks," she meowed to Feathertail and Tawnypelt. "That was a brilliant idea!"

She was right; Brambleclaw wished he had been the one to think of it. But at least they could go on now, straight into the path of the setting sun—and quickly, before that dog reached them. He led the way across the next field, confident that StarClan were guiding them.

When he woke the next morning, Brambleclaw was dismayed to see the sky covered by a thick layer of cloud. His confidence in StarClan's guidance faltered. This was what he had been afraid of; perhaps it was just luck that had kept the sky clear until now. How was he supposed to know which way to go if he couldn't see the sun?

Scrambling to his paws, he saw that his companions were still sleeping. The night before they had found no better shelter than a hollow place in a field under a couple of scrawny thorn trees. Brambleclaw found that he was growing more and more nervous without the familiar forest canopy overhead. He had never realized before how much he and his Clan mates relied on the trees: for prey, for shelter, and for concealment. Anxiety over Bluestar's prophecy bit even more sharply, as if badger's teeth were closing in his neck.

Paws itching to be on their way, he climbed the side of the hollow and looked around. The sky was unbroken gray; the air felt damp, as if there were rain to come. In the distance was a belt of trees, and the walls of more Twoleg nests. Brambleclaw hoped that their path would not lead them back among Twolegs.

"Brambleclaw! Brambleclaw!"

Some cat was calling his name excitedly. Brambleclaw turned to see Feathertail racing toward him up the side of the hollow.

"I've had it!" she exclaimed as she drew closer.

"Had what?"

"My saltwater sign!" Feathertail let out a delighted purr. "I dreamed of padding along a stretch of stony ground, with water washing over it. When I bent down to take a drink, the water was all salty, and I woke up tasting it."

"That's great, Feathertail." Brambleclaw's anxiety faded a little. StarClan were still watching over them.

"That means that Crowpaw is the only one of us who hasn't had a sign," Feathertail went on, glancing down into the hollow where Brambleclaw could just see the gray-black curve of Crowpaw's back as he slept in a clump of grass.

"Maybe we shouldn't tell him about your dream, then?" he suggested uneasily.

"We can't do that!" Feathertail looked shocked. "He'd find out sooner or later, and then he'd think we were deliberately deceiving him. No," she added after pausing to think, "let me tell him. I'll wait to catch him in a good mood."

Brambleclaw snorted. "You'll wait a long time, then."

Feathertail let out a faint mew of distress. "Oh, Brambleclaw. Crowpaw's not so bad. It was hard for him, leaving the forest just when he was about to be made a warrior. I think he's lonely—I have Stormfur, and you have Tawnypelt and

Squirrelpaw. We all knew each other before this, but Crow-paw is on his own."

Brambleclaw hadn't thought of that before. It was worth thinking about, though it wouldn't make it any easier to get on with Crowpaw the next time he started arguing the smallest point.

"We're all loyal to our Clans," he meowed. "And to the forest and the warrior code. Crowpaw is no different. He'd be fine if he didn't want to be leader all the time, when he's no more than an apprentice."

Feathertail still looked uneasy. "Even if you're right, it won't make it any easier for him, knowing he's the only one who hasn't had a vision."

Briefly Brambleclaw touched Feathertail's muzzle with his own. "You tell him, then, when you think best." Glancing around, he added, "We'd better wake them all and get moving. If we can work out which way to go."

"That way." Feathertail sounded confident as she waved her tail toward the belt of trees on the far side of the field. "That's where the sun went down last night."

And after that? Brambleclaw wondered. If there was no sun, how could they find their way? Would StarClan send them something else to help them find the sun-drown place? As he padded down into the hollow to wake his companions, he sent up a quick prayer to his warrior ancestors.

Show us the way, please. And guard us all when the trouble comes— whatever it is.

CHAPTER 18

"We're running short of celandine." Cinderpelt poked her head out of the cleft in the rock. "I've used nearly all of it to soothe Longtail's eyes. Do you think you could go out and get some more?"

Leafpaw looked up from the daisy leaves she was chewing into a paste. "Sure," she meowed, spitting out the last scraps. "This is just about ready. Do you want me to take it along to Speckletail?"

"No, I'd better check on her myself. Her joints have been aching badly since the weather turned so damp." Cinderpelt came out of her den and let out a purr of approval as she nosed the chewed-up leaves. "That's fine. Off you go—and take a warrior with you. The best celandine grows near Fourtrees, along the RiverClan border, and RiverClan aren't happy that WindClan are still coming down to drink at the river."

Leafpaw was surprised. "Still? But there's been so much rain—they must have water of their own by now."

Cinderpelt shrugged. "Try telling that to WindClan."

Leafpaw put the news out of her mind as she brushed through the fern tunnel into the main clearing. That quarrel had nothing to do with ThunderClan, and most of her thoughts were taken up with anxiety about Squirrelpaw and Brambleclaw. The sun had risen four times since she saw them leave. Her private sense of Squirrelpaw told her that her sister was still alive, but she knew nothing about where they were or what they were doing.

She had not eaten that morning, so she padded across to the fresh-kill pile, where Sorreltail was finishing off a vole.

"Hi." The young tortoiseshell warrior flicked her tail in greeting as Leafpaw chose a mouse for herself and settled down to eat.

Leafpaw returned her greeting. "Sorreltail," she asked, "are you busy this morning?"

"No." Sorreltail gulped down the last of her vole and sat up, swiping her tongue appreciatively around her jaws. "Did you want something?"

"Cinderpelt has asked me to go up toward Fourtrees, by the RiverClan border, to collect some celandine. She said I should take a warrior with me."

"Oh, *yes!*" Sorreltail sprang to her paws, excitement gleaming in her amber eyes. "In case WindClan accidentally stray into our territory, yes? Just let them try!"

Leafpaw laughed and quickly ate the rest of her mouse. "Right, I'm ready. Let's go!"

As they approached the end of the gorse tunnel, Firestar appeared, followed by Brackenfur and Rainwhisker. Leafpaw felt a thorn stabbing at her heart when she looked at her father; his head was down and his tail drooping, and even his flame-colored pelt seemed dull.

"Nothing?" Sorreltail asked him quietly; Leafpaw realized that she knew exactly what their leader had been doing.

Firestar shook his head. "Not a trace of them. No scent, no pawmarks, nothing. They've gone."

"They must have left the territory days ago," Brackenfur meowed somberly. "I don't think there's any point in sending out more patrols to look for them."

"You're right, Brackenfur." Firestar let out a heavy sigh. "They're in the paws of StarClan now."

Leafpaw pressed her muzzle against his side, and his tail curled around to brush her ears before he padded off across the clearing. Leafpaw saw Sandstorm meet him at the base of the Highrock, and the two cats went off together toward Firestar's den.

Guilt swept over her as she remembered how much she was hiding—most of all, the certainty that Squirrelpaw was safe, though far from ThunderClan territory—and every hair on her pelt prickled so much that it seemed impossible that no other cat noticed as she followed Sorreltail out of the camp.

As the sun rose higher the morning mists cleared away; the day promised to be hot, although the red-gold leaves on the trees showed that leaf-fall had taken over the forest. Leafpaw and Sorreltail headed toward Fourtrees. The medicine cat apprentice purred with satisfaction as she watched Sorreltail dashing ahead to investigate every bush and hollow that they passed. There was no sign of the shoulder injury that had kept Sorreltail from her warrior ceremony for so long, and no trace of bitterness that she had waited twice as long as other apprentices to receive her warrior name. Though she was older than Leafpaw, she still had all the joyful energy of a kit.

As they drew close to the RiverClan border, Leafpaw heard the soft rush of the river, and caught glimpses of it sparkling through the undergrowth at the edge of the trees. She found huge clumps of celandine where Cinderpelt had suggested, and settled down to bite off as many stems as she could carry.

"I can take some too," Sorreltail offered, glancing back as she padded up to the border. "Yuck—RiverClan scent marks! They make my fur curl."

She stood gazing out over the slope that led down to the river, while Leafpaw got on with her task. It was almost finished when she heard her friend calling to her.

"Come and look at this!"

Bounding to Sorreltail's side, Leafpaw looked down the slope to see a large group of WindClan cats gathered beside the water to drink. She recognized Tallstar and Firestar's friend Onewhisker among them.

"They *are* still drinking at the river!" she exclaimed.

"And look at that." Sorreltail pointed with her tail to where a RiverClan patrol was crossing the Twoleg bridge. "If you ask me, there's going to be trouble."

Mistyfoot was at the head of the patrol; she had brought with her the new warrior Hawkfrost and an older cat Leafpaw did not know, a tom with a black pelt. They padded down the slope and stopped a few foxlengths away from the WindClan cats. Mistyfoot called out something, but she was too far away for Leafpaw to hear what she said.

Sorreltail's tail twitched. "I wish we could get a bit closer!"

"I think crossing the border would be a really bad idea," Leafpaw mewed nervously.

"Oh, I know that. It looks like it could be interesting, that's all." She sounded resigned, as if the thought of helping RiverClan settle their border dispute had appealed to her.

By now, Mistyfoot's fur was bristling furiously, her tail fluffed out to twice its size. Tallstar left his Clan mate and came closer to talk to her. Hawkfrost said something urgently to the RiverClan deputy, but she shook her head and he took a pace back, looking angry.

Eventually Tallstar returned to his Clan mates, who finished drinking and set out for their own territory. They took their time; it looked to Leafpaw as if they were leaving because they had finished, not because Mistyfoot had ordered them off. Several of the WindClan cats hissed at the RiverClan patrol as they passed, and Leafpaw could tell that Mistyfoot had her work cut out holding back her two companions from a fight. They were badly outnumbered—Leafpaw could only guess how frustrated Mistyfoot must feel that she couldn't enforce her territory boundaries, thanks to the agreement at the last Gathering.

When the WindClan cats had vanished in the direction of Fourtrees, Mistyfoot gathered her patrol together to lead them down beside the river. Impulsively, Leafpaw called out to her; the RiverClan deputy turned and spotted her, and after a heartbeat's hesitation padded up the slope to join her and Sorreltail on the border.

"Hello, there," she meowed. "How's the prey running with you?"

"Fine, thank you," Leafpaw replied. She flashed a warning glance at Sorreltail, thinking it would be as well not to mention the confrontation with WindClan they had just witnessed. "Is all well in RiverClan?"

Mistyfoot inclined her head. "Yes, everything's fine, except . . ." She paused and then went on: "Have you seen anything of Stormfur and Feathertail? They disappeared from our territory four dawns ago. No cat has seen them since."

"We tracked them as far as Fourtrees, but of course we couldn't search on other Clans' territories," Hawkfrost added, coming up in time to hear what his deputy was saying. The black warrior stayed where he was, keeping watch beside the riverbank.

Hawkfrost dipped his head courteously to Leafpaw and Sorreltail. He was a powerful tabby with a glossy dark pelt, and for a heartbeat Leafpaw thought he reminded her of some cat she had seen before—but no other cat in the forest had such icy, piercing blue eyes.

"What do you mean?" she asked. "Feathertail and Stormfur have left RiverClan?"

"Yes." Mistyfoot's eyes were troubled. "We thought they must have decided to go to ThunderClan to be with their father."

Leafpaw shook her head. "We haven't seen them."

"But we've lost cats too!" Sorreltail exclaimed, lashing her tail eagerly. "And . . . yes, that was four dawns ago."

"What?" Mistyfoot stared at her in disbelief. "Which cats?"

"Brambleclaw and Squirrelpaw," Leafpaw replied, wincing. She wished Sorreltail hadn't blurted that out; her instinct had been to keep their disappearance secret from other Clans, but there was no taking the words back now.

"Is something taking them away?" Mistyfoot spoke almost to herself. "Some predator?" She shuddered. "I remember those dogs. . . ."

"No, I'm sure that's not what has happened." Leafpaw wanted to reassure her without giving away the secret that only she knew. "If it was a fox or a badger, there would be traces. Scent, droppings . . . something."

The RiverClan deputy still looked doubtful, but Sorreltail's eyes brightened.

"If they all decided to leave the forest, perhaps they've gone together," she suggested.

Mistyfoot looked even more confused. "I know Feathertail and Stormfur sometimes felt the Clan still blamed them for having a father in RiverClan," she meowed. "And Brambleclaw has to bear the burden of being Tigerstar's son. But Squirrelpaw . . . What reason could there be for her to leave her home?"

Only the fire-and-tiger prophecy, Leafpaw thought, and then remembered that Squirrelpaw herself had no knowledge of it—only what must have seemed to be unfair criticism from their father. It was the prophecy in Brambleclaw's dream that had sent Squirrelpaw on her journey. But for now Leafpaw could say nothing about either prophecy.

"Perhaps other Clans have lost cats too," Hawkfrost meowed. "We should try to find out. They might know more than we do."

"True," Mistyfoot agreed. Casting a grim look back toward the bank where the WindClan cats had gathered to drink, she added, "It will be easy enough to ask WindClan. But no cat will be able to speak to ShadowClan until the Gathering."

"That's not long now," Leafpaw remarked.

"Are you sure it will be easy to speak with WindClan?" Sorreltail ventured boldly, as if she were challenging Mistyfoot to admit that WindClan still drank freely inside RiverClan borders.

Mistyfoot drew back a pace, suddenly taller and with eyes like cold fire. From anxiously sharing her worries with Leafpaw, she had become the RiverClan deputy again, guarding her Clan's weaknesses. "I suppose you saw what happened," she hissed. "Tallstar has broken the spirit of his agreement with Leopardstar. She allowed them to come down to the river only because they had no water in their own territory, and he knows it."

"We should drive them off!" Hawkfrost's voice was hard, and his pale blue eyes stared stonily in the direction where the WindClan cats had disappeared.

"You know Leopardstar has forbidden that." Mistyfoot's tone suggested she had gone over this argument before. "She says that she'll keep *her* word no matter what Tallstar does."

Hawkfrost bowed his head in agreement, but Leafpaw noticed that his claws flexed in and out as if he itched to rake them over the pelts of the cats who had invaded his Clan's territory. Forest-born or not, he was growing into a formidable warrior, she reflected, as exceptional in his way as his sister, Mothwing.

"Say hi to Mothwing for me," she mewed to him, and with a sudden thought darted back to the clumps of celandine. Grabbing up a few of the stems she had bitten off, she hurried back and dropped them at Hawkfrost's paws. "She might like to have those," she told him. "Cinderpelt uses it to help cats with weak eyes. I think it grows much better on our side of the border."

"Thank you," Hawkfrost replied with a nod of gratitude.

"We'd better be on our way," meowed Mistyfoot. "Leafpaw, tell your father about Stormfur and Feathertail, and ask him to let us know if he hears anything."

"Yes, Mistyfoot, I will."

Guilt swept over Leafpaw yet again as she watched the RiverClan patrol pad away upriver. She felt again the burden of being the only cat to know about both prophecies—one that had sent Brambleclaw and Squirrelpaw on a journey who knew where, and one that left Firestar convinced they would be involved in the destruction of his Clan—and yet her knowledge was not enough. StarClan had not chosen to tell her about the destiny of the forest, and Leafpaw did not feel that even the full moon, shining

down on the next Gathering, would shed much light on
her dark questions.

By the time Leafpaw and Sorreltail returned to camp,
loaded with celandine, it was almost sunhigh.

"We'd better report to Firestar," Sorreltail meowed when
they had taken the herbs to Cinderpelt. "He'll want to know
about those missing RiverClan cats."

Leafpaw nodded and led the way to her father's den beneath
the Highrock. The clearing was full of cats enjoying the last
heat of early leaf-fall. Spiderpaw and Whitepaw were sprawled
in the shade of the ferns that sheltered their den, while
Cloudtail and Brightheart shared tongues in a patch of sunlight. Ferncloud was sitting outside the nursery with Dustpelt
beside her, watching their kits as they played together.

A wave of sadness swept over Leafpaw. It was almost as if
Brambleclaw and Squirrelpaw had never been part of
ThunderClan, as if they had sunk out of sight as a drowning
cat might sink in the river, the waters closing over its head.

The feeling ebbed a little when they reached Firestar's den
and called out to him. Leafpaw heard his voice telling them to
enter, and she brushed past the curtain of lichen to see him
curled up in his nest; Graystripe was sitting next to him, and the
anxiety in the eyes of both cats was enough to reassure Leafpaw
that her sister and Brambleclaw had not been forgotten.

"We've brought news," Sorreltail meowed immediately,
and poured out what Mistyfoot had told them about
Feathertail and Stormfur going missing.

Firestar's and Graystripe's eyes narrowed, and the deputy sprang to his paws as if he wanted to dash out and look for his missing children right away.

"If a fox has taken them I'll track it down and flay its skin!" he snarled.

Firestar remained in his nest, but he unsheathed his claws as if he were sinking them into the pelt of whatever had stolen his daughter. "Surely the dogs can't have come back?" he muttered. "We couldn't have to deal with them more than once in a lifetime?"

"No, there's no sign of that," Leafpaw reassured him. "Feathertail and Stormfur must have gone with Brambleclaw and Squirrelpaw, and that . . . that suggests they had a reason for leaving." She tried desperately to think how much information she could give to the anxious fathers without revealing that she knew more than she was supposed to. So far she had kept her Moonstone vision of the traveling cats even from her mentor, Cinderpelt, but now she knew she would have to reveal it. She was not breaking her promise, she told herself; she would not betray anything of what Brambleclaw and Squirrelpaw had told her when they met in the forest.

"Firestar," she went on hesitantly, "you know how close I am to Squirrelpaw? Well, sometimes I can tell what she's doing, even when she's a long way away."

Firestar's eyes opened wide in amazement. "That's impossible!" He gasped. "I always knew you were close, but this . . ."

"It's true, I promise. When I went to the Moonstone, StarClan gave me a vision of her," Leafpaw went on. "She was safe, and there were other cats with her." She met her father's intense gaze, and saw how much he wanted to believe her. "Squirrelpaw is alive," she finished, "and the others must be with her. Four cats together will be safer than two."

Firestar blinked, bewildered. "May StarClan grant you're right."

Graystripe's amber eyes remained full of fear and uncertainty. "Even if that's true, why did they leave without telling us where they were going, or why?" he meowed. "If Stormfur and Feathertail had a problem, why didn't they come to me first?"

"We think the other Clans might have lost cats too," Sorreltail meowed. "We should ask them."

Firestar and Graystripe exchanged a glance. "Perhaps," mewed Firestar; Leafpaw could tell how hard he was struggling to sound decisive, to act like a Clan leader instead of a desperately worried father. "The next Gathering is only a few days away."

"StarClan keep them all safe!" Graystripe added fervently.

Leafpaw suspected that he had little faith in his prayer; he knew well enough the dangers that stalked outside the forest. As she left her father's den, she felt the burden of her knowledge weighing even more heavily on her. She was the only cat in the forest who had heard that there were two prophecies, and knew what each of them said.

But I'm only an apprentice, she told herself anxiously. *I know them by accident, not because our warrior ancestors chose to tell me themselves. What do StarClan expect me to do?*

Leafpaw found it hard to sleep that night, fidgeting in her bed of ferns while Silverpelt glittered coldly above her. She longed to know what was happening to the journeying cats, but she could think of no way to find out.

When she finally drifted into unconsciousness, she found herself in some dim place, racing panic-stricken among the trunks of shadowy trees.

"Squirrelpaw! Squirrelpaw!" She gasped.

She was answered only by the hoot of an owl and the bark of a fox. Death panted hard on her paws, drawing closer with every footfall, and for all her twisting and turning, Leafpaw knew that there was no escape.

CHAPTER 19

Brambleclaw raced panic-stricken among the trees, bolting back and forth in a frantic effort to escape. Behind him he could hear the throaty bark of the dog that had leaped out from a thicket as he and his companions reached the wood. Glancing back, he saw the lean black shape crash through a clump of bracken, its tongue lolling. He could almost feel its sharp white teeth meeting in his pelt.

"StarClan help us!" Feathertail gasped as she dashed beside him.

They had fallen behind the other cats, though Brambleclaw heard a yowl of terror coming from somewhere just ahead.

"Dodge!" he called. "Try to lose it!"

The dog barked again, and from farther off Brambleclaw heard a Twoleg shouting. He lost sight of his pursuer, and he slowed down as a wave of relief swept over him; the creature must have gone back to its Twoleg.

Then he heard the dog's snuffling breath, and it shot out from behind a fallen tree trunk. For a heartbeat Brambleclaw stared into eyes like flames. Whirling around, he fled through the trees as the barking started up again.

Confused by fear, he remembered how Firestar and the other cats of ThunderClan had led the dog pack through the forest until they fell into the gorge and drowned. But how could he and his friends lead this dog away, here in unknown territory?

"Climb trees!" he yowled, hoping his friends could hear him above the fierce barking that sounded louder than ever.

He glanced upward as he ran, but every tree seemed to have a smooth trunk with no low-growing branches. He could not stop and search; the beast would be on him at once. Had it already caught one of the others? Was he about to find one of his companions terribly injured like Brightheart, or worse, dead?

His breath was rasping in his throat and his paws burned with every step; he knew he could not keep up this pace for much longer. Then a voice hissed at him from somewhere above his head. "Up here—quick!"

Brambleclaw skidded to a halt beside a tree that was covered with ivy. A pair of eyes gleamed down at him. In the same heartbeat the dog crashed through a tangle of briars behind him. With a terrified yowl, Brambleclaw launched himself upward, clawing frantically at the ivy stems. They gave way under his weight, and for a heart-stopping moment he swung helplessly; the dog leaped up and he heard the snap of its teeth and felt hot breath on his fur.

Then he managed to sink his claws into a stronger ivy stem and hauled himself upward again. Squirrelpaw appeared below, shot past the nose of the dog, and clawed her way up the tree, overtaking Brambleclaw to crouch shivering on a branch. Brambleclaw scrambled up beside her.

He spotted Stormfur and Tawnypelt clinging to another branch just above his head, and Crowpaw scrabbled his way up to join them from the other side of the trunk.

"Feathertail!" gasped Brambleclaw. "Where's Feathertail?"

The dog was on its hind legs at the bottom of the tree, less than a foxlength below him. Its claws tore at the ivy while it snarled furiously, drool spilling out of its jaws. The sound of the Twoleg shouting came again, but a long way off.

Then Brambleclaw noticed Feathertail crouching in the briars just behind the dog, staring out in terror. If she tried to run for the safety of the tree, the dog would cut her off. How long, Brambleclaw wondered, before it scented her?

Suddenly he heard Crowpaw spit furiously. "Fox dung! I've had enough of this." The WindClan apprentice hurled himself out of the tree, narrowly missing the dog, and hit the ground just beyond it. The dog spun around and gave chase, its paws scrabbling on the dry leaves. While it was distracted, Feathertail bolted out of the briars and across the clearing to make a desperate leap for a thin branch that swung alarmingly under her weight.

"Crowpaw!" Brambleclaw yowled.

The gray-black tom had vanished into the bushes. Brambleclaw could hear the dog crashing about, barking wildly, and the shouts of the Twoleg growing closer. Then Crowpaw appeared again, his belly close to the ground as he ran all-out for the tree. The dog was panting just behind him. Brambleclaw squeezed his eyes tight shut and opened them again in time to see Crowpaw take a flying jump and dig his claws into the ivy.

At the same moment the Twoleg lumbered into the clearing and made a dive for the dog's collar. He was red-faced and yelling furiously. The dog dodged to one side, but the Twoleg managed to grab it and clip a lead onto its collar. The dog's barks changed to whining as it was dragged away, clawing the grass and leaf mold as it struggled to return to its prey.

"Thank you, Crowpaw!" Feathertail gasped, still clinging to the swaying branch. "You saved my life!"

"Yes, you did," meowed Brambleclaw. "Well-done."

Crowpaw scrambled higher until he reached the branch beside Brambleclaw and Squirrelpaw. "Big brute," he muttered, looking embarrassed. "Tripped over its own paws."

Feathertail's blue eyes were fixed on him, huge as moons with shock. "It would have caught me for sure if you hadn't come to help me," she whispered.

As Brambleclaw's fear ebbed, he remembered for the first time the voice that had called him up into the tree. It wasn't one of the Clan cats. Looking up again, he saw a pair of eyes gleaming from the leaves a little way above his head. Then the leaves rustled and an unfamiliar cat emerged.

It was a tabby tom, old and plump with rumpled fur that looked as if he never bothered to groom himself. His movements were slow and careful as he clambered down the tree to join the six journeying cats.

"Well," he rasped. "You're a fine bunch, an' no mistake.

Don't you know that that dog runs loose every day, 'round about sunrise?"

"How would we know that?" Tawnypelt spat. "We've never been here before."

The tom blinked at her. "No need to get so snippy. You'll know another time, won't you? Get out o' the way then."

"There won't be another time," Stormfur meowed. "We're just passing through."

"Thank you for helping us," Brambleclaw added. "I was beginning to think we'd never escape."

The tabby ignored his thanks. "Just passin' through, eh?" he mewed. "I'll bet you've a story to tell. Why not stay awhile an' share it wi' me?" He stood up and braced himself, ready to jump down into the clearing.

"Down there?" Squirrelpaw sounded nervous. "What if that dog comes back?"

"It won't. It's gone home now. Come on."

The old cat scrambled down the ivy-covered trunk and ungracefully dropped the last foxlength to the ground. Looking up, he opened his jaws wide in a yawn. "Comin'?"

Brambleclaw leaped down after him; he wasn't going to let this elder, or kittypet, or whatever he was, show more bravery than warriors. His companions joined him, clustering around to gaze uncertainly at the stranger.

"Who are you?" Stormfur asked. "Are you a kittypet?"

The old tom looked blank. "Kittypet?"

"Living with Twolegs," Squirrelpaw mewed impatiently.

"Twolegs?"

"Oh, let's go," Crowpaw's ears twitched in contempt. "There are bees in his brain. We won't get any sense out of him."

"Who're you callin' senseless, young fellow?" The tabby tom's voice was a deep rumble, and his claws extended to sink into the leaves under his paws.

"Sorry," Brambleclaw meowed hastily, with a glare at Crowpaw; the apprentice might have shown amazing courage, but that didn't make him any less annoying. Turning to the old cat, he began to explain. "Twolegs, like the one who came to fetch the dog."

"Oh, you're talkin' about Upwalkers. Why didn't you say so? No, I don't live with Upwalkers. Used to once, mind you. Those were the days!" He settled down at the foot of the tree, gazing into the distance as if he were looking back at the young cat he had once been. "A fire to sleep by, an' all the food I could eat."

Brambleclaw wasn't sure he liked the sound of that. Firestar always said that kittypet food was nowhere near as tasty as fresh-kill you caught yourself. As for sleeping beside a fire . . . Brambleclaw remembered the fire that had swept through the ThunderClan camp, and the very thought of it made his fur prickle.

"Talking of food," Crowpaw meowed loudly, "we need to get on and hunt. There should be prey somewhere among these trees. Here, you . . ." He stretched out a paw and prodded the old cat, who had drifted into a doze. "What's the prey like around here?"

The tabby opened one amber eye. "Young cats," he muttered.

"Always dashin' off. There's no need to catch your own squeakers in these parts. Not if you know where to go."

"Well, we don't." Squirrelpaw flicked her ears back irritably.

"Please, won't you tell us?" Feathertail asked the old cat. "We're strangers here, so we don't know the good places. We've been traveling a long way, and we're all very hungry."

Her gentle tone, and the pleading look she gave him from liquid blue eyes, seemed to win over the old cat. "I might show you," he replied, scratching himself vigorously behind the ear with one hind paw.

"That would be very kind of you," Stormfur added, coming to stand beside his sister.

The old cat's gaze traveled over them, coming to rest at last on Brambleclaw. "Six of you," he mewed. "That's a powerful lot to feed. Who are you, anyway? Why don't you have Upwalkers of your own?"

"We're warriors!" Brambleclaw explained. He introduced himself and his companions. "I suppose you must be a loner," he finished, "if you don't live with Twolegs—I mean Upwalkers." Trying to sound as polite as Feathertail, he added, "Won't you tell us your name?"

"Name? Don't rightly reckon I've got one. Upwalkers feed me, though I don't stay with them none. They call me different names—a cat can't be expected to remember them all."

"You must have had a name to begin with," Squirrelpaw insisted, rolling her eyes at Brambleclaw.

"Yes, what was your name when you lived with the . . . the Upwalker who had the fire?" Feathertail asked.

The old cat gave the other ear a good scratch. "Well, now . . . that was a long time ago." He let out a gusty sigh. "A long time and a good time. I caught more squeakers in that Upwalker den than you youngsters have seen in your whole lives."

"So why did you leave, if it was as good as all that?" Tawnypelt asked; Brambleclaw could see by her twitching tail that her patience was running out.

"My Upwalker died." The tabby shook his head as if he were trying to flick away a clinging burr. "No more food . . . no more strokin' by the fire, dozin' on his lap. . . . More Upwalkers came after that, an' set traps for me, but I was cunnin', see. I went away."

"But what was your name?" Squirrelpaw hissed at him through clenched teeth. "What did the Upwalker call you?"

"Name . . . oh, yes, my name. Purdy, that's right. He called me Purdy."

"At last!" Squirrelpaw muttered.

"We'll call you Purdy, then, shall we?" Brambleclaw meowed, batting Squirrelpaw's muzzle with the tip of his tail.

The old tabby heaved himself to his paws. "Suit yourselves. Now, do you want food or don't you?"

He padded off through the trees. Brambleclaw exchanged a doubtful glance with his friends. "Do you think we should trust him?"

"No!" Crowpaw replied at once. "He was a *kittypet*. Warriors can't trust kittypets."

Tawnypelt murmured agreement, but Feathertail meowed, "We're all so hungry, and we don't know these woods. Would it do any harm, just for once?"

"I'm starving!" added Squirrelpaw, her claws flexing impatiently.

"StarClan know we could do with some help," Stormfur mewed. "I can't say I like it, but so long as we keep our eyes open . . ."

"Okay, then," Brambleclaw decided. "We'll risk it."

He led the way, bounding quickly through the undergrowth to catch up to the old tom, who was ambling ahead as if he did not care whether they followed him or not. To Brambleclaw's surprise, Purdy didn't show them anywhere in the wood where they could catch prey. Instead he made straight for the far side, where a narrow strip of grass separated the last of the trees from a row of Twoleg nests. Purdy strolled confidently across the grass toward the nearest fence without even looking to see if there was danger.

"Hey!" Crowpaw halted on the edge of the wood. "Where's he taking us? I'm not going into a Twoleg nest!"

Brambleclaw halted too. For once he agreed with Crowpaw. "Purdy, wait!" he called. "We're warriors—we don't go into Upwalker places."

The old cat paused at the bottom of the fence and looked back, his face creased in amusement. "Scared, are you?"

Crowpaw took a single step forward, his legs stiff and his neck fur bristling. "Say that again!" he hissed.

To Brambleclaw's surprise, Purdy didn't flinch a single whisker, even though Brambleclaw would bet that Crowpaw could have ripped him apart.

"Touchy, ain't he?" the old cat mewed. "Don't you worry none, young fellow. There'll be no Upwalkers around just yet. And there's good food in their garden."

Brambleclaw looked at the others. "What do you think?"

"I think we should give it a try," meowed Stormfur. "We need food."

"Yes, let's just get *on*," Tawnypelt muttered.

Feathertail nodded eagerly and Squirrelpaw gave a little excited bounce. Only Crowpaw stayed apart, staring ahead without replying to Brambleclaw's question.

"Let's go, then," Brambleclaw meowed.

After a cautious glance from side to side he crossed the grass to join Purdy, and the rest of his companions followed, even Crowpaw, though Brambleclaw noticed he trailed behind with his gaze on the ground.

"Crowpaw knows about my saltwater dream," Feathertail murmured into Brambleclaw's ear. "He seemed in a good mood when he woke up, so I told him, before the dog started chasing us. I think he's upset."

"Well, he'll have to get over it." Brambleclaw's patience was running short; he had enough to worry about without making allowances for Crowpaw's wounded pride.

Feathertail shook her head doubtfully, but just then they caught up with Purdy, so she said no more.

When they were all together the old tabby pushed his way through a gap in the fence and led the way into the Twoleg garden. Brambleclaw's nose wrinkled at the unfamiliar smells: at least two Twolegs, the acrid reek of a monster, though to his relief that was stale, and a whole mixture of unfamiliar plant scents. Some of the plants had huge, shaggy flower heads that bent under their own weight; Squirrelpaw sniffed one, and jumped back in surprise as it shed a shower of petals over her fur.

Purdy padded across the grass and sat in the middle of it, waving his tail invitingly. Coming up beside him, Brambleclaw saw a pool of water edged with some hard Twoleg stuff. Pale flowers and green leaves floated on the water, and in the depths he spotted a flash of gold, so bright that he instinctively glanced upward to see if the sun had appeared, but all the sky was still covered with cloud.

"It's a fish!" Feathertail exclaimed. "A golden fish!"

"What? Fish aren't golden!" Crowpaw sounded irritable.

"No, but these are." Stormfur was sitting beside his sister, gazing into the water. "I've never seen anything like it. We don't get those in the river."

"Can you eat them?" Tawnypelt asked.

"Aye, there's good eatin' on one of those," Purdy told her.

"I'm going to try!" Squirrelpaw gave the water an experimental dab with her paw.

"Not like that!" meowed Stormfur. "You'll just disturb them and send them all to the bottom. Let me and Feathertail show you."

The two RiverClan cats sat poised by the edge of the pool, their gazes fixed on the water. Then Feathertail flashed out a paw. A bright golden fish flew into the air in an arc of glittering raindrops and fell on the bank, where it lay wriggling and flopping.

"Someone grab it, before it falls back in," Stormfur ordered.

Squirrelpaw, who was nearest, pounced on the fish and bit it behind the head. "It's good!" she announced, swallowing.

Stormfur had already caught another fish, and soon Feathertail caught a third, so that Tawnypelt and Brambleclaw could feed. Brambleclaw tasted his fish with some suspicion, not knowing what he expected, but the flesh was succulent, and he polished it off rapidly.

When Stormfur hooked out the next one, he patted it over to Crowpaw. "Come on . . . it's okay."

Crowpaw gave the fish a contemptuous look. "We should be on our way, not messing about with Twoleg stuff. I would never have come if I'd thought the journey to the sun-drown place—or wherever—would take so long. I'm missing out on warrior training with my mentor."

"I reckon you're getting some pretty good warrior training here," Stormfur pointed out.

"Come sit with me," Feathertail meowed persuasively, "and I'll teach you how we catch them."

"Teach me as well, please!" Squirrelpaw demanded eagerly.

Crowpaw glanced scornfully at the ThunderClan apprentice. He padded across to Feathertail, and sat beside her on the side of the pool.

"That's right," she meowed. "The trick is not to let your shadow fall on the water. When you see a fish, scoop it up as quick as you can, before it has time to swim away."

Crowpaw bent over the water, a paw half extended, and a moment later flashed it down into the pool. He scooped out a fish, but it turned in the air and fell back into the water, spattering Crowpaw with a shower of drops. Squirrelpaw let out a snicker and Brambleclaw glared at her.

"That was very good for a first try," Feathertail soothed the angry apprentice. "Try again."

But Crowpaw had backed away from the pool. He dipped his head and began licking the splashes of water from his fur, only to stop in disgust. "What sort of water is this? It's salty!"

"No, it's not," mewed Stormfur in surprise.

Whatever he was going to say was drowned in a crash and an angry Twoleg yell. Brambleclaw looked up to see a Twoleg standing in the open doorway of the nest, shouting. He gripped something in one hand and hurled it at the cats; it landed in among the shaggy flowers just beyond Purdy.

"Uh-oh," mewed the old tabby. "Time to go."

He lumbered back to the gap in the fence. Brambleclaw and Stormfur followed; Tawnypelt and Squirrelpaw streaked ahead to slip through the gap first, with Feathertail on their heels. Crowpaw came last; as he emerged from the garden and raced across the grass to the shelter of the trees, he was spitting fury.

"Why did you take us there?" he demanded, turning on Purdy. "We should never have trusted you. Did you want that Twoleg to catch us? The filthy fish weren't even worth it."

"Crowpaw, don't," Feathertail pleaded, dropping the fish she was carrying. "There's nothing wrong with the fish or the water."

"I tell you it tasted salty!" Crowpaw snapped.

Brambleclaw was about to intervene—they had wasted far too much time, first in fleeing from the dog and now in arguing—until he saw the glow in Feathertail's eyes.

"You know why it tasted salty to you and not the rest of us, don't you?" she meowed quietly, resting the tip of her tail on his flank. "It's your saltwater sign, Crowpaw. You've had it at last!"

The gray-black cat opened his mouth to reply, but nothing came out. He stared at the fish and then at Feathertail. "Are you sure?" he meowed, sounding astonished.

"Of course, you stupid furball," Feathertail purred. Brambleclaw thought that no other cat but Feathertail could call Crowpaw a stupid furball and get away unclawed. "Why else would water in a Twoleg pool taste salty? It's StarClan's sign that we're still on the right track."

Crowpaw blinked and let his fur lie flat along his spine.

"What's all this about signs and salt water?" Purdy growled.

"We're on a really important journey!" Squirrelpaw informed him excitedly. "StarClan sent us to find out something vital for our Clans."

"Journey . . . where from? What Clans?"

Brambleclaw sighed. Even though he wanted to keep going, he guessed the old tabby was lonely; it seemed unkind to abandon him without even telling him why they were there. He had saved them from the dog, after all, and then led them to the shining golden fish.

"Come here into the bracken," he meowed. "We won't be seen there, and then we can tell you all about it."

All the cats followed him; even Crowpaw didn't object. Stormfur and Feathertail shared the fish and Tawnypelt kept watch while Squirrelpaw poured out their story. Brambleclaw chipped in to correct her or explain when Purdy didn't understand.

"StarClan?" the old tom meowed with a doubtful look when Squirrelpaw told him about Brambleclaw's dream. "Talking to you in dreams? I never heard o' that before."

The young apprentice gaped at him, her green eyes filled with disbelief that there could be a cat who did not know about StarClan.

"Just carry on," Brambleclaw meowed to her, not willing to waste time in long explanations.

Squirrelpaw rolled her eyes at him, but went on without arguing. When she finished, the old loner was silent for a while—so long that Brambleclaw wondered if he had fallen asleep. Then he straightened up and opened his yellow eyes wide, with a fire in them that had not been there before. "I know about this sun-drown place," he meowed unexpectedly. "I've spoken to cats who've been there. It's not far from here."

"Where?" Squirrelpaw leaped to her paws. "How far?"

"Two, maybe three days' travel," Purdy replied. His eyes gleamed. "Tell you what, I'll come with you an' show you."

His expression faded to disappointment when the forest cats said nothing. At last, Crowpaw voiced what Brambleclaw was thinking. "No way. You won't be able to travel fast enough."

"And I don't remember inviting you," Tawnypelt muttered.

"But if he knows the right way . . ." Stormfur mewed. "Maybe we should let him come."

"He's bound to know the way through this Twolegplace," Feathertail added, twitching her tail toward the rows and rows of dull red Twoleg nests that blocked their view of the horizon.

That was true enough, Brambleclaw thought, remembering the trouble they had met in the last Twolegplace. If Purdy really did know the way to the sun-drown place it might be quicker to go with him, even if he couldn't move so fast. Perhaps he was the guide StarClan had sent in response to Brambleclaw's prayer. He seemed an unlikely savior, but he certainly had the courage of any forest cat.

"Okay," he meowed, realizing with a jolt of surprise that the other cats were looking at him as if they expected him to make the decision. "I think he should come."

CHAPTER 20

❧

Purdy led the forest cats along the edge of the wood. It was the day after their narrow escape from the dog, and Brambleclaw was still struggling with doubts about his decision to follow the old cat; he knew that Crowpaw and Tawnypelt were unhappy about it, too. But there seemed no other choice; more and more Twoleg nests filled the horizon, and clouds still covered the sky, so there was no sun to guide them to the sun-drown place.

"Is there any chance of more food?" he asked Purdy as they left the trees behind and began to cross a grassy space dotted with clumps of brightly colored flowers. "The fish yesterday weren't really enough, and Crowpaw didn't eat at all."

"Sure, I can take you to a place," Purdy replied with a hostile glance at Crowpaw, who had been the most outspoken in voicing his distrust of the old cat.

He led them to the other side of the grassy place, where there was yet another row of Twoleg nests. Brambleclaw watched uneasily as the old cat flattened his belly to the ground and heaved himself under a wooden gate, grunting with the effort and shaking himself vigorously on the other side.

"More Twolegs?" Crowpaw hissed. "I'm not going in there."

"Suit yourself," Purdy meowed, beginning to pad up the path to the door with his tail held straight up.

"We'd better all stay together," Brambleclaw murmured. "Remember what happened last time."

Crowpaw snorted but said nothing, and none of the other cats disagreed. One by one they squeezed under the gate and followed Purdy up the path. Crowpaw came last, casting wary glances behind him.

Purdy was waiting for them by the half-open door of the Twoleg nest. A harsh glow lit up the space inside it, which was full of strange shapes and scents that Brambleclaw had never encountered before.

"In there?" he mewed to Purdy. "You're expecting us to go into an Upwalker nest?"

Purdy twitched his tail impatiently. "That's where the food is. I know this place. I often come here."

"This is wasting time," Tawnypelt meowed. Brambleclaw thought his sister sounded scared; her claws were flexing anxiously on the hard stuff of the path. "We *can't* go in there. We're not kittypets. Eating kittypet food is against the warrior code."

"Oh, come on." Stormfur gave Tawnypelt's ear a friendly flick with his tail. "There's no harm in it. We're on a long journey, and if we can get food easily it saves time we would have to spend hunting—time we might need for something else. StarClan will understand."

Tawnypelt shook her head, still unconvinced, but Feathertail looked reassured by her brother's reasoning, and both RiverClan cats ventured cautiously inside.

"That's right," Purdy encouraged them. "There's the food, see, in bowls over there, all ready for us."

Brambleclaw's stomach growled; the fish he had eaten had been small, and it had been a long time ago. "Okay," he meowed. "I think Stormfur's right. Let's go, but make it quick."

Squirrelpaw didn't wait for his decision, bounding inside hard on Purdy's paws. Brambleclaw followed her, but Crowpaw and Tawnypelt stayed outside.

"We'll keep watch!" Tawnypelt called after him.

Stormfur and Feathertail were already crouched beside the bowls, gulping eagerly. Brambleclaw peered suspiciously at the food; it was hard, round pellets like rabbit droppings, but the scent that came from it told him it would be safe to eat.

Squirrelpaw thrust her muzzle into the other bowl; when she looked up her fur was plastered into spikes by something white, and her green eyes were glowing. "It's *good!*" she exclaimed. "Purdy, what is it?"

"Milk," Purdy replied. "A bit like the milk you suck from your mother."

"And kittypets drink this every day?" Squirrelpaw was astonished. "Wow! It's nearly worth being a kittypet." She plunged her muzzle back into the bowl.

Brambleclaw crouched beside her and lapped up a few drops of the white liquid. Squirrelpaw was right—it was good, rich and full-tasting with hardly any tang of Twolegs about it. He settled down and tucked in.

The first hint he had of trouble was the sound of a door

opening and a high-pitched Twoleg voice crying out above his head. Brambleclaw sprang to his paws in time to see a Twoleg kit run through the door and scoop up Feathertail in her arms.

Taken by surprise, Feathertail let out a startled yowl and began struggling, but the young Twoleg had her in a tight clasp. Stormfur stretched up with his forepaws, trying to reach his sister, but the Twoleg kit took no notice. Brambleclaw stared in dismay. *Feathertail!* He glanced around for Purdy, only to see the old cat padding calmly toward a full-grown Twoleg that stood in the doorway, waving his tail in welcome.

Then Crowpaw appeared from the garden, a black whirlwind with glaring amber eyes. "See?" he hissed at Brambleclaw. "This is your fault! You let that old mange bag bring us here."

Brambleclaw gaped at the accusation, but Crowpaw did not wait for an answer. He spun around to face the Twoleg kit, lips drawn back in a snarl. "Let her go, or I'll claw you to shreds!" he spat.

The little Twoleg, happily stroking Feathertail with loud squeaking noises, hadn't noticed Crowpaw, nor understood his threat. The black apprentice was ready to spring when Squirrelpaw slipped in front of him. "Wait, mouse-brain! It's only a kit. Do it this way."

She padded up to the Twoleg. Raising her green eyes pleadingly, she let out a purr and rubbed herself against the Twoleg's legs.

"Good idea!" Stormfur exclaimed, and crowded up to the

Twoleg kit on the other side, purring.

The little Twoleg's eyes gleamed. It let out a cry of delight and bent down to stroke Squirrelpaw; at the same instant Feathertail, feeling the grip on her slacken, managed to wriggle free and leap to the ground.

"Let's go!" Brambleclaw yowled.

The forest cats shot out of the door and streaked down the path to the gate. As Brambleclaw squeezed underneath he heard the little Twoleg yowl loudly but he did not stop to listen. "This way!" he shouted, heading for a clump of shrubs.

As he dived under the low-hanging, glossy-leaved branches, he realized to his relief that all his companions were with him. A moment later, with a lot of puffing and blowing and scrabbling, Purdy joined them.

"Get out of here!" Crowpaw spat at the old tom. "It was you who took us in there, to be caught by Twolegs." With a pointed glance at Brambleclaw he added, "If you had listened to me, it wouldn't have happened."

Purdy twitched an ear, and showed no signs of leaving. "I don't know what you're worried about. They're decent Upwalkers. They wouldn't hurt a cat none."

"Just keep her prisoner," Tawnypelt growled. "That Twoleg kit obviously wanted to turn Feathertail into a kittypet."

"I wasn't in any danger," Feathertail pointed out. "I could have escaped by myself, except I didn't want to claw the little Twoleg." She blinked gratefully at the ThunderClan apprentice. "But Squirrelpaw had the best idea."

Squirrelpaw ducked her head, looking embarrassed. "If

ever *any* of you tell the cats back home that I purred at a Twoleg," she mewed through gritted teeth, "I'll turn you into crowfood, and that's a promise."

In spite of Crowpaw's protests, the journeying cats trekked on with Purdy as their guide. All day the old tabby led them along hard Twoleg paths that made their paws burn, where they had to slink along in the shelter of walls or dart across Thunderpaths under the noses of monsters roaring down on them.

By the end of the day Brambleclaw was exhausted, finding it hard to put one paw in front of the others. His companions were no better. Squirrelpaw was limping and Crowpaw's tail drooped; Brambleclaw remembered that the black-pelted apprentice still hadn't eaten, and he wondered if there would be any prey to be found so deep in Twoleg territory.

"Purdy!" he called, forcing himself to quicken his pace and catch up with the old cat. "Is there anywhere safe we can spend the night? Anywhere we can find food—not kittypet food," he added. "We need somewhere to hunt."

Purdy flopped down in the angle where two Thunderpaths met, and raised one hind paw to scratch his ear. "Don't know about prey," he rasped. "There's a place we can spend the night just up ahead."

"How far?" Tawnypelt growled. "My paws are dropping off."

"Not far." Purdy heaved himself to his paws again; Brambleclaw had to admit the old cat was showing more stamina than he would have expected on the seemingly endless journey. "Not far at all."

As Brambleclaw braced himself to set off again, he spotted a faint reddish gleam falling on the hard surface of the Thunderpath. His head whipped around and he stared in horror. The clouds were clearing away on the horizon, and now, in the gap between two of the Twoleg nests, he could see the setting sun. It was behind them. They had been traveling in completely the wrong direction!

"Purdy!" His voice was a strangled yowl. "Look!"

The old cat blinked at the red light in the sky. "Fine weather tomorrow, I shouldn't wonder."

"Fine weather!" Crowpaw hissed. "He's been leading us wrong all day."

Squirrelpaw sank down on the hard ground and put her head on her paws.

"We're supposed to be going *toward* the sunset," Brambleclaw pointed out. "Purdy, do you *really* know how to find the sun-drown place?"

"'Course I do," Purdy defended himself, his rumpled fur beginning to bristle. "It's just . . . well, goin' through Upwalker places, you get turned around on yourself now and then."

"He doesn't know," Tawnypelt mewed flatly.

"Of course he doesn't," Crowpaw scoffed. "He couldn't find his own tail. Let's leave him here and carry on by ourselves."

Another monster roared by; Stormfur, who had been standing nearest the edge of the Thunderpath, jumped back as a shower of grit spattered his fur.

"Look," he meowed, "I agree that Purdy's leading us the

wrong way. But we can't go off on our own now. We'd never get out of this Twolegplace."

Feathertail nodded glumly, padding over to stand beside her brother and lick the grit off his fur.

Brambleclaw knew they were right; he forced down frustration at the thought of how much time they were wasting.

"Okay," he meowed. "Purdy, show us this place where we can sleep. Everything will look better in the morning."

Ignoring a contemptuous noise from Crowpaw, he set out once again in the pawsteps of the old tabby.

By the time they reached Purdy's sleeping place, the sky was almost completely dark, but their path was lit up with a harsh glare from Twoleg lights like small, dirty suns. The old tabby led them to a stretch of shrubs and grass, surrounded by a spiky fence with gaps between the posts where a cat could easily slip through. There was shelter, water in shallow puddles, and even the scent of prey.

"There!" Purdy meowed, twitching his whiskers with satisfaction. "This isn't so bad, is it?"

It wasn't bad at all, Brambleclaw decided, wondering whether Purdy had really meant to lead them here, or if finding the place was just a lucky accident. Tired though they were, they hunted at once; the mice they caught were scrawny and reeked of Twolegplace, but they tasted like the juiciest voles to the hungry forest cats.

Squirrelpaw polished hers off, looked around for more, and sighed. "What wouldn't I give for a bowl of kittypet milk! I'm *joking,*" she added, as Crowpaw curled his lip at her. "Lighten up, will you?"

Crowpaw turned his back, too exhausted for a real quarrel.

To Brambleclaw's relief, it was not long before all his companions settled down to sleep. He curled up under some low-growing branches, where he could almost imagine himself back in the warriors' den. Gazing through the gaps between the leaves, he looked up at the sky, but the harsh Twoleg lights cut off the glitter of Silverpelt. StarClan seemed very far away.

The next day they struggled on under Purdy's directions. Brambleclaw felt as if he had been plodding along for the length of an elder's life, at the base of tall Twoleg walls that were as steep as the cliff at the sun-drown place. By now he was pretty much convinced that the old tabby was ambling along at random, not caring if they were going the right way or not. But the forest cats had no hope of finding their own way out of the Twolegplace. Cloud covered the sun again, so there was no help there, and now and again rain fell in a cold spatter.

"We'll never get out of this." Tawnypelt echoed Brambleclaw's thoughts as they lined up to cross another Thunderpath.

"You might as well stop complaining," Stormfur retorted. "There's nothing we can do about it."

Brambleclaw was surprised to hear such a hostile response from the easygoing RiverClan warrior. But they were all still tired, even after the night's sleep, and hope was trickling away like water falling onto sand. As Tawnypelt glared, her neck fur bristling, he stepped in front of her. "Take it easy, both of you," he meowed.

He broke off when Stormfur whipped around and pelted across the Thunderpath, almost straight under the paws of an approaching monster. Feathertail let out a distressed mew and sprang after him.

"And don't take stupid risks!" Brambleclaw yelled after them. The RiverClan warriors ignored him. Shrugging, Brambleclaw turned to Squirrelpaw, who was crouching beside him at the edge of the Thunderpath, watching for her chance to cross. "I'll tell you when it's safe to go," he told her.

"I can do it!" Squirrelpaw spat. "Stop trying to sound like my father." She leaped out onto the hard surface of the Thunderpath; fortunately no monsters were in sight.

Brambleclaw raced behind her, catching up as she reached the other side. He bent over her so they stood nose-to-nose, and his words came out in a hiss of fury. "If you ever do something so stupid again, you'll wish I *was* your father! I'll be tougher with you than he ever was."

"I wish you were my father *now!*" she retorted. "Firestar would know which way to go."

There was nothing Brambleclaw could say to that. She was right—the heroic ThunderClan leader would never have made such a mess of this journey. Why had StarClan chosen him, *why?*

He turned to the old tabby, who was strolling across the Thunderpath as if he had all the time in the world. "Purdy, how much farther is it to the edge of this Twolegplace?"

"Oh, not far, not far at all." Purdy let out an amused purr. "You youngsters are too impatient."

A faint growl came from Crowpaw's throat, and he took a step toward their guide. "At least age hasn't cracked our wits," he snapped. "Get a move on!"

Purdy blinked at him. "All in good time." He stood still, scenting the air, and then turned decisively alongside the Thunderpath. "This way."

"He hasn't got the faintest idea," Crowpaw snarled, but he still followed. As with all of the forest cats, it was no longer a question of faith or courage. They just didn't have any choice.

The day seemed to drag on forever, and when the light began to fade again they were limping painfully beside a tall Twoleg fence. Brambleclaw thought the skin on his pads must have been worn off with so much walking on stone; he longed for the soothing coolness of growing things under his paws.

He opened his mouth to ask Purdy to find them another place to stop, only to realize that he could taste a sharp, unfamiliar smell on the air. He paused, trying to identify it; at the same moment Tawnypelt came hurrying up to him.

"Brambleclaw, have you noticed that smell? It's like the carrionplace, on the edge of ShadowClan territory. We'd better watch out. There'll be rats."

Brambleclaw nodded. Now that his sister had reminded him, he could clearly detect the scent of rat among the other foul reeks of Twoleg rubbish. Glancing back the way he had come, he saw that the rest of his companions were spread out behind, worn out by fear and uncertainty and the hard slog of their journey.

"Hurry up!" he called. "Keep together!"

A dry chittering sound interrupted him. Whirling around, he saw three huge rats squeezing under the fence to stand in his path, their naked tails curled high over their backs. Their eyes glinted in their evil, wedge-shaped faces, and he could just make out the gleam of their sharp front teeth.

In a heartbeat, the leading rat sprang at him; Brambleclaw leaped back and felt its teeth snap a hairbreadth from his leg. He swung a paw and raked his claws down the side of the rat's head. It fell back, squealing, but at once another one took its place. More appeared from the other side of the fence, streaming onto the path like a vicious, squealing river. Brambleclaw caught a glimpse of Tawnypelt snarling fiercely as a rat sank its teeth into her shoulder. Then two more of them struck him and he went down under a writhing mass of bodies.

At first he could hardly get his breath. The disgusting stink of the rats filled his nostrils, choking him. He kicked out with his hind paws and felt his claws sink into fur and flesh. A rat squealed and the weight on him vanished, letting him scramble to his paws again to slash at another of the vile creatures as its teeth met in his ear.

Just beside him Squirrelpaw was writhing underneath a rat almost as big as she was; before Brambleclaw could make a move to help her she threw it off and hurled herself at it, ears flattened and jaws parted in a furious yowl. The rat fled; Squirrelpaw let it go and turned to aim her claws at another that was clinging onto Feathertail's back, sending streams of bright red blood running from its sharp claws.

Brambleclaw threw himself back into the battle beside Crowpaw, who was being dragged along the ground with his teeth embedded in a rat's leg. Brambleclaw dispatched the rat with a single blow of his paw, and spun to meet the next attacker. Stormfur and Feathertail were fighting side by side at the base of the fence, and Tawnypelt, one shoulder bleeding heavily, shook a rat by its tail before dropping it and biting hard at its throat. Purdy had come back too, wading into the mass of rats and tossing them aside with one powerful forepaw.

As quickly as it had begun, the fight was over. The surviving rats retreated through the hole in the fence; Crowpaw aimed a blow at the last of them as its tail vanished.

Brambleclaw was left gasping for breath, feeling a sharp sting in his tail and one hind leg, as he gazed at the remaining rats strewn across the ground, some of them still feebly twitching. *Fresh-kill*, he thought dully, but he could not summon the energy to gather the bodies together or to eat. The rest of his companions huddled around him, gazing at each other with huge eyes, all their quarrels forgotten in their shared fear.

"Purdy," Brambleclaw mewed exhaustedly. "We've got to rest. What about over there?"

He pointed with his tail to a gap in the wall on the other side of the Thunderpath from the carrionplace where the rats were. Beyond, everything was dark. He could pick up the scent of Twolegs, but it was stale.

Purdy blinked. "Sure, that'll do."

This time it was Brambleclaw who led the way across the Thunderpath. Every cat was so worn out that if a monster had appeared it could have flattened them all, but StarClan watched over them and everything was quiet. Crowpaw, Stormfur, and Feathertail dragged rats across with them, while Squirrelpaw lent her shoulder to help support Tawnypelt, who was limping badly and left a trail of blood drops behind her.

Through the gap in the wall there was a dark enclosed area behind a dead-looking Twoleg nest. Rough stones were stuck out of the ground; puddles of greasy water had gathered among them. Crowpaw bent his head to drink and grunted in disgust, but did not have the strength to complain out loud.

There was nothing to use as bedding. The cats huddled together in one corner, except for Squirrelpaw, who went nosing around the wall and came back with cobwebs plastered over one paw, which she pressed onto Tawnypelt's wound.

"I wish I could remember the herb Leafpaw uses for rat bites," she meowed.

"No herbs here anyway," Tawnypelt murmured, wincing. "Thanks, Squirrelpaw, that really helps."

"We'd better keep watch," Brambleclaw announced. "Those rats might be back. I'll go first," he added, worried that some cat would start protesting. "The rest of you get some sleep, but if you've got any bites, give them a good lick first."

All his companions, even Crowpaw, obeyed without question. Brambleclaw guessed that they were so frightened, they were just glad to have some cat tell them what to do.

He padded back to the gap in the wall and sat in shadow,

gazing out across the Thunderpath to the place where the rats had appeared. Everything was quiet, leaving Brambleclaw nothing to do but worry about how the journey had gone so disastrously wrong. Most of all he worried about Tawnypelt. They all had scratches from the battle with the rats, but his sister's was the only deep bite; it looked nasty, and he knew that of all bites, those from a rat were feared most by his Clan mates. How would they cope if the bite became infected, or if her leg stiffened so that Tawnypelt couldn't go on?

A whisper of movement beside him made him jump, until he saw that it was Squirrelpaw. Her ginger fur stood on end and blood was oozing from a scratch on her nose, but her eyes were still bright. Brambleclaw braced himself for criticism or some clever remark, but when she spoke her voice was quiet. "Tawnypelt's asleep."

"Good," Brambleclaw meowed. "You . . . you fought well today. Dustpelt would have been proud of you, if he could have seen." He let out a long sigh, full of weariness and uncertainty.

To his surprise, Squirrelpaw pushed her nose comfortingly into his fur. "Don't worry," she mewed. "We'll be fine. StarClan are watching over us."

Breathing in her soft, warm scent, Brambleclaw wished that he could believe her.

CHAPTER 21

❧

Leafpaw jumped up from her nest in the ferns outside Cinderpelt's den. The sun was just rising, its rays glittering on drops of water that trembled on each fern frond and blade of grass. There was a chill in the air, reminding Leafpaw that leaf-fall would give way to leaf-bare before many moons.

At first she was not sure what had awakened her. There was no sound except for the gentle sigh of wind in the tree-tops and the distant murmur of the warriors rousing in the main clearing. Cinderpelt had not called her, yet Leafpaw's fur prickled with the certainty that there was something she had to do.

Almost of their own accord her paws took her to the mouth of Cinderpelt's den. Peering into the cleft in the rock, she meowed softly, "Cinderpelt, are you awake?"

"I am now." The medicine cat's voice was sleepy. "What's the matter? ShadowClan attacking? StarClan walking among us?"

"No, Cinderpelt." Leafpaw shuffled her paws. "I just wanted to check if we have any burdock root."

"Burdock root?" Leafpaw heard her mentor scramble to her paws, and a heartbeat later Cinderpelt poked her head

253

out of the den. "What do you want that for? Come on, Leafpaw, what do we use burdock root for?"

"Rat bites, Cinderpelt," Leafpaw meowed. She sat down and wrapped her tail around her paws, trying to calm her heart, which was pounding as if she'd just run all the way from Fourtrees. "Especially if they're infected."

"That's right." Cinderpelt slipped out of the den and made a quick tour of the clearing, prodding the clumps of fern with one paw. "No, just as I thought. No rats here," she pronounced at last.

"I know there aren't any rats," Leafpaw mewed helplessly. "I just needed to check that we have burdock root, that's all."

Cinderpelt's eyes narrowed. "Have you been dreaming?"

"No, I—" Leafpaw broke off. "Actually, I think perhaps I have, but I don't know what it means. I can't even remember what the dream was about."

Cinderpelt's blue eyes considered her calmly for several heartbeats. "This may be a sign from StarClan," she meowed at last.

"Then can you tell me what it means?" Leafpaw begged. *"Please!"*

To her dismay Cinderpelt shook her head. "The sign—if it is a sign—is yours," she explained. "You know that StarClan never speak to us in plain words. Their messages come in little things . . . the prickling of fur, a tugging in our paws—"

"The feeling that something's right—or wrong," Leafpaw put in.

"Exactly." Cinderpelt nodded. "Part of being a medicine

cat is learning to read those messages by instinct . . . and we both know how hard it can be to make a leap of faith. That's what you have to do now."

"I'm not sure I know how," Leafpaw confessed, scraping the ground with one forepaw. "Suppose I get the meaning wrong?"

"Do you think I'm never wrong?" Cinderpelt's gaze suddenly grew intense. "You must trust your own judgment. Believe me, Leafpaw, one day you will make a wonderful medicine cat—perhaps even as good as Spottedleaf."

Leafpaw's eyes flew open. She had heard many stories of the gifted young medicine cat who had been killed not long after Firestar had joined ThunderClan. She had never in her wildest dreams thought that she might be compared with her. "Cinderpelt, you can't mean that!"

"Of course I mean it," Cinderpelt mewed dryly. "I don't talk for the pleasure of hearing my own voice. As for burdock, you'll find it growing on the edge of the training hollow. Why don't you go and dig up a few roots—so we'll have plenty, just in case."

As Leafpaw trotted out of the camp, she tried to remember what she had dreamed about. But nothing came into her mind except for a picture of dark Twoleg nests and harsh light shining on a Thunderpath. She wondered if the dream had really been a sign from StarClan; instead, she had a sense that Squirrelpaw was trying to tell her something, though the strength of their link had dwindled with distance. Leafpaw had not seen her sister and the other journeying cats in her

dream, but somehow she became convinced that Squirrelpaw
had been bitten by a rat.

If only I'd gone with her, she thought helplessly. *They need a medicine cat. Oh, Squirrelpaw, where are you?*

In the sandy hollow, Mousefur and Thornclaw were training their apprentices. Leafpaw paused for a few moments to watch, but somehow she could not summon up much interest. She felt as if the sunlight were draining all her energy away, so that she could hardly manage to put one paw in front of the others.

The tall stems of the burdock were easy to find. Leafpaw burrowed under the dark, sharp-scented leaves to dig up the roots. When she had scraped off most of the clinging earth, she carried them back to Cinderpelt's den and laid them in a neat pile beside the other herbs.

Tonight was the Gathering, she remembered. When Cinderpelt had first told her she would be going she had been excited, especially at the thought of seeing Mothwing again. Now she did not feel she had enough strength for the journey to Fourtrees. She would have given up every Gathering from now until she went to join StarClan, if only she could have been sure that her sister was safe.

By the time the ThunderClan cats reached the Gathering, Leafpaw felt better. She had snatched a brief nap after sunhigh, her nose filled with the scent of burdock clinging to her fur, and woken with energy in her paws again.

As she emerged from the bushes in the clearing at Fourtrees, she saw Mothwing pushing her way toward her.

"Hi, there," Leafpaw meowed. "How are you getting on?"

Mothwing paused. "Fine, I think, but there's so much to learn! And there are times I don't feel any closer to StarClan than before I went to Mothermouth."

Leafpaw let out a wry meow. "We all feel that. I think every medicine cat in the forest has felt it at some time."

Mothwing's huge amber eyes were confused. "But I thought I'd be wise now that I'm a medicine cat. I thought I'd walk closely with StarClan and always know the answer to everything."

She looked so dejected that Leafpaw leaned over and gave her ear a comforting lick. "One day perhaps you will. We walk closer to StarClan every day." When Mothwing still looked uneasy she added, "Mothwing, is there something in particular bothering you?"

Mothwing started. "Oh, no," she replied, shaking her broad golden head. "Nothing at all, only—"

Leafpaw never found out what she was going to say. A loud yowling drowned out Mothwing's voice as Tallstar, on the top of the Great Rock, called for silence. Leopardstar stood beside him, while Firestar and Blackstar, the leader of ShadowClan, sat a little way behind.

Leopardstar was the first of the leaders to speak. "Tallstar," she meowed, "rain has fallen many times on the forest since the last Gathering. Do the streams run freely again in WindClan territory?"

Tallstar inclined his head toward her. "They do, Leopardstar."

"Then I take back the permission I gave to you and your Clan to enter RiverClan territory to drink. From now on, my warriors will drive out any WindClan cats we find across our borders."

She said nothing about the way that WindClan had gone on visiting the river even when they no longer needed to, but her voice was sharp, and Leafpaw could see the displeasure she was not expressing in words.

Tallstar faced the RiverClan leader, unblinking. "Leopardstar, WindClan thanks you for your help and will not abuse your trust."

The RiverClan leader gave him a sharp little nod and stepped back. Suddenly there was a disturbance among the cats in the clearing, and a sleek tabby cat with massive shoulders rose to his paws. It was Mothwing's brother, Hawkfrost.

"With your permission, Leopardstar, I would like to speak," he meowed.

Leafpaw was surprised; young warriors did not usually speak at Gatherings.

"Well?" Leopardstar mewed.

Hawkfrost hesitated, scuffling the ground in front of him with one paw in apparent shyness, though Leafpaw noticed that his ice-blue eyes flicked from side to side as if making sure that every cat was watching him. "I'm not sure I should say this, but . . . well, when WindClan came to the river, they didn't just drink. I've seen them stealing fish."

"What?" Tallstar sprang to the edge of the rock and crouched there as if he were about to pounce on the RiverClan warrior. "How dare you! No WindClan cats have stolen prey!"

Leafpaw knew that was a lie; she remembered Squirrelpaw telling her about catching a WindClan patrol on Thunder-Clan territory with a stolen vole.

"Did any other cats see this?" Leopardstar asked Hawkfrost.

"I don't think so." Hawkfrost sounded apologetic. "I was on my own at the time."

Leopardstar's gaze raked the clearing, but no cat spoke. Leafpaw wondered if she should say anything, but she had not seen the theft for herself; Squirrelpaw and Brambleclaw were long gone, and Dustpelt, who had also seen it, had not come to this Gathering. She kept silent.

Tallstar turned to the RiverClan leader. "I swear by StarClan that WindClan have taken nothing but water from the river. Are you going to condemn us on the word of one warrior?"

Leopardstar's neck fur bristled. "Are you saying that my warrior is lying?"

"Are you calling my Clan thieves?" Tallstar's lips drew back in a snarl, his teeth bared and his claws unsheathed.

Yowls of protest broke out in the clearing from both RiverClan and WindClan cats. Leafpaw watched the warriors turn on each other, spitting challenges. She felt her fur stand on end, suddenly terrified that the sacred truce of the Gathering would be broken.

"Did Hawkfrost *have* to start this?" she murmured, half to herself.

"What should he do?" Mothwing's voice was sharp as she

defended her brother. "Keep quiet and let WindClan get away with it? Every cat in RiverClan knows that for a couple of mousetails those cats would steal the pelt off your back." Her amber eyes blazed and she sprang to her paws as if she were ready to join in a fight the moment it started.

A furious hiss came from her mentor, Mudfur, reminding her that medicine cats were meant to keep peace, and Mothwing shot him a glance, half-angry, half-ashamed.

"Wait!" The single word carried clearly across the hollow. Leafpaw saw that Firestar had come forward to the edge of the rock. "StarClan is angry—look up at the moon!"

With every other cat, Leafpaw gazed upward. The full moon floated above the trees; not far away a single cloud was being driven toward it, even though there was barely a breath of wind in the clearing. She shivered. If StarClan were angry enough to cover the moon, the Gathering would have to break up.

The warriors crouched down, their hostility fading to fear.

Firestar's voice rang out again. "Leopardstar, Tallstar, will you lead your Clans into battle on the word of one warrior? Hawkfrost, is it possible that you were mistaken in what you saw?"

Hawkfrost paused for a moment, his eyes narrowing to slits as he stared at the ThunderClan leader. "I believe what I said," he replied at last, "but I suppose it's possible I got it wrong. I might have been dazzled by the sun on the water, or something."

"Then let there be friendship between RiverClan and

WindClan," Firestar meowed. "Tallstar has already promised not to come down to the river again."

"And I'll keep my promise," Tallstar spat. "But you should teach your young warriors to show a bit of respect, Leopard-star."

"Don't tell me what to do!" Leopardstar was still angry, but Leafpaw recognized that the threat of battle was over. Above their heads the cloud was carried away from the moon, as though StarClan's anger were fading.

"Remember how good life is in the forest just now," Firestar urged both leaders. "Prey is plentiful, and the streams are full again. We are all well prepared for leaf-fall and leaf-bare. There is no need for us to invade one another's territories." He flashed a glance at Blackstar, who had been sitting with a knowing look on his face, as though he were enjoying the disagreement between the other Clans. "That doesn't mean my borders are not well guarded," he added pointedly.

"And so are RiverClan's," Leopardstar hissed, but she took a pace back, as if acknowledging that the dispute was over.

Tallstar moved away, too, leaving Firestar at the front of the rock. Leafpaw knew what was coming; her father paused before he began to speak, and she guessed that he was choosing his words with care. He would not want the other Clans to think that he had driven out his own cats.

"A quarter moon ago," he began, "the warrior Brambleclaw and Squirrelpaw, an apprentice, left ThunderClan. We do not know where they have gone, but we have reason to believe that they did not go alone." Turning to the other leaders, he went on. "Have any of your warriors gone missing?"

Leopardstar replied willingly enough; Leafpaw guessed that Mistyfoot had told her she had already passed on the news about Stormfur and Feathertail. "Two warriors left RiverClan—Stormfur and Feathertail—just before the half-moon. At first we assumed they had crossed the river to live in your territory, Firestar. Since they have connections in ThunderClan"—she spoke with icy disapproval of her warriors' half-Clan heritage—"we can assume they have all gone together."

There was a pause; then Tallstar cleared his throat and mewed quietly, "WindClan has lost an apprentice, Crowpaw. It would have been about the same time." He added, "I thought a fox or a badger might have gotten him, but it looks as if he might be with your lot."

A murmur of uneasiness broke out in the clearing. Some cat called out, "How do you know? Maybe there's something in the forest picking us off one by one."

The murmur grew louder, and a cat on the edge of the throng let out a wail of terror. Leafpaw could see cats exchanging fearful glances or springing to their paws as if they were ready to flee from the clearing.

"What about the dogs?" another voice yowled. "Maybe the dogs have come back!"

Firestar paced to the edge of the Highrock and looked down. For a moment he caught Leafpaw's eye. She shivered; surely he wasn't going to talk about her link with Squirrelpaw in front of the whole Gathering?

She relaxed as her father began to speak. "We wondered about predators too," he meowed. "But there are none of the signs we would expect to see in the forest—and believe me, ThunderClan would know if the dogs were back. We are sure these cats left of their own accord."

His calm voice seemed to reassure his listeners; the cats who had sprung up sat down again, though many of them still looked uneasy.

"What about ShadowClan?" Firestar turned to Blackstar. "Have you lost cats too?"

The ShadowClan leader hesitated; it was always the nature of that Clan to be secretive, as if information were as precious as prey.

"Tawnypelt," he meowed at last. "I assumed she had gone back to ThunderClan to be with her brother."

Murmurs filled the clearing, as the cats tried to make sense of what they had just learned.

"That's at least one cat from every Clan!" Mothwing exclaimed. "What does it mean?" Sounding frustrated, she added, "Why hasn't StarClan shown this to me?"

Leafpaw longed to tell her friend what Squirrelpaw and Brambleclaw had told her before they left. She wondered if Cinderpelt would mention the omen she saw in the burning bracken, that fire and tiger would join together, somehow connected to trouble for the whole forest. But when she spotted the medicine cat, crouched beside Littlecloud at the base of the Highrock, her head was lowered and she did not speak.

"What do you suggest we do, Firestar?" Tallstar asked.

"There's not much we can do," Leopardstar interrupted before Firestar could reply. "They're gone. They could be anywhere."

Tallstar looked troubled. "I don't understand why they had to go all together like that, but they must have had some idea in their heads. I'd swear Crowpaw was loyal to his Clan."

Firestar nodded. "They are all loyal cats." Leafpaw knew he must be thinking of his quarrels with Brambleclaw and Squirrelpaw before they left, and his worries about the prophecy.

"There must be something we can do," Tallstar asserted. "We can't just pretend they never existed."

"Your concern honors you, Tallstar," Firestar meowed. "But I agree with Leopardstar. There's nothing we can do. They are all in the paws of StarClan. And may StarClan grant that one day soon they will come back safely."

Blackstar, who had made no suggestions so far, added derisively, "Hope is easy, but it catches no prey. If you ask me, we've seen the last of them."

From somewhere behind Leafpaw some cat muttered, "He's right. It's dangerous out there."

Leafpaw felt as though a huge talon were squeezing her heart. Her fears for Squirrelpaw flooded over her again, and she remembered her dream about the rat bites. *Squirrelpaw,* she murmured to herself, *there must be something I can do to help you.*

She found it hard to listen as Blackstar reported more

Twoleg activity around the Thunderpath, even harder when it seemed that the new monsters were all gathered around a boggy piece of ground where the cats never went.

What does it matter? she thought distractedly. *Who cares what Twolegs do?*

When the meeting was brought to a close she said good-bye to Mothwing and hurried to find Cinderpelt. An idea had come to her; she was eager to get back to camp and try it out.

On the way back to the ThunderClan camp she made herself keep to Cinderpelt's slower pace, until the two medicine cats were walking alone, behind the others.

"Cats from all four Clans have disappeared, have they?" Cinderpelt mused. She paused briefly to gaze up at the full moon, now sinking below the trees. "Leafpaw, you're worried about Squirrelpaw, aren't you? Do you know anything about where she is now?"

The direct question startled Leafpaw, and for a couple of heartbeats she did not know how to reply.

"Come on, Leafpaw." Cinderpelt narrowed her eyes. "Don't try to tell me you know *nothing.*"

Leafpaw stopped and faced her mentor, grateful for the chance to tell the truth. "I know that she's alive, and that she's with the other cats who have left. But I don't know where they are, or what they're doing. They're very far away, I think—farther than any of the forest cats have gone before."

Cinderpelt nodded; Leafpaw wondered if StarClan had told her anything about the journey, but if they had the medicine cat said nothing.

"You might tell your father that," she meowed. "It will help reassure him."

"Yes, I will."

They reached the ravine at last; Leafpaw's paws felt weary as she followed her mentor down the gorse tunnel and into the camp.

"Cinderpelt," she meowed, "will it do me any harm to eat some of the burdock root?"

"It might give you a bellyache if you eat too much," Cinderpelt replied. "Why?"

"Just an idea I had." *If I can tell what Squirrelpaw is thinking,* she added to herself, *maybe she can pick up something from me.* She almost felt that she was stupid to hope she could reach her sister across such great distances, but she knew she had to try.

Warmth glimmered in Cinderpelt's eyes, and she did not press her apprentice to say more. Before she went to her nest in the ferns, Leafpaw bit hard into one of the burdock roots stored in the den, and settled down to sleep with the bitter mouthful in her jaws.

Burdock root. Burdock root, she whispered. *Squirrelpaw, can you hear me? Burdock root for rat bites.*

CHAPTER 22

❧

Brambleclaw crouched in the bushes and watched the full moon suspended in the dark blue sky. Back at Fourtrees, the Clans would have met for their Gathering. The thought of the clearing thronged with cats, of gossip exchanged and stories told, made him feel lonelier than ever.

For another endless day they had struggled through the Twolegplace, along Thunderpaths, through fences, over walls. At least they had left the worst of the hard ground behind them; now the Thunderpaths were edged with grass, and gardens surrounded the Twoleg nests. They had found shelter for the night beneath some shrubs, and had even managed to hunt. Yet the sharp teeth of his anxiety kept Brambleclaw awake.

He still did not know if they were going the right way. Purdy led them on confidently, but the twisting route he took among the Twoleg nests took no account of the sun, and Brambleclaw felt as if the sun-drown place were as far away as it had ever been.

"I think we're farther away than ever." Crowpaw had scornfully echoed his thoughts before he settled down to sleep.

Worst of all were his worries about Tawnypelt's shoulder.

Though his sister was too proud to admit she was in pain, by the time they stopped for the night she could barely walk. The rat bite had stopped bleeding, but her shoulder was swollen and the flesh where her fur had been torn away was red and puffy. Brambleclaw didn't need to be a medicine cat to know that the bite was infected. Squirrelpaw and Feathertail had taken turns licking the wound while Tawnypelt slipped into an uneasy, shallow sleep, but every cat knew that it would take more than that to heal her.

Brambleclaw jumped at a scrabbling sound close by in the bushes, then relaxed when Stormfur appeared and crouched down beside him.

"I'll watch for a bit if you like," the gray warrior meowed.

"Thanks." Brambleclaw arched his back and drove his claws into the ground in a stretch. "I'm not sure I can sleep, though."

"Try," Stormfur advised him. "You'll need your strength for tomorrow."

"I know." With another glance at the moon, he added, "I wish we were all safely back at Fourtrees."

To his surprise Stormfur blinked at him sympathetically. "We will be soon. Don't worry. StarClan are with us here just as much as if we were at the Gathering with the rest of our Clans."

Brambleclaw let out a sigh. Somehow, tangled as they were in Twolegplace, it was hard to imagine the starry warriors weaving among them. With a last look at the moon, he curled up and closed his eyes, and at last managed to sink into sleep.

❈ ❈ ❈

The barking of a dog woke him. He sprang up, quivering, only to realize with relief that it was too distant to be a threat; there was no dog scent close by. A gray light filtered through the bushes, and the leaves stirred in a chill breeze with a damp tang to it, as if rain was not far off.

Brambleclaw's companions were sleeping around him, all except Stormfur, who was not in sight. Brambleclaw braced himself, preparing to wake them and get them moving again, when Crowpaw lifted his head and scrambled to his paws, shaking the leaf mold off his pelt.

"Listen, Brambleclaw," he meowed, sounding less aggressive than usual. "We've *got* to get out of here today. Things would be better if we could find a forest, or even farmland. We might need to stop for a bit to let Tawnypelt rest, and we can't do that in the middle of all these Twolegs."

Brambleclaw hoped he hid his surprise at how reasonable the younger cat sounded, especially at how concerned he was for Tawnypelt. "You're right," he agreed. "But I'm not sure. We've no choice but to trust Purdy to get us out of here."

"It's a pity we ever let him come with us," Crowpaw growled. He padded across to where Purdy was sleeping, an untidy heap of tabby fur, snoring and twitching. Crowpaw prodded him hard in the ribs with one paw. "Wake up!"

"Hey? Wha'?" Purdy blinked and then heaved himself up until he was sitting. "What's all the hurry?"

"We need to get moving." Crowpaw's abrasive tone was back. "Or had you forgotten?"

Leaving him to get some sense out of Purdy, too tired and anxious to go over and soothe the festering quarrel, Brambleclaw went to wake the others. He left Tawnypelt until last, bending over to sniff her wound and examine it closely.

"It's no better," Feathertail murmured at his shoulder. "I'm not sure she'll be able to go far today."

As she spoke, Tawnypelt opened her eyes. "Brambleclaw? Is it time to go?" She struggled to sit up, but Brambleclaw could see that her leg would barely support her.

"Lie still for a bit," Feathertail told her. "Let me give that bite another lick."

She crouched down and her tongue rasped in a comforting rhythm over the swollen flesh. Tawnypelt let her head drop onto her paws again. As Brambleclaw watched, Stormfur reappeared with a mouse in his jaws, which he dropped close to Tawnypelt's muzzle.

"There you are," he mewed. "Fresh-kill."

Tawnypelt blinked up at him. "Oh, Stormfur . . . thank you. But I should catch my own."

Brambleclaw's belly clenched with pity. No cat had ever looked less able to hunt.

Stormfur just touched her ear with his nose. "You eat that one," he murmured. "You need to keep up your strength. I can catch more later."

With a little nod of gratitude, Tawnypelt began to eat. Ignoring the argument that was developing between Purdy and Crowpaw, Brambleclaw went to see what Squirrelpaw was doing.

The ginger apprentice was sitting up in the nest of leaves she had made the night before. She was muttering something under her breath, and she kept passing her tongue over her lips as if she could taste something foul.

"What's the matter?" Brambleclaw asked. Trying to joke, he added, "Have you been eating your own fur?"

For once Squirrelpaw did not react. "No," she replied, still licking her lips. "It's just this funny taste. I keep thinking I should remember what it is."

"Not salt, I hope?" Brambleclaw suggested lightly. He had never thought he would miss Squirrelpaw's smart remarks, but this seriousness made him anxious.

"No . . . something else. Just let me think about it, and I'll remember in a bit. Something tells me it might be important."

They set off again, with Purdy in the lead. The night's sleep seemed to have helped Tawnypelt, and she limped along valiantly, managing to keep up with Purdy's ambling pace. Brambleclaw kept an eye on her, determined to stop for a rest if he thought his sister needed it.

The old tabby led them through more Twoleg gardens and out onto a narrow Thunderpath bordered on one side by a wooden fence and on the other by a high wall. Two or three monsters crouched at the edge of the Thunderpath, their huge eyes gleaming. Brambleclaw eyed them suspiciously as he and his companions passed, ready to flee if they roared into life.

The Thunderpath bent sharply to one side; Purdy rounded the corner and Brambleclaw saw Feathertail halt and stare disbelievingly in front of her.

"No!" she spat with uncharacteristic fury. "That's too much! We can't go that way, you furball!"

As if in answer, a dog started barking on the other side of the wall. Brambleclaw glanced around in alarm, but he could see no way for the dog to reach them. Anxiously he bounded forward, and when he reached Feathertail he saw what had upset her. A few foxlengths in front of them the Thunder-path ended abruptly in a high wall, blocking the path ahead with the same dull red stone that had surrounded them for days. They couldn't go any farther that way. Every muscle in Brambleclaw's body shrieked in protest at the thought of having to retrace their steps.

Purdy had stopped to look back, an injured expression on his face. "There's no call to be like that, now."

"You have no idea where we are, do you?" Feathertail demanded. She had flattened herself against the hard surface of the ground; Brambleclaw wasn't sure whether she was try-ing to hide, or preparing to attack their hopeless guide. And if she did, would he stop her? "We've got an injured cat with us. We can't spend all day traipsing after you up and down this . . . this vile place!"

"Steady." Crowpaw came up and bent over Feathertail, rasping his tongue over her ear. "Just ignore the old fool. We'll make a plan to get out of here by ourselves."

Feathertail bared her teeth at him. "How can we? We

don't know where we are."

Behind the wall the dog was going crazy, letting out a flurry of high-pitched barks. Brambleclaw tensed, ready to run if it found a way out of its garden. Behind him, Stormfur bounded around the corner, checked his pace as he realized the dog was no immediate danger, and went over to his sister. A moment later Squirrelpaw arrived with Tawnypelt.

"What's going on?" asked the ThunderClan apprentice. "Where's Purdy?"

Brambleclaw realized that the old cat had vanished. He wasn't sure whether to feel relieved or angry.

"Good riddance," growled Crowpaw.

The words had hardly left his mouth when Purdy's head reappeared, poking through a gap beside the wall that Brambleclaw had not noticed until now.

"Well?" the old cat meowed. "You comin' or not?"

He withdrew again; Brambleclaw padded over to the broken fence panel and looked out. He was ready for yet more Twoleg nests, and gaped in astonishment. Across a narrow, dusty track was a grass-covered slope dotted with clumps of gorse, and beyond that—trees! Trees as far as Brambleclaw could see, with not a Twoleg nest in sight.

"What is it?" Squirrelpaw called impatiently from behind him.

"A forest!" Brambleclaw's voice squeaked like a kit. "A real forest at last. Come on, all of you."

He slid through the gap to stand beside Purdy. The old tabby was looking at him with a knowing gleam in his eye.

"Satisfied now?" he purred. "You wanted out; I've brought you out."

"Er . . . yes. Thanks, Purdy, this is great."

"Not so much of the 'stupid furball' now, hey?" Purdy asked, with a meaningful look at Crowpaw as the WindClan apprentice slipped through the gap.

Brambleclaw and Crowpaw exchanged a glance. Brambleclaw suspected that Purdy had been as surprised as the rest of them to find the way out of the Twolegplace, but the old cat would never admit it. Anyway, it didn't matter now. Twolegplace was behind them, and they could start looking for the sun-drown place again.

They crossed the track and began to climb the slope. Brambleclaw reveled in the feel of fresh grass on his pads, and the forest scents wafting toward him on the faint breeze. When they stood underneath the trees, it was almost like coming home.

"This is more like it!" Stormfur meowed, gazing around at the clumps of bracken and the long, cool grass. "I vote we stay here for the rest of today and tonight. Tawnypelt can get a good sleep, and the rest of us can hunt."

Brambleclaw bit back a protest; his compulsion to make for the sun-drown place was growing stronger as time slipped away, but he knew they would make better progress if they stopped to recover their strength.

The other cats murmured agreement, except for Tawnypelt. "You don't have to stop for me."

"It's not just for you, mouse-brain." Squirrelpaw pushed

her nose affectionately into the ShadowClan cat's fur. "We all need to rest and eat."

Slowly the cats began to move deeper into the wood, clustered together and alert for danger as they looked for a good place to rest. Brambleclaw stopped every few paces to taste the air, but he could not scent fox, or badger, or other cats—nothing that was likely to give them trouble. But the air was full of prey-scent; his mouth began to water at the thought of sinking his teeth into a plump mouse, or better still, a rabbit.

Before long, they came to a spot where the ground fell away toward a thin trickle of water beneath dense hawthorn bushes.

"Couldn't be better," Crowpaw meowed. "There's water and shelter, and if there are predators about they won't find it easy to sneak up on us."

Tawnypelt, who was limping badly again, half slid, half scrambled down the slope and dragged herself into a mossy nest between two twisted roots. Her green eyes were clouded with pain and exhaustion. Feathertail settled down beside her and began to lick her wound again. Purdy flopped down on her other side and immediately curled up and went to sleep.

"Right, you three stay here," Crowpaw mewed, "and the rest of us will hunt."

Brambleclaw opened his mouth to challenge him for ordering everyone else around, then decided it wasn't worth it. Besides, it made a nice change not to be expected to make all the decisions for once. Instead, he padded over to Squirrelpaw. "Fancy hunting with me?" he asked.

Squirrelpaw just nodded, as if half her mind were on something else. She followed Brambleclaw up the stream, and they were hardly out of sight of their temporary camp when Brambleclaw spotted a mouse scuffling among the grass near the water's edge. In one smooth movement he dropped into the hunter's crouch and sprang, killing his prey with a swift blow. Turning to show Squirrelpaw, he saw her standing with her head lifted and her jaws parted to drink in the forest scents.

"Squirrelpaw, are you okay?"

The apprentice jumped. "What? Oh, yes, fine, thanks. There's something I can't quite . . ." Her voice trailed off and she licked her lips again.

Guessing that he wouldn't get any more sense out of her, Brambleclaw scraped earth over his fresh-kill to keep it safe until he came to collect it, and padded farther into the wood. The whole place was rich in prey, and they hardly seemed to know what a predator was. It was one of the easiest hunts he had ever known.

Squirrelpaw helped, but it was clear her mind wasn't on the task. Usually she was a skillful hunter, but today she let a blackbird escape by hesitating too long, and completely missed a squirrel that was nibbling a nut barely a foxlength away.

Then as Brambleclaw was stealthily creeping up on a rabbit, she cried out, "That's it! Over there!"

At once the rabbit shot upright in the grass, and a heartbeat later all Brambleclaw could see of it was its white tail bobbing up and down as it fled.

"Hey!" he exclaimed indignantly. "What did you do that for?"

Squirrelpaw wasn't listening. She had darted down toward the waterside, where clumps of tall plants with dark green leaves were growing. As Brambleclaw stared, mystified, she began to scrape vigorously at the base of the stems.

"Squirrelpaw, what are you doing?" he asked.

The apprentice paused long enough to give him a glance from green eyes that glowed with triumph. "Burdock!" She panted, attacking the stems again. "It's what Tawnypelt needs for her rat bite. Help me to dig up the roots."

"How do you know?" Brambleclaw asked as he began to dig.

"You know that taste I told you about? I've been trying to think of it all morning. Leafpaw must have mentioned it when she was saying good-bye to us."

Brambleclaw paused and looked at her. Leafpaw had certainly told them about several herbs that she thought they might need, but he couldn't remember burdock root being one of them. Then he shrugged and dug harder. There was no other way that Squirrelpaw could have found out about it.

Once they had dug up three or four of the roots, Squirrelpaw pushed them into the water to wash off the earth and then gripped them in her teeth to carry them back to the camp. Brambleclaw followed more slowly, collecting as much of their prey as he could carry.

When he reached their resting place again he found that Squirrelpaw had already chewed up some of the root and was gently pressing the pulp onto Tawnypelt's injured shoulder. The ShadowClan warrior lay still, watching, but as the juice from the root seeped into her wound she relaxed and let out a long sigh.

"That's better," she mewed. "It's going numb. I can't feel the pain anymore."

"That's brilliant," Brambleclaw meowed.

"I think you must be a secret medicine cat," Tawnypelt said to Squirrelpaw, settling herself more comfortably into the moss. "Perhaps you're carrying a bit of your sister's spirit." Blinking drowsily, she sank back into sleep.

Squirrelpaw was watching Tawnypelt with shining eyes, and Brambleclaw felt his fur prickle. Had Leafpaw really mentioned the burdock root back in the forest, or was there something more mysterious going on between her and her sister?

He went back into the wood to collect the rest of the prey. By the time he returned, Stormfur and Crowpaw had also brought back a good catch. For the first time in many days, they were able to eat as much as they wanted. Purdy woke up and gulped down the fresh-kill enthusiastically, as if he found it much tastier than the kittypet food he was used to.

They all slept well. When he woke, Brambleclaw saw that the clouds had vanished and sunlight was angling through the trees, bathing the forest in a reddish glow. Springing up, he climbed as high as he could above the stream and managed to find a gap in the trees so that he could see where the sun was going down.

"That's the path we have to take." Stormfur scrambled up the slope to stand beside him, and his voice was as calm and determined as if he had shared the visions himself. "That's where we will find what midnight tells us."

Brambleclaw's paws itched to race toward the setting sun, as if he knew for certain that Bluestar was waiting there to tell him exactly how he could save the forest. But he knew that it was more sensible to stick to their original plan and spend the night in the wood. Carefully noting the direction they needed to travel, he went back to his friends beside the stream.

Tawnypelt was tearing ravenously into a rabbit. She paused to nod a greeting at Brambleclaw as he appeared. "I'm famished," she admitted. "And my shoulder feels much better. What did you say that was you put on it, Squirrelpaw?"

"Burdock root." Brambleclaw noticed that Squirrelpaw did not try to explain how she knew that burdock root was the right remedy for the infected bite. Perhaps she was wondering about it, too.

She began chewing up another of the roots, and when Tawnypelt had finished eating she applied more of it to her wound. Brambleclaw noticed that the swelling had gone down and the angry red color had faded. He breathed silent thanks to StarClan—and to Leafpaw—for his sister's recovery.

By the time they set out the next morning, after another good meal, Tawnypelt looked almost like her old self. She was barely limping at all and her eyes were bright again.

Long before sunhigh they came to the edge of the forest.

Ahead of them was open country for as far as they could see. The ground rose and fell in a series of gentle slopes. Wind rippled over short, springy grass interspersed with creeping trefoil and wild thyme. It looked to be easy going, and the air had a fresh tang.

"Like home!" Crowpaw murmured, obviously remembering the open moorland of WindClan.

Unlike the WindClan apprentice, Brambleclaw was reluctant to leave the trees behind. The shelter of the canopy had been comforting. But the food and rest had given them all new strength, and he hoped that at last they were coming to the end of their journey.

To his surprise, Purdy said good-bye to them before they left the trees. "I don't feel right under the open sky," he confessed, echoing Brambleclaw's own thoughts. "I guess I've had too many Upwalkers chasing me. I like to be somewhere I can hide. Besides, you don't need me anymore. StarClan, whatever they might be, won't be waiting for *me* at midnight," he added with a glint in his eye.

"Maybe not," meowed Brambleclaw. "Thanks for everything, anyway. We'll miss you." Surprisingly he realized that was true; he had come to feel something like affection for the exasperating old cat. "If you're ever in our forest, you'll be welcome to visit ThunderClan."

As he finished speaking, he couldn't help hearing Crowpaw mew under his breath to Tawnypelt, "Your brother might miss him, but I won't!"

Brambleclaw curled his lip in warning at the WindClan cat,

but Purdy hadn't caught the apprentice's muttered words. "I'll wait here two or three days for you," he promised. "In case you need help to find your way back."

Brambleclaw glanced at Crowpaw in time to see him rolling his eyes at Feathertail, who just shrugged.

"Always supposin' you come back of course," Purdy went on as he padded away with his tail high. "You wouldn't catch me so close to the sun-drown place. Shouldn't wonder if you all end up drowned."

"That's right," Squirrelpaw muttered into Brambleclaw's ear. "Way to keep our hopes up!"

But by the end of that day, even Brambleclaw's hopes were fading. The heat of the sun had drained his energy, and with no water on these rolling uplands his mouth felt like the floor of the sandy training hollow. His companions were no better off, plodding along with their heads down and tails drooping. Tawnypelt was limping again; though she didn't want any cat to examine her wound, Brambleclaw could see the swelling had returned, and wondered how much longer she could keep going. There was no more burdock root here.

Straight in front of them, the sun was sinking in a blaze of scarlet fire, tongues of flame spreading halfway across the sky.

"At least we're heading the right way," Feathertail murmured.

"Yes, but how far do we still have to go?" Brambleclaw had tried not to share his doubts, but his anxiety was becoming too much for him. "The sun-drown place could be days away."

"I always said this was a mouse-brained idea," Crowpaw remarked, though he sounded too exhausted to be aggressive.

"Well, how long do we carry on?" asked Stormfur. As all the other cats turned to look at him, he went on: "If we don't find the place, sooner or later we have to decide . . . do we give up or keep trying?"

Brambleclaw knew he was right. At some point they might have to admit defeat. But what would that mean for their Clans, to ignore the will of StarClan and go home with the journey unfinished?

Then Squirrelpaw, who had been facing into the wind to drink in the scents it carried, spun around to face the others, her eyes blazing with excitement.

"Brambleclaw!" She gasped. "I can smell salt!"

CHAPTER 23

❧

Brambleclaw stared at the apprentice for a moment before opening his mouth and tasting the air for himself. Squirrelpaw was right. The salt tang was unmistakable, carrying him right back to his dream, and the bitter taste of the water that had surged around him.

"It *is* salt!" he meowed. "We must be close. Come on!"

He raced into the wind with the sun dazzling his eyes. A swift glance behind showed that his companions were following. Even Tawnypelt was managing to hobble faster. Brambleclaw felt new strength pouring into his limbs, as if he could go on running forever until he soared into the fiery sky like one of the white birds that wheeled and screamed above them.

Instead, he came to a skidding, terrified halt on the edge of a huge cliff. Steep sandy slopes fell away barely a mouse-length in front of his paws. Waves crashed at the bottom, and stretching out ahead of him was a heaving expanse of blue-green water. The sun was sinking into it on the horizon, its flames so bright that Brambleclaw had to narrow his eyes against them. The orange fire burned a path like blood across the water, almost reaching the foot of the cliff.

For a few moments no cat could do anything but stare. Then Brambleclaw shook himself. "We've got to hurry," he meowed. "We have to find the cave with teeth before it gets dark."

"And then wait for midnight," Feathertail added.

Brambleclaw glanced from side to side, but he couldn't see anything to tell him which way to go. Choosing a direction at random, he led the way along the cliff top. From time to time they stopped and peered over the edge to look for the cave. Brambleclaw dug his claws firmly into the tough grass; it was too easy to imagine slipping over and falling, falling, falling into the hungry waves.

Gradually the land sloped down until the water was only the height of a tree below them. The cliff top jutted out so they could not see the bottom, and the almost sheer surface was deeply scored with ancient runnels of rain. As the cliff grew less steep, the cats scrabbled a little way down and made their way along closer to the water, sometimes even within reach of a salty burst of wave. Clefts, riven by ancient streams, split the rock, sometimes so wide that the cats had to leap over them, and the grass frequently gave way to hollows where a few twisted shrubs clung to the scant soil.

"There are plenty of places to shelter for the night if we don't find the cave," Stormfur pointed out.

Brambleclaw was beginning to think they might need to find somewhere to stop. The sun had sunk beneath the water by now, though great orange flares still streaked the sky. The breeze was growing colder. Tawnypelt at least could lie down, he thought, while the rest of them went on searching.

His sister had fallen a little way behind. Brambleclaw was just bounding back to her, skirting the edge of one of the clefts, when his paws slipped and he found himself sliding helplessly into the hollow. He scrabbled at the loose soil but it gave way under his claws, showering him with dirt. He kept on sliding; in the shadows he could not see the bottom and he let out a yowl of alarm.

"Brambleclaw!" Stormfur leaped into the hollow beside him and tried to sink his claws into Brambleclaw's shoulder, but Brambleclaw felt more of the soil give way and they both slid downward more rapidly than before. Soil spattered over Brambleclaw's face, stinging his eyes and choking him. From somewhere above he heard an earsplitting yowl and Squirrelpaw launched herself practically on top of him.

"No—go back!" he choked out, getting a mouthful of soil.

Then even the shifting soil vanished and there was nothing beneath him at all; he fell, howling, for a few terrified heartbeats and landed with a thump on damp pebbles.

For a moment he lay stunned. A booming echo thundered in his ears, and he felt as if the whole world were spinning around. Then he opened his eyes and stared in horror as he saw the shape of a massive gaping mouth with teeth closing on him, outlined against the red evening sky. He tried to scramble up, but a sudden rush of water swept him off his paws. His yowl of terror was cut off abruptly as water swirled into his mouth, with the terrifying salt taste of his dream.

Brambleclaw flailed with all his strength but the waves

hurled him mercilessly toward the teeth and then tossed him back again, far under the cliff. He did not know where he was or which way he should try to swim. Water filled his eyes and ears, roaring around him. He gasped for breath, only to swallow more of the salt water.

His frantic struggles were growing weaker, and the cold, stifling waves were closing over his head when he felt a sharp pain in one shoulder. Suddenly the pressure on his fur vanished and he could breathe again. Coughing up water, he turned his head and saw Squirrelpaw's eyes blazing at him, her teeth fastened firmly in his fur.

"No!" He gasped. "You can't—you'll drown. . . ."

Squirrelpaw could not reply without letting go of him. Her only response was to kick out strongly with all four paws. Brambleclaw felt pebbles shifting underneath his feet, and then the waves washed them back toward the teeth.

Summoning the last scrap of his strength he thrashed at the water, trying to drive himself and Squirrelpaw away from those spiky rocks. The water surged and lifted them up; he got a brief glimpse of sodden dark gray fur—Stormfur— beside him, before the waves sent them crashing down on hard ground.

The breath driven out of him, Brambleclaw scrabbled among the rolling pebbles while the shallow, sucking water threatened to drag him back again. Squirrelpaw, still gripping his shoulder, pulled him up, and he felt another cat give him a shove from behind. At last he collapsed on solid rock and lay still, letting the world drift away.

A paw prodding against his flank roused him.

"Brambleclaw?" It was Squirrelpaw, sounding desperately anxious. "Brambleclaw, are you all right?"

Brambleclaw opened his mouth and let out a moan. His fur was soaked and he was ice-cold. He felt too exhausted to move; every muscle shrieked with pain, and his stomach felt distended from all the water he had swallowed. But at least he was alive.

He managed to raise his head. "I'm fine," he rasped.

"Oh, Brambleclaw, I thought you were dead!"

As his vision cleared he could make out Squirrelpaw bending over him. He could not remember ever seeing her look so upset, not even when her father had been angry with her back in the forest. The sight of her troubled eyes urged him to make an effort: he sat up, and instantly vomited up several mouthfuls of salt water.

"I'm not dead." He coughed. "Thanks to you. You were great, Squirrelpaw."

"She took a huge risk." That was Stormfur's voice; the gray warrior was standing over Brambleclaw. With his fur plastered to his body he looked much smaller than Brambleclaw was used to. He sounded disapproving, and yet there was a glow in his eyes as he looked at Squirrelpaw. "But it was a very brave thing she did."

"And a stupid one." With a start of surprise Brambleclaw realized that Tawnypelt was there as well, standing close by with water washing around her paws and her eyes narrowed in anger. "What if you'd both drowned?"

"Well, we didn't," Squirrelpaw flashed at her.

"I could have helped."

"With that infected bite?" Stormfur pressed his muzzle briefly against Tawnypelt's flank. "StarClan know how you managed to get down here at all."

"I fell, like the rest of you." Tawnypelt's voice was wry, and she relaxed a little as she looked at Squirrelpaw. "I'm sorry," she meowed. "You *were* brave. It's just that I'm finding it hard being injured and not able to help. Like you, I . . . I thought we'd lost Brambleclaw for good."

By now Brambleclaw was beginning to feel better, enough to look around and recognize the cave of his dream. He was *inside* it. The gaping mouth with its ring of teeth was at one end. Water washed through it in a strange, ceaseless rhythm, crashing in with a roar and then hissing out again, rolling the pebbles over the floor as it went. The rock walls were smooth and rounded. The ground sloped upward to the back of the cave, which was lost in shadows; the only light came through the mouth and from a small hole high in the roof, where Feathertail and Crowpaw were peering anxiously down.

"Are you all right?" Feathertail called.

"I'm fine." Brambleclaw rose shakily to his paws. "I think we've found what we were looking for."

"Hold on, we're coming down," meowed Crowpaw.

Brambleclaw almost called out an order to stay where they were—which Crowpaw would certainly have disobeyed—but when he looked more closely he could see a series of ledges and clefts in the rock wall where it would be possible to climb safely down and then to get out again. Feathertail and Crow-paw picked their way down carefully until they reached the cave floor and stood looking around, blinking.

"Do we have to stay here until midnight?" Squirrelpaw asked, raising her head from licking her damp chest fur. Her voice echoed strangely around the walls.

"I suppose—" Brambleclaw began, then stopped, his muscles tensing.

From the darkness at the back of the cave came a heavy scratching noise. A powerful, rank scent reached his nostrils. A shadow moved, not wholly black, but patched with white. Then lumbering into the dim light came a shape that was terrifyingly familiar: one of the deadliest enemies of the forest cats.

A badger!

CHAPTER 24

Brambleclaw glanced wildly over his shoulder, but there was nowhere to flee except into the water; the difficult climb back to the hole in the cave roof would take too long. Guilt crashed over him with the cold force of the waves that had almost drowned him. All his visions, all his certainty, had led his companions to this dreadful place, where they would find no knowledge, no vision from StarClan, only a pointless and horrible death. What use were faith and courage now, when they were trapped like rabbits in a hole?

Crowpaw had flattened himself to the ground and was creeping forward with his teeth bared in a snarl. Stormfur was edging around the badger to attack it from the side. Despairingly Brambleclaw knew that they were heading to meet their death. Even all six of them, weak and starving as they were and worn out by their travels and the struggle in the water, could not hope to defeat a badger. Caught as they were by the choking waves, it would not be long before the blunt claws and snapping jaws picked them off one by one.

The badger had paused on the edge of the shadows that filled the back of the cave. Its powerful shoulders were hunched and its claws scraped on rock. Its head swung to and fro, the white stripe glimmering, as if it were deciding which of them to attack first.

Then it spoke.

"Midnight has come."

Brambleclaw's mouth fell open, and for a moment he felt as if the ground had given way beneath him again. That a badger could speak, could say words he understood, words that actually meant something . . . He stared in disbelief, his heart pounding.

"I am Midnight." The badger's voice was deep and rasping, like the sound of the pebbles turning under the waves. "With you I must speak."

"Mouse dung!" Crowpaw spat. The WindClan apprentice was still crouched ready to spring. "Make one move and you'll have my claws in your eyes."

"No, Crowpaw, wait—"

The badger's throaty laughter interrupted Brambleclaw. "Fierce, is he not? StarClan have chosen well. But there will be no clawing this day. Here is talk, not fight."

Brambleclaw and his companions uncertainly looked at each other, their tails bristling. Crowpaw put words to what they were all thinking. "Are we going to trust it?"

"What else can we do?" Feathertail responded, blinking.

Brambleclaw weighed up the badger again. It was smaller than the one he had seen at Snakerocks—probably a female— but no less dangerous for that. Believing what she said went against everything he had been taught as a kit. Yet so far she had made no move to attack them; he even thought that he could make out a gleam of humor in her eyes.

He glanced back at his friends. Crowpaw, Stormfur, and Feathertail might have managed to fight well, but he and Squirrelpaw were exhausted from their near-drowning, while Tawnypelt had sunk down onto the floor of the cave with her injured shoulder held awkwardly, and hardly seemed to be conscious.

"Come," the badger rasped. "All night we cannot wait."

Brambleclaw knew for certain that this was no ordinary badger. Never before had he heard of a badger who could speak in a language that cats understood—still less one that spoke of StarClan, as if she knew more of their wishes than any cat alive.

"Feathertail's right," he hissed. "What choice do we have? She could have turned us all into crowfood by now. This must be what Bluestar meant in my dream when she told me to listen to midnight. She didn't mean a *time* at all." Turning to the badger, he asked out loud, "You are Midnight? And you have a message for us from StarClan?"

The badger nodded. "Midnight am I called. And it was shown to me that here I would meet with you . . . though four were numbered to me, not six."

"Then we'll listen to what you have to say," Brambleclaw told her. "You're right; four were chosen, but six have come, and all deserve to be here."

"But make one wrong move . . ." Crowpaw threatened.

"Oh, shut up, mouse-brain!" Squirrelpaw growled. "Can't

you see, this is what we came here to find? 'Listen to what midnight tells us.' *This* is Midnight."

Crowpaw glared at her through the gathering darkness, but did not reply.

Midnight turned with the single word, "Follow," and headed for the back of the cave. Brambleclaw could just make out the dark opening of a tunnel. Taking a deep breath, he meowed, "Okay, let's do it."

Stormfur took the lead, with Crowpaw just behind him; Brambleclaw hoped that the apprentice would stop looking for a fight long enough to hear what the badger had to say. Feathertail gently nudged Tawnypelt to her paws and lent her shoulder for support as she staggered into the tunnel. Brambleclaw exchanged a glance with Squirrelpaw and was surprised to see that in spite of her wet, exhausted state her eyes were sparkling with excitement.

"What a story we'll have to tell when we get home!" she meowed, getting up and trotting into the tunnel after Feathertail.

Brambleclaw brought up the rear, with a final glance over his shoulder at the rocky teeth that framed the mouth of the cave and the waves that still surged back and forth. The last crimson rays of the drowned sun still stained the sky; in a single heartbeat Brambleclaw seemed to see an endless river of blood pouring down upon him, filling his ears with the screams of dying cats.

"Brambleclaw?" Squirrelpaw's voice cut through the terrified sounds. "Are you coming?"

The vision was gone; Brambleclaw found himself back in the wave-filled cave to see that the color was rapidly fading from the sky and a single warrior of StarClan shone down on him. Shivering, he followed his friends and Midnight.

The tunnel sloped upward. Brambleclaw could see nothing in the pitch darkness, but he felt sandy soil beneath his paws, rather than pebbles or rock. As well as the wary cat-scent of his friends, there was a powerful reek of badger.

Then he came out into another cave. Fresher air moved against his fur, and at the far end a hole led into the open. A faint silvery gleam filtered through it, telling Brambleclaw that outside, the moon was crossing the sky. By its light he saw that this cave had been dug out of the earth, with twisting roots entangled in the roof and the floor covered with a thick layer of bracken. Feathertail was already helping Tawnypelt to make a nest among the soft fronds, and settled down beside her to lick her wound again.

"You have injury?" Midnight asked the ShadowClan warrior. "What gave it?"

"It's a rat bite," Tawnypelt replied through gritted teeth.

The badger made a spitting noise. "Is bad. Wait." She vanished into the shadows at one side of the cave and returned a moment later with a root clamped in her jaws.

"Burdock root!" Squirrelpaw exclaimed, with a triumphant glance at Brambleclaw. "You use it too?"

"Good for bite, good for infected paw, good for all sores." The badger chomped up the root and laid the pulp on Tawnypelt's wound, just as Squirrelpaw had done in the wood.

"Now," she went on when she had finished, "is time for talk."

She waited until all the cats had settled themselves among the bracken. Brambleclaw felt his excitement rising. He was only just beginning to realize that they had reached the end of their journey. They had found the place where StarClan had sent them, and now they were about to hear what Midnight had to tell them.

"How is it you can speak to us?" he asked curiously.

"I have traveled far, and many tongues have learned," Midnight told him. "Tongues of other cats, who speak not same as you. Of fox and rabbit also." She grunted. "They speak not of interest. Fox talk is all of kill. Rabbit has thistledown for brain."

Squirrelpaw let out a *mrrow* of laughter. Brambleclaw could see that her fur lay flat again and her ears were pricked. "So what do you want to tell us?" she meowed.

"Much, in good time," replied the badger. "But first, tell me of your journey. How came you from your tribes?"

Stormfur looked puzzled. "Tribes?"

Midnight shook her head irritably. "My brain thistledown also. Forget which sort of cats here. You say Clans, not?"

"That's right," meowed Brambleclaw. He nudged away the uneasy thought that there were other cats like them, not loners, who lived in Clans known as tribes. They had not seen them on their journey—they probably lived far in a different direction.

With the others to help him, he began the story of their journey, from the first dreams that four of them had shared, to his own dream of the sun-drown place and the decision to leave the forest. Midnight listened intently, with a low chuckle as the cats told her of their misadventures with Purdy, and an understanding nod when they described how they had all, in the end, received their own saltwater sign.

"So here we are," Brambleclaw finished. "We are ready to know what StarClan's message is."

"And why we had to come here to find out," Crowpaw added. "Why couldn't StarClan have told us what we needed to know back in the forest?"

His tone was still hostile, as if he had not accepted that Midnight was not a threat, but that didn't seem to bother the badger. Feathertail flicked her tail out in a calming gesture, and at her touch the WindClan apprentice relaxed a little.

"Think, small warrior," Midnight replied to his question. "When you set out, you were four. Six with friends who would not stay behind. Now you are one." Her voice grew deeper and seemed to Brambleclaw to be full of foreboding as she went on, "In days coming now, all Clans must be one. If not, trouble destroy you."

Brambleclaw felt icy claws rake down his spine. The shudder that ran through him had nothing to do with his sodden fur. "What *is* the trouble?" he whispered.

Midnight hesitated, her deep, dark gaze resting on each cat in turn. "You must leave the forest," she growled at last. "All cats must leave."

"What?" Stormfur leaped to his paws. "That's mouse-brained! There have always been cats in the forest."

The badger heaved a long sigh. "No longer."

"But why?" Feathertail asked, anxiously kneading her paws on the bed of bracken.

"Twolegs." Midnight sighed again. "Always is Twolegs. Soon they come with machines . . . monsters is your word, not? Trees will they uproot, rocks break, the earth itself tear apart. No place left for cats. You stay, monsters tear you too, or you starve with no prey."

There was silence in the moonlit cave. Brambleclaw struggled with the dreadful vision the badger had summoned. He imagined Twoleg monsters—huge shining things in bright unnatural colors, roaring through his beloved camp. He could almost hear again the screams he had heard in the cave with teeth, though now they were the terrified cries of his Clan mates as they fled. Everything in him strained against what he had heard, yet he could not tell Midnight that he did not believe her. Every word she had spoken was filled with truth.

"How do you know all this?" Stormfur meowed quietly; there was no challenge in his voice, only a desperate need for an explanation.

"It happened to my sett, many seasons ago. I have seen all before; I can see what will come now. Just as the stars speak to you, they talk to me also. All that you need to know is written there. Is not hard to read, once you know."

"No more Sunningrocks?" Squirrelpaw mewed in a small voice; she sounded as scared as a kit without its mother. "No more training hollow? No more Fourtrees?"

Midnight shook her head, her eyes tiny bright berries in the shadows.

"But *why* would the Twolegs do that?" Brambleclaw demanded. "What harm have we ever done them?"

"Is no harm," Midnight replied. "Twolegs hardly know you there. They do it for build new Thunderpath—go here, there, more faster."

"It won't happen." Crowpaw stood up with a fierce gleam in his eyes, as if he were ready to take on the whole race of Twolegs single-pawed. "StarClan won't allow it."

"StarClan cannot stop it."

Crowpaw opened his mouth to protest again, but nothing came out. He looked utterly bewildered to think of a disaster that was beyond the power of StarClan to stop.

"Then why did they bring us here?" mewed a faint voice. Tawnypelt had raised her head from her nest of ferns to fix her gaze on Midnight. "Are we supposed to go home and watch our Clans being destroyed?"

"No, indeed, injured warrior." The badger's voice was suddenly gentle. "For hope is given to you. Hope you shall bring. You must lead your Clans away from the forest and find new home."

"Just like that?" Crowpaw let out a snort of disgust. "I'm supposed to go to my Clan leader and say, 'Sorry, Tallstar, we've all got to leave'? He would claw my ears off, if he didn't die laughing first."

Midnight's reply rumbled from deep in her chest. "When you reach home I think you will find that even your Clan leaders will listen."

Terror seized Brambleclaw. What more had the badger seen in the stars? When they returned to the forest, would they find that the destruction had already begun?

He sprang to his paws. "We must go now!"

"No, no." Midnight shook her head from side to side. "Time is for rest tonight. Hunt in moonlight. Eat well. Let injured friend sleep. Tomorrow is better for travel."

Brambleclaw glanced at his friends and nodded reluctantly. "That makes sense."

"But you haven't told us where to go," Feathertail pointed out, her blue eyes full of trouble. "Where can we find another forest where all the Clans can live in peace?"

"Fear not. You will find, far from Twolegplaces, where is peace. Hills, oak woods for shelter, running streams."

"But how?" Brambleclaw persisted. "Will you come with us and show us?"

"No," Midnight rasped. "Much have I traveled, but no longer. Now enough is this cave, roar of sea, wind in grasses. But you will not be without a guide. When return, stand on Great Rock when Silverpelt shines above. A dying warrior the way will show."

Fear clutched harder at Brambleclaw. Midnight's words sounded more like a threat than a promise. "One of us will die?" he whispered.

"I did not say. Do so, and you will see."

Evidently the badger was not prepared to say more, if indeed she knew. Brambleclaw did not doubt her wisdom, but he realized that not everything had been revealed to her. His breath grew shaky as he caught a glimpse of other powers beyond StarClan—perhaps a power so great that the whole blaze of Silverpelt was no more than the dazzle of moonlight on water.

"Okay," he meowed, letting out a long breath. "Thank you, Midnight. We'll do as you say."

"And now we'd better hunt," added Stormfur.

Dipping his head in deep respect to the badger, he padded past her up the tunnel and out into the night. Crowpaw and Feathertail followed him.

"Squirrelpaw, you stay with Tawnypelt," Brambleclaw mewed. "Rest and get your fur dry."

To his surprise, Squirrelpaw agreed without question, even giving his ear a quick lick before settling down in the bracken beside his sister. Brambleclaw watched them for a moment, realizing how much they meant to him—even the pesky ginger apprentice whom he had tried so hard to leave behind. Stormfur and Feathertail, too, were true friends, and even Crowpaw had become an ally he would want beside him in any battle.

"You were right," he meowed thoughtfully to Midnight. "We have become one."

The badger nodded gravely. "In days to come, you need each other." She pronounced the words with all the force of a prophecy from StarClan. "Your journey not end here, small warrior. It only just begin."

EPILOGUE

❧

The long grass beside the Thunderpath parted and Firestar prowled into the open, the weakening leaf-fall sun shining on his flame-colored pelt. Beside him Graystripe sniffed suspiciously at the air.

"Great StarClan, it smells foul today!" he exclaimed.

Cloudtail and Sandstorm padded up to join them, and Leafpaw, the last member of the patrol, turned away from the clump of marigold she was examining. Cloudtail let out a snort of disgust. "Every time I come up here, it takes me all day to get the reek out of my fur," he complained.

Sandstorm rolled her eyes but said nothing.

"You know, there's something strange about today," Firestar meowed, glancing up and down the Thunderpath. "There aren't any monsters in sight, but the smell's worse than ever."

"And I can hear something," Leafpaw added, her ears pricked.

The wind carried a deep-toned roaring sound toward the group of cats, faint with distance but growing gradually louder.

Cloudtail turned to his Clan leader with a puzzled look in

his blue eyes. "What's that? I've never heard . . ." His voice trailed off and he stood gaping.

Over a rise in the Thunderpath came the biggest monster any of the cats had seen in their lives. Sunlight dazzled off its gleaming body, and its shape rippled in the heat rising from the surface of the Thunderpath. Its throaty roaring grew and grew until it seemed to fill the whole forest.

It came slowly, followed by another and yet another. Twolegs swarmed over them like ticks, yowling at each other, their words all but drowned by the roar of the monsters.

Then as the leading monster drew abreast of the five watching cats, the unthinkable happened. Instead of going past it swerved, crunched over the narrow strip of grass that edged the Thunderpath, and headed straight for them.

"What's going on?" Graystripe gasped as Firestar howled, "Scatter!"

He dived for cover into a clump of bracken while his deputy fled deeper into the forest and turned to stare out from underneath a thornbush. Cloudtail shot up the nearest tree and crouched in the fork between two branches, gazing down. Sandstorm headed into a narrow gully with a trickle of water at the bottom, pausing to look back only when she reached the other side, her fur bristling in mingled shock and anger. Leafpaw followed her, and flattened herself in the long grass.

The monster barreled forward on huge black paws that crushed everything in its path. As all five cats watched, frozen with horror, it rammed its shoulder up against an ash tree; the tree shook under the impact, and then, with a shriek like all the prey in the forest dying at once, its roots tore out of the earth.

The tree crashed to the ground. The monster rolled on.

The destruction of the forest had begun.

KEEP WATCH FOR

THE NEW PROPHECY

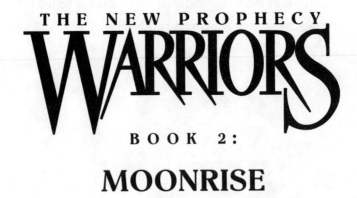

BOOK 2:

MOONRISE

As the questing cats journey through the harsh mountains, they encounter a tribe of wild cats who have their own set of warrior ancestors . . . and their own mysterious prophecy to fulfill. Stormfur can't understand their fascination with him, but he senses that they are hiding a deadly secret.

THE NEW PROPHECY

WARRIORS

MOONRISE

WARRIORS

WARRIORS:
THE NEW PROPHECY

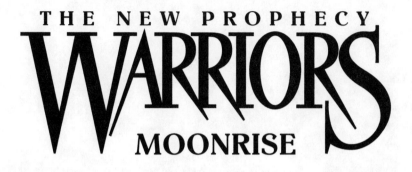

THE NEW PROPHECY

WARRIORS

MOONRISE

ERIN
HUNTER

HARPERCOLLINS*PUBLISHERS*

Moonrise

Copyright © 2005 by Working Partners Limited

Series created by Working Partners Limited

www.harperchildrens.com

Library of Congress Cataloging-in-Publication Data
Hunter, Erin.
    Moonrise / Erin Hunter— 1st ed.
        p. cm — (Warriors, the new prophecy ; 2)
    Summary: As they journey home to warn their clans of the coming
destruction, the six cats, guided by StarClan's prophecy, meet an unfamiliar
tribe of cats with their own set of beliefs—and their own mysterious
prophecy.
    ISBN-10: 0-06-074452-9 — ISBN-10: 0-06-074453-7 (lib. bdg.)
    ISBN-13: 978-0-06-074452-6 — ISBN-13: 978-0-06-074453-3
(lib. bdg.)
    [1. Cats—Fiction. 2. Fantasy.] I. Title. II. Series.
PZ7.H916625Mo 2005
[Fic]—dc22   2004029893

Typography by Karin Paprocki
11 12 13 14 15
❖
First Edition

Special thanks to Cherith Baldry

ALLEGIANCES

THUNDERCLAN

LEADER FIRESTAR—ginger tom with a flame-colored pelt

DEPUTY GRAYSTRIPE—long-haired gray tom

MEDICINE CAT CINDERPELT—dark gray she-cat
APPRENTICE, LEAFPAW

WARRIORS (toms, and she-cats without kits)

MOUSEFUR—small dusky brown she-cat
APPRENTICE, SPIDERPAW

DUSTPELT—dark brown tabby tom
APPRENTICE, SQUIRRELPAW

SANDSTORM—pale ginger she-cat
APPRENTICE, SORRELPAW

CLOUDTAIL—long-haired white tom

BRACKENFUR—golden brown tabby tom
APPRENTICE, WHITEPAW

THORNCLAW—golden brown tabby tom
APPRENTICE, SHREWPAW

BRIGHTHEART—white she-cat with ginger patches

BRAMBLECLAW—dark brown tabby tom with amber eyes

ASHFUR—pale gray (with darker flecks) tom, dark blue eyes

RAINWHISKER—dark gray tom with blue eyes

SOOTFUR—lighter gray tom with amber eyes

APPRENTICES (more than six moons old, in training to become warriors)

SORRELPAW—tortoiseshell and white she-cat with amber eyes

SQUIRRELPAW—dark ginger she-cat with green eyes

LEAFPAW—light brown tabby she-cat with amber eyes and white paws

SPIDERPAW—long-limbed black tom with brown underbelly and amber eyes

SHREWPAW—small dark brown tom with amber eyes

WHITEPAW—white she-cat with green eyes

QUEENS (she-cats expecting or nursing kits)

GOLDENFLOWER—pale ginger coat, the oldest nursery queen

FERNCLOUD—pale gray (with darker flecks) she-cat, green eyes

ELDERS (former warriors and queens, now retired)

FROSTFUR—beautiful white she-cat with blue eyes

DAPPLETAIL—once-pretty tortoiseshell she-cat, the oldest cat in thunderclan

SPECKLETAIL—pale tabby she-cat

LONGTAIL—pale tabby tom with dark black stripes, retired early due to failing sight

SHADOWCLAN

LEADER   **BLACKSTAR**—large white tom with huge jet-black paws

DEPUTY   **RUSSETFUR**—dark ginger she-cat

MEDICINE CAT   **LITTLECLOUD**—very small tabby tom

WARRIORS   **OAKFUR**—small brown tom
APPRENTICE, SMOKEPAW

TAWNYPELT—tortoiseshell she-cat with green eyes

CEDARHEART—dark gray tom

ROWANCLAW—ginger she-cat
APPRENTICE, TALONPAW

TALLPOPPY—long-legged light brown tabby she-cat

ELDERS   **RUNNINGNOSE**—small gray and white tom, formerly the medicine cat

WINDCLAN

LEADER   **TALLSTAR**—elderly black and white tom with a very long tail

DEPUTY   **MUDCLAW**—mottled dark brown tom
APPRENTICE, CROWPAW—dark smoky gray, almost black tom with blue eyes

MEDICINE CAT   **BARKFACE**—short-tailed brown tom

WARRIORS **ONEWHISKER**—brown tabby tom

WEBFOOT—dark gray tabby tom

TORNEAR—tabby tom

WHITETAIL—small white she-cat

ELDERS **MORNINGFLOWER**—tortoiseshell she-cat

RIVERCLAN

LEADER **LEOPARDSTAR**—unusually spotted golden tabby she-cat

DEPUTY **MISTYFOOT**—gray she-cat with blue eyes

MEDICINE CAT **MUDFUR**—long-haired light brown tom
APPRENTICE, MOTHWING—beautiful golden tabby she-cat with amber eyes

WARRIORS **BLACKCLAW**—smoky black tom

HEAVYSTEP—thickset tabby tom

STORMFUR—dark gray tom with amber eyes

FEATHERTAIL—light gray she-cat with blue eyes

HAWKFROST—broad-shouldered dark brown tom

MOSSPELT—tortoiseshell she-cat

QUEENS **DAWNFLOWER**—pale gray she-cat

ELDERS **SHADEPELT**—very dark gray she-cat

LOUDBELLY—dark brown tom

CATS OUTSIDE CLANS

BARLEY—black and white tom that lives on a farm close to the forest

RAVENPAW—sleek black cat that lives on the farm with Barley

PURDY—elderly tabby tom that lives in woods near the sea

CARRIONPLACE

SHADOWCLAN
CAMP

THUNDERPATH

THUNDERCLAN
CAMP

GREAT
SYCAMORE

SANDY
HOLLOW

SNAKEROCKS

TALLPINES

TREECUT PLACE

TWOLEGPLACE

THUNDERCLAN

RIVERCLAN

SHADOWCLAN

WINDCLAN

STARCLAN

North Allerton
Amenity Tip

Windover Road

White Hart Woods

Chelford Forest

Chelford Mill

Chelford

Deciduous Woodland

Conifers

Marsh

Cliffs and Rocks

Hiking Trails

NORTH

PROLOGUE

One by one, the cats crept into the cave. Their fur was streaked with mud and their eyes stretched wide with fear, reflecting the cold moonlight that filtered through a crack in the roof. They crouched low with their bellies close to the ground, their gazes flickering from side to side as if they expected to see danger lurking in the shadows.

The glimmer of moonlight was caught in pools of water on the cave floor. It lit up a forest of pointed stones, some rising from the ground and others hanging from the cave roof. Some of the stones joined in the middle to form slender trees of gleaming white rock. Wind gusted through them, ruffling the cats' fur. The air smelled damp and clean, and was filled with the distant roar of falling water.

A cat stepped out from behind one of the pointed stones. He was long-bodied, with lean, muscular limbs, and his pelt was completely covered in mud that had dried into spikes, so that he looked like a cat carved in stone.

"Welcome," he meowed in a rasping voice. "Moonlight lies on the water. It is time for a Telling, according to the laws of the Tribe of Endless Hunting."

One of the cats crept forward, dipping his head to the mud-covered cat. "Stoneteller, have you had a sign? Has the Tribe of Endless Hunting spoken to you?"

Another cat spoke from behind him. "Is there hope at last?"

Stoneteller bowed his head. "I have seen the words of the Tribe of Endless Hunting in the pattern of moonlight on rock, in the shadows cast by the stones, in the sound of raindrops as they fall from the roof." He paused, letting his gaze sweep over the cats around him. "Yes," he went on. "They have told me there is hope."

A faint murmur, like the rustle of leaves in the wind, passed through the group of cats. Their eyes seemed to grow brighter, and their ears pricked. The one who had come forward first mewed hesitantly, "Then you know what will rid us of this dreadful danger?"

"Yes, Crag," Stoneteller replied. "The Tribe of Endless Hunting has promised me that a cat will come, a silver cat not from this Tribe, who will rid us of Sharptooth once and for all."

There was a pause, then: "Are there other cats, not in the Tribe of Rushing Water?" a voice asked from the back of the group.

"There must be," another cat replied.

"I have heard tell of strangers," meowed Crag, "though we've seen none here in our lifetimes. But when will the silver cat come?" he added desperately, and other mews rose from all around him.

"Yes, when?"

"Is it really true?"

Stoneteller signaled for silence with a twitch of his tail. "Yes, it is true," he meowed. "The Tribe of Endless Hunting has never lied to us. I have seen the sheen of his silver fur myself, in a moonlit pool."

"But *when?*" Crag persisted.

"The Tribe of Endless Hunting has not shown that to me," Stoneteller replied. "I do not know when the silver cat will come, or from where, but we will know it when he arrives."

He raised his head toward the cave roof, and his eyes shone like two tiny moons. "Until then, cats of my Tribe, we can only wait."

CHAPTER 1

Stormfur opened his eyes, blinking away sleep, and struggled to remember where he was. Instead of his nest of reeds in the RiverClan camp, he was lying curled in dry, crunchy bracken. Above his head was the earth roof of a cave, crisscrossed with tangled roots. He could hear a rhythmic roaring sound faintly in the distance. At first it puzzled him; then he remembered how close they were to the sun-drown water, washing endlessly onto the edge of the land. He flinched as a vision burst into his mind, of how he and Brambleclaw had struggled in the water for their lives; he spat, still tasting the salty tang at the back of his throat. At home in RiverClan he was used to water—his was the only Clan that could swim comfortably in the river that ran through the forest—but not this surging, salty, pushing-and-pulling water, too strong even for a RiverClan cat to swim in safely.

Other memories came rushing back. StarClan had sent cats from each of the four Clans on a long, dangerous journey, to hear what Midnight had to tell them. They had fought their way across unknown country, through Twoleg nests, facing attacks from dogs and rats, to make the last incredible discovery: that Midnight was a badger.

Stormfur felt ice creeping along his limbs as he recalled Midnight's dreadful message. Twolegs were destroying the forest to make a new Thunderpath. All the Clans would have to leave, and it was the task of StarClan's chosen cats to warn them and lead them to a new home.

Stormfur sat up and looked around the cave. Faint light filtered down the tunnel that led out onto the clifftop, along with a gentle current of fresh air that carried the scent of salt water. Midnight the badger was nowhere to be seen. Close beside Stormfur, his sister, Feathertail, was sleeping, her tail curled over her nose. Just beyond her was Tawnypelt, the fierce ShadowClan warrior; Stormfur was relieved to see that she was resting quietly, as if the rat bite she had suffered in the Twolegplace was troubling her less. Midnight's store of herbs had yielded something to soothe the infection and help her sleep. On the opposite side of the cave, a little way apart, was the WindClan apprentice Crowpaw, his dark gray pelt barely visible among the fronds of bracken. Nearest the cave entrance, Tawnypelt's brother, Brambleclaw, was stretched out beside Squirrelpaw, who slept in a tight ball. Stormfur felt a stab of jealousy at the sight of the two ThunderClan cats close together, and tried to push it away. He had no right to admire Squirrelpaw, and her courage and bright optimism, as much as he did, when they came from different Clans. Brambleclaw would make her a much better mate.

Stormfur knew that he ought to rouse his companions so that they could begin their long journey back to the forest.

Yet he was strangely reluctant. *Let them sleep a little longer*, he thought. *We'll need all our strength for what lies ahead.*

Shaking scraps of bracken from his pelt, he picked his way across the sandy floor of the cave and out through the tunnel. A stiff breeze ruffled his fur as he emerged onto the springy grass. He was dry at last, after his near-drowning the night before, and sleep had refreshed him. He stood gazing around him; just ahead was the edge of the cliff and beyond it lay an endless stretch of shimmering water, reflecting the pale light of dawn.

Stormfur opened his jaws to drink in the air and catch the scent of prey. Instead his senses were flooded by a strong reek of badger. He caught sight of Midnight sitting on the highest point of the cliff, her small, bright eyes fixed on the fading stars. In the sky behind her, on the far side of the moorland, a strip of creamy light showed where the sun would rise. Stormfur padded over, dipping his head respectfully before sitting beside her.

"Good morning, gray warrior," Midnight's voice rumbled in welcome. "Sleep you have enough?"

"Yes. Thanks, Midnight." Stormfur still found it strange to be exchanging friendly greetings with her, when badgers had always been deadly enemies of the warrior Clans.

Yet Midnight was no ordinary badger. She seemed closer to StarClan than any warrior, except perhaps the medicine cats; she had traveled far and somehow had found the wisdom to foretell the future.

Stormfur gave her a sidelong glance, to see her eyes still

fixed on the remaining stars in the dawn sky. "Can you really read signs there from StarClan?" he asked curiously, half hoping that her terrible predictions from the night before would vanish in the light of morning.

"Much is to be read everywhere," the badger replied. "In stars, in running water, in flash of light on waves. Whole world speaks, if ears are open to listen."

"I must be deaf, then," Stormfur meowed. "The future seems dark to me."

"Not so, gray warrior," rasped Midnight. "See." She pointed with her snout across the sun-drown water to where a single warrior of StarClan still shone brightly just above the horizon. "StarClan has seen our meeting. Pleased they are, and help they will give in dark days coming."

Stormfur gazed up at the brilliant point of light and let out a faint sigh. He was no medicine cat, accustomed to sharing tongues with their warrior ancestors. His task was to offer his strength and skill in the service of his Clan—and now, it seemed, of all the forest cats. Midnight had made it clear that each and every Clan would be destroyed if they could not ignore the ancient boundaries and work together for once.

"Midnight, when we go home—"

His question was never finished. A yowl interrupted him, and he turned to see Squirrelpaw burst out of the tunnel that led down into the badger's sett. She stood in the entrance, her dark ginger fur fluffed up and her ears pricked.

"I'm starving!" she announced. "Where's the prey around here?"

"Budge up, and let the rest of us out." Crowpaw's irritable voice sounded behind her. "Then we might be able to tell you."

Squirrelpaw bounced forward a few paces, and the WindClan apprentice emerged, followed closely by Feathertail. She stretched with pleasure in the sunlight. Stormfur got up and bounded over the tough moorland grass so he could touch noses with his sister. He had not been one of StarClan's original chosen cats, but he had insisted on coming on the journey to protect Feathertail. With their mother dead and their father living in a different Clan, the two cats were much closer than ordinary siblings.

Midnight lumbered after him and nodded a greeting to the cats.

"Tawnypelt's much better this morning," Feathertail reported. "She says her shoulder hardly hurts at all." To Midnight she added, "That burdock root you gave her really helped."

"Root is good," the badger rumbled. "Now injured warrior travel well."

As she spoke, Tawnypelt herself appeared from the tunnel; Stormfur was relieved to see that she looked stronger after her long sleep and was scarcely limping at all.

Following Tawnypelt, her brother, Brambleclaw, pushed his way out of the tunnel and stood blinking in the growing light. "The sun's nearly up," he meowed. "It's time we were on our way."

"But we have to eat first!" Squirrelpaw wailed. "My belly is growling louder than a monster on the Thunderpath! I could eat a fox, fur and all."

Stormfur had to agree with her. Hunger clawed at his own belly, and he knew that without food they would not be able to face the long and exhausting journey back to the forest. Yet he shared Brambleclaw's urgency; how would they feel if they delayed too long, and then discovered cats had died because of it?

A look of exasperation flitted over Brambleclaw's face. His voice was firm as he replied, "We'll pick up some prey as we go. And once we get back to the woods where we made camp, we'll have a proper hunt."

"Bossy furball," Squirrelpaw muttered.

"Brambleclaw's right," Tawnypelt meowed. "Who knows what's happening at home? There's no time to waste."

A murmur of agreement rose from the other cats. Even Crowpaw, who usually challenged Brambleclaw's decisions even more than Squirrelpaw, had nothing to say. With a slight shock, Stormfur realized that their long journey, and the threat to all their Clans, had changed them from a group of squabbling rivals into a unified force with a single purpose, to save their Clanmates and the warrior code that had protected them for so long. A warm feeling of belonging swept over Stormfur. His loyalty toward RiverClan was complicated—knowing how their half-Clan heritage made other warriors suspicious of him and Feathertail—but here he knew he had found friends who judged him without thinking about Clan differences all the time.

Brambleclaw paced forward until he stood in front of Midnight. "The thanks of all the Clans go with you," he mewed.

Midnight grunted. "Time is not yet for farewell. I come with you as far as woods, make sure you know right path."

Without waiting for the cats to agree or thank her, she lumbered off across the moor. Ahead of her, the sky had become too bright to look at as the sun began to edge its way above the horizon. Stormfur blinked gratefully at the yellow light. The setting sun had guided them on their journey to find the sun-drown place; now the rising sun would guide them home.

The four chosen cats—along with Stormfur and Squirrelpaw, who had come with Brambleclaw after an argument with her father, Firestar—had set out from the forest blindly following a half-understood prophecy from StarClan. Now that they had discovered what the prophecy meant, it was easier to decide what to do next, but at the same time it was terrifying to know just how much danger their Clans were in.

"Well, what are we waiting for?" Squirrelpaw asked, dashing off to overtake Midnight.

Her Clanmate Brambleclaw followed more slowly, looking deep in thought, as if he were imagining all the difficulties they would have to face on their way back to the forest. At his side, Tawnypelt seemed refreshed from her night's rest, and even though she was still limping, her eyes showed nothing but determination to make the long journey home. Feathertail trotted with her tail up, clearly enjoying the bright morning, while Crowpaw loped along beside her, keeping his ears pricked and his muscles tense, as if he were already anticipating trouble.

Stormfur, bringing up the rear, breathed a swift prayer to StarClan. *Guide our paws, and bring us all safely home.*

As the sun climbed higher, the sky became a deep, clear blue, dotted with fluffy scraps of cloud. The weather was warm and kind for so late in leaf-fall. A breeze swept over the grass, and Stormfur's mouth watered as he caught the scent of rabbit. Out of the corner of his eye, he spotted a white tail bobbing as the rabbit vanished over the crest of a gentle slope.

Instantly Crowpaw darted after it.

"Wait! Where are you going?" Brambleclaw called after him, but the WindClan apprentice was gone. The tabby warrior's tail lashed irritably. "Does he ever listen?"

"He won't be long," Feathertail soothed him. "You could hardly expect him to ignore a rabbit when it pops up right under our noses."

Brambleclaw's only reply was another swish of his tail.

"I'll fetch him back," Stormfur meowed, bunching his muscles to spring in pursuit.

Before he could move, the dark gray apprentice reappeared at the top of the rise. He was dragging the rabbit with him; it was almost as big as he was.

"Here," he meowed ungraciously as he dumped it on the ground. "That didn't take long, did it? I suppose we're allowed to stop and eat it?"

"Of course," Brambleclaw replied. "Sorry, Crowpaw. I'd

forgotten how fast WindClan cats can be. This . . . this moorland must feel like home to you."

Crowpaw acknowledged the apology with a curt nod as all
six cats crowded around the fresh-kill. Stormfur stopped
short when he noticed a glow of admiration in Feathertail's
eyes. Surely his sister couldn't be interested in Crowpaw? All
he ever did was argue and push himself forward as if he were
already a warrior. A cat from another Clan—and an apprentice at that!—had no right to start padding after Feathertail.
And whatever did Feathertail see in him? Didn't she know
the problems this sort of thing could cause—hadn't she
learned that from their own parents?

Then Stormfur's gaze slid across to Squirrelpaw. Had he
any right to criticize Feathertail, when he liked Squirrelpaw
so much? But then, he told himself, any cat would like the
brave, intelligent ThunderClan apprentice. And he knew
better than to start something with a cat from another Clan,
when they couldn't possibly have a future together.

Stormfur sighed and began gulping his share of the rabbit.
He hoped he was imagining things; after all, any cat might
admire Crowpaw's speed in catching them prey when they
were all hungry. Surely that was all Feathertail was feeling.

While the cats ate, Midnight waited a few paces away.
Stormfur saw her tearing at the moorland grass with her
strong, blunt claws, snuffling up the grubs and beetles she
disturbed. Her eyes were screwed up, as if she found it
hard to search for food in the strong sunlight, but she said
nothing, and as soon as the cats had eaten all they could of

Crowpaw's prey, she set off once more toward the rising sun.

Even with Midnight to lead them by the most direct route, it was sunhigh by the time they reached the crest of a gentle hill and saw the edge of the woods in front of them. The shade underneath the trees looked as inviting as running water to Stormfur after traveling through the heat of the unprotected moorland. For one brief moment, he let himself imagine an afternoon of hunting, then settling down full-fed for a sleep under the arching fronds of bracken, but he knew there was no chance of that.

As they drew closer to the woods, he spotted what looked like a heap of mottled brown fur in the long grass underneath a bush. His tail twitched in rueful recognition at the sight of the elderly tabby who had guided them—and nearly lost them forever—in the Twolegplace.

"Hey, Purdy!" Brambleclaw called. "We're back!"

A large round head emerged from the bundle of fur, whiskers twitching and eyes blinking in confusion that gradually turned to welcome. The old cat scrambled to his paws and took a couple of paces toward them, shaking bits of dead leaf from his untidy pelt.

"Great StarClan!" he exclaimed. "I never reckoned I'd see you again." Suddenly he broke off, his eyes fixed on something over Stormfur's shoulder. "Don't move a whisker!" he hissed. "There's a badger behind you. Just let me deal with it. I know a few fightin' moves that—"

"It's okay, Purdy," Stormfur interrupted, while Squirrel-paw's tail curled up with amusement. "This is Midnight. She's a friend."

The old tabby stared at Stormfur, his jaws gaping in astonishment. "A friend? You don't make friends with a badger, young fellow. You can't trust 'em a single mouselength."

Stormfur gave Midnight an anxious look, wondering if the badger was offended by Purdy's words. To his relief, she looked as amused as Squirrelpaw, her tiny black eyes gleaming.

"Come and meet Purdy," Stormfur mewed to her. "He guided us through Twolegplace."

Midnight plodded forward until she stood in front of the old tabby tom. Unconvinced, Purdy crouched down with his neck fur bristling and his lips drawn back in a snarl to reveal snaggly teeth. Stormfur felt a twinge of admiration for his courage, even though the badger could have flattened him with one swat of her powerful front paws.

"Here is not fight," Midnight assured him. "Friend of my friends is my friend also. Much of you they have told me."

Purdy's ears twitched. "Can't say I'm pleased to meet you," he muttered. "But I suppose you must be all right if they say so." Backing away, he turned to Brambleclaw. "Why are we hangin' around here?" he demanded. "There are Upwalkers and dogs all over the place. Say good-bye and let's be on our way."

"Hang on!" Squirrelpaw protested loudly to Brambleclaw. "You said we could hunt."

"We can," he mewed.

He paused to taste the air; Stormfur did the same, and was relieved to find that although he could distinguish several different dog scents, they were all stale. He guessed that Purdy was using the danger of dogs as an excuse to get away from Midnight.

"Okay," Brambleclaw went on, "let's split up and hunt quickly. We'll meet in that place where we camped last time. Tawnypelt, do you want to go straight there?"

The ShadowClan warrior's eyes flashed as she replied, "No, I can hunt as well as any of you."

Before any of the cats could respond, Midnight padded up to her and gave her a gentle nudge. "Foolish warrior," she rumbled. "Rest while able. Show me camping place. I will stay while sun is high, go home in dark."

Tawnypelt shrugged. "Okay, Midnight." She headed farther into the woods, following the stream to the hollow where the cats had rested on the outward journey.

The air was cooler in the dappled shade of the trees. Stormfur began to relax, feeling safer here than on the open moorland, though the chattering stream, too shallow for fish, was no substitute for the river he loved. A pang of loss stabbed through him at the thought that, even if he saw the river again, it would not be for long; Midnight had told them that the Clans would have to leave the forest as soon as the six cats returned.

A rustle in the undergrowth reminded him of how hungry he was. It would be good to go off for a while and hunt with

Feathertail, just as they did at home. But when he swung around to speak to his sister, he saw that Crowpaw was saying something in her ear.

"Do you want to hunt with me?" the apprentice muttered, sounding half grudging, half embarrassed. "We'd do better together."

"That would be great!" Feathertail's eyes shone; then she spotted Stormfur, and looked even more embarrassed than the WindClan cat. "Er—why don't we all hunt together?"

Crowpaw looked away, and Stormfur felt the hairs on his neck begin to prickle. What right did this apprentice have to invite Feathertail to be his hunting partner? "No, I'm fine on my own," Sormfur retorted, spinning around and plunging into the undergrowth, trying to pretend he hadn't seen the hurt in his sister's blue eyes.

But once he slipped beneath the lowest branches of the bushes his irritation faded. His ears pricked up and all his senses were alert in the hunt for prey.

Before long he spotted a mouse scrabbling among fallen leaves, and dispatched it with one swift blow. Satisfied, he scraped earth over the little brown body until he was ready to collect it, and looked around for more. Soon he added a squirrel and another mouse to his hoard—which was as much as he could carry—and set off for the meeting place.

On the way he began to wonder how Feathertail was getting along, asking himself if he should have stayed with her after all. He was not one of StarClan's chosen cats; he had come on this mission especially to look after his sister. He had been wrong to abandon her in this strange place, just because Crowpaw had annoyed him. What would he do if something happened to her?

When he reached the camping place he saw Tawnypelt stretched out in the shade of a hawthorn bush, her tortoise-shell fur hardly visible in the dappled sunlight. Midnight was beside her, dozing, and there was more chewed-up burdock root laid on Tawnypelt's injured shoulder. The badger must have found some growing by the stream. Brambleclaw was perched above Tawnypelt on a steeply arching tree root, obviously keeping watch, while Feathertail and Crowpaw shared a squirrel just below. As Stormfur dropped his catch on the small pile of fresh-kill in the center of the hollow, Squirrelpaw appeared at the top of the slope, dragging a rabbit, and Purdy followed with a couple of mice in his jaws.

"Good, we're all here," meowed Brambleclaw. "Let's eat and then get moving."

He leaped down into the hollow and chose a starling from the pile. Stormfur took one of his mice over to Feathertail, settling down next to her on the opposite side from Crowpaw.

"Good hunting?" he asked.

Feathertail blinked at him. "Brilliant, thanks. There's so much prey here! It's a pity we can't stay longer."

Stormfur was tempted to agree, but he knew that the danger to their home was too desperate for them to delay. He began to devour his mouse in famished gulps, his paws already itching for the next stage of their journey.

He had swallowed the last of the fresh-kill and was beginning to groom his thick gray pelt when he heard a low snarling behind him. He saw Brambleclaw raise his head, alarm flaring in his yellow eyes.

Stormfur whipped around to see what had spooked the ThunderClan warrior. A familiar smell hit his scent glands a heartbeat before two slender, tawny shapes emerged from the bracken beside the stream.

Foxes!

CHAPTER 2

♣

Leafpaw wrinkled her nose at the foul scent and tried not to hiss in disgust. Shaking her head, she parted Sorreltail's tortoiseshell fur with one paw and dabbed the wad of bile-soaked moss on the tick clinging to her shoulder.

Sorreltail wriggled as she felt the bile soak through her fur. "That's better!" she meowed. "Has it gone yet?"

Leafpaw opened her mouth and dropped the twig that held the moss. "Give it time."

"There's only one good thing about ticks," Sorreltail mewed. "They hate mouse bile just as much as we do." Springing to her paws, she gave herself a vigorous shake and flicked the tick off her shoulder. "There! Thanks, Leafpaw."

A breeze rustled through the trees that surrounded the medicine cat's den. A few leaves drifted down; there was a chill in the morning air that warned Leafpaw of how few moons there were before leaf-bare. This time there would be more than the cold and shortage of prey to face. Leafpaw closed her eyes and shuddered as she remembered what she had seen the day before on patrol with her father, Firestar.

The biggest monster the cats had ever seen had been

forging a dreadful path through the forest, scoring deep ruts into the earth and tearing up trees by their roots. The huge, shiny monster had rolled inexorably through the bracken, roaring and belching smoke while the cats scattered helplessly before it. For the first time, Leafpaw began to understand the danger to the forest, which had been prophesied twice now, once in Brambleclaw's dream that had sent him on the journey with Squirrelpaw, and once in Cinderpelt's vision of fire and tiger. The doom that had been foretold was coming upon the forest, and Leafpaw did not know what any cat could do to stop it.

"Are you okay, Leafpaw?" meowed Sorreltail.

Leafpaw blinked. The vision of smoke, splintered trees, and shrieking cats faded away, to be replaced by soft green ferns and the smooth gray rock where Cinderpelt made her den. She was safe, ThunderClan was still here—but for how long? "Yes, I'm fine," she replied. Firestar had ordered the patrol to keep quiet about what they had seen until he had decided how to break the news to the Clan. "I've got to go and wash this mouse bile off my paws."

"I'll come with you," Sorreltail offered. "Then we could go along the ravine and pick up some fresh-kill."

Leafpaw led the way into the main clearing. Whitepaw and Shrewpaw were scuffling outside the apprentices' den in warm shafts of early morning sunlight, while Ferncloud's three kits watched them with huge admiring eyes. Their mother sat at the entrance to the nursery, washing herself while keeping one eye on her litter. The dawn patrol—Dustpelt, Mousefur, and

Spiderpaw—were just pushing their way into the clearing through the gorse tunnel, Dustpelt's eyes narrowing with pleasure as he caught sight of Ferncloud and his kits. Leafpaw gazed at the busy, peaceful camp, and could hardly keep back a wail of despair.

As soon as the apprentices spotted Leafpaw, they stopped their practice fight and stared at her, then started whispering urgently together. Even the cats in the returning patrol gave her an uneasy look as they padded over to the fresh-kill pile. Leafpaw knew that rumors about yesterday's patrol were starting to fly around the camp. At daybreak Firestar had called his deputy, Graystripe; Leafpaw's mother, Sandstorm; and Cinderpelt into a meeting in his den, and every cat had begun to suspect that something unusual had happened the day before.

Before she and Sorreltail could reach the gorse tunnel, Firestar appeared from his den at the foot of the Highrock. Graystripe and Sandstorm followed him out into the clearing with Cinderpelt limping after them. Firestar leaped to the top of the rock, leaving the other three cats to find comfortable places to sit at its base. In the slanting leaf-fall sun, his flame-colored pelt blazed like the fire that gave him his name.

"Let all those cats old enough to catch their own prey join here beneath the Highrock for a Clan meeting," he called.

Leafpaw felt her belly lurch as Sorreltail nudged her gently toward the front of the gathering cats. "You know what he's going to say, don't you?" the tortoiseshell warrior murmured.

Leafpaw nodded bleakly.

"I knew something weird happened yesterday," Sorreltail went on. "You all came back looking as if the whole of ShadowClan were clawing at your tails."

"I wish it were just that," Leafpaw muttered.

"Cats of ThunderClan," Firestar began, then paused to take a deep breath. "I . . . I don't know if any Clan leader has ever had to take his Clan into the darkness that I see ahead." His voice faltered and his eyes met Sandstorm's, seeming to draw strength from the she-cat's steady gaze. "Some time ago, Ravenpaw warned me about more Twoleg activity on the Thunderpath. Back then, I didn't think it was important, and there was nothing we could do anyway because that is not our territory. But yesterday . . ."

A tense silence had fallen in the clearing. Firestar did not often sound so serious; Leafpaw could see how reluctant he was to go on, how he had to force himself to speak.

"My patrol was not far from Snakerocks when we saw a Twoleg monster leave the Thunderpath. It tore into the earth and pushed trees over. It—"

"But that's ridiculous!" Sootfur interrupted. "Monsters *never* leave the Thunderpath."

"This isn't another of his dreams, is it?" Dustpelt's question was too low for Firestar to hear, though Leafpaw caught the muttered words. "A tough bit of fresh-kill too late at night?"

"Shut up and listen." Cloudtail, Firestar's kin, glared at Dustpelt.

"I saw it too," Graystripe confirmed from his place at the foot of the rock.

Dead silence followed his words. Leafpaw watched the cats glance at one another with uncertainty and fear in their eyes. Sorreltail turned to Leafpaw. "Is that really what you saw?"

Leafpaw nodded. "You can't imagine what it was like."

"What does Cinderpelt have to say?" Speckletail called from where she sat among the elders. "Has StarClan shown you anything?"

The medicine cat rose to her paws and faced the Clan, her blue eyes steady. Of all the cats, even Firestar, she seemed the calmest.

Before she replied, she looked up to meet Firestar's gaze; Leafpaw could almost see flashing between them the memory of the prophecy of fire and tiger that Cinderpelt had seen in a clump of blazing bracken. She wondered how much they had decided to tell the Clan, in the meeting that had just ended. Then Firestar nodded as if he was giving Cinderpelt permission to speak; she acknowledged his signal with a brief dip of her head.

"The signs from StarClan are not clear," she admitted. "I see a time of great danger and change for the forest. A terrible doom hangs over us all."

"Then you have had warnings about this! Why haven't you told us before?" Mousefur challenged with a lash of her tail.

"Don't be mouse-brained!" Cloudtail growled. "What good would it have done? What could we do? Leave the forest—and go where? Wandering around in strange country with leaf-bare coming on? You might fancy that, Mousefur, but I don't."

"If you ask me, Brambleclaw and Squirrelpaw had the right idea," Sootfur muttered to his brother Rainwhisker. "Getting out when they did."

Leafpaw wanted to leap to the missing cats' defense, but she made herself sit still and keep quiet. She was the only cat in the Clan who knew that Squirrelpaw and Brambleclaw had left on a mission from StarClan to try to save the forest from this terrible danger. Stormfur and Feathertail, Graystripe's RiverClan children, had gone with them, and cats from WindClan and ShadowClan too. However much their Clanmates missed them, Leafpaw knew it was for the good of all the Clans that they had gone.

Yet the danger was here now, she thought, apprehension gripping her belly, and the missing cats had not returned. Did that mean they had failed? Did it mean StarClan had failed, in spite of the warnings they had sent?

Cinderpelt's calm gaze rested on the hushed and waiting Clan. "There will be great danger," she repeated. "But I do not believe that ThunderClan will be destroyed."

The Clan cats looked at one another, bewildered and afraid. The silence seemed to stretch out for a thousand heartbeats, until it was broken by a single eerie wail rising from the group of elders. As if that were a signal, more yowls and cries of terror broke out. Faced with the terror of approaching monsters, few of the Clan could believe Cinderpelt's reassurances.

Ferncloud swept her tail protectively around her three kits, drawing them into the shelter of her flecked gray fur. "What are we going to do?" she cried.

Dustpelt got up and pressed his nose comfortingly into her side. "We'll do something," he promised. "We'll show the Twolegs this is *our* place."

"And how do you propose doing that?" Mousefur asked, her voice harsh. "When have Twolegs ever cared about us? They do what they want."

"Their monsters will frighten all the prey," Ashfur added. "We already know the forest is emptier than it's ever been, and leaf-bare is coming. What are we going to eat?"

More terrified caterwauling broke out, and several heartbeats went by before Firestar could make himself heard again.

"We can't decide what to do until we know more," he meowed, when the noise had died to apprehensive muttering. "What happened yesterday was near Snakerocks, well away from here. It's possible that the Twolegs won't come any farther."

"Then why would StarClan send any warnings at all?" Thornclaw asked. "We've got to face it, Firestar—we can't pretend this isn't happening."

"I'll arrange extra patrols," Firestar assured him, "and I'm going to try speaking to ShadowClan. This was near their border, and they may have had trouble too."

"You can't believe anything ShadowClan tells you," Cloudtail growled. "They wouldn't give you a mousetail if you were starving."

"Maybe not," Firestar replied. "But if the Twolegs have invaded their territory, they might be prepared to talk if it meant we could help one another."

"And hedgehogs might fly," Cloudtail grunted. He turned away from Firestar and muttered something into the ear of his mate, Brightheart, who pushed her nose into his fur as if she were reassuring him.

"Everyone must keep alert," Firestar continued. "If you see anything unusual, I want to know. We survived the flood and the fire. We survived Tigerstar's dog pack, and the threat from Scourge and BloodClan. We will survive this too."

He leaped down from the rock to show that the meeting was at an end.

Immediately the cats in the clearing broke into anxious little knots, discussing what they had just heard. Firestar and Cinderpelt spoke briefly together, and then Cinderpelt padded over to Leafpaw.

"Firestar is going to see ShadowClan right away," the medicine cat announced. "He wants you to come too."

Mingled excitement and apprehension clawed at Leafpaw. "Why me?"

"He wants both medicine cats with him. He thinks that if we're there Blackstar will realize that ThunderClan isn't looking for a fight." Cinderpelt's blue eyes flashed. "All the same, Leafpaw, I hope you've practiced your fighting moves recently."

Leafpaw swallowed. "Yes, Cinderpelt."

"Good." With a wave of her tail, she led the way to where

Firestar was waiting at the entrance to the gorse tunnel. Graystripe and Brackenfur were with him.

"Let's go," meowed Firestar. "And remember, I don't want any trouble. We're only going to talk."

Graystripe snorted. "Try telling that to ShadowClan. If a patrol catches us on their territory, they'll claw us as soon as they see us."

"Let's hope not," Firestar replied with feeling. "If the Twolegs are threatening both our Clans, we can't afford to waste our strength in fighting one another."

Graystripe still looked doubtful, but he said nothing more as Firestar led them up the ravine toward the ShadowClan border. Leafpaw kept her ears pricked for any unusual sounds, and every hair on her pelt stood on end. The forest that had been safe for as long as she could remember was suddenly a frightening place, invaded by the Twolegs and their monsters.

Firestar led his patrol directly toward Snakerocks, and soon Leafpaw realized that he was heading for the spot where the monster had left the Thunderpath. Before they came in sight of it she picked up the reek of the monster and the rich earthy smell of the torn ground. When she came to the top of the slope above the Thunderpath, she stopped and peered through a clump of bracken.

Just below her, a swath of churned-up grass stretched as far as the Thunderpath. Trees lay on the ground, their roots tangling in the air. Everything was silent; Leafpaw couldn't hear a single bird, or the scuffling of prey in the grass. But the monster had gone, and when she opened her jaws to drink in the air, the scent of Twolegs was stale. Even the reek of the monster was beginning to fade.

"They haven't been here today," Graystripe meowed. "Perhaps they've finished whatever they were doing."

"I wouldn't count on it," Firestar replied tersely.

"This is . . . terrible." Brackenfur sounded stunned. He had not been on the original patrol. "Why are they destroying the forest, Firestar?"

The tip of Firestar's tail twitched back and forth. "Why do Twolegs do anything? If we knew that, our lives would be a lot easier."

Skirting the edge of the damaged area, he led the way along the Thunderpath. Leafpaw's belly lurched as she saw that more trees had been felled in ShadowClan's territory, and more ground had been churned up.

Every one of the ThunderClan cats stopped to stare across the hard black surface. Brackenfur dropped into a crouch as if he were about to spring into attack, but there was no enemy to fight.

"Look at that!" Graystripe's voice shook with horror. "You were right, Firestar. ShadowClan is having exactly the same trouble."

"Then that should make it easier to talk to Blackstar." Firestar was trying to sound confident, but his ears were laid flat against his head.

Cinderpelt gave the scarred area a long look before turning away, shaking her head. Though she said nothing, her blue eyes were filled with dread and confusion.

A monster roared by on the Thunderpath, smaller than the tree-eating monsters but still deafeningly noisy. Leafpaw flinched, half expecting it to veer into the forest where they were standing. But it stayed on the Thunderpath and growled away until it vanished among the trees. Another monster followed it; then a third raced along in the opposite direction.

"I don't want to cross here," Graystripe muttered, blinking grit out of his eyes.

Firestar nodded. "We'll cross the stream by Fourtrees and go through the tunnel," he decided. "And just hope we don't meet any ShadowClan warriors on this side of the Thunderpath."

When they reached the stream, Firestar crossed in a couple of bounds by a stepping-stone in the middle. Leafpaw kept an eye on her mentor, making sure that Cinderpelt crossed safely in spite of the old injury to her leg from a Thunderpath accident seasons before. Then she followed her across as Firestar climbed the opposite bank.

A light breeze was blowing toward them, carrying the rank scent of ShadowClan. At the border, Firestar and Graystripe renewed the scent markings, before Firestar led the way toward the tunnel under the Thunderpath.

To Leafpaw's relief, there was no sign of ShadowClan cats in this section of their territory. The elders had told her many stories about that Clan's dark-hearted history, from the murderer Brokenstar, who had killed his own father, to treacherous Tigerstar, who had made himself ShadowClan leader when he was exiled from ThunderClan. The present leader, Blackstar, hadn't caused any trouble so far, but Leafpaw knew that Firestar didn't really trust him. As she followed him into the tunnel, she admired him even more for his courage in trying to make allies of his old enemies for the sake of the forest.

Leafpaw shivered as she plunged into the gloomy silence beneath the Thunderpath, broken only by the drip of water and the plashing of their paws in the mud that covered the bottom of the tunnel. On the ShadowClan side the harsh scent was stronger than ever. The ground under Leafpaw's paws was dank and marshy, covered with coarse scrubby grass. Here and there were pools fringed with reeds; there were few tall trees, unlike those that sheltered the ThunderClan camp. It felt like another world.

"The ShadowClan camp is this way," Firestar meowed, heading for a clump of bushes. "Leafpaw, Cinderpelt, keep close to me. Graystripe and Brackenfur, spread out and keep watch. And remember that we're not looking for trouble."

Leafpaw padded behind Firestar as they headed deeper into ShadowClan territory. She hated the way her paws sank into mud at every step. She kept wanting to stop to flick away the moisture. It was hard to imagine ShadowClan cats putting up with it every day of their lives. Surely they would have grown webbed paws by now? Her muscles began to ache from the strain of keeping alert; when Brackenfur called out she jumped nervously and then hoped that no cat had noticed.

"Firestar, come and look at this." Brackenfur pointed with his tail to a thin piece of wood, too smooth and regular to be the branch of a tree, standing upright in the ground about the height of a cat. Firestar padded over to and sniffed at it suspiciously. "It reeks of Twolegs," he reported.

"There's another over there," Leafpaw called, spotting a matching stick a few foxlengths farther away. "And another—all in a line! What are they—"

Her voice died away. As she bounded toward the next piece of wood, the bushes in front of her rustled and three cats stepped out into the open. She quickly recognized Russetfur, the dark ginger she-cat who was ShadowClan's deputy; the other warriors, a dark gray tom and a lean tabby with a torn ear, were strangers to her.

Leafpaw swallowed nervously.

Firestar was already bounding up to her. "Greetings, Russetfur," he meowed.

"You're trespassing on our territory," snarled the Shadow-Clan deputy.

With a flick of her tail she summoned her warriors forward. Leafpaw barely had time to dodge, as the dark gray tom sprang at her; she felt claws rake down her side as she rolled away and scrambled to her paws, trying to remember her fighting moves. She caught a glimpse of Cinderpelt and Russetfur stalking around each other; a tail-length away, Graystripe had the tabby pinned down, while Brackenfur and the other tom writhed together in a screeching bundle of gray and ginger fur.

For a moment she could not see Firestar. Glancing around wildly, she saw that he had leaped onto one of the fallen tree trunks. His voice rose in a yowl above the hissing and spitting.

"Stop!"

CHAPTER 3

"You lot stay here," Purdy ordered in an undertone. "Let me deal with this."

Stormfur stared in dismay as the old tom shuffled forward toward the foxes, his rumpled fur on end, his tail lashing back and forth. Frozen by shock, the others might have let Purdy attack and be torn to pieces if Stormfur had not stepped forward at the last moment and pushed him aside.

"Wha'?" Purdy protested. "Let me get at 'em. I've chased off more foxes than you've had mice, young fellow."

"Then give the rest of us a chance," Stormfur retorted grimly.

The two foxes were creeping slowly up the bank, their eyes flicking from one cat to the next. Too late Stormfur realized that he and his friends had been wrong to assume the woods held no danger for them.

He saw that Crowpaw had stepped forward to shield Feathertail, while Brambleclaw tried to do the same for Squirrelpaw. But the ThunderClan apprentice slipped out from the shelter of his flank and stood beside him with her ears flattened and one paw extended threateningly.

"What are you doing, treading on my tail?" she growled. "I can take care of myself!"

"You did say you could eat a fox," Tawnypelt pointed out wryly. "Now's your chance."

The foxes crept nearer. Stormfur braced himself, his gaze fixed on their narrow snouts and coldly glittering eyes, trying to guess where they would attack first. Back home, foxes weren't much of a threat to cats who kept alert. They could be avoided, but these were obviously young and spoiling for a fight, eager to defend their territory. Stormfur was sure that the six of them could drive the creatures off eventually, but not without serious injuries. And what would that mean for their journey? *StarClan help us!* he prayed desperately.

Crowpaw, who was nearest to the foxes, crouched to spring. There was barely a tail-length between him and the first of them when Stormfur heard a strange sound behind him, half growling and half barking. The leading fox abruptly lifted its head and stood very still.

Stormfur flicked a glance over his shoulder. Midnight had lumbered forward, thrusting her way between Purdy and Feathertail until she stood in front of the foxes. She said something else in the same mixture of barks and growls. Although Stormfur could not understand what she was saying, there was no mistaking the threat in the way her shoulders hunched, or the hostility in her black eyes.

Then his ears pricked in shock as the first fox barked what was obviously a reply. "I'd forgotten Midnight told us she could speak fox," he muttered, glancing at Brambleclaw. The

ThunderClan warrior nodded without taking his eyes off the foxes.

"They say this is their place," Midnight reported. "To come here is to be their prey."

"Fox dung to that!" Crowpaw burst out. "Tell them if they try anything, we'll rip their fur off."

Midnight shook her head. "No, small warrior. Cat fur be ripped also. Wait."

Crowpaw backed off a pace or two, still looking furious, and Feathertail pressed her nose against his flank.

Midnight said something else to the foxes. "I tell them you only pass through," she explained to the cats when she had finished. "I tell them much prey is here in woods, easier prey that does not rip fur."

The leading fox was looking confused now, perhaps out of surprise at hearing a badger speak fox, perhaps because it was taking her arguments seriously. But the second—a lean dog fox with a scarred muzzle—was still glaring past Midnight at the group of cats, his teeth bared. He snarled out something that was a threat in any language.

Midnight barked a single word. Taking a step forward, she raised a paw, her massive body poised to strike. Every hair on Stormfur's pelt prickled as he braced himself for a fight. Then the dog fox started to back away, growling a last curse at Midnight before turning and vanishing into the bracken. Midnight's gaze swiveled to his companion, but the other fox paused only to bark out something rapidly before following.

"And don't come back, if you know what's good for you!"

Crowpaw yowled after them.

Stormfur relaxed, feeling his fur lie flat again. Squirrelpaw flopped down on the ground with a noisy sigh. All the cats, even Purdy, were looking at the badger with new respect.

Brambleclaw padded over to her and dipped his head. "Thanks, Midnight," he meowed. "That could have been nasty."

"They might have killed us," Feathertail added.

"I suppose it's a bad time for a fight," Crowpaw admitted. Stormfur sighed at the aggressive note in the apprentice's voice as he went on, "All the same, I'd like to know why you didn't warn us about the foxes. You said you can read everything in the stars, so why didn't you tell us they'd be here?"

Even though he would never have asked the question, Stormfur waited tensely for Midnight's reply. She had told them so much already about the threat to the forest and how they must go home and lead the Clans to safety. If they did not trust her, they and all their Clanmates would be helpless in the face of destruction. Could she have warned them about the foxes?

For a moment the badger loomed over the WindClan apprentice, her black eyes furious. Crowpaw could not hide a flash of alarm in his eyes, though to his credit he did not back down. Then Midnight relaxed. "I not say everything. Everything indeed StarClan not want me to say. Much, yes, how Twolegs tear up forest, leave no place for cats to stay. But many answers lie within ourselves. This you have already learned, no?"

"I suppose," Crowpaw muttered.

Midnight turned away from him. "Foxes say you must go now," she told the cats. "If you still here at sunset, they attack. That dog fox, he says he tasted cat once, liked it fine."

"Well, he's not going to taste it again!" snapped Tawnypelt.

"We have to leave anyway," Brambleclaw pointed out. "And we're not looking for trouble from foxes. Let's go."

They paused for a few moments to gulp down the rest of the prey. Then Midnight took the lead, and brought them after a short time to the edge of the forest. The sun was dipping below the trees, and where they stood was already in shadow. In front of them, Stormfur saw yet more open moorland, with a range of mountains in the distance; over to one side were the hard reddish shapes of the Twolegplace they had traveled through on the outward journey.

"Which way now?" he asked.

Midnight raised one paw to point straight ahead. "That quickest way, path where sun rises."

"It's not the way we came," Brambleclaw mewed uneasily. "We came through Twolegplace."

"And I'm not going back there!" Crowpaw put in. "I'll climb as many mountains as you like before I face all those Twolegs again."

"I'm not sure," Feathertail meowed. "At least we know the way through Twolegplace, and we've got Purdy to help us."

Crowpaw replied only with a contemptuous snort. Stormfur half agreed with him; they had spent many frightening, hungry days wandering in Twolegplace, and Purdy had seemed as lost as any of them. But the mountains were unfamiliar too; even from here, Stormfur could see that their upper slopes were bare gray rock, with a streak of white here and there that must be the first snow of the approaching leaf-bare. They were far higher than Highstones, and he wondered how much shelter or prey they would find there.

"I agree with Feathertail," he meowed at last. "We made it through Twolegplace once, so we can do it again."

Brambleclaw glanced from one to another, undecided. "What do you think, Tawnypelt?"

His sister shrugged. "Whatever you like. There'll be problems whichever way we go; we all know that."

True enough, Stormfur thought grimly.

"Well, *I* think—" Squirrelpaw began, and broke off with a gasp. Her green eyes had widened with an expression of horror; they seemed to be fixed on something in the distance that no other cat could see.

"Squirrelpaw? What's the matter?" Brambleclaw meowed urgently.

"I . . . I don't know." Squirrelpaw gave herself a shake. "Just make your mind up, Brambleclaw, and let's be off. I want to go that way if it's the quickest route—" She flicked her tail toward the distant mountains. "We'll waste days and days going through Twolegplace again."

Stormfur's whiskers began to tingle. Squirrelpaw was right. They already knew that the route among the Twoleg nests was confusing and difficult. What dangers could there be in the mountains that could be worse than the rats and

monsters they knew they would meet in Twolegplace? All
that mattered was to get back to the forest without delay.

"I think she's got a point," he meowed. "I've changed my
mind. I vote we should go through the mountains."

Squirrelpaw's dark ginger tail twitched to and fro, and she
flexed her claws into the grass. "Well?" she spat at Brambleclaw.
"Are you going to make up your mind or not?"

Brambleclaw took a deep breath. "Okay, the mountains
it is."

"Eh? Wha'?" Purdy had been scratching one ear with his
hind paw. But when Brambleclaw made his decision he
looked up in alarm, blinking his wide amber eyes. "You can't
go that way. It's dangerous. What about the—"

"Danger is all around," Midnight broke in, silencing Purdy
with a fierce glare. "Your friends great courage will need. The
path has been laid out for them in the stars."

Stormfur shot a sharp look at the old tabby. What had
Purdy been trying to say when Midnight interrupted him?
Did he know of some particular danger in the mountains?
And if so, why had Midnight stopped him from telling the
rest of them? He thought that he could see wisdom in her
face, and something like regret. Just what did she mean by
"the path has been laid out"?

"Choice is hard, young warrior." The badger spoke in a low
tone to Brambleclaw. Stormfur edged a pace closer so that he
could hear. "Your path before you lies, and many challenges
you will have to return safe home."

Brambleclaw gazed into the badger's eyes for a long

moment before padding forward a few paces across the moorland. Whatever these challenges might be, he seemed ready to face them, and Stormfur couldn't help admiring his resolve, even though he came from a rival Clan. When Purdy scrambled to his feet to follow, Midnight put out a paw to hold him back.

The old tom bristled, his amber eyes glaring. "Get out o' my way," he rasped.

Midnight did not move. "With them you cannot go," she rumbled. "The way is theirs alone." Her black eyes gleamed in the dusk. "Young and rash they are, and tests will be many. Their own courage they need, my friend, not yours. Too much on you they would rely."

Purdy blinked. "Well, if you put it like that . . ."

Feathertail darted up to him and gave his ears a quick lick. "We'll never forget you, Purdy, or everything you've done for us."

Just behind her, Crowpaw opened his mouth with his eyes narrowed, as if he was about to say something cutting. Stormfur froze him with a glare. He doubted they would see the old cat again, and although Purdy had made mistakes, he had stood by them and brought them safely to Midnight in the end.

"Good-bye, Purdy. And thank you. We could never have found Midnight without you." Brambleclaw echoed Stormfur's thoughts. "And thank you, too, Midnight."

The badger inclined her head. "Farewell, my friends. May StarClan light your path."

The rest of the cats said their own good-byes, and began to follow Brambleclaw out onto the moor. Stormfur brought up the rear. Glancing back, he saw Midnight and Purdy sitting side by side under the outlying trees, watching them go. It was impossible to read their expressions in the gathering dusk. Stormfur waved his tail in a last farewell, and turned his face toward the mountains.

CHAPTER 4

❧

At *Firestar's yowl of command, Brackenfur* and the gray ShadowClan warrior broke apart. Graystripe looked up from the tabby, but still kept a paw firmly on his neck.

"Let him go," Firestar ordered. "We're not here to fight."

"It's hard to do anything else when they jump us like that," Graystripe hissed. He stepped back, and the skinny tabby scrambled to his paws and shook his ruffled fur.

Leafpaw bounded across the marshy ground to stand beside Cinderpelt, half afraid that Russetfur might still attack the medicine cat. ShadowClan's deputy was not likely to take orders from the leader of a rival Clan.

Russetfur flicked her tail toward the dark gray tom. "Cedarheart, get back to camp. Warn Blackstar that we have been invaded, and fetch more warriors."

The gray warrior streaked off into the bushes.

"There's no need for that," Firestar pointed out, keeping his voice mild. "We're not invading your territory, and we're not trying to steal prey."

"Then what *do* you want?" Russetfur demanded bad-temperedly. "What are we supposed to think when you trespass on our territory?"

"I'm sorry about that." Firestar leaped down from the tree trunk and padded across to her. "I . . . I know we shouldn't be here. It's just that I have to speak to Blackstar. Something has happened, something that's too urgent to wait for the next Gathering."

Russetfur sniffed disbelievingly, but sheathed her claws. Leafpaw felt her racing heart begin to slow down. The ShadowClan deputy was too badly outnumbered to launch another attack, especially when she had sent away the gray tom, Cedarheart.

"What's so urgent then?" she growled.

Firestar gestured with his tail through the sparse trees, toward the swath of destruction that the Twoleg monster had left on this side of the Thunderpath. "Isn't that enough?" he asked desperately.

Russetfur silenced him with a furious hiss. "If you think ShadowClan is weakened . . ."

"I didn't say that," Firestar protested. "But you must have seen that we've had the same trouble in our territory. Now, are you going to drive us off, or are you going to let us talk to Blackstar?"

Russetfur narrowed her eyes, then gave a curt nod. "Very well. Follow me."

She led the way through the bushes. The ThunderClan cats bunched together behind her, and the tabby ShadowClan warrior brought up the rear. Leafpaw's heart began to pound again as the scents of the strange territory flowed around her.

Even the day had grown darker, clouds covering the sun so that their path was shadowed. She tried to stop herself from jumping at every sound, or staring around as if there might be a ShadowClan warrior lurking behind every tree.

Soon Leafpaw became aware of a stronger ShadowClan scent coming from up ahead. Russetfur led the way around a thick clump of hazel; following her, Leafpaw stopped dead in front of a long line of cats—lean warriors with their muscles tensed and the light of battle in their eyes. Behind them rose a tangled wall of brambles.

"That's the ShadowClan camp," Cinderpelt muttered close to Leafpaw's ear. "It doesn't look as if Blackstar is going to invite us in."

The ShadowClan leader stood in the middle of his warriors. He was a huge white cat with black paws; his pelt showed the scars of many battles. As the ThunderClan cats appeared he stepped forward and faced Firestar with narrowed eyes.

"What's this?" His voice was rough. "Does the great Firestar think he can go where he likes in the forest?"

Firestar ignored the contempt in Blackstar's tone, simply dipping his head in the courteous greeting of one leader to another. "I have come to talk to you about what the Twolegs are doing," he began. "We have to decide what we're going to do if it carries on."

"We? What do you mean, we? ShadowClan does not talk with ThunderClan," Blackstar retorted. "We make our own decisions."

"But the forest is being destroyed!"

Leafpaw heard the exasperation in her leader's tone, and knew how hard it was for Firestar to stay calm when the ShadowClan leader insisted on treating him like an enemy.

The ShadowClan leader shrugged his powerful shoulders. "Firestar, you're panicking over nothing. Twolegs are mad. Even the smallest kit knows that. True, they knocked down a few trees—but now they've gone away again. Whatever was going on, it's over."

Leafpaw wondered if Blackstar really believed that. Surely he couldn't be such a fool? Or was this just a show of bravado to convince Firestar that ShadowClan had nothing to worry about?

"And if it's not over?" Firestar asked steadily. "If it gets worse? Prey has been frightened away from where the Twolegs have been. What if the Twolegs claw up more of our territories? What will you do in leaf-bare, Blackstar, if you can't feed your Clan?"

One or two of the ShadowClan warriors looked uneasy, but their leader stared defiantly at Firestar.

"We have no reason to fear leaf-bare," he meowed. "We can always eat rats from Carrionplace."

Cinderpelt twitched her ears impatiently. "Have you forgotten what happened last time you tried that? Half your Clan died from sickness."

"That's true." A small tabby tom, crouched at the end of the line, spoke up boldly. Leafpaw recognized Littlecloud, the ShadowClan medicine cat. "I was ill myself. I would have died if it hadn't been for you, Cinderpelt."

"Be quiet, Littlecloud," Blackstar ordered. "The sickness was a punishment from StarClan because Nightstar was not a properly chosen leader. There's no danger in eating food from Carrionplace now."

"There's danger if a leader silences his medicine cat," Cinderpelt retorted tartly. "Or pretends to know more than they do about the will of StarClan."

Blackstar glared at her, but said nothing.

"Listen to me," Firestar began again desperately. "I believe that great trouble is coming to the forest, trouble that we'll survive only if we work together."

"Mouse dung!" Blackstar snarled. "Don't try to tell me what to do, Firestar. I'm not one of your warriors. If you have anything to say, you should do what we have always done, and bring it to the next Gathering at Fourtrees."

Part of Leafpaw felt that the ShadowClan leader was right. The warrior code dictated that the business of the forest should be discussed at Gatherings. There was nowhere else that cats could meet under the sacred truce of StarClan. At the same time, she knew that the Twolegs wouldn't wait until after the next full moon to continue their destruction of the forest. What else might happen by the time of the next Gathering?

"Very well, Blackstar." Firestar's voice was hollow with defeat. *It's happening*, Leafpaw thought in panic. *He's giving up. The forest is going to be destroyed.* "If that's the way you want it. But if the Twolegs come back, you have my permission to send a messenger into ThunderClan territory, and we will talk again."

"Generous as always, Firestar." Blackstar meowed scornfully. "But nothing's going to happen that we can't handle ourselves."

"Mouse-brain!" Graystripe hissed.

Firestar shot Graystripe a warning glance, but the ShadowClan leader did not reply. Instead, he swept his tail toward Russetfur.

"Take some warriors and escort these cats off our territory," he ordered. "And in case you were thinking of paying us another uninvited visit," he added to Firestar, "we'll be increasing our patrols along that border. Now go."

There was nothing to do but obey. Firestar turned and signaled to his own cats to follow him. Russetfur and her warriors gathered around them in a threatening semicircle, letting them walk away but keeping them bunched tightly together. Leafpaw was glad when the tunnel under the Thunderpath came into sight, and more relieved still to be through it and heading for their own part of the forest.

"And don't come back!" Russetfur spat as they crossed the border.

"We won't!" Graystripe hurled a parting shot over his shoulder. "We were only trying to help, you stupid furball."

"Leave it, Graystripe." Now that they were back in their own territory, Firestar let his disappointment show. Leafpaw felt a sharp stab of compassion for him; it wasn't his fault that ShadowClan had refused to listen to reason.

"Maybe we should try talking to WindClan?" she suggested quietly to Cinderpelt as the patrol headed for camp. "Perhaps they've had trouble too. That could be why they've been stealing fish from RiverClan." She was referring to the furious accusations made by Hawkfrost, a RiverClan warrior, at the last Gathering.

"*If* they have. It was never proved," Cinderpelt reminded her. "All the same, Leafpaw, you might have a point. Ravenpaw said there were more Twolegs than usual on that part of the Thunderpath."

"Then perhaps Firestar should talk to Tallstar?"

"I don't think Firestar will be talking to any more Clan leaders for a while," Cinderpelt meowed, with a sympathetic glance at the flame-colored tom. "Besides, Tallstar is a proud leader. He'd never admit that his Clan is starving."

"But Firestar has to do *something!*"

"Perhaps Blackstar was right, and he should wait for the Gathering. But if I get the chance"—Cinderpelt interrupted her apprentice's protest—"I'll have a word with him." She lifted her blue gaze to the cloud-covered sky. "And let's just pray that StarClan has mercy on us, whatever happens."

"Sorreltail, are you there?"

Leafpaw stood outside the warriors' den and tried to peer through the branches. It was early the following morning; a thick fog covered the camp and misted her fur with tiny droplets of water.

"Sorreltail?" she repeated.

There was a scuffling sound inside the den, and Sorreltail poked her head out, blinking sleep from her eyes.

"Leafpaw?" Her jaws gaped wide in a yawn. "What's the matter? The sun's not up yet. I was having this terrific dream about a mouse. . . ."

"Sorry," Leafpaw mewed. "But I want you to do something with me. Are you due to go out with the dawn patrol?"

"No." Sorreltail squeezed out between the branches and gave the fur on her shoulders a quick lick. "What's all this about?"

Leafpaw took a deep breath. "I want to go and visit WindClan. Will you come with me?"

Sorreltail's eyes stretched wide, and her tail curled up in surprise. "What if we meet a WindClan patrol?"

"It should be okay—I'm a medicine cat apprentice, so I'm allowed to go into the territories between here and Highstones. Please, Sorreltail! I really need to know whether WindClan is having trouble too." Though she couldn't tell Sorreltail, Leafpaw knew that a cat from every Clan had been chosen by StarClan for the journey. Because of that, she suspected that every Clan would be invaded by the Twolegs, but she wanted to be sure.

The light of adventure was already sparkling in Sorreltail's eyes. "I'm up for it," she declared. "Let's get a move on, before any cat catches us and starts asking questions."

She darted across the clearing and into the gorse tunnel. Leafpaw followed, with a last glance back at the silent, sleeping camp. The fog hung thickly in the ravine, deadening the sound of their pawsteps. Everything was gray, and though the dawn light was strengthening, there was no sign of the sun. The bracken was bent double with the weight of water drops, and soon the two cats' pelts were soaked.

Sorreltail shivered. "Why did I ever leave my warm nest?" she complained, only half joking. "Still, if it's like this on the moor, the fog will help to hide us."

"And muffle our scent," Leafpaw agreed.

But before she and Sorreltail reached Fourtrees, the mist had begun to thin out. It still lay heavy on the stream, but when they climbed the opposite bank they broke out into sunlight. Leafpaw shook the moisture from her fur, but there was little heat in the sun's rays; she looked forward to a good run across the moor to warm herself up.

As they skirted the top of the hollow at Fourtrees, Leafpaw felt a breeze blowing directly off the moorland. She and Sorreltail paused for a moment at the far side of the hollow, their fur blown back and their jaws parted to scent the air.

"WindClan," Sorreltail meowed. She put her head to one side, uncertainly. "There's something odd about it, though."

"Yes. And there's no sign of any rabbits," Leafpaw added.

She hesitated for a couple more heartbeats, then led the way across the border. The two cats darted from one clump of gorse to the next, making what use they could of the scant cover on the moorland. Leafpaw's fur prickled; her tabby-and-white pelt would show up starkly against the short grass. In the ThunderClan camp she had been confident that as a medicine cat she would not be challenged; now she felt small and vulnerable. She wanted to find out what she could, then hurry back to the safety of her own territory.

She headed for the crest of a low hill that looked down over the Thunderpath, and flattened herself in the grass to peer down. Beside her, Sorreltail let out a long hiss.

"Well, there's not much doubt about that," she mewed.

Leading from the Thunderpath on the far side of the territory was a long scar where the moorland grass had been torn away. The track was marked by short stakes of wood like the ones Leafpaw had seen in ShadowClan territory the day before. It gouged a path across the moor and came to an abrupt halt at the foot of the hill where she and Sorreltail were crouching. A glittering monster sat silent where it ended. Leafpaw's breath came in short gasps as she imagined it scanning the moorland, ready to leap on its prey with a roar.

"Where are its Twolegs?" Sorreltail muttered.

Leafpaw glanced from side to side, but everything was quiet; an air of menace lay thick as fog on the scarred landscape. There was still no scent of rabbits—had they been frightened away, Leafpaw wondered, or had the Twolegs taken them? Perhaps they had moved to a different part of the moor when the monster dug up their burrows.

"Yuck!" Sorreltail exclaimed suddenly. "Can you smell that?"

As she spoke, Leafpaw picked it up too, a harsh tang like nothing she had ever scented before. Instinctively her stomach churned and she curled her lip. "What is it?"

"Probably something to do with the Twolegs," Sorreltail meowed disgustedly.

A distant yowl interrupted her. Leafpaw sprang to her paws and spun around to see three WindClan warriors racing toward them.

"Uh-oh," murmured Sorreltail.

Before Leafpaw could decide whether to run or stay to talk, the WindClan cats had surrounded them. With a sinking heart she recognized the aggressive deputy Mudclaw, with the tabby warrior Tornear and another tabby tom she did not know. She would rather have dealt with the Clan leader, Tallstar, or Firestar's friend Onewhisker, who were both more likely to listen to her explanations.

"Why are you trespassing on our territory?" the WindClan deputy demanded.

"I'm a medicine cat apprentice," Leafpaw pointed out, bowing her head respectfully. "I came to—"

"To spy!" That was Tornear, his eyes blazing with anger. "Don't think we don't know what you're up to!"

Now that the WindClan cats were up close, Leafpaw could see how thin they were. Their bristling pelts hardly covered their ribs. Fear-scent came off them in waves, almost drowning the scent of their fury. They were obviously short of food, but that didn't explain why they were so much more hostile than ShadowClan had been.

"I'm sorry, we were only—" she began.

Mudclaw interrupted with a frenzied shriek. "Attack!"

Tornear hurled himself at Leafpaw. The ThunderClan cats

were outnumbered and outclassed; besides, she and Sorreltail
had not come to fight.

"Run!" Leafpaw yowled.

She leaped back from Tornear's outstretched claws.
Spinning around, she fled for the border, her belly close to
the ground and her tail streaming out behind her. Sorreltail
raced along at her side. Leafpaw dared not look over her
shoulder, but she could hear the shrieks of the pursuing cats
hard on their paws.

The border was in sight, but she barely had time to realize
that they were bearing too far toward the river when scent
markers flooded over her, WindClan and RiverClan scents
mixed together.

"Oh, no!" she exclaimed. "We're in RiverClan territory
now."

"Keep going," Sorreltail panted. "It's only a narrow strip
between here and ThunderClan territory."

Leafpaw risked a glance to see if the WindClan patrol was
still pursuing them. They were—they must be so furious that
they hadn't noticed the border, or did not care.

"They're gaining on us!" she gasped. "We'll have to fight.
We can't lead them onto our territory."

She and Sorreltail whirled to face their attackers. Leafpaw
braced herself, wishing desperately that she had never
thought of entering WindClan territory, and especially that
she had not brought Sorreltail into danger with her.

As Mudclaw leaped at her, Leafpaw saw a streak of golden
fur shoot out from a nearby bush. It was Mothwing, the

medicine cat apprentice from RiverClan. Then Mudclaw's body crashed against her and she was rolling on the ground, squirming to escape the flurry of raking claws. She tried to twist around and sink her teeth into his neck, but there was a wiry strength in the deputy's lean body that trapped her helplessly like a piece of prey. Leafpaw felt his claws rake across her side and bury themselves in her shoulder. With a massive effort she shook him off, trying to bring her hind paws up to attack his belly.

Suddenly the weight lifted and Mudclaw was scrabbling for a foothold beside her. Leafpaw staggered to her paws to see Mothwing cuffing him hard over both ears. "Get off our territory!" she spat. "And take your mangy friends with you."

Mudclaw aimed a final blow at her, but he was already backing away. Sorreltail sprang up from where she had Tornear pinned down and bit hard on his tail before releasing him. He fled, yowling after the Clan deputy; the other tabby warrior had already vanished.

Mothwing turned back to the ThunderClan cats. Her golden tabby fur was hardly ruffled and her amber eyes gleamed with satisfaction. "Having trouble?" she murmured.

Leafpaw fought for breath and shook leaves and scraps of twig from her pelt. "Thanks, Mothwing," she replied. "I don't know what we'd have done without you." Turning to her friend, she added, "Sorreltail, have you met Mothwing? She's Mudfur's apprentice, but she was trained as a warrior first."

"A good thing she was," Sorreltail mewed, with a nod of thanks to the RiverClan cat. "We bit off more than we could chew there."

"I'm sorry we're on your territory," Leafpaw went on. "We'll go right away."

"Oh, there's no hurry." Mothwing did not try to question them about why they were there, or what they had done to annoy WindClan. "You look pretty shaken. Rest for a bit and I'll find you some herbs to calm you down."

She vanished among the bushes, leaving Leafpaw and Sorreltail with nothing to do but sit and wait for her.

"Is she always this careless about the warrior code?" Sorreltail muttered. "She doesn't seem to understand that we shouldn't be here!"

"I think it's because I'm a medicine cat apprentice too."

"Even medicine cats have to stick to the warrior code," mewed Sorreltail. "And I can't see Cinderpelt being so welcoming to other Clans! Of course, Mothwing's mother was a rogue, wasn't she? That could explain it."

"Mothwing is a loyal RiverClan cat!" Leafpaw fired up in defense of her friend. "It doesn't matter who her mother was."

"I never said it did," Sorreltail soothed her, touching Leafpaw's shoulder with her tail-tip. "But that might be why she's more relaxed about Clan boundaries."

Mothwing returned at that moment with a wad of herbs in her jaws. The ThunderClan apprentice drank in the scent of thyme; she remembered Cinderpelt telling her how good it was for calming anxieties.

"There," Mothwing meowed. "Eat some of that and you'll soon feel better."

Leafpaw and Sorreltail crouched down and chewed up some of the leaves. Leafpaw imagined the juices soaking into every scrap of her body, healing the shock of their terrifying encounter with WindClan.

"Are you hurt at all?" Mothwing asked. "I can fetch some cobwebs."

"No, there's no need, thanks," Leafpaw assured her. She and Sorreltail both had a few scratches, but they would stop bleeding by themselves without need for a poultice of cobwebs. "We really ought to be going."

"So what was all that about?" Mothwing queried, as Leafpaw and Sorreltail swallowed the last of the herbs. She wasn't quite as uninterested as the ThunderClan cats had thought. "What were you doing on WindClan territory?"

"We went to see what the Twolegs are up to," Leafpaw explained. When Mothwing still looked mystified, she described how she had seen the monster roaring into the forest two days before, tearing up the ground, and then found evidence that WindClan and ShadowClan were being destroyed in the same way. She was aware of a doubtful glance from Sorreltail; the young warrior was clearly unhappy about revealing ThunderClan's problems to a cat from a rival Clan. Leafpaw shook her head impatiently; there could be no harm in taking another medicine cat into her confidence.

"Firestar wants to ask the other Clans what they think," she finished. "But ShadowClan won't admit anything is wrong, and—well, you've seen how WindClan reacted."

"What can you expect?" Sorreltail broke in. She passed her tongue over her lips as if she didn't much like the taste of the herbs. "No Clan is going to be in a hurry to tell us they're starving and losing their territory to Twolegs."

"We've seen nothing of these monsters in RiverClan," Mothwing meowed. "Everything's fine here. But it explains one thing. . . ." Her amber eyes widened. "I've sensed panic over WindClan territory. Their scent markers on the border are filled with fear."

"I'm not surprised," Sorreltail mewed. "They're thin as anything, and there's no scent of rabbits anywhere."

"Everything's changing," Leafpaw murmured.

"And inside the Clans, as well. An ambitious cat might take the chance of—" Mothwing spoke quickly, urgently, and then broke off awkwardly.

"What do you mean?" Leafpaw prompted.

"Oh . . . no . . . I don't know." Mothwing trailed off and looked away.

Leafpaw stared at her, wondering what was going on inside that beautiful golden head. She was too young to remember Tigerstar, the bloodthirsty cat who had plotted to make himself leader of ThunderClan. When his murderous plans failed, he had been prepared to destroy the whole Clan for vengeance. She shivered. Did Mothwing know of another cat with ambition like this? Surely the forest could never produce another Tigerstar?

Her thoughts were interrupted when Mothwing sprang to her paws, her head turned toward the river. "A patrol is coming!" she exclaimed. "Come this way—quickly!"

She slipped between two bushes; Leafpaw and Sorreltail followed. A few moments later they came into the open and found themselves on the slope that led up to the ThunderClan border.

"If your Clan is short of prey, come and see me," Mothwing mewed. "We can always spare a few fish. Now run!"

Leafpaw and Sorreltail streaked up the slope and plunged for cover into more bushes. Though Leafpaw braced herself for accusing snarls behind her, they reached the border unseen.

"Thank StarClan for that!" Sorreltail exclaimed as they crossed into their own territory.

Leafpaw looked back through the branches. Mothwing was standing where they had left her; a moment later the undergrowth parted and a large, sleek-furred tabby warrior emerged. Leafpaw recognized Mothwing's brother Hawkfrost; two other warriors followed him. Hawkfrost stopped to talk to his sister, but never once glanced in the direction of the ThunderClan cats.

Looking at the warrior's massive shoulders and strong muscles, Leafpaw was relieved that he had not caught them trespassing. Unlike Mothwing, he kept strictly to the warrior code, and he was unlikely to listen to explanations. Not for the first time, Leafpaw felt that he reminded her of some other cat, but however hard she stared at him, she could not remember who.

"Come on," Sorreltail meowed. "Are you going to stare at those RiverClan warriors all day? It's time we were getting back, and then you can decide how much you're going to tell Firestar."

CHAPTER 5

Stormfur's paws scrabbled on smooth gray rock. Heaving himself upward, he reached the top of the boulder and turned to look down at his friends, his fur buffeted by the icy breeze.

"Come on," he meowed. "It's not so bad if you take a leap at it."

Following the rising sun, he and the other cats had left the moorland behind and begun to climb. Now, as sunhigh approached on the second day of their homeward journey, the mountains they had seen from a distance stretched up in front of them even bigger than they had imagined, their sheer slopes black and forbidding, with wisps of cloud floating around their peaks. The soil beneath the cats' paws was rough with pebbles, and little grew there except sparse grass and twisted thorn trees. There was no clear path; instead they followed winding narrow clefts and often had to turn back when they came up against rock walls with no way through. Thinking wistfully of the river sliding through deep, cool grasses at home, Stormfur half wished they had decided to return through Twolegplace instead.

Squirrelpaw bunched her hind legs and launched herself in

a massive leap, following Stormfur up the boulder that blocked their path. "Mouse dung!" she gasped as she missed the top and began to slide back. Stormfur leaned over and sank his teeth into her neck fur, steadying her until her scraping claws propelled her up the last tail-length to sit beside him.

"Thanks!" Her green eyes glowed at him. "I know my name's Squirrelpaw, but I never thought I'd wish that I *was* a squirrel!"

Stormfur let out a *mrrow* of laughter. "We'll all wish we were squirrels if we get much more of this."

"Hey!" Crowpaw's voice rose aggressively from below. "Stand back, will you? How can I get up there with you two furballs standing in the way?"

Stormfur and Squirrelpaw stepped back from the top of the boulder, and a moment later Crowpaw joined them, his long limbs managing the jump easily. Ignoring the others, he turned back to help Feathertail, who scrambled up with a muttered curse as one of her claws snagged on the rock.

Stormfur was worried that the rat bite in Tawnypelt's shoulder would stop her from climbing the boulder, and wondered if they would have to try finding a way around it, but to his relief her leap brought her almost to the top, where Crowpaw grabbed her by the scruff and hauled her up. Brambleclaw joined them last of all, shaking his ruffled tabby fur as he stood on top of the boulder and looked around. This close to sunhigh, there were few shadows to point them in the right direction and nothing but a sheer precipice in front of them, hiding what lay ahead.

"I suppose we go that way," he meowed, flicking his tail toward a narrow ledge leading across the face of the rock. "What do you think?" he asked Stormfur.

Stormfur felt his pelt prickle as he looked at the ledge. A few straggling bushes had rooted themselves in cracks, but apart from that the rock was bare and if they slipped there would be nothing to hold on to.

"We can try," he mewed doubtfully, rather surprised that Brambleclaw had asked his opinion. "There's nowhere else, unless we go back."

Brambleclaw nodded. "Bring up the rear, will you?" he asked. "We don't know what might be lurking around here, and we need a strong cat to watch our back."

Stormfur murmured agreement, feeling a warm glow that spread from his ears to his tail-tip at the ThunderClan cat's praise. Brambleclaw was neither his leader nor his mentor, but Stormfur couldn't help feeling strong admiration for the young warrior's courage and the way he had taken the lead on this difficult journey.

"I've changed my mind," Squirrelpaw announced as Brambleclaw squeezed his way along the ledge. "I don't want to be a squirrel anymore. I'd rather be a bird!"

Stormfur brought up the rear as Brambleclaw had asked, his ears pricked for danger while he tried to hide his nervousness about the sheer drop, which tugged at him like an invisible weight. He hugged the rock face, placing each paw carefully and using his tail for balance. After a little while the breeze grew stronger, and Stormfur's mind filled with terrifying images of himself or one of his friends blown right off the ledge and down to the ground below.

After a short while the ledge curved around the rock face, out of sight. Before Stormfur reached the turn, Tawnypelt, who was just in front of him, stopped abruptly, and from farther ahead he heard Feathertail exclaim, "Oh, no!"

"What's the matter?" Stormfur asked.

Tawnypelt edged forward more slowly, and Stormfur followed until he could see what was ahead. His belly lurched. A gap had opened up between their ledge and the rock face; the ledge became a spur of rock, jutting out from the side of the mountain and narrowing to a point. On both sides was a dizzying drop to a valley below where a mountain stream flowed, looking thin as a mousetail.

"Do you want to go back?" he called to Brambleclaw.

"Hang on a minute," the ThunderClan warrior replied. "There might be a way. Look over there."

Stormfur looked where his tail was pointing: On the mountainside beyond the gap the rock face had broken away, and a narrow rift had opened up between two steep slopes. Bushes were growing there and one or two small trees. A stream trickled down one side, overhung by grasses.

"The going looks easier there," Feathertail meowed. "But can we get across?"

Squirrelpaw lifted her head and tasted the air. "I can smell rabbits," she mewed longingly.

Stormfur measured the gap. It was wider than he liked, especially from a standing start. He thought he could manage it, but what about Tawnypelt? The ShadowClan warrior had started to limp again since they had started their climb, and even though she hadn't said anything, it was obvious the wound hadn't healed properly yet.

Before he could voice his doubts he heard Crowpaw mew, "What are we waiting for? Are we going to stand around here until we grow wings?"

Without any more hesitation the WindClan apprentice launched himself across the gap. For a heartbeat his gray-black body seemed to hang in the air; then he was across, landing lightly on the loose stones at the edge of the drop.

"Come on!" he called. "It's easy."

Catching Brambleclaw's eye, Stormfur knew that the tabby warrior shared his annoyance that the apprentice hadn't waited for the rest of them to agree. Now they all had to try the leap, whether they wanted to or not, because Crowpaw would never manage to jump back onto the narrow spur of rock, and they could not leave him on his own over there.

He was even less pleased when he saw Feathertail crouching at the edge of the rock with the wind buffeting her fur. Crowpaw was waiting to steady her at the other side, and she waved her plumy tail with pleasure as she realized that she had made it safely.

The remaining cats bunched together on the rock. Stormfur's pelt pricked with fear as he felt the breeze grow stronger.

"Okay, who's next?" Brambleclaw asked steadily.

"I'll go," Squirrelpaw meowed. "See you over there."

She pushed herself off from the rock in a tremendous leap, landing a tail-length from the edge on the other side.

"She's quite something," Brambleclaw murmured, then looked confused, as if he hadn't meant to speak his thoughts aloud.

"She certainly is," Stormfur agreed.

"Tawnypelt, are you ready?" Brambleclaw asked, turning away. "Is your shoulder okay?"

"I'll be fine," Tawnypelt mewed grimly.

She measured the distance with a glance and then took off. For one horrible instant, Stormfur thought she had jumped short. Her body slammed into the edge of the rock and her front paws scrabbled frantically for a grip among the loose stones. A heartbeat later Feathertail was on one side of her, and Squirrelpaw on the other, sinking their teeth into her neck fur and pulling her up the rest of the way.

"Well done!" Brambleclaw called, his voice high-pitched from worry.

Tawnypelt did not reply. Her tail had fluffed out with terror; Stormfur saw Feathertail coaxing her over to the stream and encouraging her to drink.

"You next?" Brambleclaw asked Stormfur.

"You go; I'm fine."

But as Stormfur watched the strong tabby warrior leaping the gap, he couldn't help wishing he hadn't waited to go last. He was just about to jump when Squirrelpaw shrieked, "Stormfur! Look out!"

At the same instant a dark shadow fell over him and he

heard the beating of wings thudding through the air. Without pausing to look up, he launched himself across the gap, catching a glimpse of his friends on the other side scattering to the sides of the valley.

He hit the ground awkwardly, falling to one side, and froze with horror as he looked up to see an enormous bird swooping down on top of him, talons extended.

A cat yowled his name. Rolling away from the claws and stabbing beak he felt the draft from the beating wings and smelled a reek of carrion. Then he was aware of Brambleclaw and Feathertail hurtling toward him, hissing and spitting with their fur standing on end. The bird veered to one side; Stormfur had a couple of heartbeats to scramble away. Then the talons hit the ground, throwing up spurts of dust. The bird let out a frustrated screech. Its wings beat strongly, carrying it up again. All three cats streaked into the shelter of a bush where Squirrelpaw and Tawnypelt were waiting.

"What in StarClan's name was *that*?" Stormfur gasped, watching the bird climb higher until it was no more than a dot in the sky. "I've never seen such a big bird."

"An eagle." Crowpaw wormed his way under the lower branches to join them. "We see them in WindClan territory now and then. They prey on lambs, but the elders say they've taken cats before."

"In another heartbeat it would have taken me," Stormfur muttered. "Thanks, both of you," he added to Brambleclaw and Feathertail.

Feathertail shuddered. "Imagine what would have hap-

pened if it had spotted us a bit earlier, when we were all stuck
out on that rock!"

"I don't *want* to imagine it!" Squirrelpaw retorted.

"I think we need to take a break after that," Brambleclaw
meowed. "What about finding some prey? I scented rabbits
out there."

"I'll go," Crowpaw offered. "*I* don't need to rest. Coming,
Feathertail?"

Stormfur opened his mouth to object as his sister pushed
her way out of the bush behind Crowpaw. In the end, all he
said was, "Watch out for that eagle!"

When they had gone, Tawnypelt closed her eyes with an
exhausted sigh and within a couple of heartbeats she was
asleep. Stormfur curled up beside her, but he found it hard to
rest. He could hear Brambleclaw and Squirrelpaw murmuring quietly together, and found he was straining his ears to
make out what they were saying, envying their closeness and
wishing not for the first time that Squirrelpaw was in his
Clan and not Brambleclaw's. He was worried about his sister
too, out there alone with that apprentice. They should keep
moving while they could; if they delayed too long, darkness
would overtake them and they would be forced to spend the
night here.

At last he drifted into an uneasy doze; a paw prodding him
in the ribs brought him back to consciousness. He blinked up
into Squirrelpaw's green eyes and his senses were flooded by
the scent of rabbit.

"They're back," Squirrelpaw meowed. "And they've

brought enough fresh-kill for every cat. Of course," she added, her eyes glinting with amusement, "I can eat yours if you don't want it."

"Don't you dare!" Stormfur growled, flicking her ear with his tail as he scrambled up.

Crouching over his share of rabbit, he saw Feathertail and Crowpaw sitting close together as they ate. He suppressed a growl as he wondered yet again how Feathertail could possibly forget what happened when cats from different Clans tried to be together.

Once all the journeying cats were relaxing with full bellies, he managed to edge his sister away from the rest. "Listen, Feathertail, you and Crowpaw—" he murmured.

"What about Crowpaw?" Feathertail's blue eyes flashed and her voice was uncharacteristically sharp. "You others are so unfair to him!"

Stormfur wanted to point out that the young cat asked for trouble with the way he argued about everything, but he had enough sense not to say so to Feathertail. "That's not the point," he mewed. "What's going to happen when we get back home? Crowpaw's in a different Clan."

"We don't even know if there will be Clans anymore," Feathertail pointed out. "We'll be leaving the forest, remember?"

Stormfur snorted. "Do you think all the Clan boundaries will vanish, just because we have to leave? I doubt it."

He was surprised by the flash of anger in Feathertail's eyes.

"Have you forgotten already what Midnight said?" she

spat. "The Clans won't *survive* if they can't work together."

"And have you forgotten what happens when cats from different Clans get together?" Stormfur growled. "Look at the way our own father has been torn between two Clans. You and I nearly *died* because we're half-Clan! Tigerstar would have killed us if the ThunderClan cats hadn't rescued us."

"But Tigerstar's gone now," Feathertail mewed stubbornly. "There won't be another cat like that in the forest. And Midnight said all the Clans will have to find somewhere else to live. Everything will be different."

"But you and Crowpaw . . ."

"I'm not going to talk about me and Crowpaw." Feathertail's anger died. "I'm sorry, Stormfur, but this doesn't have anything to do with you."

Stormfur started to deliver a stinging reply, then realized that she was right. Awkwardly he stroked her shoulder with the tip of his tail. "I worry about you, that's all."

Feathertail gave his ear a quick lick. "I know. But there's no need. Really."

Even though he did not agree with her, Stormfur said nothing. She was his sister and he would do anything to make her happy. He wished Crowpaw could make her happy too, if that was what Feathertail really wanted, but he couldn't believe that all the rivalry between the Clans would vanish, whatever happened, and let them be together.

When the cats emerged from the shelter of the bush to continue their journey they saw that the sky had grown darker. The wind had dropped but there was a chill in the air and clouds surged around the mountaintop, hiding the sun.

"Rain on its way," Tawnypelt commented. "That's all we need."

"Then let's push on while we can," meowed Brambleclaw.

They set off up the rift in the side of the mountain, keeping close to the sides and making what use they could of the cover from bushes, in case the eagle returned. Stormfur kept an eye on the sky; once, he saw a tiny dot, drifting lazily above the mountainside, and knew that the fierce bird was still on the watch.

They passed the source of the tiny stream, bubbling up from a crack between two rocks, and took a last drink before they pressed on. Stormfur gazed up the slope ahead, scanning it for something familiar that would show him the next source of food or shelter, and saw nothing but lifeless, gray rock.

The valley grew narrower and there was even less vegetation. Stormfur felt uncomfortably exposed, but the eagle did not return. As twilight gathered, a thin, cold rain began to fall. The cats' fur was soon soaked, and there was nowhere to shelter.

"We've got to stop soon," Squirrelpaw announced loudly. "My paws are falling off."

"Well, we can't stop here." Brambleclaw sounded irritable. "We need to get out of the rain."

"No, Squirrelpaw's right," Stormfur objected, facing up to

the ThunderClan warrior. "We can't go on in the dark; we risk falling."

Brambleclaw's neck fur rose and he fixed Stormfur with a furious glare. Behind him, Stormfur heard a faint murmur of distress from Feathertail. He realized they were within a couple of heartbeats of fighting among themselves. His growing respect for the ThunderClan cat meant that a fight was the last thing he wanted, but he could not back down and let Brambleclaw lead them on to slip over some precipice in the darkness.

Then he saw Brambleclaw's fur begin to lie flat again as the tabby seemed to understand Stormfur's concerns. "You're right, Stormfur. Let's shelter under the rock over there. It's better than nothing."

He led the way to an overhanging rock, open on one side to the wind and rain that grew heavier still as the cats settled down, huddling together in an attempt to keep warm and dry.

"Shelter?" Crowpaw muttered. "If this is shelter, then I'm a hedgehog!"

You're just as prickly, Stormfur thought, but he kept the words to himself.

That night he slept only in brief, uncomfortable snatches, and whenever he woke, he could feel his friends shifting uneasily around him. When at last the darkness began to lift he heaved himself to his paws, feeling stiff and bleary-eyed, and peered out of the overhang to see dense white mist swirling around them.

"We must be in the clouds," Brambleclaw murmured, coming to join him. "I hope it lifts soon."

"Do you think we should go on?" Stormfur asked hesitantly, wanting to avoid another confrontation with the ThunderClan cat. "If we can't see where we're going, we could walk straight over a cliff."

"We manage when the mist comes down on the moors," Crowpaw pointed out, yawning as he staggered to his paws. Then he added doubtfully, "But we know our own territory by scent as well as sight."

"And what about fresh-kill?" Squirrelpaw mewed. "There's no rabbit scent up here. I'm starving!"

Stormfur tried to ignore his own growling belly while Brambleclaw ventured out of their shelter and stood looking upward. "I can see for a few foxlengths," he reported. "This cleft seems to go on and on. I think we'll be safe if we follow it."

He glanced at Stormfur as he spoke, a questioning look in his eyes, as if he regretted their recent argument and wanted to be sure that the RiverClan cat agreed with him.

Stormfur stepped out to join him, shivering as the mist began to soak into his fur. "Okay," he meowed. "Lead the way. It's not like we have much choice."

Reluctantly the other cats followed Brambleclaw out into the cold, clinging mist and padded after him up the rift. Stormfur noticed that Tawnypelt was limping worse today, as if her leg had stiffened in the night. Midnight's burdock root had cured the infection, but Stormfur suspected her muscles had been damaged. She needed a medicine cat to look at it, but that was impossible out here.

Daylight gradually grew stronger, and the swirls of cloud became paler, as if somewhere above them the sun was rising. The rift grew steadily narrower, with walls of rock closing in on either side.

"I hope this isn't a dead end," Feathertail mewed. "We can't go back to that ledge."

She had hardly spoken when the clouds began to thin out and the cats could see farther ahead. Stormfur found himself staring up at a sheer rock face where the sides of the valley came to a point. There didn't seem any way of climbing up, not unless they all grew wings and flew. His fur was plastered to his body by the mist and he felt hollow with hunger.

"Now what?" Tawnypelt meowed, sounding as defeated as Stormfur felt.

The six cats stood looking upward, a fine rain drifting around them as if the drops were light enough to be blown by the wind. Stormfur struggled with black despair. What was the point of all this? Even if they reached home, the forest was going to be destroyed. Their hopes of helping their Clans rested on the word of a badger—a creature whom the cats had always regarded as an enemy. Stuck here among rain-wet rocks, it was hard to remember his trust in Midnight's wisdom. And if Stormfur doubted her, what would his Clanmates say when he tried to pass her message on? They had never completely trusted him or Feathertail because of their half-Clan heritage, so why should they listen now?

Then Stormfur realized that he could hear a steady roaring sound. It reminded him of the river pouring through the ravine in his home territory.

"What's that?" he meowed, lifting his head. "Can you hear it?"

"Over here, I think," Brambleclaw called.

Stormfur followed him up to the valley's point, and discovered a split in the rock winding upward, just wide enough for one cat at a time. Brambleclaw led the way into it, gesturing with his tail for the others to follow. Stormfur waited to bring up the rear, his fur brushing the rock on either side, with unpleasant thoughts going through his head of what would happen if the path became so narrow that they got stuck.

The roaring grew louder, and after a little while the path came out on an open ledge. Broken rocks lay in front of them, rising to a ridge above their heads. A stream poured over the ridge, foaming down past the place where the cats were standing until it vanished behind a jutting boulder.

"Hey, at least we can have a drink!" Squirrelpaw mewed.

"Be careful," Brambleclaw warned her. "One slip, and you'll be crowfood."

Squirrelpaw shot him a glare, but said nothing. She crept forward cautiously to the edge of the stream and crouched to lap. Stormfur and the other cats followed her. The water was ice-cold, refreshing Stormfur and giving him new courage. Perhaps their scramble over these hostile mountains would soon be over.

Rising to his paws again, he glanced downstream and froze in shock. Just below where the cats were drinking, the rocks fell away into a precipice. Padding warily a few paces toward it Stormfur stretched his neck to peer over the edge and saw the stream pounding down in a waterfall until it crashed into a pool many tail-lengths below. The sound of thundering water filled his ears, making him dizzy, so that he instinctively tried to dig his claws into the rain-wet rock.

The rest of the cats gathered around him, their eyes wide and horrified.

"Awesome!" Squirrelpaw murmured. Peering over, she added, "There's prey down there, I bet."

Through the mist of spray that rose from the pool Stormfur caught a glimpse of another valley like the one they had just left, where grass grew up between broken rocks and bushes lined the rock walls. Squirrelpaw was right—if there were any other living things to be found around here, it would be down there.

"But we need to go up," Brambleclaw pointed out, flicking his ears toward the place far above their heads where the stream poured over the lip of the rock. "It doesn't look too difficult to climb. If we go down, we might never get back again."

"Big deal, if it meant we got something to eat," Squirrelpaw muttered, but so softly that Stormfur wondered if her Clanmate had heard.

With Brambleclaw in the lead again, they began the scramble upward. They were all exhausted, their soaked fur making them clumsy. Tawnypelt in particular found the going tough, hauling herself painfully over every rock as if she had hardly any strength left.

The stream bubbled up beside them, splashing over the rocks that were already wet and slippery with rain, which was falling more heavily again. Stormfur kept a wary eye on the stream, half expecting it to overflow and sweep them off the rocks. He stayed to the back of the group, trying to watch every cat, well aware that if any of them slipped they could be washed into the pool below the waterfall.

Almost as soon as that thought crossed his mind he saw Feathertail's paws skid from under her. She slid sideways into the stream; water surged around her as she clung to the rocks by a single paw, her jaws wide in a silent wail of shock.

Stormfur bounded toward her, pushing past Tawnypelt, but before he reached her, Crowpaw had leaned out precariously over the foaming water, sunk his teeth into the scruff of Feathertail's neck, and dragged her back onto the path.

"Thank you, Crowpaw," she gasped. Stormfur saw with annoyance that her blue eyes were glowing with gratitude— and something more.

"You should be more careful," Crowpaw meowed gruffly. "Do you think you're a Clan leader, with nine lives to throw away? I saved you this once—don't make me save you again."

"I won't." Feathertail blinked and pressed her nose against Crowpaw's muzzle. "I'm sorry for not watching out."

"So you should be," Stormfur snapped, not sure whether he was more annoyed by his sister's carelessness or by the fact that Crowpaw had been the one to save her. He shouldered the apprentice away so that he could examine Feathertail more closely. "Are you okay?"

"Yes, fine," Feathertail replied, trying to shake water from her fur.

A louder rumbling from farther up the mountain interrupted her, drowning even the roar of the waterfall below. Stormfur looked up and froze in horror at the sight of a wall of mud, branches, and water hurtling down on them. His worst fears had come true: The mountain stream was in flood. Squirrelpaw let out a terrified yowl and Brambleclaw sprang back toward her.

But the water was upon them before they could do anything. It struck Stormfur like a blow, carrying him off his paws. His legs flailed as the flood carried him down, driving him against rocks where he clawed in vain for a grip before the water swept him on again. He choked as water filled his mouth and one of his paws caught painfully against a rock. Then there was nothing beneath him at all, and he knew he was plunging over the waterfall.

There was a moment of eerie silence, broken by the whisper of rushing water. Then the roaring and pounding started up again, waiting to swallow him as he plummeted into the pool. Whirled around in the icy water, he caught a brief glimpse of Crowpaw floundering wildly before the surge closed over his head. Then more water crashed down on him, driving him under and filling his senses with churning white foam, a deafening roar, and then nothing.

I'm sorry, StarClan, Stormfur thought desperately as his senses faded. *I know it wasn't my mission, but I tried so hard. Please look after our Clans. . . .*

CHAPTER 6

Leafpaw burst up through the surface of the water, gasping for air as she scrambled to find solid ground. Managing to stand in spite of the river flowing strongly around her legs, she shook icy drops of water from her pelt. The riverbank was only a couple of tail-lengths away. She shivered in the pale sun of leaf-fall as she looked up to see Mothwing peering down at her from an overhanging rock.

The RiverClan cat's amber eyes were narrowed in amusement. "You don't fish by jumping in the river," she pointed out.

"I know that!" Leafpaw retorted crossly. "I slipped, that's all."

"I believe you," Mothwing purred, giving her golden chest fur a quick lick. "Now come out, and we'll have another go. I'll teach you to fish if it's the last thing I do."

"I'm still not sure we should be doing this," Leafpaw meowed as she waded back to the bank.

"Of course we should. The rabbits and squirrels are starting to disappear, thanks to the Twolegs, but there's still plenty of fish for every cat."

"But I had to come onto RiverClan territory to get it," Leafpaw pointed out anxiously. "What would Leopardstar say if she knew?"

Mothwing blinked. "We're both medicine cats, so Clan boundaries don't matter for us like they do for other cats."

Leafpaw didn't think that was how the warrior code worked. Her friend had said much the same a couple of days earlier, when she had rescued Leafpaw and Sorreltail from the pursuing WindClan warriors. This morning she had called to Leafpaw while she was gathering herbs near Sunningrocks, and offered to give her a fishing lesson. Leafpaw had felt very nervous about crossing the Clan border, but her hunger had driven her on now that prey was becoming even scarcer in ThunderClan territory. All the same, her ears and nose were alert for the first signs of a RiverClan patrol.

"Okay," Mothwing went on, "crouch here beside me, and look down into the water. When you see a fish, scoop it out with your paw. It's easy."

A couple of glittering fish lying on the bank showed just how easy it was for Mothwing. Leafpaw gave them a longing glance, wondering if she would ever learn.

"Want some?" Mothwing offered, following her gaze.

Leafpaw felt guilty at the thought of being full-fed while the rest of her Clan went hungry. But she had not tasted fresh-kill since the night before, and that had been only a stringy vole. "I shouldn't . . ." she murmured, trying to convince herself that it wouldn't help her Clan if she starved as well.

"Of course you can. Where's the harm?"

Leafpaw did not wait to be asked again. She crouched down in front of the fish, tucking her paws in, and sank her teeth into the cool flesh. "Delicious," she mumbled.

Mothwing looked pleased. "Learn how to do it, and you can take lots more for your Clan." She took a few dainty bites, as if she were full-fed already and didn't care whether or not she ate.

Gulping down the rest of the fish, Leafpaw told herself that she would find food for her Clan to make up for it. As soon as she had finished, she settled down on the rock beside Mothwing and concentrated on the water just below, to wait for a fish of her own.

An unfamiliar scent swept over her at the same instant as Mothwing hissed, "Hawkfrost!" Leafpaw felt a paw jab hard into her ribs, tipping her over the edge of the rock and back into the river. She thrashed wildly, wondering why Mothwing was trying to drown her. Then as her head broke the surface she saw the huge tabby shape of Hawkfrost approaching the bank, and realized that Mothwing had done the only thing she could to hide her quickly.

Her paws working gently to keep her nose just above the water, Leafpaw let herself drift downriver for a few tail-lengths until she came to a clump of reeds where she could crawl out on the ThunderClan side of the river and hide.

Hawkfrost had stopped to talk to his sister, and Leafpaw realized that she would have to crouch where she was, soaked and shivering, until he went away and she could make a break across open ground to the ThunderClan border.

". . . keeping my eyes open for WindClan," she heard him meow when her ears were clear of water. "I know very well they're stealing fish, and one day I'll catch them at it."

"Not down here, surely?" Mothwing replied innocently. "WindClan would fish closer to Fourtrees—if they're fishing at all."

"WindClan *and* ThunderClan," Hawkfrost growled. He added, "I can scent a ThunderClan cat now."

Leafpaw shivered and shrank down in her clump of reeds.

"So? The border's over there," Mothwing pointed out. "It would be odd if you *didn't* scent ThunderClan."

Hawkfrost grunted. "There's something not right in the forest. Cats have gone missing from all the Clans, for one thing. Do you remember what the other leaders said at the last Gathering? That's four more cats, beside Stormfur and Feathertail. I don't know what's going on, but I'll find out."

Leafpaw tensed. She had told Mothwing about the Twoleg monsters, but obviously Mothwing had not passed on the news to the rest of her Clan. Chilled by the hunger in Hawkfrost's voice, Leafpaw prayed to StarClan that she would say nothing about it now. To her relief, her friend meowed calmly, "There's nothing wrong in RiverClan, so why should we care?"

"Have you got bees in your brain?" Hawkfrost snapped. "This could be our chance to make RiverClan great. If the other Clans are weak, we could rule over the whole forest."

"*What?*" Mothwing sounded disgusted. "You're the one with bees in your brain. Who do you think you are— Tigerstar?"

"There are worse cats to imitate," Hawkfrost meowed.

Pure icy fear lanced through Leafpaw. Tigerstar had been prepared to kill any cat who opposed him in his quest for supreme power. And now another cat was preparing to follow in his pawsteps.

Another thought sprang into her mind. This was what Mothwing must have meant when she talked about a cat with ambitions, on the day she rescued Leafpaw and Sorreltail from WindClan. She had been worried about her own brother! A few days before, Leafpaw had been sure that the forest would never produce another Tigerstar; now she could only strain her ears, horrified, to make out what Hawkfrost would say next.

"Have you forgotten what happened to Tigerstar?" Mothwing snapped. "He failed, and now he's just a name to frighten kits with."

"I shall learn from his mistakes." Hawkfrost's voice rumbled deep in his chest. "Our mother told us enough about him, after all. He broke the warrior code, and he deserved to fail. I shall know better."

Leafpaw stared at the reeds in front of her, puzzled. Hawkfrost's mother, Sasha, the rogue cat, had told them about Tigerstar? How did she know? Leafpaw had never met Sasha—the Clanless she-cat had stayed in RiverClan for only a short while, long enough to decide that she wanted her kits to be raised as part of the Clan. No cat knew where she had been before then.

In her bewilderment Leafpaw had not noticed that the

wind had changed, and that a playful breeze, twisting its way upriver, had carried her scent with it.

"I *can* smell ThunderClan," Hawkfrost declared suddenly. Leafpaw's heart nearly jumped out of her chest. "The scent's fresh too. If one of their warriors is on our territory, I'll claw his fur off."

Above her head, Leafpaw heard Mothwing scramble to her paws. "You're right!" she exclaimed. "It's this way. Come on!"

Leafpaw heard her voice growing fainter as she bounded away in the opposite direction. "Mouse-brain!" Hawkfrost argued. "It's *downstream.* . . ."

Leafpaw didn't wait to hear any more. While he was following Mothwing, she broke out of the reeds and streaked up the bank toward the ThunderClan border. She plunged thankfully into thick bracken just on the ThunderClan side of the border.

Turning to peer out again, she saw Hawkfrost padding downstream, stopping to give the clump of reeds where she had just been hiding a good sniff before turning back to Mothwing with a frustrated growl. Once again Leafpaw was struck by the powerful tabby's resemblance to some other cat; the thought bothered her like a tick she couldn't reach, because she still couldn't remember who.

She was too far away to hear what the two RiverClan cats said to each other, but after a few moments, they both continued downstream to the stepping-stones and crossed to the RiverClan side of the river. When they finally disappeared into the reeds, Leafpaw drew a huge breath of relief and started trotting back to camp.

The guilt she felt about her full belly was almost forgotten amid pricklings of unease about what Mothwing had said. Hawkfrost sounded as ambitious as Tigerstar—and there was no place for that when the forest was on the brink of destruction.

A gleam of dying sunlight pierced the clouds and lay like a streak of blood on the forest floor. Leafpaw guessed that Cinderpelt would be wondering where she was, but she needed time to figure out how Hawkfrost and Mothwing knew so much about Tigerstar. She sat down and began to groom her drying fur.

Sasha had been a rogue cat wandering the forest, until she had come to RiverClan with her kits and settled briefly there. She might have visited ShadowClan when Tigerstar was leader. It was possible. . . .

Leafpaw froze. She realized which cat Hawkfrost resembled so strongly. Brambleclaw! And every cat knew who Brambleclaw's father was. Could it be possible that *Tigerstar* was Hawkfrost's and Mothwing's father as well? If he was, that would make Hawkfrost and Brambleclaw half brothers.

She was staring into the trees as if she could see the answer there when her thoughts were interrupted by the frantic beating of wings. She looked up to see a magpie fluttering out of the bushes to land on a branch above her head. At the same time a loud voice exclaimed, "Mouse dung!"

The bushes just ahead of her rustled violently and

Graystripe appeared, glaring up at the magpie with frustration in his yellow eyes. "Missed it," he muttered. "I don't know what's the matter with me."

Leafpaw rose to her paws as the deputy approached, dipping her head respectfully and letting out a sympathetic purr. She hoped that her pelt was dry enough for Graystripe not to notice that she had been swimming.

"Hello, Leafpaw," he meowed. "Sorry if I startled you. Actually, I do know what's wrong with me," he went on, the tip of his tail twitching uneasily. "I can't get Feathertail and Stormfur out of my head. I wish I knew where they've gone. Brambleclaw and Squirrelpaw too."

Leafpaw felt another pang of guilt. She could save Graystripe so much worry if she told him what she knew about the prophecy, but she had promised the journeying cats that she would keep silent.

"I feel that they're all safe," she ventured, "and that they'll come back to us."

Graystripe looked up with a flicker of hope in his amber eyes. "Has StarClan told you that?"

"Not exactly, but—"

"I can't help wondering if it has something to do with the Twolegs," Graystripe interrupted. "Cats go missing—Twolegs invade us. . . ." His paws worked against the ground, tearing up the grass with his claws.

"Graystripe, can I ask you something?" Leafpaw meowed, desperate to change the subject.

"Sure, go ahead."

"Did you ever meet Sasha—Hawkfrost and Mothwing's mother?"

Graystripe looked at her in surprise. "Once. At a Gathering."

"What was she like?" Leafpaw asked curiously.

"Nice enough," Graystripe told her. "Quiet and ready to be friendly. A lot like Mothwing to look at. But it was clear that being among a lot of cats spooked her. I wasn't surprised when she left the forest as soon as Mothwing and Hawkfrost were old enough to do without her."

"Does any cat know who their father was?"

The deputy shook his head. "No. I always assumed it was another rogue."

"Rogues?"

There was the sound of pawsteps behind them, and Leafpaw spun around to see Firestar approaching from the direction of the camp.

"Have you seen rogues?" he demanded, tension clear in every hair on his flame-colored pelt. "For StarClan's sake, that's the last thing we need right now."

"No, no, not at all." Graystripe meowed quickly. "Leafpaw was just asking about Sasha, and which cat fathered Mothwing and Hawkfrost."

Firestar turned to look at Leafpaw, his green eyes puzzled. "Why do you want to know?"

Leafpaw hesitated. She wasn't about to admit that she had been spending time with Mothwing in RiverClan territory. "Oh, I just saw Hawkfrost," she meowed. "He was patrolling on the border." Well, she comforted herself, that was not entirely a lie. There was no way she was going to mention her suspicions that Tigerstar had fathered Hawkfrost and Mothwing, not when he and Firestar had been such bitter enemies.

Firestar nodded. "Well, I've no idea. Sasha might have told some cat in RiverClan, I suppose."

He padded across to Graystripe and touched noses with his old friend as if he guessed the thoughts that were troubling him. Both cats had lost children among the six cats that had vanished from the forest. They stared up into the trees, where a chilly wind was tugging leaves from the branches until they drifted down to join the other dead leaves on the forest floor.

"They must be cold, with no Clan to shelter them each night," Graystripe murmured.

"At least they have one another," Firestar mewed, pressing himself against Graystripe's side.

For a moment both cats remained silent; then Firestar turned to his daughter. "Leafpaw, you sometimes know what Squirrelpaw is thinking, don't you? You told us she was with the RiverClan cats. Have you any idea where they are now?"

Leafpaw blinked. She couldn't deny her father the chance to know if Squirrelpaw was alive—and she wanted to know just as fiercely. She shut her eyes and summoned up her old rapport with her sister. Emptying her mind, she concentrated fiercely. She gasped to feel a surge of cold and wet, shuddering as a blast of cold wind probed her drying fur. But there was no sign of Squirrelpaw anywhere—just water, blasting air, and endless rock.

Opening her eyes, Leafpaw blinked in confusion as she realized that her fur was dry and the forest was still. She had made contact with her sister after all!

"She's alive," she murmured. Beside her, Firestar's eyes lit up. "And wherever she is, I think it must be raining. . . ."

CHAPTER 7

Stormfur opened his eyes and blinked in light that was sharp as a claw. His breath rasped in his throat and every muscle in his body ached. He felt too exhausted even to move.

As his vision cleared he saw that he was lying on rain-wet rock, beside a pool of churning black water. His ears were ringing; when he raised his head feebly he saw a waterfall thundering down into the pool in a whirl of foam and spray, and realized that what he could hear was the roar and crash of falling water.

At once he remembered the flood that had swept him down from the rocks and plunged him into the pool. How had he survived? He remembered the roar, the foam, the darkness. . . . Fear for his friends stabbed through him.

"Feathertail? Squirrelpaw?" he mewed hoarsely.

"Over here."

The reply was so faint, it was nearly lost in the endless pounding of the waterfall. Stormfur turned his head to see Squirrelpaw splayed out on the rock beside him, her dark ginger fur sodden.

"Got to sleep . . ." she muttered, closing her eyes.

Just beyond her, Stormfur could see Brambleclaw, stretched limply on his side. The ThunderClan warrior was staring up at the sky, his breathing fast and shallow. Crowpaw was on Stormfur's other side; with a feeling of horror, he thought the WindClan apprentice was dead until he saw the faint rise and fall of his flank.

What about Feathertail and Tawnypelt? Beginning to panic, Stormfur struggled to sit up. At first he could not see either his sister or the tortoiseshell she-cat. Then a movement farther around the pool caught his eye. Near the waterfall, Feathertail was helping Tawnypelt out onto the rock. The ShadowClan warrior was tottering on three legs, and as soon as she reached solid ground she collapsed and lay without moving. Feathertail hauled herself out, her gray fur plastered to her sides so it looked almost black. She settled down beside Tawnypelt and gave her shoulder a couple of feeble licks.

"Thank StarClan!" Stormfur rasped aloud. "We all made it."

He vaguely knew they had to find shelter, that if they went on lying here they were vulnerable to predators like the eagle, but he was too exhausted to move. He gave his drying fur a few licks, but even that was too much effort. He lay still, his senses drifting, his gaze fixed unseeingly on the rocks beside the pool.

As his senses gradually returned he noticed that they were lying in a curved bowl of rock, open on the side where the stream surged out of the pool and headed down the valley. Boulders covered the ground on either bank, a couple of spindly trees rooted among them. Light shivered on the water; the rain had almost stopped and the clouds were thinning out. Above Stormfur's head, rainbows danced in the spray thrown up by the waterfall. A thin beam of sunlight splashed on the rocks a tail-length away from him; he dragged himself painfully into it and sighed with pleasure at the warmth on his fur.

A few heartbeats later he thought he saw a flash of movement. He blinked, straining to focus his eyes. For a moment all was still; then he caught another flicker on the far side of the pool. His fur prickled. They were being watched!

Stormfur narrowed his eyes, gazing hard at the boulders near the waterfall. "Brambleclaw," he whispered. "Look over there."

"What?" The ThunderClan warrior raised his head, peered around, and lay down again. "Can't see anything."

"There!" Stormfur hissed as movement flickered again, this time a tail-length closer. He flexed his claws, knowing how helpless he and his friends were to defend themselves.

Then a gray-brown shape detached itself from the rock and began padding toward him around the edge of the pool. It was a cat! Before Stormfur could move, another cat appeared and then another, a whole group of cats moving silently away from the rocks where they had been hidden, camouflaged against the boulders, as if they were carved from stone themselves. They sat on the edge of the pool, staring unblinkingly at the group of half-drowned travelers.

Stormfur swallowed hard. These cats were like none he had ever seen before, uniformly gray-brown with dull, flattened fur. Then one moved into the sunlight and he realized that their fur was covered with thick streaks of mud, helping them to blend into the rocks and hiding the real color of their pelts.

Stormfur sat up, his muscles shrieking a protest. He prodded Squirrelpaw with one paw and whispered hoarsely, "Sit up very slowly. Whatever you do, don't say anything out loud."

Squirrelpaw lifted her head, then saw the watching cats and tried to scramble up with alarm flaring in her green eyes. Her movement disturbed Brambleclaw, who jumped up at once. Stormfur managed to get to his paws and stand beside him, thankful to have the strong ThunderClan warrior with him as they faced danger.

Brambleclaw glanced around for the other cats. "Feathertail, Tawnypelt—over here, now." There was a commanding rasp in his voice, even though it shook with exhaustion. "You too, Crowpaw."

Crowpaw struggled up, for once not arguing, and went to help Feathertail. Tawnypelt was leaning against her shoulder, hardly able to move. The three of them limped around the pool until they could bunch together with Stormfur and the others, their eyes wide and scared as they watched the strange cats.

Stormfur knew they were too shaken and exhausted to defend themselves. But in spite of his fear a pang of curiosity stabbed him. He wanted to know more about these strangers who looked so different from any other cats he had known.

The thought even flashed through his mind that they might help with food and shelter—then he reminded himself that he and his friends were unlikely to be made welcome after trespassing on the strange cats' territory, and the best they could expect was to be driven off.

He hardly dared to breathe as the first cat approached and studied them all carefully. Padding close to Stormfur, he gave him an especially long scrutiny, barely sparing a glance for the cats on the other side of him. Stormfur tried to meet the staring yellow eyes, wondering uneasily what it was about him that interested the mud-clad cat so much.

"Is this the one?" A tabby she-cat stepped forward eagerly. She spoke in the same language as the Clan cats, though the sound of the words was strange to Stormfur's ears, and the question more confusing still. He watched her as she drew closer, her lithe body balancing easily on the slippery stones at the edge of the pool. "Is this what we've hoped for?" she persisted, reaching her Clanmate's side.

The first cat's head whipped around and he glared at the speaker. "Silence, Brook!" Turning back to Stormfur he asked roughly, "Who are you? Have you traveled far?"

Stormfur heard Tawnypelt mutter, "What are these—mud warriors? We're more than a match for them," and felt heartened by the ShadowClan cat's abrasive courage.

"Yes, we've come a long way," Squirrelpaw answered. "Can you help us?"

"Careful," Brambleclaw interrupted with a warning look. To the strange cat he added, "We are travelers trying to cross the mountains. We're not looking for trouble, but if you are enemies, we can fight."

The cat narrowed his eyes. "We have no wish for fighting. Your journey has brought you to the Tribe of Rushing Water."

"You are welcome if you come in friendship," the tabby she-cat added, a glow in her amber eyes as she looked at Stormfur.

Stormfur remembered that Midnight the badger had spoken of cats who lived in Tribes instead of Clans. These must be the cats she meant, though she had said nothing to suggest the Clan cats would encounter them on their journey home. Surely she must have known that they would come across the Tribe as they crossed the mountains. Stormfur reminded himself that he had instinctively trusted Midnight; if the Tribe had been dangerous, she would have warned them, or told them to go the other way. Instead she had implied that this route had been laid down for them. Did that mean she thought that they were destined to meet the Tribe?

As the she-cat spoke, another of the strangers came padding up to look at Stormfur with a gleam in his eyes. "Come on, Crag," he meowed to the first cat. "We should take this one to Stoneteller."

"What?" Brambleclaw stepped forward to confront Crag, while Stormfur tensed his muscles in readiness for a fight. "You're taking him nowhere without us. We want to talk to your leader." As Crag motioned the other cat back with an angry flick of his tail, the ThunderClan warrior relaxed slightly. "We only want to travel in peace," he went on. "My name is Brambleclaw of ThunderClan."

Crag bowed his head while stretching out one paw, an odd but polite gesture. "My name is Crag Where Eagles Nest," he announced.

"And I am Brook Where Small Fish Swim," the tabby she-cat added, stretching out a paw as Crag had done.

Crag gave her a disapproving look, as if he was not happy that she had put herself forward. His gaze flicked past Brambleclaw and rested again on Stormfur. "What is this one's name?"

"I'm Stormfur." He tried to push down the uncomfortable feeling that these cats' fascination gave him. "I come from RiverClan."

"Stormfur," Crag repeated.

"I'm Squirrelpaw." The tense moment was broken as the ThunderClan apprentice spoke up.

"And I'm Crowpaw."

"I'm Feathertail, and this is Tawnypelt." Stormfur's sister fixed anxious blue eyes on Crag. "Please, can you help her? Her shoulder is badly injured."

Brambleclaw glared at Feathertail with a hiss of disapproval; this was no time to be admitting weakness to strangers.

Instantly Crowpaw stepped forward. "She's right," he defended Feathertail. "This Clan might have a medicine cat who can help."

"Your words are strange to us," Crag responded. "But we will help. Come with us now and our leader will speak with you."

"Hang on," Crowpaw meowed. He was still shaky on his legs but he was obviously trying hard to sound fit to defend himself. "How far are we going?"

"Not far," meowed Brook.

Stormfur glanced at the watching cats around the edge of the pool. "What else can we do, except go with them?" he murmured to Brambleclaw. "We need to rest."

He said nothing of his own misgivings about Crag's penetrating gaze. After all, any cat would stare if he found six half-drowned strangers in his territory.

Brambleclaw nodded. "All right," he meowed to Crag. "We'll come."

"Good." Crag led the way along the edge of the pool, leaped up the first few rocks beside the waterfall, and then vanished behind the sheet of foaming water.

Stormfur stared in astonishment, half expecting the strange cat to come hurtling down into the pool again, knocked off his paws by the waterfall.

Then Brook stepped forward, gesturing with her tail. "This is the Path of the Rushing Water. Come—it is safe."

The rest of the cats had risen to their paws and gathered around them; Stormfur felt uneasy that he and his friends were being herded after Crag as if they were prisoners. But he had no choice but to follow the mud-covered cats and scramble up the rocks. It was a hard climb after their fall, especially for Tawnypelt, who was limping heavily. Halfway up, she stumbled and almost slipped back into the pool, until Brook darted forward to steady her.

The ShadowClan warrior flinched away from her. "I'm fine," she growled.

As Stormfur hauled himself up to where Crag had disappeared, he saw the Tribe cat waiting for him on a narrow ledge of rock leading behind the waterfall. A dark hole gaped at the end of it.

"I'm not going in there!" Squirrelpaw exclaimed.

"You'll be fine." Brambleclaw spoke reassuringly behind her.

"There is no danger," Crag meowed, padding confidently along the path and standing at the mouth of the hole.

Stormfur swallowed. They had to trust these cats—there was no way they could make it through the mountains without food and rest. "Come on."

Taking the lead, he edged along the path, pressing himself against the rock as far as possible from the sheet of thundering water. It was barely a tail-length away from him; spray misted his fur, and the rock underneath his paws was cold and slippery. Too tense to turn around, he could not be sure that the other cats were following him. He felt as if he were walking alone into endless, thundering darkness.

But the gaping hole led into a cave with steep rocky walls, stretching nearly to the top of the waterfall. Stormfur paused on the threshold, peering past Crag at soaring walls that ran with water. The scent of many more strange cats drifted out to him, hidden in the shadows around the edge of the cave.

"What's in there?" Feathertail murmured nervously, trying to peer inside. She was shivering, her pelt so sodden that it looked almost as dark as Crowpaw's.

Crowpaw brushed against her flank. "Whatever happens, we'll be there together," he murmured.

Stormfur suspected he was not supposed to hear that; he had to stop himself from spitting at Crowpaw or shooting an angry glare at his sister. There were far more pressing things to think about right now.

Crag waved his tail once again and padded into the cave, turning back to check that the others were behind him.

"I don't like this," Squirrelpaw muttered. "How do we know what we're going to find in there?"

"We don't," Brambleclaw replied. "But we've got to face it. Everything on this journey happens for a reason. We owe it to the Clans to see this through."

"We never thought it would be easy," Stormfur agreed, trying to shake off the deep sense of dread that overcame him at the thought of setting paw inside the cave.

"Well, if we have to do it, let's get on with it." Crowpaw pushed forward and led the way inside.

Stormfur followed, the other cats crowding behind him. As he gazed around he heard Tawnypelt mew quietly, as much to reassure herself as the rest of them, "StarClan will be with us, even here."

CHAPTER 8

"If a cat leaps at you, roll onto your back," Cinderpelt instructed. "Then you can attack his belly with your claws. Try it."

Leafpaw waited as her mentor crouched in front of her and then leaped into the air. Rolling over as Cinderpelt had told her, she dug her hind paws into the medicine cat's belly and flung her off to one side.

"Good," Cinderpelt meowed. She scrambled to her paws, awkward because of her injured leg. "That's enough for now."

The two cats had been training all morning in the sandy hollow, and though thick, gray clouds covered the sky Leafpaw's rumbling belly told her it must be close to sunhigh. She had enjoyed the session with her mentor. The exercise had been a good distraction from her worries about the Clan and the Twolegs, not to mention Squirrelpaw and the other cats who were traveling with her.

She followed Cinderpelt down into the ravine. Before they reached the entrance to the gorse tunnel, Leafpaw heard a patrol returning close behind them. Turning, she saw Firestar, Dustpelt, and Sorreltail. Firestar looked more worried than ever, while Dustpelt's brown tabby fur was bristling and his tail lashed furiously from side to side.

Cinderpelt limped over to meet Firestar, while Leafpaw hurried to Sorreltail's side. "What in StarClan's name is going on?"

"WindClan," Sorreltail mewed, with a glance at the older warriors. "They've been stealing prey from us."

Leafpaw remembered the thin, desperate cats who had chased them out of their territory, and knew that she was not surprised at the news.

"We found scraps of rabbit fur and bones by the stream near Fourtrees," Sorreltail went on. "They reeked of WindClan scent."

"It's because their rabbits have vanished," Leafpaw meowed. She pushed aside a guilty memory of how she had taken fish from RiverClan.

"It's still against the warrior code," Sorreltail pointed out. "Dustpelt was furious."

"So I see," meowed Leafpaw.

She followed her friend down the gorse tunnel to find Firestar and Dustpelt standing beside the fresh-kill pile. Her belly lurched when she saw how small it was.

"Look at it!" Dustpelt gestured with his tail. "How is that going to feed the Clan? You'll have to do something about WindClan, Firestar."

Firestar shook his head. "We all know that Tallstar wouldn't allow his warriors to steal prey unless his Clan was in real trouble."

"Tallstar might not know what's going on. Besides,

ThunderClan is in trouble too. It's not as if we have prey to spare."

"I know," Firestar sighed.

"I'm worried about Ferncloud," the brown warrior added. "She's already lost a lot of weight, and she still has three kits to feed."

"If this goes on, I'll have to start rationing," Firestar decided. "But meanwhile, we *will* do something about Wind-Clan, I promise."

Whirling around, he bounded across the clearing and leaped to the top of the Highrock. As he yowled out the summons, the rest of the Clan began to appear at once. Leafpaw was shocked to see how lean they were; she had never really noticed before the gradual change from day to day as prey got harder to find. But now they looked more like skinny WindClan cats than sturdy, forest-born ThunderClan warriors. Dustpelt was right that Ferncloud in particular looked gaunt and exhausted; her kits were thinner, too, and they trailed after their mother as if they had no energy left to play. Were all the Clans—apart from RiverClan—slowly going to starve?

Leafpaw listened anxiously as Firestar told the rest of the Clan what the patrol had discovered. Wails of indignation broke out at the news that WindClan cats had trespassed onto ThunderClan territory and stolen prey.

"WindClan needs to be taught a lesson!" Cloudtail called out. "I haven't had the sniff of a rabbit for days."

"We should attack now," Mousefur put in, her brown fur bristling.

"No," Firestar meowed firmly. "Things are bad enough without us looking for a battle."

Mousefur didn't argue, though she muttered something under her breath, and Cloudtail lashed his tail. Leafpaw saw Brightheart meow a few words to him, trying to calm him down.

"What are you going to do?" Speckletail called out from the entrance to the elders' den. "Go and ask them nicely not to steal our food? Do you think they'll take any notice?"

More voices were raised in protest, with more than one cat echoing Mousefur's demand to attack.

"No," Firestar repeated. "I'm going to talk to Tallstar. He's a noble, trustworthy cat; maybe he doesn't know that his warriors have been stealing prey."

"And what good will talking do?" Cloudtail snorted. "Blackstar didn't listen when you went to talk to *him*."

"If you ask me," Speckletail rasped, "you're crossing Clan boundaries far too often. The last cat to ignore borders like that was Tigerstar."

Leafpaw winced at the old she-cat's suggestion that their leader was anything like the murderous Tigerstar. She wasn't the only cat to be shocked. Several cats turned on Speckletail, hissing fiercely, but when Firestar replied, his voice was calm.

"Tigerstar wanted to satisfy his greed for power. All I want is to make peace. And as for Blackstar," he added to Cloudtail, "Tallstar has always been more reasonable."

"That's right." Graystripe supported his leader from where he sat at the base of the Highrock. "Remember when Bluestar wanted to fight WindClan? Tallstar was ready to make peace then."

"But there wasn't a shortage of prey back then," Thornclaw reminded him.

"Right." Mousefur's tail lashed again. "Some cats will do *anything* if their bellies are empty."

Leafpaw listened in dismay as yowls broke out around her, agreeing with Mousefur. She spotted her mother, Sandstorm, exchanging an anxious glance with Graystripe.

Firestar signaled with his tail for silence. "That's enough! My mind's made up. All the Clans are in trouble together now. This is no time to start fighting one another."

"Be careful, Firestar," Sorreltail warned him, as the yowls of protest died into discontented muttering. "You may go in peace, but the other clans might not see it that way." She glanced at Leafpaw, reminding her of their of their narrow escape from WindClan only a few days ago.

Firestar nodded. "WindClan will have to respect a patrol that looks strong enough to fight back," he meowed. "I'll make it clear to Tallstar that there'll be trouble if he can't control his warriors and keep them on their own side of the border. But we won't be looking for a fight. With StarClan's help we can avoid that."

Leafpaw's mind filled with images of the scarred moorland she had seen when she visited WindClan territory, and the desperation of the warriors who had chased her. Every hair on her pelt shrank from the idea of attacking WindClan and making their plight even worse.

"This is a bad time for all of us," she began hesitantly. "We should be trying to help one another. Why don't we all share the fish in the river? There are still plenty of those."

"That's for RiverClan to say, not us," Graystripe pointed out, while Ashfur added, "Fishing's too difficult."

"No, it's not," Leafpaw protested. "We can learn how."

She noticed that some of the other cats were giving her suspicious looks, as if they were wondering what she knew about fishing. Embarrassed, she scuffled her forepaws on the ground. "It was just an idea," she mumbled.

"But not one we can use," Firestar mewed decisively.

Anxious not to draw any more attention to herself, Leafpaw bowed her head, and sat looking at her paws while Firestar chose the cats who would make up the patrol going to WindClan.

"Graystripe, of course," he began. "Sandstorm, Dustpelt, Thornclaw. Ashfur. And you, Cinderpelt. Tallstar will listen to a medicine cat if he won't listen to me."

Leafpaw realized that he had not chosen any of the cats who had been arguing for an attack straight away, though he had included some formidable fighters. This patrol would not need to run!

She stayed where she was while the meeting broke up. With her eyes still fixed on the ground, she was aware of Firestar leaping from the Highrock and padding over to her.

"Well, Leafpaw," he began. When she lifted her head, she was relieved to see warm affection in her father's eyes, and felt even more ashamed of herself. "What's all this about fishing?"

Leafpaw knew she would have to tell the truth. "Mothwing taught me how," she explained. "She said it was okay, because we're both medicine cats. . . ."

"You are medicine cat *apprentices*," Firestar meowed. "And it sounds as if you both have a lot to learn. You know that it's against the warrior code to take prey from another Clan. Even medicine cats have to respect that."

"I know." Guilt swept over Leafpaw again, making her feel like a naughty kit. She just hoped that RiverClan had not found out what Mothwing had done, and punished her for her generosity. "I'm sorry."

"I shall have to punish you, you realize that?" Firestar went on. His tail-tip touched her shoulder gently as he added, "I can't have any cat saying I favor you because you're my daughter."

"Oh, come on, Firestar." Cinderpelt had limped up to join them, and was regarding her Clan leader with amusement in her blue eyes. "I remember a couple of cats who took ThunderClan prey across the river to RiverClan, when the Twolegs poisoned the fish. Surely you haven't forgotten?"

"No. And Graystripe and I were punished for it," Firestar retorted. Then he sighed. "Leafpaw, I know it's hard to see other cats hungry and do nothing about it. But the warrior code is what makes us what we are. If cats can break it when they feel like it, where does that leave us? Whatever is going to happen to the forest—whatever is happening now—we can't forget everything we believe in."

"I'm sorry, Firestar," Leafpaw repeated. She managed to stand up straight and look her father in the eye.

"Let her come with the patrol to WindClan," Cinderpelt meowed before Firestar could speak. "It'll be good experience for her."

Leafpaw looked hopefully at her Clan leader.

"Honestly, Cinderpelt." Firestar sounded exasperated. "There are cats who would say that's a *reward*, not a punishment. Oh, very well," he added. "We're leaving right away. I'll just go and get the others."

He touched Leafpaw's shoulder once more before padding away with his tail high.

"Thanks, Cinderpelt," Leafpaw meowed. "I know I was stupid. It's just that . . . well, when Mothwing said it, it sounded okay to take the fish."

Cinderpelt snorted. "Like Firestar said, you've both got a lot to learn."

"I don't know if I *ever* will!" Leafpaw burst out. "There are warrior rules, and medicine cat rules, and it's all so confusing!"

"It's not just about rules," Cinderpelt murmured sympathetically, touching her nose to Leafpaw's muzzle. "Your sympathy for other Clans, and your willingness to see that sometimes rules have to be ignored, will make you a great medicine cat in the end."

Leafpaw's eyes widened. "Really?"

"Really. 'Medicine cat' means nothing on its own, without an understanding of what should be done—which isn't always what you first think. Remember what I've told you about Yellowfang? She never followed the rules, but she was one of the best medicine cats the forest has ever seen."

"I wish I'd known her," Leafpaw murmured.

"So do I. But I can pass on to you what she taught me. To truly *be* a medicine cat lies in a cat's heart, and all its five senses. You must be braver than warriors, wiser than a Clan leader, humbler than the tiniest kit, more willing to learn than any apprentice. . . ."

Leafpaw gazed up at her mentor. "I'm not sure I can be all that," she whispered.

"Well, I *am* sure." Cinderpelt's voice was low and intense. "For we do not achieve this by ourselves, but by the strength of StarClan within us." Suddenly the intensity was gone and the humor back in Cinderpelt's eyes. She swatted Leafpaw lightly with her tail. "Come on. Firestar will never forgive us if we aren't ready for the patrol on top of everything else."

Sunhigh was long gone and a brisk wind was breaking up the clouds by the time Firestar led his patrol toward Fourtrees. Before they were very far from the camp Leafpaw could hear the roar of Twoleg monsters as they forced their way even farther into ThunderClan territory. In contrast, the usual forest sounds—the calling of birds, the rustle of prey in the undergrowth—were silent. Even though leaf-fall had well and truly arrived, Leafpaw knew there should be much more prey than this. The small creatures that the cats depended on for their survival were gone, frightened away by Twolegs or even killed as the monsters tore up their forest homes.

As they drew closer to Fourtrees the roar of the monsters died away, and Leafpaw could make out the faint scrabblings of prey among the bushes, but it was still much less than usual. She swallowed nervously as she imagined a harsh and hungry leaf-bare.

A yowl from Thornclaw jerked her out of her thoughts. "Look!"

There was a flash of movement in the thick undergrowth beside the stream. Two cats—a dark brown tom and a tabby—leaped across the stream and streaked up the slope toward Fourtrees. One of them had a small piece of prey, a vole or a mouse, in its jaws.

"WindClan cats!" Sandstorm meowed, her pale ginger fur bristling. "That was Mudclaw and Tornear, I'm sure of it."

Dustpelt and Ashfur sprang after the fleeing warriors, but Firestar called them back sharply. "We mustn't look as if we're attacking WindClan," he told them. "I'm coming in peace, not fury, to speak with Tallstar."

"You mean you're letting them go?" Ashfur asked disbelievingly. "With our fresh-kill in their mouths?"

"It's more proof that they're stealing prey," Firestar pointed out. "Tallstar won't be able to ignore what we have to tell him now."

"But they'll warn Tallstar," Dustpelt protested. "WindClan could ambush us before we get anywhere near their camp."

"No. Tallstar isn't like that. If he fights us, he'll do it in the open."

The two warriors exchanged doubtful glances before falling in behind Firestar. Leafpaw could see that Dustpelt was still smoldering with anger, but he expressed it with no more than an irritable twitch of his tail-tip.

The patrol crossed the stream, the water still churned and muddy from the WindClan warriors' paws, and climbed the slope to Fourtrees. Leafpaw's heart started beating uncomfortably as Firestar led them around the top of the hollow. Remembering her doomed visit with Sorreltail, she wondered whether they would be able to speak to Tallstar at all.

As they approached the border, the breeze carried a strong scent of cats toward them. Leafpaw looked out over the windblown grass to see a ragged group of WindClan warriors racing over the crest of the moorland. In the lead she recognized the Clan leader, Tallstar, by his black-and-white pelt and long tail. He must have spotted the ThunderClan patrol, for he slackened his pace and signaled with his tail. His warriors slowed to a walk and spread out to form a long line facing the ThunderClan cats.

"See?" Dustpelt hissed. "They're ready for us."

On an unspoken command, the WindClan cats stalked up to the border and halted a couple of tail-lengths from the ThunderClan patrol. They were even thinner than Leafpaw remembered, the sharp lines of their ribs plainly visible. Hostility burned in their eyes, and it was clear that not one of them wanted the ThunderClan visitors to set paw on their territory.

"Well, Firestar?" Tallstar growled. "What do you want with us this time?"

CHAPTER 9

❧

Stormfur stared in amazement. The cave was at least as broad as the waterfall that screened it from the outside world, and stretched far back into the mountainside, until the farthest recesses were lost in shadow. He could just make out a narrow passage leading off on either side of the wall opposite the sheet of water. The roof, far above his head, was shadowed too; here and there, stones like fangs emerged to point straight down at the cave floor.

The only light came through the rushing water, pale and wavering, so that it was like standing in the depths of a pool. As the cats ushered them farther into the cave, Stormfur heard more running water beneath the roar of the falls, and saw a stream trickling over a mossy rock to fall into a shallow pool on the floor of the cave. Two or three cats—a skinny elder and a couple who looked young enough to be apprentices—were crouched beside it to drink. All of them looked up warily at the arrival of the newcomers, as if they were expecting danger.

Just beyond the pool was a pile of fresh-kill and, as Stormfur watched, a couple more of the mountain cats came in and deposited prey. It was the first thing he had seen that looked at all familiar, and his belly growled with hunger at the sight of the rabbits.

"Do you think they'll let us eat?" Squirrelpaw muttered close to his ear. "I'm starving!"

"For all you know, they think *we're* fresh-kill," Crowpaw hissed from Squirrelpaw's other side.

"They haven't done anything to harm us yet," Brambleclaw pointed out.

Stormfur tried to share his optimism, but Crag and Brook had vanished, and for a few moments none of the other cats came up to speak to them. Instead, the cats who had been drinking sidled over to their guards, and the elder whispered something, all the while darting glances at him. The two apprentices murmured excitedly to each other. The roar of the waterfall drowned their voices, though Stormfur noticed that the mountain cats seemed to have no trouble hearing one another.

Trying to ignore the muttering—most of which seemed to be directed at him, though he told himself to stop being so paranoid—Stormfur identified what looked like sleeping places beside the cave walls: shallow scoops in the earth floor, lined with moss and feathers. One cluster of sleeping places lay close to the entrance and the other two were farther back, at opposite sides of the cave. He wondered if one set was for warriors, one for apprentices, and one for elders. Spotting a couple of kits scuffling outside the entrance to one of the passages, he guessed that led to the nursery. Suddenly he saw the dark, noisy, frightening cave in a different way: This was a camp! The Tribe shared some of the ways of the Clans in the forest; Stormfur began to feel much more hopeful of getting food and rest, and help for Tawnypelt, who had sunk shivering to the floor.

Then he spotted Crag again, emerging from the far passage and padding across the cave floor toward the tight group of forest cats. He was followed by another cat, long-bodied and skinny as a WindClan warrior. So much mud plastered his fur that Stormfur couldn't make out what color it was underneath, but his eyes were a deep and glowing green, and a few white hairs around his muzzle betrayed the fact that he was older than the cats they had seen so far.

"Greetings," he meowed in a deep voice that seemed to echo around the cave. He made the odd gesture with one paw extended that Crag and Brook had used outside. "My name is Teller of the Pointed Stones, though you will find it easier to call me Stoneteller. I am the Healer of the Tribe of Rushing Water."

"Healer?" Brambleclaw glanced uncertainly at his friends. "Do you mean the medicine cat? Where is the leader of your Clan—I mean, Tribe?"

Stoneteller hesitated for a moment. "I am not sure what you mean by a medicine cat, and there is no other leader of this Tribe. I interpret the signs of rock and leaf and water, and that shows me what the Tribe should do—with the help of the Tribe of Endless Hunting."

Stormfur picked out the bit of Stoneteller's speech that he

understood. "Then he's medicine cat *and* leader," he muttered to Brambleclaw. "That's pretty powerful!"

In reply, Brambleclaw dipped his head politely. "We come from a forest a long way from here," he began, repeating his own name and the names of his friends. "We have a difficult journey ahead of us, and we need food and shelter before we can go on."

More of the Tribe cats crowded around as he spoke, openly curious. Stormfur picked out kits and apprentices by their sizes, and noticed that the warriors seemed to divide into two groups, one with massive shoulders and powerful muscles, the other more slender, with wiry strength and long limbs for speed. He noticed too how anxious they all looked; they seemed to be on edge, as if they were poised to flee.

A brown tabby she-cat, her eyes fixed on Stormfur, murmured, "Yes! This is the one—it must be!"

Stormfur started. Brook had said something similar, when they first met beside the pool. He opened his mouth to ask what she meant, but the Tribe's Healer had turned to the young brown tabby. "Be silent!" he hissed. More smoothly he went on to the Clan cats, "You are welcome to our cave. Here is caught-prey in plenty." He flicked his tail toward the fresh-kill pile. "Eat your fill, and rest. We have much to say to one another."

Brambleclaw looked at the other Clan cats. "We might as well eat," he meowed quietly. "I don't think they're going to hurt us now."

As Stormfur followed him toward the pile, he felt once

more dozens of eyes burning into his fur. It wasn't his imagination—they were definitely watching him more closely than the others. His fur prickled from nose to tail-tip as he settled down to eat.

As he bit into the rabbit he had chosen, he heard a gasp from somewhere behind him and a shocked voice whispering, "They don't share!"

Glancing up, he saw a young gray cat giving him a hostile stare, while an older tabby bent her head to him and murmured, "Shh. It's not their fault if they haven't been properly taught."

Stormfur didn't know what they meant. Then he spotted two of the Tribe cats who were eating side by side; each of them took a bite from the piece of fresh-kill they had taken, then exchanged pieces before they settled down to finish it off. Embarrassment flooded over him as he realized how rude he and his friends must look to the cats of the Tribe.

"We don't do that," he meowed directly to the young cat who had spoken at first. "But we *do* share." He flicked his tail toward Feathertail, who was gently coaxing Tawnypelt to eat a mouse. "None of us would let our friends go hungry, and the hunting patrols always feed the Clan before taking food for themselves."

The gray cat backed away a pace or two, looking confused, as if he hadn't intended the newcomers to hear his comments. The tabby dipped her head with a friendlier look. "Your ways are strange to us," she meowed. "Perhaps we can learn from one another."

"Perhaps," Stormfur agreed.

He began gulping down his rabbit again. After a few moments one of the bolder kits pattered right up to the group of Clan cats, urged on by his littermates. "Where do you come from?" he asked.

"A long way away," Squirrelpaw mumbled with her mouth full. Swallowing the bite of prey she added more clearly, "Across these mountains and lots of fields and then a forest."

The kit blinked. "What are fields?" Before Squirrelpaw could reply, he added, "I'm going to be a cave-guard."

"That's nice," Feathertail mewed.

"'Course, I've got to be a to-be first."

"Tooby? What's a tooby?" asked Crowpaw.

Stormfur hid his amusement at the scornful look the kit gave the WindClan apprentice. "To-be a cave-guard, of course. You know, training and stuff. Don't you new cats know *anything?*"

"He means an apprentice," Stormfur explained, and couldn't resist adding, "Like you."

Crowpaw curled his lip as the kit stared at him and exclaimed, "You're only a to-be? You're *way* old!"

"It sounds as if they have some of the same traditions as us," Tawnypelt murmured.

"I wonder if they believe in StarClan?" Squirrelpaw whispered.

"It's too far for them to go to Mothermouth," meowed Stormfur, "and no cat has ever seen them there."

"Stoneteller mentioned the Tribe of Endless Hunting,"

Feathertail remembered. "Perhaps that's what they call StarClan." Her blue eyes stretched wide and her voice was uneasy as she added, "Or do you think they have different warrior ancestors?"

"I don't know," Brambleclaw replied. "But I guess we'll find out."

When he finished eating, Stormfur had not felt so comfortably full since they left the woods where they said goodbye to Midnight and Purdy. He would have liked to sleep, but as he swallowed the last mouthful and swiped his tongue around his jaws he spotted Stoneteller making his way toward them with three other cats. One of them was Crag; the others were she-cats, though neither of them was Brook. Stormfur felt faintly disappointed. The young she-cat had shown courage and friendliness when they first met, and he had looked forward to seeing her again.

"You have eaten well?" Stoneteller asked as he approached.

"Very well, thanks," Brambleclaw replied. "It's good of you to share prey with us."

"Why wouldn't we?" Stoneteller sounded surprised. "The prey is not ours—it belongs to the stones and the mountain."

He sat down in front of the forest cats, wrapping his tail neatly around his paws. The other three cats gathered around him, but remained standing. Brambleclaw looked expectantly at them.

"Crag you already know," meowed Stoneteller, introducing his companions. "He is the leader of our cave-guards, the cats who protect this place," he added, when the Clan cats looked confused. "This"—he flicked his tail toward the younger of the two she-cats—"is Mist Where Sunlight Shimmers. She is one of our best prey-hunters."

Mist dipped her head and blinked with friendly interest at the forest cats.

"And this," Stoneteller went on, indicating the other she-cat, "is Star That Shines on Water. For now she is a kit-mother, though when her kits are grown she will go back to being a cave-guard."

"You all have different duties, then?" Tawnypelt questioned, as the other forest cats murmured greetings.

"We do," Stoneteller replied.

"Do you choose the best fighters to be cave-guards, and the fastest cats to be prey-hunters?" Stormfur asked, fascinated in spite of his wariness.

Stoneteller twitched his whiskers in disagreement. "No. All the cats in our Tribe are born to their duties. That is our way. But tell us something more of yourselves," he went on, interrupting Squirrelpaw as she was about to ask another question. "Why are you making this long journey? We have never seen cats like you before."

Brambleclaw gave Stormfur a sideways glance and muttered, "What do you think? Do we tell them?"

"I think we have to tell them we were sent by StarClan." Stormfur breathed his reply close to the tabby warrior's ear, aware of how acute the mountain cats' hearing was. "Otherwise they might think we're outlaws. But don't tell them why we had to make the journey in the first place," he added. "We don't want to sound weak."

Brambleclaw nodded. Clearing his throat self-consciously he began to explain about the dreams each of the four chosen cats had received from StarClan, and the saltwater signs that had led them to the sun-drown place where they had met Midnight.

More of the Tribe cats gathered warily around to listen. Stormfur spotted admiring glances from them as Brambleclaw spoke of the dangers they had faced, but there were a few suspicious mutterings too, as if some of them found it hard to trust the strangers.

"Don't worry," he put in, when Brambleclaw paused in his story. "StarClan hasn't sent us to fight you. They didn't say anything about meeting you, in fact."

"StarClan?" Mist echoed, glancing at Stoneteller in bewilderment. "What is StarClan?"

Stormfur heard Tawnypelt stifle an exclamation of surprise. Feathertail was right after all; these cats were not guided by StarClan. His fur prickled as he suppressed a shiver at the thought that perhaps StarClan was not watching over him and his friends in this strange place.

"Do not be troubled," Stoneteller meowed, touching Mist's shoulder with the tip of his tail in a reassuring gesture. "Not all cats believe as we do, and we must respect that which we do not know. Ignorance is nothing to be afraid of. Please"—he gestured toward Brambleclaw with one paw—"continue."

"So at last we came to the sun-drown water and discovered

that Midnight is a badger," Brambleclaw explained. "She told us the meaning of StarClan's prophecy, and now we're going home to tell our Clans."

"A prophecy?" Stoneteller meowed. His green gaze was fixed on Stormfur in a stare of eerie intensity. "Then you too have visions of what is hidden?"

"Well, sometimes we have dreams," Tawnypelt explained. "But mostly our medicine cats interpret signs for us—clouds, the flight of birds, the fall of leaves. . . ."

"This I do also," Stoneteller mewed.

He broke off as a group of cats appeared in the cave entrance. Rising to his paws, he murmured, "Forgive me. These are cave-guards, returning from patrol. I must hear what they have to tell me." Dipping his head, he walked off to meet the leader of the group.

Mist and Star stayed with the forest cats. Stormfur was struck again by how anxious the Tribe cats looked, and he realized that so far he had not seen any of them enjoying themselves: no apprentices play-fighting, no warriors sharing tongues, or elders gathering to exchange gossip and stories. The whole Tribe seemed to live in an atmosphere of suppressed fear.

"Are you okay?" Tawnypelt meowed to Mist, echoing Stormfur's thoughts. "You look worried. Is something wrong?"

"Are you being attacked by another Tribe?" Squirrelpaw added.

"No, there are no cats to attack us," Star replied. "There are no others in the mountains that we know of. How could there be another Tribe when we guard the Cave of the Pointed Stones?"

"What's that?" meowed Crowpaw.

His question was ignored.

Mist exchanged a swift glance with Star and murmured, "Should we tell them?" Stormfur barely caught the words and realized that he had not been meant to hear.

A hiss came from one of the Tribe cats who had crept closer to listen to the conversation. More than one of them looked scared or angry with Mist.

"What are you afraid of?" Stormfur persisted, his fur beginning to prickle with dread of the unknown.

"Nothing," Star replied. "Or nothing we may speak of." Rising to her paws, she dipped her head and began to walk away, gesturing with her tail for Mist to follow her. Mist gave the forest cats a backward glance, her eyes filled with fear, before she vanished into the shadows at the back of the cave. The other cats too began to creep away.

Mystified, Stormfur turned to Brambleclaw, and saw his own apprehension reflected in the ThunderClan cat's amber eyes. "What was all that about?" he muttered.

Brambleclaw shook his head. "StarClan knows. But whatever it is, it's obvious that something is frightening them. I wonder why they don't want to tell us what it is."

CHAPTER 10

Leafpaw gazed along the line of hostile WindClan cats, and locked eyes with a bracken-colored apprentice. The young cat drew its lips back in a snarl; Leafpaw's fur prickled. She was a medicine cat and supposed to be outside normal Clan rivalries. But she found her claws instinctively flexing into the soft moorland grass; if it came to a fight, that apprentice would soon discover that she was not lacking in warrior skills.

"Well?" When Firestar did not immediately answer his question, Tallstar repeated it. "Why have you come? Do you think we're so weak that you can drive us out as Brokenstar did?"

Defiant yowls and hisses broke out from the warriors behind him, and it was a moment before Firestar could make himself heard.

"Tallstar, you have known nothing but friendship from me since the time that Graystripe and I found you and brought you home," he replied. "Have you forgotten that? I think you must have, or you wouldn't accuse me of being like Brokenstar."

Leafpaw thought she detected a flash of guilt in the older

cat's eyes, but there was still a challenge in his voice as he meowed, "Then why have you come here with so many warriors?"

"Don't be absurd, Tallstar," Firestar growled. "I haven't enough warriors to take on your whole Clan. We want to talk to you, that's all. WindClan have been stealing prey from ThunderClan territory, and you know as well as I do that that's against the warrior code."

Tallstar looked taken aback, as if he genuinely hadn't known what his warriors were up to. Before he could reply, his deputy Mudclaw called out, "Prove it! Prove that WindClan has stolen so much as a sniff of prey!"

"*What?*" Leafpaw saw Graystripe's whole body stiffen. "We saw you ourselves just now! And we found prey bones reeking of WindClan scent."

"So you say," Mudclaw sneered. "If you ask me, it's just an excuse to attack us."

Furious, Graystripe launched himself across the border, his claws reaching out as he bowled over the WindClan deputy. Mudclaw let out a screech and the two cats rolled on the short moorland grass.

Tallstar gazed down at the two battling warriors with a look of contempt, as if he had found maggots in his fresh-kill. Warriors on both sides were poised to spring, their teeth bared and the light of battle in their eyes. Leafpaw's heart beat faster as she tried to remember the fighting moves her mentor had taught her.

Firestar stepped forward with a fierce hiss. "Stop!"

At once Graystripe broke away from Mudclaw's raking claws and stood back, breathing heavily. Mudclaw scrambled to his paws and glared at him.

"Graystripe, I told you we were not here to fight," Firestar meowed.

The deputy's yellow eyes were smoldering. "But did you hear the lies he told?"

"Yes. But that doesn't change my orders. Get back onto our side of the border. Now."

His tail twitching angrily, Graystripe obeyed. Leafpaw understood how he must feel, especially when he was still worrying about his missing children, but she could also guess how uncomfortable it must be for Firestar when his friend and deputy disobeyed a direct order, and in full view of WindClan. She stifled a sigh. Was this part of being a medicine cat, to understand every cat so clearly and want to sympathize with them all?

Cinderpelt limped forward to stand beside Firestar. "You know that medicine cats do not lie," she meowed to Tallstar. "You know, too, that it is not the will of StarClan for warriors to trespass on the territory of other Clans and steal their prey."

"And is it the will of StarClan for my Clan to starve?" Tallstar asked bitterly. "Yesterday one of our elders died, and he will be the first of many if we don't do something."

"If we could help you, we would," Cinderpelt replied with feeling. "But ThunderClan is short of prey too. The whole forest is suffering because of the Twolegs."

"We should work together," Firestar added. "I swear to you by StarClan that if ThunderClan finds an answer to these problems, we will share it with WindClan."

Tallstar met his gaze with a long, thoughtful look, his bitterness dying away and leaving deep sorrow behind it. "An answer? Firestar, I don't think that even you can find an answer to our troubles. Unless you let us hunt on your territory." Even while he was speaking, he shook his head, to show Firestar he did not make that suggestion seriously. "No, you are right to keep your own prey. The warrior code demands that you feed your own Clan first. WindClan does not look to you for help."

Firestar dipped his head to the WindClan leader. "Tallstar, we promise you that ThunderClan has not lied to you. There will be no fighting now, but if the prey-stealing doesn't stop, you know what to expect."

He turned and walked away, gesturing with his tail for his warriors to follow him. As they withdrew, yowls of derision rose from the WindClan warriors, as if they had fought a battle and driven invaders away from their territory.

Leafpaw felt her neck fur rise, half expecting the rival Clan to pursue them like the warriors had pursued her and Sorreltail a few days before. But the sounds died away behind them as Firestar led the way around the top of the hollow at Fourtrees and down the slope toward the stream.

"Why didn't we fight it out?" Dustpelt demanded. "We could have taught them a lesson that they wouldn't forget in a hurry!"

"I know," Firestar sighed. "But as I said before, the Clans cannot afford to turn on one another."

"And when our patrols catch WindClan stealing prey again?" Dustpelt's tail twitched; he was short-tempered at the best of times, and Leafpaw knew how anxious he was about Ferncloud and their kits.

"We'll see them off if we catch them trespassing," Firestar promised. "But let's pray to StarClan that Tallstar sees sense and keeps his warriors on their own territory. I don't think he knew what was going on until today."

"Maybe not. But he'll back his own warriors now." Dustpelt paused, his brown tabby fur bristling as if he could see his enemy in front of him.

"Why don't you go and hunt for a bit?" Firestar suggested. "See if you can find a bit of fresh-kill for Ferncloud."

Dustpelt glanced at him, his neck fur beginning to relax. "Okay, I will." In a reluctant growl he added, "Thanks." Swiftly he turned and disappeared into the thicker vegetation beside the stream.

Firestar watched him go, his expression full of sorrow. Leafpaw could hardly bear to see his frustration and hope-lessness. She knew he would never give up, not before the monsters had destroyed every last tree in the forest. But it looked like the time when that might happen was drawing near, and what would Firestar do then?

As she followed him across the stream toward the ThunderClan camp, she struggled yet again with the guilt she felt about not telling her father what she knew about

Squirrelpaw and Brambleclaw. Perhaps now was the time to speak up, to relieve some of his anxieties about them, and to assure him that StarClan knew about the suffering in the forest and had their own plan to relieve it. But what would Firestar say to her, when she had kept silent for so long? Leafpaw shrank at the thought of his anger.

Seeing that Cinderpelt had dropped a little way behind the other cats, she wondered if her mentor might have the answer. She could tell Cinderpelt; the medicine cat would understand, and perhaps help her to pass the news on to Firestar.

Leafpaw waited for her mentor to catch up to her. "Cinderpelt . . ." she began, anticipating the medicine cat's usual sensible, no-nonsense advice.

But when Cinderpelt turned to her, her blue eyes were clouded with pain. "I've heard nothing from StarClan," she mewed without giving Leafpaw the chance to speak first. "Have they abandoned us? It *can't* be their will for the Twolegs to destroy us all."

As if to emphasize her desperation, the roar of the Twoleg monsters thundered in the distance. Though she couldn't see them from here, Leafpaw could picture all too clearly the garish, glittering pelts and the vast black paws that tore up the forest as easily as Dustpelt's claws had torn the grass moments before.

She brushed comfortingly against her mentor. "Suppose StarClan spoke to us in another way?" she suggested, feeling her heart begin to pound. The whole forest was turned upside down, if apprentices knew about prophecies that had not been sent to older cats.

"What other way? They haven't sent me a single dream or a sign."

"They might have sent it to another cat."

"To you?" Cinderpelt rounded on Leafpaw with her blue eyes blazing. "Have they?"

"No, but—"

"No, StarClan are silent." Cinderpelt's brief flash of energy vanished and her tail drooped. "They must want something from us, but what?"

Leafpaw found it impossible to go on. Perhaps this wasn't the right time to speak after all. How would Cinderpelt feel if she found out that StarClan had chosen to speak to inexperienced warriors, and send them on the journey instead of the medicine cats? She felt so lonely and confused that she instinctively tried to reach out to Squirrelpaw and share her sister's thoughts. But she found no comfort there. All she could sense was darkness, and the noise of rushing water.

"Leafpaw! Are you coming?"

With a jump, Leafpaw realized that Cinderpelt was several tail-lengths ahead of her.

"Sorry!" she called back, and plodded on at the rear of the patrol, her head bowed down by her fears for StarClan's chosen cats and for all the forest. And, most of all, for Squirrelpaw—wherever she was.

CHAPTER 11

❧

Moonlight shone into the cave, turning the waterfall into a sheet of rippling silver. Stormfur felt as though the day had lasted for a moon, and now even the shallow, sandy dips in the cave floor were looking as comfortable as his nest among the reeds back home.

Stoneteller had returned and shown the forest cats to sleeping hollows at the side of the main cave, their curved sides lined with a sparse layer of moss and feathers. "You may rest here," he meowed. "Stay many days—for as long as you want. You are all welcome."

Once he had gone, Brambleclaw beckoned with his tail for all his friends to gather around. "We need to talk," he mewed. "How long do you think we should stay here?"

Crowpaw's tail lashed from side to side. "I don't know how you can ask that!" he rasped. "I thought we were on a mission. What about taking Midnight's news to the forest?"

"Crowpaw's right," Stormfur meowed, stifling a brief stab of annoyance that he had to agree with the WindClan apprentice. "I think we should leave right away."

"Me too," mewed Tawnypelt. "Leaf-bare's coming, and

there'll be snow up here."

"But what about your shoulder?" Brambleclaw reminded her. Since their plunge over the waterfall, she'd been limping on three legs, and a trickle of dried blood ran down her shoulder, seeping between her claws. "We've got to stay until the rat bite is better. We'd all get on faster after that."

Tawnypelt's neck fur bristled. "I knocked it again, that's all. If you think I'm holding you back," she spat, "then just come out and say so."

"Brambleclaw didn't mean that." Feathertail brushed her side comfortingly against Tawnypelt's flank, taking care to avoid the injury. "That's more than just a knock. It looks like you've done as much damage as before, and it won't heal if you don't rest."

Squirrelpaw looked thoughtful. "It sounded as if the Tribe cats don't think we should leave at all. What are they all so frightened of? Are we going to meet more danger farther on?"

The other cats looked uneasily at one another. Stormfur admitted to himself that the thought had crossed his mind too. Part of him wanted to stay safely in the cave for as long as they could, if the alternative was unknown terror among the rocks and precipices of the mountains.

"It'll be risky whenever we leave," Crowpaw pointed out. "Okay, I agree about Tawnypelt, but let's get Stoneteller to fix her shoulder, and then go."

"That's all very well," Squirrelpaw broke in, her green eyes sparkling in the moonlight. "But we're all assuming we can leave whenever we want."

"What do you mean? They wouldn't dare stop us!" Crowpaw exclaimed.

Squirrelpaw snorted. "I'll bet you my next piece of freshkill that they *would*. Look over there."

She flicked her ears toward the cave entrance. A caveguard was seated on either side, making no secret of the fact that they were keeping an eye on the newcomers.

"Perhaps they're guarding the cave from enemies outside," Feathertail meowed.

"We could always try leaving," Crowpaw suggested, the tip of his gray-black tail twitching. "Then we'd see what happened."

"No." Brambleclaw's voice was firm. "It would be mousebrained to leave right now. We're all tired out, and we need to sleep. Tomorrow we'll see how Tawnypelt's shoulder is, and figure out when we can leave."

There was a murmur of agreement. Not even Crowpaw wanted more trouble just then, and it was not long before the forest cats were settling into their sleeping hollows, huddled together against the curious stares that darted at them from all around the cave.

As Stormfur prodded his bedding into place, he heard a pawstep behind him, and turned to see one of the mountain cats padding across the cave toward him. Warm recognition swept through his pelt as he recognized Brook by her soft tabby fur and lithe walk. She carried a wad of feathers in her jaws.

Dropping them in the sleeping hollow Stormfur had chosen,

she dipped her head to him. "Stoneteller sent me to make sure you're comfortable."

"Er, thanks," Stormfur replied. Did Brook mean that Stoneteller had sent her to all the cats, or to him in particular? She showed no signs of going to fetch more feathers for the rest of them. True, Stormfur still felt battered from the fall into the pool, but so did all his friends. He was not their leader either, who would get special treatment.

"I . . . I hope you'll be happy here," Brook went on hesitantly. "This must be very different from what you're used to. Do you have caves for sleeping in your forest?"

"No, we sleep in nests of reeds and bushes. RiverClan's camp—that's my Clan—is on an island." A pang of home-sickness stabbed Stormfur as he spoke, and he wondered if he would ever again lie curled up in the warriors' den, listening to the soft sighing of the wind in the reeds. If Midnight was right, and all the Clans had to leave the forest, he might never find another home that was so peaceful.

Brook's eyes shone in the moonlight. "Are you a cave-guard or—" She broke off, scuffling her paws in embarrassment. "No, of course not, if you have no caves there will be no cave-guards. Do you guard your camp, or are you a prey-hunter?"

"Our Clans don't work like that," Stormfur told her. "We all guard and hunt and patrol."

"That must be hard," Brook meowed. "We are born to our duties, so we know exactly what we have to do. I am a prey-hunter," she added. "If Stoneteller allows it, perhaps you would like to hunt with me tomorrow?"

Stormfur swallowed. It sounded as if Brook assumed that the forest cats would be staying for a while. He was not sure either that he liked the idea of asking Stoneteller's permission for everything; they would respect the Tribe's leader while they stayed in his territory, but he had no right to give them orders. All the same, it would be fun to hunt with Brook.

He wondered whether to ask her outright if they were prisoners, but before he could speak, the pretty young tabby dipped her head in farewell. "You're tired; I'll leave you alone now," she mewed. "Sleep well. I hope we will hunt together soon."

Stormfur said good-bye to her and watched her retreat across the cave before he settled into the feathers. All around him were the soft murmurs of his sleeping friends. But although his muscles ached and his head spun with exhaustion, it was some time before sleep claimed him as well.

The sound of pawsteps padding past his sleeping hollow woke Stormfur the next morning; he opened his eyes to see sunlight spilling through the cascade of water and into the cave. It reminded him of how they should be following the rising sun back to the forest, and he scrambled out of his hollow, shaking off a feather that clung to his pelt.

Brambleclaw was already up, standing a few tail-lengths away and watching a patrol of cave-guards leaving through the main entrance. Their quiet sense of purpose reminded

Stormfur of the patrols at home. He padded over to Brambleclaw, who twitched his whiskers in greeting.

"Tawnypelt's shoulder started bleeding in the night. I think the muscles have torn open again," the ThunderClan warrior meowed. "I told her to get some more sleep, but it means we'll have to stay here for a day or two at least."

Stormfur glanced back to where he could see the smooth curve of Tawnypelt's tortoiseshell fur as she lay curled in her sleeping hollow. Feathertail was anxiously bending over her, examining her injured shoulder, while Crowpaw looked on. Squirrelpaw was still sleeping.

The sight of his sister so close to the WindClan apprentice did nothing to improve Stormfur's temper. "Well, if we must, we must," he muttered. "But sooner or later we'll have to find out why these Tribe cats have been quite so welcoming. We know there's something they're not telling us."

"True." Brambleclaw was calm, his amber eyes meeting Stonefur's in a level stare. "But we'll learn more if we cooperate with them—to begin with, anyway."

"You could be right," Stormfur grunted.

Movement at the back of the cave caught his eye, and he spotted Stoneteller emerging from one of the tunnels and heading toward them. Crowpaw and Feathertail spotted him too; Crowpaw prodded Squirrelpaw to wake her, and all three cats came bounding over to Stormfur and Brambleclaw.

Tawnypelt raised her head as Feathertail moved away. "Are we leaving?" she meowed; Stormfur could hear the pain grating in her voice. "I can go on if I have to."

Feathertail glanced back at her. "No, we're not going anywhere yet. Try to get some sleep."

"Are you going to ask Stoneteller to let us out of here?" Crowpaw hissed to Brambleclaw. "If he thinks he can keep us prisoner, I'll claw his ears off!"

"No, you won't," Brambleclaw said swiftly. "You know very well Tawnypelt needs to rest until that rat bite is better. Besides, the last thing we want to do is offend any of these cats. Let me do the talking."

Crowpaw shot the tabby warrior a glare, but said nothing more.

"I'm sure we're not prisoners." Stormfur spoke more confidently than he felt, trying to convince himself that he had imagined the eerie interest the Tribe cats took in him. "Why should we be? We've done them no harm."

"Maybe we have something they want," Squirrelpaw suggested.

That idea was so close to what Stormfur himself had been thinking that he found nothing to say in reply. Besides, Stoneteller was approaching; there was no more chance to talk among themselves.

"Good morning," the Healer meowed. "Have you slept well?"

"Very well, thank you," Brambleclaw replied. "But Tawnypelt's shoulder is badly hurt, so we'd like to stay for a day or two until she's better, if that's all right with you."

"Good." Stoneteller's head swiveled toward Stormfur as he spoke, and the glow in his green eyes made Stormfur even more apprehensive. "I will look at your friend's shoulder, and find some herbs to heal her."

"The rest of us would like to go hunting," Brambleclaw continued. "We need to stretch our legs, and we'd like to catch our own prey. You can't go on feeding six of us while we sit around doing nothing."

Stoneteller's ears pricked forward, and his eyes narrowed. Stormfur got the idea that he was not pleased by Brambleclaw's request.

However, the Healer scarcely hesitated. "Of course," he meowed. "We will be glad for your help. Some prey-hunters are about to leave, so you can go with them."

As he spoke, Stormfur saw several of the Tribe cats gathering beside the cave entrance; Brook was among them, and Mist, the prey-hunter they had met the day before. Stoneteller led the Clan cats over to them.

"Our new friends want to go hunting," he announced. "Take them with you, and teach them the way we hunt."

The order given, he padded away again. Stormfur glanced after him, slightly stung that he thought Clan warriors would need to be taught how to hunt. Then he realized that Brook was beside him again.

"Greetings," she mewed. "There are so many of us, we'd better split into two groups. Will you hunt with me?"

"Yes, I'd like that," Stormfur replied, slightly surprised at how pleased he felt that Brook had remembered her invitation of the previous night.

Quickly the Tribe cats divided into two groups. One of

them, with Mist in the lead, took Crowpaw and Feathertail, while Stormfur joined Brook's group, along with Brambleclaw and Squirrelpaw.

Tawnypelt watched them go with a brief flash of fear in her eyes, but as Stormfur left the cave, he spotted the kit-mother Star padding over to her with a piece of fresh-kill.

"She'll be fine," Brambleclaw murmured. "With any luck, she'll sleep until we get back. It doesn't look like the Tribe cats mean her any harm."

Seeing the friendliness with which Star spoke to Tawnypelt, Stormfur realized that the tabby warrior was right. He stepped cautiously along the ledge behind the waterfall, shivering as the spray soaked into his fur, and out onto the rocks beside the pool.

As he shook off most of the moisture, he noticed that Crag and a number of other cats were already waiting, their fur streaked with fresh mud. They were strong cats with massive shoulders, unlike the lithe prey-hunters. Stormfur guessed they were all cave-guards.

Catching Brambleclaw's eye, he muttered, "What are they doing here?"

Brook heard his low-voiced comment. "We take cave-guards with us on our hunts," she explained. "We need them to watch for eagles, and—"

She broke off with a nervous glance at Stormfur, who wondered what she had been about to say. Still, he felt relieved at her explanation. The thought had crossed his mind that the cave-guards might be there to keep an eye on him and his friends, and make sure that they did not try to escape. Of course, they would never leave Tawnypelt, but Stoneteller didn't know that.

When Brook had explained to Crag that the visitors were joining them for the hunt, the cave-guards joined the two groups. One of them, with Crowpaw and Feathertail, began to climb the rocks where Stormfur and the others had fallen the day before, while Brook led Stormfur's group farther down into the valley.

The ground here was hard earth, where a few scanty clumps of grass poked up among broken rocks. A few bushes straggled here and there beneath the steep rock walls. Though the rain had stopped, the boulders gleamed wet in the morning light. The prospects for prey looked meager to Stormfur's eyes, and he wondered how the Tribe cats had managed to find the fresh-kill they had shared so generously. He tasted the air, and picked up only the faintest traces of prey-scent.

Brook led her group along one side of the valley, in the shadow of the bushes. Now Stormfur could see why they streaked their pelts with mud; it made them blend into the rock so that when they were still it was hard to see them at all. In contrast Squirrelpaw's dark ginger fur looked like a splash of blood, though Stormfur's gray pelt and Brambleclaw's dark tabby were inconspicuous enough. All the Tribe cats moved silently; Stormfur had to concentrate to make sure his paw-steps were just as quiet.

Before long he saw Squirrelpaw halt, her ears flicking up in excitement. "Look—a mouse!" she whispered.

Stormfur spotted it too, nibbling on a grass-seed a few tail-lengths ahead. Squirrelpaw dropped into the hunter's crouch, but instantly Brook swung her tail in front of her, barring her way. Her jaws formed the word, "Wait."

Stormfur expected Squirrelpaw to make an indignant protest, but the ThunderClan apprentice obviously figured that if she did she would frighten the prey. She glared at Brook instead, but the young she-cat didn't notice. Her eyes were fixed on the mouse.

A shadow flicked over Stormfur. A heartbeat later a falcon swooped down from the sky and gripped the mouse in its powerful talons. At the same moment Brook launched herself forward. She sprang onto the bird's back, sinking her claws into its shoulders. Its wings beat furiously; for a couple of heartbeats it lifted Brook off the ground, only to fall back under her weight. A second prey-hunter ran up, and helped Brook finish the falcon off. Its wings stopped beating and it lay limp on the rocky ground.

"And we get the mouse too," Crag pointed out to Stormfur, swiping his tongue around his jaws.

Stormfur's eyes stretched wide with admiration at Brook's hunting skills. What a warrior she would make, if she'd been forest-born! Briefly he imagined her in RiverClan, teaching them this new way of hunting, but he banished the picture almost at once. Brook belonged here in the mountains, and within the next day or two he would have to part from her. He felt a strange stab of regret at the thought and was surprised. How could he already feel attached to a cat he barely knew?

Squirrelpaw was staring in disbelief at the dead falcon, all her indignation forgotten. "That was *brilliant!*" she meowed. "I want to try it." To Brambleclaw she added, "Could we hunt like this at home, do you think?"

"There aren't as many hawks," Brambleclaw pointed out. "WindClan might try, I suppose—Crowpaw said he'd seen eagles on the moors."

Stormfur noticed that instead of scraping earth over her prey until she was ready to collect it, Brook hid the mouse and the falcon by dragging both of them into a crevice in the rock. Then she set off again at the head of her group.

This time she led them up the wall of the valley, bounding over some loose rocks and then along a ledge. Stormfur couldn't think what prey she hoped to find out here, but by now he was content to wait and see, aware that these mountain cats had tricks he and his friends had never heard of.

They came to a flattened heap of twigs and dried grass, blocking the ledge. There was a strong reek of stale prey. Brook sprang nimbly over it, and the rest of the cats followed.

"This is a hawk's nest," she explained. "In the freed-water season, we can sometimes find hawk chicks."

"'Freed water'?" Squirrelpaw echoed.

"I expect she means newleaf," Brambleclaw replied in a low voice. "When the water's freed from ice, I guess. That's when there would be chicks in the nest."

"Very good they are, too," Crag added, coming up from

behind. "And it means there are fewer hawks to grow up and prey on us. Like this one," he added, with a massive leap into the air.

Stormfur jerked his head up with a gasp. Just above him a huge hawk had swooped down, its talons extended, but as Crag leaped upward it veered off, shedding air from under its wings as it slid sideways.

Crag came down perilously close to the edge of the rock, regaining his balance with the ease of long practice. Stormfur's respect for him increased; the courage and speed with which the cave-guard had attacked the fierce bird matched any skills possessed by the best Clan warriors.

"Thanks," he gasped as he crouched on the ledge and watched the falcon swoop away, many tail-lengths below.

Crag turned to him, amber eyes gleaming. "That's the first thing a to-be learns," he meowed with a purr of amusement. "Never forget to look up!"

CHAPTER 12

Stormfur crouched on a jutting spur of rock and looked down into the valley a couple of tail-lengths below. The sun was going down on the fourth day since he and his friends had come to the cave of the Tribe cats. Although the thought of what was happening in the forest hung over their heads like a swollen rain cloud, they had been unable to move on. Tawnypelt's shoulder was healing again, thanks to the herbs Stoneteller had given her, but it was still too stiff for her to walk.

Meanwhile, Stormfur was beginning to think he had gotten the hang of the Tribe cats' way of hunting. It depended much more on keeping still and silent than on stalking prey, for among the rocks there was not as much cover as in the forest or even by the river where he used to fish.

His ears pricked as he caught the faint sound of fluttering wings, and he peered down into the shadows. A bird had landed just below him and was pecking at the ground. Bunching his muscles, Stormfur sprang. His claws met feathers, and the bird's frantic alarm call was cut off as he killed it with one blow of his paw.

Stormfur stood up, his prey in his jaws, and saw the dim

shape of one of the mud-covered cave-guards approaching up the valley. The fresh-kill in his mouth masked the scent, and he did not recognize Crag until the cat spoke.

"Good catch! You'll make a great prey-hunter."

Stormfur nodded his thanks, but Crag's words made him slightly anxious; did he really mean "you *will* make a good prey-hunter," or had he meant to say "you *would*"? The cave-guard sometimes seemed to assume that Stormfur intended to stay with the Tribe for good. But there was no opportunity to ask him what he meant; Brook and the rest of the prey-hunters had just appeared, and the whole patrol set off back to the cave, collecting the prey they had caught earlier on their way.

When they reached the pool, Stormfur set down his load for a brief rest before climbing the rocks and negotiating the ledge behind the waterfall. The sun had set and the peak was outlined against a sky the color of blood. Stormfur shivered, trying not to picture blood being shed back home in the forest. However happy he felt to be hunting with the Tribe, they had to move on as soon as they could.

Brook padded up beside him, her eyes shining in the evening light. "A good day's hunting," she purred. "You have learned our ways well, Stormfur."

A warm glow spread through him from ears to tail-tip. Even more than before, he knew how much he would miss her when he had to leave. In these last few days she had become a friend; even her strange accent had begun to sound familiar. He guessed she felt the same; at least, she always asked him to go hunting with her, while the rest of the forest cats, if they hunted at all, went with other groups. Stormfur wondered what Brook really thought of him. Would she miss him when he had to go?

He opened his jaws and picked up a strong rank scent. It was like nothing he had ever smelled before: a bit like a cat's, but harsher and tinged with carrion. He felt his neck fur rise with a premonition of danger.

"What's *that*?"

Brook's eyes stretched wide with fear, but she did not reply. Already the rest of the hunting patrol were gathering up their prey, hurrying for the safety of the cave. Crag bounded over and almost pushed Stormfur up the rocks. Glancing up, Stormfur thought he spotted a shadowy movement near the top of the waterfall, but he wasn't sure. Then he had to concentrate on keeping his footing on the slick, wet stones of the ledge, struggling to see around the half-grown falcon in his jaws. No cat tried to explain the reason for the sudden panic, and Stormfur had learned by now that there would be no point in asking.

In the cave, he carried his prey over to the fresh-kill pile and went to find his friends. Spotting them near their sleeping hollows, he headed toward them, dodging around a couple of to-bes who were training with one of the cave-guards. They were using unfamiliar fighting moves; Stormfur's pelt itched to join in and learn, and teach the Tribe cats a few RiverClan tricks too. *Maybe later*, he promised himself.

The other Clan cats were all gathered around Tawnypelt, who was on her paws, twisting her head to examine her shoulder. Feathertail's tongue rasped busily over her fur.

"It's much better," she meowed. "There's no swelling at all, and the wound's healing cleanly. How does it feel, Tawnypelt?"

The ShadowClan warrior flexed the injured shoulder, then dropped into the hunter's crouch and crept a few tail-lengths along the cave floor. "Stoneteller certainly knows his stuff," she reported. "I don't know the herbs he used, but they're just as good as burdock root. The shoulder's a bit stiff, that's all," she added, springing up again. "It'll be fine if I keep exercising it. I just wish I could get my claws on that rat!"

"Then it's time we were leaving," Brambleclaw mewed. "I'll have a word with Stoneteller, and we'll set off first thing tomorrow."

"Right!" Crowpaw's eyes flashed. "And they'd better not try to keep us here."

"They won't." Feathertail pressed her muzzle against his side. "I'm sure you're worrying about nothing. The Tribe cats have been nothing but kind to us ever since we got here."

"They'll probably be glad to see the back of us," Squirrelpaw agreed cheerfully. "They're bound to be short of prey when leaf-bare comes."

"It's nearly here," mewed Feathertail. "The rocks were white with frost this morning."

"Right." Squirrelpaw waved her tail. "So they won't want us sitting here stuffing ourselves."

Stormfur could see from the look Brambleclaw gave his Clanmate that he was still worried, but he said nothing.

Instead, it was Crowpaw who spoke, noticing for the first time that Stormfur had padded up to join them.

"There you are!" he exclaimed, his lip curling unpleasantly. "Decided to join us, have you? Getting bored with your new friends in the Tribe?"

"Don't," Feathertail murmured, flicking him with her tail.

Stung, Stormfur stalked up to the young WindClan apprentice. "If he's got something to say, let him say it."

"Only that you spend all your time with them. Maybe you'd like to stay with them for good. After all, things are going to be pretty tough when we get back to the forest."

"Don't be stupid," Stormfur retorted. Turning his back on Crowpaw, he saw that all the others were looking at him gravely, as if they half agreed with what the WindClan cat had said. "Come on," Stormfur went on, alarmed. "What have I done? Gone out hunting a couple of times, that's all. You said yourself, Brambleclaw, that we should catch our own prey while we're here. What makes you think that I care any less than you about what happens to the forest?"

"No cat thinks that," Feathertail mewed soothingly.

"*He* does." Stormfur twitched his ears at Crowpaw. "This isn't about the dreams, is it? Just because I wasn't chosen by StarClan . . . You haven't had more dreams, have you, and not told me?"

He unsheathed his claws, hating that they scraped against stone rather than soft riverside earth or a tangle of reeds. Crowpaw he could understand; the apprentice had always been difficult, and he would fight with StarClan themselves.

But that the others might think him less than loyal—even his own sister . . . It was almost as bad as the time when Tigerstar had merged two Clans together, and he and Feathertail had nearly been killed for being half-Clan. Feathertail at least should remember that and understand. Stormfur stifled a flash of guilt as he remembered how comfortable he felt among the Tribe, but he was determined to remain loyal to RiverClan.

"No, we haven't had any more dreams," Brambleclaw replied. "Settle down, Stormfur, and Crowpaw, stop annoying him. We have problems enough without that."

"It's that waterfall," Tawnypelt meowed unexpectedly. "The noise of it, day and night, is driving me mad. StarClan could be sending us every sign under the sun, but we'd never hear them. I'll be glad when we're out in the open again, and well away from this place."

There was a soft snarl in Crowpaw's voice. "We need to go back to the forest, and defend it like warriors should. Stormfur can come or not."

"Shut up, mouse-brain," Squirrelpaw snapped. "Stormfur's just as loyal as you."

Stormfur blinked gratefully at her. "Of course I'm coming with you," he meowed.

"Then let's eat, and get a good night's sleep," Brambleclaw growled. "It might be our last chance for a while."

Stormfur looked up and flinched, surprised to see that while they had been talking several of the Tribe cats had gathered and were watching them with serious faces.

Crag stepped forward. "Why do you talk about leaving?" he meowed. "You'll never make it through the mountains in the season of frozen-water. Stay with us until the sun returns."

"We can't do that!" Squirrelpaw exclaimed. "There's trouble back home—we told you that when we arrived."

"We're grateful for the offer," Brambleclaw meowed more diplomatically, brushing his tail across Squirrelpaw's mouth to silence her. "But we have to go."

The Tribe cats glanced at one another, their neck fur starting to bristle. Suddenly they looked threatening. Several of the powerful cave-guards moved to stand between them and the entrance, and two or three of the kit-mothers began anxiously herding their kits toward the nursery tunnel. The meaning was clear; Stormfur knew that if they tried to leave now they would have a fight on their paws.

Spotting Brook near the back of the group, he thrust past a cave-guard to stand in front of her. "What's going on?" he demanded. "Why are you treating us like prisoners?"

Brook would not meet his eyes. "Please . . ." she murmured. "Are you so unhappy here that staying is such a terrible thing?"

"'Unhappy' isn't the point. We're on a mission; we don't have any choice." Stormfur whirled around to question Crag, but the cave-guard avoided his gaze, and he knew that their friendship was being brushed aside out of loyalty to the Tribe, for reasons he could not begin to guess. He had believed that the Tribe cats liked him for himself, and pain at their betrayal tore him like an eagle's talons.

"Fox dung to this!" Crowpaw muttered, trying to force his way past the cave-guards.

Crag raised his paw, and another cave-guard thrust Crowpaw back with a furious hiss. The WindClan apprentice's bristling fur and lashing tail showed that he was ready to attack both of them at once.

"Wait," Feathertail murmured, pushing between Crowpaw and the guards. "Let's find out what all this means."

"It means trouble," Crowpaw snarled. "No cat is going to stop me from leaving."

He shouldered his way past Feathertail and leaped on Crag, bowling the huge cave-guard over. Crag's hind paws battered his belly, but before the fight could go any further, Brambleclaw fastened his teeth into Crowpaw's scruff and dragged him off.

The apprentice spun around to face him, eyes blazing. "Get off me!" he snarled.

"Then stop being so mouse-brained!" Brambleclaw hissed, just as furious. "These guards could turn you into crowfood. We have to find out what they want."

Stormfur hated to admit defeat, but if they fought their way out tonight—even supposing they could—they would have to face a cold night on an unfamiliar mountainside. And looking around at the lean, well-muscled cave-guards, barely out of breath from the tussle with Crowpaw, Stormfur knew they could not hope to survive a fight without injury, and that would make their journey harder than ever. *Why didn't Midnight foresee this?* he wondered desperately. Or had she foreseen it, and kept it hidden from them?

He saw that Stoneteller had emerged from his tunnel. *Now perhaps we'll get some answers*, he thought.

The cave-guards stepped back to allow their leader to come closer to the Clan cats; Brambleclaw padded forward to face him. "I think there must be some misunderstanding," he began. Stormfur could see his efforts to stay calm. "We have to leave tomorrow, and your Tribe doesn't seem to want us to go. We're grateful for your help and shelter, but—"

He broke off; Stoneteller wasn't listening. His eyes glimmered like pebbles on a streambed as he gazed around the group of cats. Raising his voice, he meowed, "I have received a sign from the Tribe of Endless Hunting. It is time for a Telling."

"A Telling? What's that?" Squirrelpaw mewed.

"Maybe it's like a Gathering," Stormfur murmured.

"But there aren't any other Tribes to meet with."

"Then maybe it's something to do with the Tribe of Endless Hunting." In spite of his fears that they would not be allowed to leave the cave, Stormfur couldn't help feeling curious about discovering more of the Tribe's strange beliefs.

The cave-guards gathered more closely around the Clan cats and began to herd them toward the tunnel from where Stoneteller had just emerged.

"Back off!" Tawnypelt snapped at one of them. "Where are you taking us?"

Stormfur wondered that too. Until now he had assumed

that the second tunnel just led to Stoneteller's private den.

"To the Cave of Pointed Stones," Stoneteller replied. "There, many things will be made clear to you."

"And what if we don't want to go?" Without waiting for a reply, Crowpaw launched himself at the nearest cave-guard, a cat almost twice his size. The cave-guard casually swatted him with a huge paw, sending him half stunned to the floor of the cave. Feathertail spat at the guard and lashed out a paw, claws extended.

Stormfur felt his neck fur stand on end, but before a real fight could break out Brambleclaw hissed, "No! If we're going to get an explanation, we'll listen to it. Then we'll decide what to do. Do you hear me, Crowpaw?"

The apprentice, scrambling to his paws with his fur torn and his tail fluffed out, glared at him but said nothing.

"Get a move on," growled one of the guards.

Stormfur stumbled, almost losing his balance as the nearest guard butted him toward the tunnel. It took all his self-control to move on quietly. Then he realized that Brook was beside him. There was something like relief in her eyes as she mewed, "Don't worry. Everything will become clear soon."

"I'm not worried." Stormfur's voice was cold. He had thought they were friends, and she had betrayed him. "You can't keep us here forever."

He was almost pleased when she winced. "Please . . ." she whispered. "You don't understand. It's for the sake of the Tribe."

Stormfur curled his lip and turned away. He padded after

Tawnypelt into the passage, with a couple of cave-guards close behind.

In the darkness he heard Stoneteller's voice raised in a soft chant. "When the Tribe of Endless Hunting calls, we come to listen."

More voices answered him from behind Stormfur, not just the cave-guards but more of the Tribe cats pressing into the tunnel. "In rock and pool, in air and light on water, through fall of prey and cry of kit, through scrape of claw and beat of blood, we hear you."

The voices echoed through the shadows. Stormfur saw moonlight filtering in from somewhere ahead, and Tawnypelt's pricked ears outlined in gray. He stepped out into another cave, and for a moment all his fears and frustrations vanished and he stood with his mouth dropped open in awe.

This cave was much smaller than the one they had just left. A jagged rift high in the roof let in a shaft of moonlight that bathed the floor in watery gray light. Stormfur was standing amid a forest of pointed stones, many more than in the main cave; some of them grew up from the floor while others hung down above his head. A few of them had joined together as if they were propping up the roof, pale yellow and rippled with tiny streams of water trickling down to pool on the hard stone floor.

Earlier that day rain had fallen through the hole to leave a pattern of puddles around Stormfur's paws. The roar of the waterfall, so loud in the outer cave, had sunk to a whisper, faint enough that he could hear drops of water falling from the roof.

All the Clan cats were silent, the same awe, which Stormfur felt, shining in their eyes. The place reminded Stormfur of Mothermouth; as well as being in a moonlit cave, there was the same sense of being in the presence of something greater than himself. But this was not the home of StarClan, but of the Tribe of Endless Hunting, and would they even care about cats from territories far away? A shiver went through him and in his mind he formed a prayer to StarClan. *Guard us and guide us, even here.*

The cave-guards nudged the Clan cats farther into the cave, while Stoneteller stalked ahead of them until he stood in the center of the forest of stones. There he turned to face the rest of the cats. "We stand in the Cave of Pointed Stones," he meowed; his voice was high and expressionless. "Moonrise is here, caught in rock and in water as it has always been and always will be. It is time for a Telling. We call on the Tribe of Endless Hunting to show us their will."

"Show us your will," the other Tribe cats responded in chorus. Almost all of them had pushed into the cave behind the Clan cats; the air was growing warm with their bodies and damp, misty breath.

Moving like a shadow, Stoneteller padded to and fro, peering into the puddles. His eyes shone in the moonlight, and the mud on his fur looked more sinister and stonelike than ever. Brook had told Stormfur that her leader had been given nine lives by the Tribe of Endless Hunting, just as the Clan leaders were given nine lives by StarClan, but he had found it hard to believe until now. Outlined in watery light and surrounded by strange points of rock, Stoneteller looked in possession of more power than all the forest cats put together.

At last the leader of the Tribe paused beside one of the biggest pools, and murmured, "We greet you, Tribe of Endless Hunting, and we thank you for your mercy in saving us at last from Sharptooth."

"We thank you," the Tribe cats murmured in response.

Stormfur tensed. Exchanging glances with his friends, he saw his own confusion reflected in their eyes. What did Stoneteller mean? What was Sharptooth, and why did the Tribe need to be saved from it?

"Why is—" Squirrelpaw began, only to be reduced to silence by a hiss from a nearby cave-guard.

Stoneteller went on. "Tribe of Endless Hunting, we thank you for sending the promised cat."

"We thank you," the Tribe cats responded again, their voices growing stronger.

Raising his head, Stoneteller commanded, "Let him stand forth."

Before Stormfur could protest, two of the burly cave-guards thrust him forward. Taken by surprise, he slid sideways into a puddle, shattering the moonlight into glittering splinters. A gasp of shock rose from the Tribe, and he heard a cat mutter, "An evil omen!"

Fighting to stay calm, he shook the water off his paws and walked forward until he stood beside Stoneteller in the center of the pointed stones.

"What are you doing?" he demanded.

Stoneteller raised a paw for silence. His eyes glowed in the moonlight with unconcealed triumph as he murmured, "Do not question. This is your fate."

Glancing around, Stormfur saw that all the Tribe cats were gazing at him with the same expectation in their eyes and a kind of joy, as if he were the most wonderful sight they had ever seen. "It is your fate," they repeated.

He had been right all along. The Tribe had singled him out as special, and now he was going to find out why.

"The time has come," Stoneteller intoned solemnly. "The promised cat is here, and at last we will be saved from Sharptooth."

"I don't understand!" Stormfur burst out. "I've never even heard of Sharptooth."

As if his words had broken a spell, his friends pressed forward to stand beside him, only to be shoved back again by the cave-guards. Squirrelpaw spat, and both Crowpaw and Tawnypelt flexed their claws on the cold stone, but Brambleclaw held them back with a word of warning. The cave-guards clearly did not want a fight either; they kept their claws sheathed, only shouldering the forest cats into a tight group.

"Sharptooth is a huge cat," Stoneteller began, his voice hushed with fear. "He lives in the mountains, and makes the Tribe his prey. For many seasons now he has been picking us off, one by one."

"He looks like a lion," Crag added, and asked, "Do you know of lions?"

"We have legends of LionClan," Stormfur replied, still wondering what Sharptooth could possibly have to do with him. "Lions are known for their strength and wisdom, and they have a golden mane like the sun's warm rays."

"Sharptooth has no mane," Stoneteller meowed. "Perhaps he lost it because he is so evil. He is the enemy of our Tribe." His voice was bleak, his eyes shining cold with memories. "We feared that he would not rest until every cat of the Tribe had been killed."

"But then the Tribe of Endless Hunting sent us the promised cat." Stormfur's head whipped around as he heard Brook's voice. She had drawn close to him, and was gazing at him, her eyes filled with admiration. "Stormfur, you're the chosen one. You'll save us all. I know you will."

"How can I?" A slow anger had begun to burn inside Stormfur, replacing his bewilderment. "What do you expect me to do?"

"Before the last full moon, the Tribe of Endless Hunting sent a prophecy to us," Stoneteller explained. "They said that a silver cat would save us from Sharptooth. We knew as soon as we saw you by the pool that you must be the cat who was promised to us."

"But I *can't* be," Stormfur protested. "I come from a forest a long way away, and I've never even seen Sharptooth."

"That's true." Brambleclaw padded forward to stand beside Stormfur. "We're sorry that Sharptooth is threatening you, but our Clans at home are in danger too."

"Maybe even worse danger," Feathertail added anxiously. "We have to go."

Stoneteller flicked his ears. Without a word, the cave-guards surrounded the forest cats and began thrusting them back toward the cave entrance—all except Stormfur, who was surrounded by a separate patrol. Feathertail desperately tried to break through to her brother, but the nearest cave-guard bowled her over with a swipe of his paw.

"Take your paws off her, you piece of fox dung!" Crowpaw spat, hurling himself at the cave-guard and raking his claws over the Tribe cat's ear. The two of them rolled on the ground in a flurry of claws until Brambleclaw hauled Crowpaw away.

"Not now," he commanded the furious apprentice. "It won't help any cat for you to get ripped to shreds."

"We should fight!" snarled Crowpaw. "I'd rather die fighting than be trapped here."

"Just say the word," Tawnypelt hissed at her brother. "I'll tear their pelts off and feed them to the eagles."

"StarClan, help us!" Feathertail cried out as she was forced back to the tunnel entrance. "Show us you haven't abandoned us!"

"Do not fear," Stoneteller meowed reassuringly. "This is the will of the Tribe of Endless Hunting."

Stormfur felt as though he were falling into deep, dark water as he saw his friends shoved away from him, back to the main cave. When he tried to follow, Crag and another cave-guard moved to block his way.

"Over there," Crag meowed, pointing with his tail to the other end of the Cave of Pointed Stones. "You'll find a sleeping hollow ready for you." As Stormfur faced him with burning eyes, Crag added awkwardly, "It won't be so bad. You'll kill Sharptooth for us—the Tribe of Endless Hunting says so—and then you can leave if you still want to."

"Kill Sharptooth!" Stormfur exclaimed, remembering the rank scent and the shadowy shape he had seen at the top of the waterfall. That must have been Sharptooth, prowling close to the cave entrance; no wonder Brook and the rest of the patrol had been so frightened. "How can I do that, if all of you have failed? This is a mouse-brained idea. You're all mad."

"No." That was Stoneteller again, padding up to stand at Stormfur's shoulder. "You must have faith in the Tribe of Endless Hunting. The sign was clear, and you came, just as they promised."

"My faith is in StarClan," Stormfur retorted, trying to hide how scared he felt inside. Had the spirits of his warrior ancestors really abandoned him?

"Go to your sleeping hollow," Stoneteller meowed. "We will bring you fresh-kill. Your coming has been long awaited, and you need have no fear that we will ill-treat you."

No, but you'll keep me prisoner, Stormfur thought desperately. He padded to the back of the cave to find the sleeping hollow Crag had indicated and found it warmly lined with dried grass and feathers. A couple of tail-lengths away was another scoop in the rock, also lined with bedding, where he guessed Stoneteller slept.

Stormfur lapped water from the nearest pool and then lay down with his head on his paws to try to figure out how to escape. But it was hard to think, with the pain of betrayal still throbbing through him. He had really believed that the Tribe cats liked him, without any of the questions that shadowed his RiverClan friendships about his parentage or his loyalty. Instead, they only wanted him to fulfill their prophecy.

A few moments later Brook appeared, a rabbit in her jaws, and set it down timidly in front of him. "I'm sorry," she whispered. "Is it really so bad, to stay with the Tribe? I . . . I want to be your friend, Stormfur, if you will let me." She hesitated, and then added, "I'll stay with you now, if you like. It is our way to groom each other's fur, especially in times of hardship. We call it the giving of close comfort."

She must mean sharing tongues, Stormfur realized. Not long before, he would have been delighted at the thought of sharing tongues with Brook. Now the idea outraged him. Did she really think he would want to be close to her, when she had betrayed him and lied to him?

"Stormfur . . . ?" Brook's eyes shone with compassion, but their glow was like a fire searing Stormfur to the heart. He turned his head away without saying anything.

He heard a faint gasp of pain from Brook, and then her pawsteps vanishing down the tunnel. When she had gone he turned the rabbit over with one paw. He had been hungry at the end of the day's hunting, but now the thought of eating made him feel sick. Still, he forced himself to choke down the fresh-kill, because he knew that whatever happened next, he would need all his strength.

He curled up in the sleeping hollow and lay staring at the tunnel where his friends had disappeared. Crag and the other cave-guard were on duty at the entrance, and as Stormfur watched, Stoneteller emerged from the shadows and slipped between the guards, back to the main cave. Between them and Stormfur lay pools of shimmering water, lit by the cold moonlight. They reminded Stormfur of the river, but he missed its endless murmuring and the glitter and splash of moving water.

As he closed his eyes and tried to sleep he reflected sadly that he need never have come on this journey at all. He hadn't been chosen by StarClan, had never been summoned by a dream. But right now he would have given anything for the whole adventure to have been a dream, if only he could wake up in the morning to find himself back home in RiverClan.

CHAPTER 13

Leafpaw shifted uneasily in a pool of moonlight and listened to the soft sighing of the wind in the oaks at Fourtrees. She and Cinderpelt were on their way to meet with the other medicine cats at Mothermouth, and already the half-moon was high in the sky.

"They're late," Cinderpelt meowed. "We're wasting moon-light."

Littlecloud, the ShadowClan medicine cat, settled himself more comfortably in a hollow in the grass. "They'll be along soon."

Cinderpelt's tail-tip twitched. "We need all the time we have at the Moonstone, especially tonight. We have to find out what we should do about the Twolegs."

Leafpaw tried to curb her own impatience with the RiverClan medicine cats, who should have met them long before now. Perhaps sharing tongues with StarClan wasn't so important to them, when their own territory hadn't been invaded by the Twoleg monsters. Everything was quiet now; the Twoleg monsters slept at night, but Leafpaw knew they were still there, squatting on the scarred ground among the trees they hadn't destroyed yet. The silence in the forest was unnatural, without the small sounds of prey that always seemed louder at night.

Her belly rumbled at the thought of prey. Cinderpelt had given her traveling herbs to quell her appetite before they set out, but they didn't help her hunger when she couldn't remember the last time she had been full-fed. All the Clan cats were suffering; lack of food had begun to weaken them so that they couldn't run as fast and catch what prey there was. With leaf-bare looming ever closer, crisping the leaves and sending them spiraling to the ground in the chill breeze, Leafpaw couldn't see what help StarClan might give.

To her embarrassment, her belly rumbled again, loud enough for the others to hear. Littlecloud shot her a sympathetic glance.

"Blackstar has sent warriors to fetch rats and crowfood from Carrionplace," he told Cinderpelt. His eyes darkened. "We haven't had any sickness yet, but it's only a matter of time."

"I hope you remember the herbs and berries I gave you when you were ill," Cinderpelt meowed.

"I've been collecting them. I know I'll need them soon."

"And tell your Clan not to touch any crowfood," Cinderpelt advised. "Fresh rats might be okay, but not carrion."

Littlecloud sighed. "I've tried, but what can I do when Blackstar gives the orders? Most of our cats are too hungry to care what they're eating."

Just then Leafpaw caught sight of Mudfur, the RiverClan

medicine cat, and his apprentice, Mothwing, climbing the slope from the river. She leaped to her paws, delighted to see her friend again, though she could not suppress a pang of envy that Mothwing looked so well fed, her long golden fur sleek with good health.

"At last!" Cinderpelt growled as the two cats came up. "I was beginning to think a fish must have jumped out of the river and swallowed you."

"Well, we're here now." Mudfur hardly paused for greetings, but led the way around the top of the hollow toward the WindClan border.

Cinderpelt and Littlecloud followed, while Leafpaw and Mothwing brought up the rear, side by side.

"I got into trouble about that fishing lesson," Leafpaw whispered. "I knew I should not have eaten your prey."

"Your leader's got no right!" Mothwing meowed indignantly. "We're medicine cats."

"Still, we shouldn't have done it," Leafpaw replied. "Medicine cats have to stick to the warrior code as much as any cat."

Mothwing just snorted. "I think I'm getting on really well," she mewed after a moment. "Mudfur taught me the herbs to use for greencough and blackcough, and the best way to get thorns out of pads. He said he'd never seen a cat do it so neatly."

"That's great!" Leafpaw purred. She didn't mind her friend boasting because she knew how insecure Mothwing felt. Because she was the daughter of a rogue, many of her own

Clan thought that she should never have been allowed to train as a medicine cat. Mothwing was desperate to prove them wrong.

As they approached the WindClan border, Leafpaw felt a twinge of nervousness. It was not long since the confrontation with WindClan, and she knew that their warriors would still be hostile. They seemed determined to keep their starvation a secret, even though it was horribly obvious from their scrawny frames and dull eyes. Would they be desperate enough to attack medicine cats if they found them on their territory? She said nothing; Firestar would be furious if she gossiped with Mothwing about that fateful encounter.

None of the medicine cats paused as they crossed the border. They hurried on, their pace set by Cinderpelt's limping gait. Coming to the top of a gentle rise, Leafpaw found herself looking down on the worst scene yet of Twoleg devastation. The scar on WindClan's territory was much longer and wider now than when she and Sorreltail had first seen it. A couple of Twoleg monsters squatted there, moonlight glinting off their shiny pelts. If a hill got in their way they just gorged a path through it, leaving earth piled high on either side. Were they going to devour the whole moor?

Shuddering, Leafpaw bounded on behind her mentor. Not far from the WindClan camp, Barkface, the WindClan medicine cat, emerged from behind a gorse bush. Even though Leafpaw had been prepared for him to look hungry, it was a shock to see how thin he was—barely more than a walking skeleton covered by his ragged pelt.

Cinderpelt went up and touched noses with him sympathetically. "StarClan be with you, Barkface," she mewed.

"And with all my Clan." Barkface heaved a great sigh. "Sometimes I think StarClan wants every one of us to join them, and not even a kit left to keep the warrior code alive."

"Perhaps they will show us what to do when we share dreams at the Moonstone," Cinderpelt tried to encourage him.

"It's getting worse for WindClan." Mothwing's amber eyes were wide as she murmured the words to Leafpaw. "They've been stealing fish from the river again, you know. Hawkfrost caught a couple of them, and chased them off."

"They have to find prey somewhere." Leafpaw knew that what the WindClan warriors were doing was wrong, but she couldn't blame them. Not when the river was full of fish, enough to feed all the Clans. Fleetingly, she realized that Firestar was right—the Twolegs were destroying the forest, but in doing so they were also destroying the invisible boundaries between the Clans as well. Maybe the cats would survive only by joining together after all.

Mothwing paused to scent the air. "Hang on, I can smell rabbit—at least, I think it's rabbit; it smells funny somehow. Yes, look, over there!"

She gestured with her tail at a dip in the moorland where a small stream chattered over stones. Lying beside it was a small, brown-furred body.

"It's dead," Leafpaw pointed out.

Mothwing shrugged. "So it's crowfood. I imagine

WindClan can't afford to be too fussy. Hey, Barkface!" she called. "Look what I found." She bounded down the slope toward the rabbit.

"Stop!" Barkface commanded. "Don't touch it!"

Mothwing skidded to a halt beside the limp bundle of fur and looked back up the slope. "What's the matter?"

Barkface padded down to join her, followed by Leafpaw and the other medicine cats. Warily he approached the rabbit and sniffed it. Leafpaw sniffed too, and recognized the harsh tang she had picked up when she and Sorreltail had visited WindClan territory. Her stomach churned and she swallowed to stop herself from gagging. Whatever had happened to this rabbit, it wasn't fit for food.

"Yes, I thought so," Barkface murmured, his eyes clouding. "There's that scent again. . . ." Facing the other cats, he explained quietly, "Twolegs have done something bad to the rabbits in the territory. They all die. And if cats eat them, they die too. We have lost half our elders and nearly all of our apprentices."

There was a horrified silence. Compassion lanced through Leafpaw. Tallstar had said nothing of this when he confronted Firestar; the proud WindClan leader would rather let other Clans think his cats could not catch prey in their territory, than that their own fresh-kill was killing them, one by one.

"And you couldn't help them?" Mudfur asked.

"Do you think I didn't try?" Barkface sounded desperate. "I gave them yarrow to make them sick, just as we do for deathberries. Two of the strongest pulled through, but most of them died." His claws tore up the grass in front of him; his eyes burned with grief and frustration. "What hope is there for us when even our prey can kill us?"

Cinderpelt limped up to him and pressed her muzzle against his side. "Let's go on," she murmured. "We'll ask StarClan for guidance about this as well as everything else."

"Shouldn't we bury the rabbit?" Leafpaw suggested as the cats began to climb the slope again. "In case some other cat finds it?"

Barkface shook his head. "There's no point. No WindClan cat would touch it now." His lips stretched in a wry snarl. "We know better than to trust fresh-kill from inside our own borders." Head bowed, tail drooping, he plodded on across the moor toward Highstones.

Leafpaw blinked in the silver light from the Moonstone, letting it soothe her until she felt like a fish sinking into deep water. Here in the cavern, far below Highstones, it was easy to believe that StarClan ruled everything, and the troubles of the world above were too far away to matter. But medicine cats came to the Moonstone only so that they could learn the wisdom of StarClan and take it back to help their Clans. In these dark days, they needed that wisdom more than ever.

The other medicine cats were lying with her around the stone. Mothwing was next to her; the RiverClan cat's eyes were wide with wonder as she gazed at the shimmering crystal surface. Trying to focus her thoughts, Leafpaw pushed away the questions that nagged her about Mothwing and her aggressive brother, Hawkfrost. Mothwing had a right to be here; StarClan themselves had approved her with a moth's wing left at the entrance to Mudfur's den before she had finally been accepted as a medicine cat apprentice.

With a quick plea to StarClan for guidance, Leafpaw closed her eyes and pressed her nose against the stone. Cold instantly seized her like a claw, the hard surface of the cave floor vanished from beneath her, and she felt as though she were floating in darkness.

Squirrelpaw! Squirrelpaw, can you hear me? she called silently. She was desperate to make sure that her sister was still alive and safe, and more than that: If the chosen cats had discovered the answer to the trouble that had come upon the forest, then seeking out Squirrelpaw might give her some hope that she could share with the others.

But tonight something seemed to be blocking her thoughts. The silence was broken by the sound of rushing water, loud as thunder, and then the darkness shifted to show her a waterfall, crashing endlessly down into a pool below. Before Leafpaw could properly understand what she was seeing, clouds swirled over it. Out of them came a terrible snarling, and she caught a glimpse of sharp fangs. She sensed the presence of warrior ancestors and reached out for the comforting presence of StarClan. But she caught only a flickering vision of lean, prowling cats, their fur streaked with mud and blood. Their eyes glared with desperation, as if they stared at some terrible sight that was hidden from Leafpaw.

She thought she cried out to them, but they did not answer, and she was not even sure that they were aware of her.

A wind howled around her, sweeping all the visions away, and Leafpaw woke up with a jolt. She blinked in confusion, staring around the cavern that was dark now except for the faint glitter of Silverpelt. In the dim light she could just make out a cat crouched beside her, a beautiful tortoiseshell with a white chest and white paws. The sweet scent of herbs clung about her fur.

For a heartbeat Leafpaw mistook the cat for Sorreltail, until she remembered that her friend was back in the ThunderClan camp. And where were Mothwing and the medicine cats? Leafpaw realized that except for herself and the strange tortoiseshell, the cavern was empty.

The tortoiseshell cat opened her eyes and turned to blink at Leafpaw. "Greetings," she mewed softly. "Do not be anxious for your sister or your Clan. A time of great trouble has come, but the Clans are strong and have the courage to meet it."

Leafpaw froze. She had woken up in another dream. Her eyes widened as she realized who the tortoiseshell cat must be. She had heard many stories of the medicine cat who had befriended her father when he first came to ThunderClan, and guided him in dreams on his path to becoming leader.

"Are you . . . are you Spottedleaf?" she meowed.

The tortoiseshell cat bowed her head. "I am. I see that Firestar has told you about me."

"Yes." Leafpaw stared curiously at the she-cat. "He told me how much you helped him."

"I loved him as well as any cat," Spottedleaf purred. "Maybe even more than I should have done, as a medicine cat. If StarClan had not chosen me to walk their path, things might have been different." Her eyes narrowed with affection. "I never had kits of my own, Leafpaw, but I cannot say how happy it makes me that Firestar's daughter will be following the path of a medicine cat. I know that StarClan has great things in store for you."

Leafpaw swallowed. "May I ask you something?" she meowed hesitantly.

"Of course."

"Can you see Squirrelpaw? Is she all right?"

There was a long pause. "I cannot see her," Spottedleaf replied at last, "but I know where she is. She is safe, and on her way home to you."

"Why can't you see her, if you know where she is?" Leafpaw challenged.

Spottedleaf's gaze shone with gentleness and compassion. "Squirrelpaw is in the paws of different warrior ancestors now."

"What do you mean?" Leafpaw remembered the fearsome, blood-streaked cats she had sensed when she tried to make contact with Squirrelpaw. In her dream, her eyes flew wide and she sprang to her paws. "Whose warrior ancestors are these? There can't be more than one StarClan!"

Spottedleaf laughed softly. "The world is wide, dear young one. There are other cats who are guided by other spirits. There is always more to learn."

Leafpaw's head whirled. She stammered, "I thought—"

"StarClan does not control the wind or the rain, do they?" Spottedleaf prompted gently. "They do not command the sun to rise or the moon to wax and wane. Do not fear, little one," she went on. "From now on, wherever you walk, I will walk with you. . . ."

Her voice began to fade; her fur paled and her shape seemed to melt into the darkness. For a heartbeat longer, Leafpaw could see her white front shining like a star and her glowing eyes. Then she was blinking awake, emerging from her dream into the cavern where Mothwing and the medicine cats were stirring around her.

Is it true? she wondered, too dazed to speak out loud. *Are Squirrelpaw and the others in the paws of another Clan? And are there really powers other than StarClan's—and does that mean that StarClan won't be able to save the forest after all?*

As she staggered to her paws, she could still catch a trace of Spottedleaf's sweet scent.

CHAPTER 14

♣

Feathertail gazed back helplessly at the tunnel entrance as the cave-guards thrust her out of the tunnel and back into the main cave. She felt unseen claws tearing into her heart with every step she took away from her brother.

What did Stoneteller mean, that Stormfur was the promised cat who would save the Tribe from Sharptooth? True, her brother was a strong and brave warrior, more skilled at fighting than any of the other cats on this journey. But if Sharptooth was as huge and terrible as the Tribe cats said, what could even the bravest warrior do?

"Please," she meowed to one of the cave-guards, a huge mud-colored tabby whose name was Scree Beneath Winter Sky, "you *can't* keep Stormfur here. He belongs with us."

There was sympathy in the Tribe cat's eyes, but he still shook his head. "No. He is the cat sent here by the Tribe of Endless Hunting. They told us a silver cat would come."

"But—"

"Don't try to argue with them," Crowpaw growled into Feathertail's ear. "There's no point. If we have to fight to get Stormfur out, then that's what we'll do."

Feathertail looked at the WindClan cat's bristling fur and the fierce courage in his eyes. "We can't," she mewed sorrowfully. "There are too many of them."

"I don't see why the Tribe is so worried about Sharptooth." Crowpaw's voice was scornful. "We haven't seen a whisker of him since we arrived, so what's the big deal?"

"Be thankful you haven't seen him," Scree meowed.

Crowpaw bared his teeth, but this time he didn't spring at the guard, just turned away and touched his nose to Feathertail's muzzle. He would have fought the whole of StarClan for her, Feathertail knew that, but he had to see that this time fighting would do no good.

The cave-guards herded the Clan cats across the cave until they reached their sleeping hollows.

"What's going on?" Brambleclaw mewed in surprise. "Aren't you throwing us out?"

"Into the night?" The mud-colored guard sounded indignant. "We're not cruel. It's cold out there and dangerous. You can eat and rest here, and leave in the morning."

"With Stormfur?" Tawnypelt challenged.

Scree shook his head. "No. I'm sorry."

The cave-guards left them, except for Scree and another who remained on watch a few tail-lengths away. A couple of to-bes trotted over with fresh-kill in their jaws.

"Isn't it great?" the first of them mewed excitedly, dropping the prey he carried. "No more Sharptooth!"

"Shut up, beetle-brain," growled his friend, giving him a sharp prod in the flank. "You know Crag told us not to talk to them."

They retreated quickly, glancing around to make sure no cat had spotted them disobeying orders.

"I'm not eating that!" Crowpaw spat, glaring at the small pile of fresh-kill. "I don't want anything from the Tribe."

"Great StarClan!" Tawnypelt let out a noisy sigh. "How's that going to help, you stupid furball? You need your strength twice as much now—to save the forest and to save Stormfur."

Crowpaw muttered something inaudible, but made no other protest as he dragged a falcon out of the heap.

"Well?" Squirrelpaw demanded when they had divided the rest of the fresh-kill and were crouched close together to eat. "We're not putting up with this, are we? What are we going to do?"

"There's not very much we can do," Brambleclaw pointed out. "There aren't enough of us to fight the cave-guards."

"You're not going to leave him?" Squirrelpaw's green eyes were wide with disbelief.

Brambleclaw paused; Feathertail could see an agony of indecision in his expression. She began to shiver. Since they left the forest she had come to respect the young warrior's skills as the unelected leader of their group; if he could not see what to do, then what hope was there for Stormfur?

"We should never have come into these mountains," growled Tawnypelt. "It's a hundred times worse than Twolegplace. Midnight mentioned cats in a Tribe, so she must have known about Sharptooth. Why did she send us this way?"

"It must have been a trick all along," Crowpaw hissed. "I

knew we should never have trusted that badger."

"But why would she trick us?" Brambleclaw objected. "StarClan sent us to her, and she warned us about the Twolegs destroying the forest. If we can't trust her, then nothing makes sense."

Feathertail wanted to agree with him, but she suddenly remembered something Purdy had said, when they were discussing which way to go at the edge of the wood. "Purdy tried to tell us not to come through the mountains," she meowed out loud. "And Midnight wouldn't let him speak. You're right. They both *knew*."

She looked around and saw her alarm reflected in the faces of her friends.

"Midnight said we would need courage," Brambleclaw reminded her after a heavy pause. "She said our path was laid out for us. So even if she knew about the Tribe and Sharptooth, there must be a way we can get through this. That makes me think that we must still be following the right path."

"So *you* say," Crowpaw sneered. "I don't suppose it matters to a ThunderClan warrior if a cat from RiverClan gets left behind."

"And what does it matter to WindClan?" Squirrelpaw fired up in defense of her Clanmate. "I'd have thought you'd be delighted if Feathertail's brother weren't here to keep an eye on you."

Crowpaw sprang to his paws, hissing a challenge. Squirrelpaw's green eyes blazed. Horrified, Feathertail forced herself to get up and shoulder Crowpaw away.

"Stop it!" she cried. "Can't you see you're making it worse?"

"Feathertail's right," meowed Tawnypelt. "What Clan we come from doesn't matter here. Four of us are half-Clan anyway—have you ever thought StarClan might have chosen us *because* of that? If we quarrel among ourselves, then we'll lose everything."

Squirrelpaw's gaze seared into Crowpaw for a moment longer before she stepped back and began to tear mouthfuls off a rabbit. Crowpaw looked into Feathertail's eyes and then ducked his head and muttered, "Sorry."

"So maybe we can discuss what to do without ripping one another's fur off?" Tawnypelt meowed tartly. When no cat answered, she went on, "Don't forget that StarClan didn't choose Stormfur in the first place. He's only here because he wouldn't let Feathertail come on this mission alone." She paused; her eyes grew troubled as she added, "What . . . what if the Tribe cats are right and he *is* the promised cat who's going to save them from Sharptooth?"

"That's mouse-brained!" Crowpaw exclaimed.

Feathertail was not so sure. Tawnypelt had put words to the fear that she had also felt squirming inside her ever since Stoneteller had first told them about the prophecy. Sure, Stormfur's fur wasn't what she would call silver—it was darker than that, more like Graystripe's—but he had come into the world of the Tribe cats just as their warrior ancestors had promised.

"Does that mean . . ." Her voice shook and she had to start

again. "Does that mean we're going to leave him here?"

"No, it doesn't." Brambleclaw sounded determined. "These are not our warrior ancestors. StarClan has nothing to do with this Tribe. But we can't get him out by fighting, so we'll have to do it another way. In the morning, when they tell us to leave, we'll go without trouble. Then we'll come sneak back and rescue Stormfur."

The cats were silent for a moment, glancing at one another as if they were weighing the idea. Feathertail began to feel the first faint stirrings of hope. Then she noticed that the cave-guards were watching them suspiciously; had they overheard? She flicked her ears, and the Clan cats, following her gaze, huddled more closely together.

Crowpaw spoke softly. "That's easy to say." He sounded doubtful, but he wasn't sneering anymore. "We'd still have to get into that inner cave, and the whole place is crawling with cave-guards."

"We could wait until it's dark," Tawnypelt suggested.

"And the noise of the waterfall will hide our pawsteps," Squirrelpaw added optimistically.

Crowpaw still looked uncertain. "I'm not sure—haven't you noticed the Tribe cats are so used to it that they can hear a kit squeak at the other end of the cave?"

Feathertail knew he was right. She looked around, wondering if the darkness or the crashing of the torrent would help them at all. Moonlight rippled into the cave through the sheet of thundering water, but shadows fell thickly around the walls. Perhaps it would be possible. But however hard it seemed, they had to try. Stormfur was her *brother*.

"I'm willing to give it a try," she announced. "You can leave me behind if you want."

"Well, I for one—" Crowpaw began.

"Don't try to stop me," Feathertail interrupted. "I know we have to get StarClan's message to the Clans before they're destroyed along with the forest, but they don't need all of us. I can stay here."

"Who said I was going to try to stop you?" Crowpaw demanded indignantly, his neck fur bristling. "I was going to say I'll help, but if you don't want me . . ."

"Don't be mouse-brained." Feathertail gave his ear a quick lick. "I'm sorry I misunderstood. Of course I want you with me."

"I don't think we should split up." Brambleclaw's eyes narrowed thoughtfully. "It's all of us or none. We came on this journey together and we'll finish it together—and that means Stormfur as well." More briskly he added, "Let's finish eating and get some sleep. We'll need all our strength."

Feathertail tried to obey him, forcing down the young hawk that the to-be had left for her, though she felt sick with apprehension. She tried to focus her thoughts on how loyal her friends from the other Clans were. It was hard to imagine that they would ever be able to separate back into their different Clans when they returned to the forest. How would she ever go back to her regular life without them?

She curled into her sleeping hollow, tired enough to sleep, then sat up again. *What was that?* She turned her head to one side and listened. She could hear voices whispering but there were no cats nearby, except for the Clan cats, and they were all asleep. Twitching her ears, Feathertail froze. The voices were coming from the *waterfall*, almost hidden among the rushing, hissing water. She strained to make out what they were saying.

The silver cat has come, they seemed to whisper. *Sharptooth will be destroyed.*

No, Feathertail argued silently, instinctively. She didn't stop to figure out who she was talking to. *You're wrong. Stormfur is not your cat. He must come with us.*

She waited for a reply, but the voices had vanished into the roar of the water, and Feathertail began to wonder if she had even heard them at all. A long time passed; moonlight crept across the floor of the cave and faded before exhaustion overcame her and she finally fell into a troubled sleep.

A paw roughly shaking her shoulder woke Feathertail, and she looked up into the stern face of Crag. "It's time to go," he announced.

Other guards were rousing her friends. As she stumbled drowsily out of her sleeping hollow, she saw Stoneteller standing at the entrance to the tunnel that led to the Cave of Pointed Stones. Two more cave-guards stood alertly beside him, and Feathertail thought she could make out more in the tunnel itself; the Tribe cats were making sure that Stormfur was too heavily guarded for any sort of rescue attempt.

"We will take you to the edge of our territory and show

you the best way through the rest of the mountains," Crag meowed.

"What about Stormfur?" Brambleclaw asked, shaking a feather from his pelt. "We can't go without him."

The ThunderClan warrior's last attempt to free his friend peacefully was doomed to failure; Crag was shaking his head before he finished speaking. "You can't take him with you," he meowed. "His destiny is to stay here and save our Tribe from Sharptooth. We will care for him and honor him."

"So that makes it all right, then?" Crowpaw muttered disgustedly.

The cave-guards gathered around the Clan cats and forced them toward the entrance. Feathertail noticed that Crowpaw was still limping from the blow he had taken from the cave-guard the night before.

"Are you okay to travel?" she murmured in his ear.

"I don't have much choice, have I?" he meowed disagreeably, only to turn to her a moment later and touch his nose to her muzzle. "Don't worry; I'll be fine."

Just before they reached the waterfall, Feathertail heard her name, and turned to see Brook bounding toward her.

"I . . . I wanted to say farewell," she mewed as she came up. "I'm sorry it turned out like this. But without your brother, Sharptooth will destroy the whole Tribe."

Feathertail gazed into the young prey-hunter's eyes. She knew Brook believed what she was saying, but she couldn't forget how Stormfur had thought that this cat was his friend. Stormfur didn't make friends easily—a legacy of being half-

Clan, always feeling as if he had more to prove than other warriors, as if he could never fight hard enough or catch enough prey. Feathertail had watched this she-cat win her brother's trust, but now she had betrayed him, and would probably see him die in a battle with Sharptooth for the sake of her Tribe.

"Come on." Crowpaw brushed his tail against Feathertail's flank, already damp from the spray of the waterfall. Feathertail turned away from Brook without another word. As she padded along the narrow path, she strained to hear the voices in the thundering water, but today she heard only the ceaseless pounding of foam.

Whoever you are, she vowed silently, *we will come back for my brother. He is ours, and his destiny lies far away from here.*

The forest cats traveled through the mountains until almost sunhigh. The cave-guards kept pace with them on either side, their gaze fixed on the path ahead. They did not even stop to hunt, and the tense silence made every hair tingle on Feathertail's pelt.

She tried to study every rock, every tree, every twist in the path, hoping that they would be able to follow their own scent trail back to the cave. The rocky slopes were more familiar to her now, but all the paths still looked the same. In contrast, the cave-guards seemed to know exactly where they were going, sometimes doubling back to avoid boulders or cliffs.

Once Crag led them down a slope of shifting scree to a mountain stream. "Drink," he ordered, flicking his tail at the tumbling water.

Crowpaw's eyes narrowed as he gazed at the slippery rocks by the waterside, and Tawnypelt exchanged a suspicious glance with her brother.

"We're not going to push you in," Crag mewed irritably. "You must learn to drink when you can in the mountains."

Still wary, the forest cats crouched down and lapped the icy water.

The air was crisp and cold, with the sun shining in a pale blue sky. Wind ruffled their fur, but there was no sign of rain to wash away the scent trail. To Feathertail's relief, Crowpaw's limp didn't seem to be bothering him, and grew less apparent as the young cat exercised his injured leg. Tawnypelt was also managing well; although Feathertail saw her flinch once or twice when she had to cope with a difficult leap, she did not complain.

After a scramble over steep rocks, Crag brought them to a halt.

"This is the edge of our territory," he announced, though there were no scent markers to indicate a border. "You must go on alone from here."

Relief stabbed through Feathertail. She couldn't wait to get away from the cave-guards and their stern, silent looks.

"Head for that mountain," Crag went on, pointing with his tail at a sharp peak, its upper slopes streaked with the white of snow. "A path winds around it to greener lands beyond. You should be safe from Sharptooth until night falls."

Feathertail thought he put too much stress on *Sharptooth*, as if there were other dangers lurking among the rocks. Her suspicions hardened when she saw one of the other guards give him a warning glance. "Go on," the Tribe cat meowed roughly, giving her no chance to ask any questions, "while there's still plenty of daylight."

He dipped his head to Brambleclaw. "Farewell," he meowed. "I wish we could have met in a happier time. Our Tribes have much to teach each other."

"There's nothing I want to learn from *you*," Squirrelpaw muttered, and for once Crowpaw looked as if he agreed with her.

"I wish that too." Brambleclaw shot an icy glance at his companions to silence them. "But there cannot be friendship between us while you keep our friend a prisoner."

Crag bowed his head again; he looked genuinely regretful. "That is our fate and his, as our warrior ancestors have promised. Just as yours have made a promise to you."

He called the rest of his patrol around him with a flick of his tail, and all the cave-guards waited while Brambleclaw led the Clan cats up a grassy slope. Soon the grass gave way to loose stones, leading upward to a ridge of spiky rock.

Brambleclaw paused at the top. Feathertail glanced back to see that Crag and the other cave-guards were still watching them with unblinking stares.

"They're making sure we leave," Tawnypelt growled. "That means they'll probably be looking out in case we come back."

Crowpaw shrugged. "Their loss." He flexed his claws against the bare rock. "If we meet a patrol out here, they're crowfood."

Brambleclaw flashed him a glance. "We'll do this *without* fighting, if we can," he mewed. "Remember that we can't afford injuries this far from home. Meanwhile," he added, "let's keep going, and make them think we've given up."

He led the way between the rocks. On the other side the land fell away sharply into a grassy hollow. A spring of water bubbled out of a crevice and fell into a small pool. Two or three bushes grew beside it. The wind brought Feathertail the scent of rabbits.

"Can't we stop here?" Squirrelpaw pleaded. "Remember what they said about drinking when we can? We could hunt, and rest until it's time to go back."

Brambleclaw hesitated. "Okay. But we'd better keep watch in case the cave-guards come to check on us."

"I'll take first watch," Tawnypelt offered. "My shoulder's fine," she added. "And I'll call you if there's any trouble."

Very cautiously, stepping as lightly as if she were stalking a mouse, she slid back between the rocks and disappeared. Squirrelpaw was already bounding down into the hollow, calling out, "Come on! I'm starving!"

"She'll frighten every scrap of prey from here to Highstones," Crowpaw grumbled as Brambleclaw took off after her.

Feathertail watched as Brambleclaw caught up to the younger cat, and the two of them went on together, their pelts brushing. They had become very close during the journey, even if they didn't quite realize it yet.

"Don't mind Squirrelpaw," she told Crowpaw. "Let's go

and see if there are any fish in that pool. I could give you a lesson, just in case you want to catch any fish when we get home." She broke off and looked awkwardly down at the ground. "It'll be a useful thing to know, whatever happens."

Crowpaw brightened. "Okay." He paused as if he wanted to say something more, then without a word bounded down the slope after the two ThunderClan cats. Feathertail followed, her mind buzzing with her feelings for Crowpaw as well as her fears for her brother. She approached the pool and gazed down into its blue depths. She and Crowpaw had plenty of time to figure out what they would do when they got back to the forest. She tried to push away the tiny, persistent voice that kept telling her that cats from different Clans couldn't be together without causing a whole heap of trouble. She shook her head impatiently; right now, the only thing any of them should be thinking about was finding prey to give them strength for Stormfur's rescue.

A silver flash caught her eye and her paw shot out, claws extended, to hook a fish.

"Come over here," she instructed Crowpaw, "so your shadow doesn't fall on the water. And when you see a fish, be quick!"

Crowpaw came to join her, picking his way with a grimace around the muddy edge of the pool. He settled down at her side, but instead of peering into the water he looked into her eyes. "I know I shouldn't ask this, but . . . will you still see me when we get home?" He glanced down at his paws and added, "I want to be loyal to my Clan, but . . . there's never been another cat like you, Feathertail."

Feathertail's pelt tingled with happiness and excitement. She touched his muzzle with her nose, sensing the uncertainty that made it hard for him to believe that she could like him enough to cross Clan boundaries for him. "I know how you feel. We'll have to wait and see. It might not be so bad. With everything that's happening in the forest, the Clans will *have* to come together."

To her surprise, Crowpaw shook his head. "I don't see how. There have *always* been four Clans."

"Well, maybe *always* is going to change," she meowed quietly. "Now, what about that fish?"

Crowpaw brushed her shoulder with his tail, and crouched down over the water. A few heartbeats later his paw shot out. A fish curved up out of the water and fell wriggling on the ground; Crowpaw grabbed it in his jaws before it could slide back into the pool.

Feathertail jumped up and pushed her nose against his shoulder. "Well done! We'll make a RiverClan cat of you yet." She broke off, confused, and Crowpaw blinked in understanding.

His eyes were shining; Feathertail wished their companions could see this side of him, eager and enthusiastic, instead of the defensive, difficult face he chose to show to them.

She was distracted by a movement at the top of the rocks and looked up to see Tawnypelt crouched on the smooth stone.

"The cave-guards have gone," the ShadowClan warrior

called down to them. "But I'll stay on watch."

Not long after, Brambleclaw and Squirrelpaw returned from their hunting expedition with a couple of rabbits and a few mice; along with Feathertail's and Crowpaw's fish there was enough fresh-kill for all of them.

They each took a turn on watch, but there was no sign of any Tribe cats. They spent the rest of the day in the shelter of the bushes. Feathertail felt more at home out here, in the silent open air, than in the stuffy, noise-filled cave.

Clouds gathered in the sky, gray and ominous, covering the sun. The wind dropped; the air became heavy and damp, as if there were a storm coming.

At last the daylight faded and shadows began to thicken in the hollow.

Brambleclaw rose to his paws. "It's time," he meowed.

He took a few pawsteps back up the slope; as the others followed, Feathertail suddenly noticed how easily they could be seen against the rocks, especially Squirrelpaw's dark ginger pelt and her own light gray fur.

"This is never going to work. They're bound to spot us coming," she mewed anxiously.

"Wait." Squirrelpaw narrowed her eyes. "Why don't we roll ourselves in the mud? Then we'd look like Tribe cats, especially in the dark. It would help to hide our scent too."

Tawnypelt gave her a look full of respect. "That has to be the best idea I've heard for a moon."

Squirrelpaw's green eyes glowed, and she hurried back to the pool and began nosing around the edge. "There's plenty of mud here!" she called, beginning to roll in a sticky patch to plaster her fur.

Crowpaw's whiskers twitched in disgust as he and the others followed. "Just the sort of idea *she* would dream up. Clever, though," he admitted grudgingly.

Feathertail winced as she padded to the edge of the pool and felt mud ooze around her paws. Cold seeped through to her skin as she lay down in the glutinous hollow, thinking that at least her thick RiverClan pelt was suited to getting wet. Crowpaw would be much more uncomfortable with his thin, wind-flattened fur, although for once he didn't complain. She blinked fondly at him, remembering what he'd said earlier about wanting to see her when they got home. Right now, she didn't want to ever let him out of her sight.

Their pelts streaked and spiky with the mud, the Clan cats climbed back to the ridge and down the slope on the other side, warily crossing back into the Tribe's territory. Feathertail pricked her ears, alert for the sound of other cats, and they all stopped every few paces to sniff the air. Even with Squirrelpaw's disguise, there was a huge risk that they would be spotted, and no cat was sure how far the Tribe cats would go to keep Stormfur. Feathertail knew how desperate they were that their ancestors' prophecy should come true. She and her friends could all be returning to their deaths.

Brambleclaw's nose was almost touching the path as he sniffed out their scent trail from that morning. Feathertail tried hard to remember the landmarks they had passed, but everything looked different in the gathering darkness. They were padding down a steep path between broken rocks when Crowpaw suddenly halted, his muzzle raised and his jaws parted. Then he whirled on Feathertail and pushed her behind a rock, signaling wildly with his tail for the other cats to hide too.

A heartbeat later, Feathertail caught the same scent: Tribe cats! Peering out cautiously, she saw a patrol of lithe prey-hunters bounding along the path in the same direction, their jaws filled with prey, their escort of cave-guards around them. She tensed, waiting for them to pick up the intruders' scent and turn to attack, but they passed her hiding place without pause and disappeared into the darkness. Squirrelpaw's mud must have masked their scent, as they'd hoped.

"That's twice I saved you," Crowpaw teased, stepping away to let Feathertail stand up straight.

She touched noses with him with a purr of amusement. "I know. I won't forget it; don't worry."

Brambleclaw emerged from among the rocks at the other side of the path, signaling to the others to move on. This time Tawnypelt brought up the rear, keeping a lookout behind in case more prey-hunters were on their way home. The moon was just rising over the topmost peaks, a fuzzy white glow behind the covering of clouds, when they came to the river. Still alert for the sound of other Tribe cats, they followed the rushing water until they heard the roar of the waterfall in the distance.

"Quiet now," Brambleclaw whispered. "We're getting close."

Silently they padded on until they reached the top of the

falls. Feathertail crouched at the edge of the river, watching the dark water slide over the lip of the rock. Then a flash of lightning split the sky overhead, and above the thunder of the water she heard a rumbling in the sky.

"Storm's coming," Crowpaw breathed into her ear.

A fat drop of rain landed on Feathertail's head, and she shook it off. The noise and confusion of a storm might help them, but then she wondered if it would drive more cats than usual into the cave. Stormfur was heavily guarded already—they couldn't hope to take on the whole of the Tribe.

"Let's *go*," Squirrelpaw muttered impatiently.

Lightning flashed and another roll of thunder crashed overhead as the cats peered down. Feathertail could just make out the foaming white of the water as it fell into the pool. Then she thought she saw a movement in the darkness at the end of the path.

"What's that?" Crowpaw had seen it too.

As if in answer, another claw of lightning crackled across the sky. Feathertail heard Tawnypelt gasp in horror. For a single heartbeat that seemed to last forever, the white flash lit up the shape of a huge tawny-colored cat slinking along the path; it paused as the thunder pounded the sky, then padded on to disappear behind the waterfall.

Sharptooth!

CHAPTER 15

A terrible shrieking broke out in the cave, slicing through the sound of the rain pattering around them and even the noise of the falls. Feathertail sprang to her paws; every hair on her pelt told her to flee as far from the cave as she could. Only the thought of the danger that Stormfur was in made her stay where she was.

"Come on!" Brambleclaw's voice was tense.

The rest of the cats stared at him in disbelief.

"Down there?" Crowpaw demanded. "Are you mouse-brained?"

"Think!" Brambleclaw was already bounding toward the cave entrance; he paused and swung around to face the apprentice. "With Sharptooth in the cave, no cat will notice us. This might be our only chance to get Stormfur out."

Without waiting to see if the others were following he leaped down the rocks toward the path.

"I still think he's crazy!" muttered Crowpaw, but he followed all the same.

Feathertail scrambled down after them, her paws sliding on the wet rocks, her claws scraping painfully as she tried to keep her balance. She ran along the ledge behind the falls with barely enough time to be afraid of slipping and falling into the turbulent pool below. The screeching grew louder. Terror surged through Feathertail as she imagined what they would find inside the cave; Sharptooth might be sinking his fangs into Stormfur's neck at that very moment, clawing her brother's pelt and turning him into fresh-kill.

She skidded into the cave and halted just behind Brambleclaw. For a moment she could hardly make sense of what she was seeing. With the moon covered by clouds, the cave was almost dark; the huge shape of Sharptooth seemed to be everywhere at once, massive paws pounding on the floor as he sprang from wall to wall, blood spattered against his flanks and saliva dripping from his jaws. This was more terrible than Feathertail had ever imagined—there was no way Stormfur could challenge this beast and survive.

The Tribe cats scattered, scrambling blindly out of their sleeping hollows. Feathertail caught a glimpse of Brook, hustling a kit down the tunnel that led to the nursery, with another dangling from her jaws. Near the other tunnel, a cave-guard was clinging to the huge lion-cat's neck, only to be thrown off and flung against the wall with a sickening thud. The cave-guard slid to the floor and lay still, a trickle of blood running from its mouth. While Feathertail stared in horror, two or three cats fled past her with shrill cries, blundering against the Clan cats without realizing who they were.

"This way!" Brambleclaw ordered. He looked at each Clan cat in turn, his gaze resting longest on Squirrelpaw. "We have to do this for Stormfur," he reminded them.

Sharptooth had pounded across to leap up the far wall of the cave, trying to reach a Tribe cat who cowered on a ledge just above the vicious claws. Skirting the cave walls, clinging to the darkest corners, Brambleclaw headed for the tunnel leading to the Cave of Pointed Stones. Feathertail and the others followed. In the blackness they stumbled against Tribe cats, some wounded, others frozen in fear, but the terror and blood-scent filling the cave were so strong that no cat recognized them.

At the tunnel entrance, two cave-guards still held their positions, their fur standing on end and their eyes stretched wide. Feathertail felt a flash of respect for their courage, to stay there when all their Tribemates were running for their lives.

"Now!" Brambleclaw and Crowpaw launched themselves at the cave-guards, their claws slashing and their teeth bared. Squirrelpaw was only a heartbeat behind them. Feathertail heard an exclamation of astonishment from one of the guards, and recognized Crag's voice. She saw Brambleclaw bowl him over and fasten his teeth in the cave-guard's neck fur, while Crowpaw cuffed the other guard on both ears, drawing him away from the tunnel entrance. Squirrelpaw sank her teeth into Crag's tail and held on.

With the entrance clear, Feathertail and Tawnypelt darted down the tunnel. Before they reached the Cave of Pointed Stones they met two other cats, barely visible in the darkness. With a surge of relief and joy Feathertail recognized Stormfur's scent. The other cat was Stoneteller; she glimpsed his blazing eyes as he pelted past her and launched himself into the outer cave.

"Quick!" the Tribe leader yowled to Stormfur. "Your time has come. Oh, Tribe of Endless Hunting, help us now!"

"Feathertail!" Stormfur exclaimed. "What's happening?"

For a moment Feathertail was content just to drink in his scent and twine her tail with his. She had been afraid they'd find the Cave of Pointed Stones empty, that Stormfur would have already been sent out to do battle with the lion-cat, and that his body had been one of those bleeding in the corners of the cave.

"There's no time for that!" Tawnypelt snapped. "Head for the entrance. Don't stop for anything."

She dashed back down the tunnel, and Feathertail and Stormfur followed. As they reached the outer cave, a shriek ripped through the darkness, louder than thunder. A flash of lightning revealed Sharptooth backing toward the entrance. His jaws were clamped around a Tribe cat; with a shudder of pure horror Feathertail recognized Star, the kit-mother who had spoken to them when they first arrived. Her mouth was open in a desperate wordless yowl, and her claws scored the earth floor as she fought vainly to free herself. Then all was dark again; Feathertail saw the faint outline of the lion-cat against the sheet of water as it whipped around and vanished through the entrance.

For a heartbeat a shocked silence filled the cave. Then a shrill wail of loss rose all around. Feathertail felt a cat nudge her roughly and spun around to see Brambleclaw.

"Out—now!" he rasped.

He bounded toward the entrance with Squirrelpaw and Tawnypelt hard on his paws. Crowpaw thrust Feathertail after him, though she did not move until she was sure Stormfur was following too. No cat tried to stop them; all the Tribe were still gripped by terror, crouched low on the cave floor or gazing after Sharptooth with bristling fur and their eyes glazed with fear.

At the entrance Brambleclaw paused, sniffed the air, and then led the way along the path. Feathertail detected Sharptooth's scent, mingled with Star's fear-scent and the reek of blood, but they were fading. The predator had gone, carrying his prey with him and leaving many more cats dead or wounded.

Sheets of rain were falling steadily, gusted by the wind, and thunder rumbled out again overhead. Feathertail was soaked within a couple of heartbeats, her fur plastered to her body, but she scarcely noticed. She followed Brambleclaw up the rocks as he led the Clan cats back the way they had come. Behind them, the Tribe's heartbroken wailing died away, drowned in the pattering rain and the endless, unchanging roar of the waterfall.

CHAPTER 16

A cold raindrop splashed onto Leafpaw's fur, and she shook it away irritably. Above her, a restless wind stirred the trees, sending brittle scarlet and gold leaves drifting into the clearing. Leaf-bare was barely a moon away, but it seemed like the least of the Clan's troubles.

"The rabbit smelled bad," Cinderpelt reported to Firestar. "Barkface said that cats who ate them died. I believe him. This rabbit we saw wasn't infected with any sort of sickness I've encountered. It must be something the Twolegs have done."

Crouched beside the fresh-kill pile in the ThunderClan camp, Leafpaw listened anxiously as her mentor told Firestar what they had discovered on their way to Highstones. Leafpaw's heart twisted with pity to see the shock in her father's green eyes as he listened.

"This means we can't eat rabbits either," he meowed. "Great StarClan, what next? We'll all starve."

"No cat has died in our territory yet," Sandstorm pointed out from where she sat a tail-length away, her tail wrapped neatly around her paws. She twitched as a falling leaf brushed against her ear. "Maybe the trouble's just in WindClan."

"But rabbits run across the border all the time," replied Cinderpelt. "It might be safe to eat rabbits from the other end of our territory, near the Treecut place, but I don't think we should take the risk even there."

"You're right." Firestar heaved a deep sigh. "I'll announce it to the rest of the Clan. No more rabbits."

"Well, we have to eat something." Sandstorm got briskly to her paws. "I'll get my hunting patrol together and see what we can find." She padded away and disappeared between the branches of the warriors' den.

"Meanwhile," mewed Cinderpelt, "we'd better get rid of any rabbits in the fresh-kill pile."

Leafpaw studied the pathetically small pile of prey. There was only one rabbit; it looked plump and inviting, and her mouth watered at the sight of it. She hadn't had such a good meal for days. Then her belly cramped at the thought of what the Twolegs might have done to it. She thought she could catch a whiff of the harsh scent that had clung to the WindClan rabbit, but this rabbit's scent was so mixed up with that of the other prey in the pile that she could not be sure.

"Take it outside the camp and bury it," Firestar directed.

"Wait—don't pick it up in your mouth," Cinderpelt added. "Push it out with your paws, and then clean them with moss."

Leafpaw had just separated the rabbit from the pile when Dappletail, the oldest cat in the Clan, came past and gave the prey an appreciative look.

"I hope that's for the elders," she rasped. "My belly's flapping like a leaf in the wind."

"No." Cinderpelt explained what she and Leafpaw had seen in WindClan territory.

"What? I've never heard such nonsense!" Dappletail snorted. "WindClan has a bit of trouble, so ThunderClan can't eat rabbits? Barkface might have been lying, just to weaken ThunderClan. They've always been a proud, deceitful Clan. Have you thought of that?"

Leafpaw exchanged a glance with her mentor. She could see there would be no point in trying to convince Dappletail. The old cat wanted the rabbit.

"The decision's been made." Firestar spoke with the authority of Clan leader. "No more rabbits. Leafpaw will take that one out and bury it."

"She'll do no such thing!" Outraged, Dappletail darted for the rabbit and began tearing into it hungrily and gulping down huge mouthfuls.

"No!" Cinderpelt exclaimed. "Stop!"

Firestar sprang forward, pushing himself between the elder and her prey, and thrusting her gently away. "Dappletail, I'm ordering you not to eat that. It's for your own good."

The old cat's eyes burned into his, her gaze full of hostility. Seeing her skinny body, her tortoiseshell pelt dull and patchy, Leafpaw could understand her desperation. The old cat was usually one of the gentlest queens; only starvation would have driven her to this.

"Do you call yourself a leader?" she spat at Firestar. "The

whole Clan will starve, and it will be your fault."

"Firestar's doing the right thing," Cinderpelt insisted. "There's no point feeding the Clan with food that could kill us quicker than any hunger."

Dappletail turned on her, with lips drawn back in the beginnings of a snarl. Then she whipped around and stalked across the clearing toward the elders' den.

Leafpaw watched her go. "Please, StarClan, let that rabbit be safe," she murmured as she began to push the half-eaten remains toward the camp entrance.

A withered brown leaf spiraled down in front of Leafpaw as she padded up the ravine beside Cinderpelt. It was the day following their return from Highstones and the argument with Dappletail over the rabbit. Cinderpelt was stocking up on the herbs the Clan would need to see them through leaf-bare—weakened by hunger, the Clan would be in danger of greencough and deadly blackcough even more than usual.

"There's no point in going anywhere near the Twoleg monsters," Cinderpelt meowed. "Nothing grows where they've been. We'll head for Sunningrocks and see what we can find there."

Dead leaves lay thickly on the ground, stirred up by a stiff breeze. When she was a kit, Leafpaw would have loved to toss them in the air and chase them. Now she hardly had the energy to go on putting one paw in front of another.

Soon Sunningrocks appeared ahead of them, smooth gray mounds rising out of the grass like the backs of sleeping animals. Almost at once Cinderpelt found a thick clump of chickweed and began carefully biting off the stems. Leafpaw cast around to see what else she could find, looking longingly down to the bank of the river where plants grew thickly, their roots fed by the water. But that was RiverClan territory, and after being punished for the fishing lesson with Mothwing, Leafpaw knew better than to trespass.

She heard a scrabbling close beside her and turned to see a vole scuttling along the base of the nearest rock. In the same heartbeat the vole sensed her and darted for a crevice, but before it could gain safety Leafpaw had sprung on it and bit down hard on its neck.

Her belly was crying out to gulp down the prey, but instead she forced herself to pick it up and go looking for Cinderpelt. Her mentor was where she had left her, arranging the stems of chickweed, ready to carry them back to camp.

"Here," Leafpaw mewed, dropping the vole in front of Cinderpelt.

Her mentor looked up at her, blinking in gratitude. "No, Leafpaw. You caught it, so you eat it."

Leafpaw shrugged, trying to sound unconcerned. "I can catch another." She knew that Cinderpelt , with her crippled leg, would have more trouble hunting than any other Clan cat. "Go on," she added, when Cinderpelt still didn't start eating. "What will happen to ThunderClan if our medicine cat falls ill?"

Cinderpelt let out a purr, and touched her nose to Leafpaw's muzzle. "All right. And thanks, Leafpaw."

She crouched in front of the vole and disposed of it in rapid, neat bites. Leafpaw was just about to go look for more herbs, when she heard a voice yowling, "Cinderpelt! Cinderpelt!"

The medicine cat sprang up, ears pricked. "Over here!" she called.

Mousefur's apprentice, Spiderpaw, burst out of the trees, his long gray-black legs a blur as he raced across the grass and skidded up to Cinderpelt. "You've got to come," he panted. "It's Dappletail!"

"What's wrong?" Cinderpelt asked, while Leafpaw's heart began to pound.

"She's complaining of feeling sick," Spiderpaw replied. "She says her belly hurts."

"That rabbit!" Cinderpelt exclaimed. "I knew it. Okay," she added to Spiderpaw. "I'm on my way. You run ahead and tell them I'm coming."

Spiderpaw dashed off again while Cinderpelt turned to Leafpaw. "You stay here; there's no need for both of us to go back," she meowed. "Collect more herbs. And bring that chickweed back with you."

She started limping as fast as she could toward the trees. Leafpaw waited until her mentor had vanished into the bracken before turning back to her search. What was it Barkface had said about treating cats who had eaten deadly rabbits? He had dosed the sick cats with yarrow, but almost all of them had died. Only the strongest pulled through—but Dappletail was old, and already weakened by hunger.

Oh, StarClan help us! Leafpaw prayed. *Show us what to do, before the Twolegs destroy us all.*

She had just begun to search for herbs again when she heard the shrill wailing of a cat coming from the river. For a moment she wondered if she ought to cross the RiverClan border. She made up her mind when the wail came again; some cat was in trouble. Without any more hesitation Leafpaw bounded down the slope.

The river surged along between its banks, swollen by leaf-fall rain. Branches and other debris were swept along in the current, bobbing and swirling on the white-tipped ripples. Leafpaw gazed out over the water, wondering where the cry had come from. Then she spotted a branch surging along close to the RiverClan side; half hidden by its few remaining leaves was the small black head of a cat. As Leafpaw watched, it opened its jaws wide to let out another terrified wail as it clung to a branch for its life.

Leafpaw tensed, ready to leap into the river even though her common sense told her that it would do no good. The current was too strong and swift, and the drowning cat was too far away.

Just before she leaped she saw another cat thrust its way through the reeds on the far bank and jump into the river, striking out with strong paws toward the floating branch. Leafpaw recognized the blue-gray fur at once: It was Mistyfoot, the RiverClan deputy.

She watched, claws flexing in and out in anguish, as Mistyfoot reached the branch and began to push it across the current toward the RiverClan bank. But before they reached it the waves rolled the branch right over, dragging Mistyfoot with it so that she disappeared into the black water. Leafpaw let out a gasp of horror. Then there was a splash and she resurfaced closer to the bank, where her paws found a foothold on the pebbles. Leafpaw shivered with relief as she watched Mistyfoot drag the other cat out by the scruff of its neck and crouch beside it. The tiny, bedraggled shape lay utterly still, water streaming from its pelt.

"Can I help?" Leafpaw called, wondering if Mistyfoot would remember that she was a medicine cat apprentice.

Mistyfoot glanced up. "Yes! Come over!"

Leafpaw raced down the bank until she reached the stepping-stones. Floodwater was lapping over them, but she launched herself onto the first without hesitating. Moments could mean the difference between life and death for the black cat.

She was leaping for the third stone when her paws slipped and she scrabbled frantically against the slick wet surface. The river bubbled around her and for a heartbeat she thought she would be swept away, drowning and tumbling in bottomless black water. In the midst of surging terror she felt a warm touch on her side, pushing her back onto the stone. A sweet scent drifted around her, strangely familiar.

"Spottedleaf?" Leafpaw whispered.

She could see nothing, but she sensed the reassuring presence close to her, the same as in her dream beside the Moonstone. As if she had grown wings, she leaped quickly over the other stones and dashed along the far bank toward Mistyfoot and the cat she had rescued.

Before Leafpaw could reach them, Hawkfrost and Mothwing pushed their way out of the reeds and stood over the black cat.

"What happened?" Hawkfrost demanded.

"Reedpaw fell in the river. We need Mudfur," Mistyfoot meowed. "Can you fetch him? Quickly!"

"He went out to collect herbs," Mothwing told her. "I'll go and look for him."

She sprang along the path that led upstream, but her brother called her back. "It'll take too long," he rasped. He flicked his ears toward the still black cat. "You see to him, you know what to do."

Just then he became aware of Leafpaw approaching. He looked up and glared at her with his eerie ice-blue eyes. Leafpaw felt a shiver run through her. "What's *she* doing here?"

"I called her over," Mistyfoot explained. "Reedpaw needs all the help he can get."

Hawkfrost let out a disgusted snort. Leafpaw ignored him as she crouched beside the black cat. He was very small—newly apprenticed, she guessed—and he lay quite still, with a trickle of water coming out of his parted jaws. There was a gash on his shoulder; blood was oozing into his sodden fur.

"He must have fallen," Mistyfoot meowed worriedly. "The apprentices are always playing too close to the river. It looks as if the branch hit him."

Leafpaw bent closer to Reedpaw. A huge sigh of relief escaped her as she detected the faint rise and fall of his chest. He was still breathing—but his breaths were fast and shallow, and seemed to grow weaker as Leafpaw watched. She glanced at Mothwing, waiting for her to start treating the injured cat.

Mothwing's huge amber eyes were fixed on the limp body of the apprentice.

"Well?" Hawkfrost meowed impatiently. "Get on with it."

Mothwing looked up, and Leafpaw saw the glare of panic in her eyes. "I—I'm not sure. I haven't brought the right herbs. I'll have to go back to camp. . . ."

"Reedpaw hasn't time for that!" Mistyfoot rasped.

Leafpaw understood her friend's panic. They were only apprentices; they weren't ready yet to hold the lives of cats within their paws. Where was Mudfur?

Then a gentle voice spoke inside her mind. *Leafpaw, you can do this. Remember what Cinderpelt has taught you. Cobwebs for the bleeding . . .*

"Yes—yes, I remember now," Leafpaw mewed out loud.

Hawkfrost stared at her with narrowed eyes. "Do you know what to do?"

Leafpaw nodded.

"Right. Do it. You—out of the way." Hawkfrost shouldered his sister to one side so that Leafpaw could get closer to Reedpaw.

Mothwing let out a faint meow of protest; Leafpaw glanced up at her to see her amber eyes still wide and shocked and her ears flat to her head.

"Go and find me some cobwebs," Leafpaw instructed her. "Quickly!"

The RiverClan apprentice shot her a frightened look, then whirled around and dashed up the riverbank to the bushes at the top of the slope.

Now get the water out of him, Spottedleaf whispered. Leafpaw bent down and worked her shoulder under Reedpaw's, propping him up until water gushed out of his mouth.

Good. Now he'll breathe properly, so you can deal with his wet fur.

The apprentice started to cough feebly and let out a faint cry of pain.

"Lie still," Mistyfoot told him, giving his muzzle a reassuring lick. "You're going to be okay."

"That's right," Leafpaw meowed urgently to the RiverClan deputy. "Keep licking him—lick his fur the wrong way to help it dry and get him warm."

At once Mistyfoot bent down beside the young apprentice and began licking vigorously; after a moment's hesitation Hawkfrost began to do the same on his other side. Leafpaw licked at the gash on Reedpaw's shoulder, cleaning it of scraps of bark and leaf. She knew she had to get it clean to avoid infection setting in.

"Here," Mothwing gasped, reappearing beside Leafpaw with a wad of cobwebs. "Is this enough?"

"That's fine, Mothwing. Put them on just there."

She almost felt like Mothwing's mentor as she checked how the RiverClan cat put the cobwebs in place, making sure they covered all the gash, and patted them down carefully.

"That's fine," she repeated. "Reedpaw, do you hurt anywhere else?"

The apprentice coughed again; under Mistyfoot's and Hawkfrost's energetic licking he was beginning to revive. "No," he rasped. "Just my shoulder."

Leafpaw examined him for other injuries anyway, but she couldn't find any. "I think you're lucky," she meowed.

"He's lucky you were here," Hawkfrost growled, with a hostile look at his sister. "Mothwing, what was the matter with you? You're supposed to be a medicine cat!"

Mothwing shrank away, and would not meet her brother's gaze.

"Reedpaw, can you stand up?" Leafpaw asked, diplomatically not reacting to her friend's embarrassment.

For an answer the apprentice staggered to his paws. Mistyfoot supported him on his other side, letting him lean against her with his uninjured shoulder.

"Think you can make it back to camp?" Hawkfrost demanded.

Reedpaw nodded. "Thanks . . ." His voice trailed off as he looked at Leafpaw and his eyes widened. "You have ThunderClan scent!"

"That's right. My name's Leafpaw. I'm Cinderpelt's apprentice. Take him straight back," she added to Mistyfoot. "If Mudfur's there, he'd better check him. If not, you can give him some thyme leaves to chew for the shock."

"And poppy seeds for the pain," Mothwing added, trying to sound confident.

"Er . . . no, I wouldn't." Leafpaw hated contradicting her friend. "It's best if he sleeps naturally for now. He'll be worn out anyway from the shock."

Mothwing's gaze dropped to her paws again as Hawkfrost shot her a contemptuous glance. He turned away to pad upstream, toward the RiverClan camp. Mistyfoot followed, supporting Reedpaw. The black apprentice was still shaky, but he kept going until a clump of reeds hid all three cats from Leafpaw's sight.

As they left, Leafpaw couldn't help feeling envious of their sleek pelts and strong muscles. Even Reedpaw, with his fur drying rapidly in the cold wind, looked healthy and well fed. RiverClan was the only Clan that still had plenty of prey, the only Clan not to be affected by the Twolegs tearing up the forest.

Shaking off her resentment, Leafpaw glanced at Mothwing, who hadn't moved. "Don't feel bad," she meowed. "It's all over, and no harm done. Reedpaw will be fine now."

"It's *not* all over!" Mothwing whirled to face her, her voice rising. "I lost it. . . . My first chance to show that I'm fit to be a medicine cat, and I totally messed up."

"Everybody makes mistakes." Leafpaw tried to soothe her. "*You* didn't."

But I had help, Leafpaw thought, wishing she could tell her friend about Spottedleaf, but knowing that she could never share such a momentous secret with a cat from a different Clan. She sent a silent prayer of thanks to her father's friend.

"*I* could have helped Reedpaw," Mothwing went on bitterly.

"I *know* all that stuff you did. I gave you and your friend thyme leaves, that time WindClan chased you. But now . . . somehow I couldn't think straight. I just panicked, and I couldn't remember."

"You will next time."

"If there is a next time." Mothwing tore fiercely at the ground with sharp, curved claws. "Hawkfrost will tell every cat how useless I was, and Mudfur will wish he'd never chosen me. And the Clan will never respect me now!"

"Of course they will." Leafpaw padded up to her friend and pushed her nose into Mothwing's beautiful golden tabby fur. "It'll all be forgotten soon, you'll see." She was shocked that Mothwing was so sure her brother would spread the news of her failure around the camp. She would have expected Hawkfrost to be more loyal to his sister.

"I know what you're thinking," Mothwing mewed bitterly, making Leafpaw jump. "Hawkfrost is loyal to the *Clan*, not to me or to any cat. He cares more for being a great warrior than anything else."

Like Tigerstar, Leafpaw thought with an inward shiver.

"You're so lucky, Leafpaw." Mothwing's voice was despairing. "You're Clanborn, and your father is a Clan leader. My mother was a rogue, and no cat will ever forget that."

She turned away, her head bowed and her tail trailing on the ground, and began plodding upstream as if every pawstep were an effort.

"I'll see you soon!" Leafpaw called, but her friend did not respond.

There was nothing more Leafpaw could do. Sadly she went back to the stepping-stones and crossed more carefully than she had done in her desperate race to save Reedpaw.

By the time she reached the ThunderClan border, she was beginning to feel better. With leaf-bare coming, Mothwing would have plenty of chances to try out her medicine-cat skills, and her Clan would forget that she had failed once. Besides, Leafpaw couldn't help feeling pleased with her own success. She had saved a cat's life—the first time, but not the last, she hoped.

"Thank you, Spottedleaf," she murmured aloud, and thought she caught just a trace of the medicine cat's sweet scent.

Feeling more optimistic than she had felt in moons, she collected Cinderpelt's chickweed and hurried back to camp. When she reached the top of the ravine she paused; her optimism vanished and an icy claw closed around her heart at the sound of the shrill wails and yowling coming from the clearing below. As she looked down, Mousefur and Rainwhisker burst out of the gorse tunnel and raced up the ravine, hurtling past Leafpaw without even noticing her.

Leafpaw bounded down to the camp and brushed through the tunnel, terrified of what she would find. Had the Twolegs reached this far already? Firestar was standing at the foot of the Highrock with Graystripe, Sandstorm, and Brackenfur clustered around him. Outside the apprentices' den Whitepaw crouched, wailing like a kit. Shrewpaw and Spiderpaw were trying to comfort her.

Leafpaw skidded to a halt, bewildered. Why was everyone so upset? There were no alien scents in the camp, and no signs of Twoleg devastation. She spotted Cinderpelt, limping wearily into the fern tunnel that led to the medicine cats' clearing.

Leafpaw raced after her. "What's the matter?" she demanded, dropping the chickweed. "What's happened?"

Cinderpelt turned and gazed at her, her blue eyes full of sorrow. "Dappletail is dead," she explained, and the lack of emotion in her voice scared Leafpaw as much as anything else. "And Cloudtail and Brightheart have disappeared."

CHAPTER 17

❧

Stormfur's legs ached and the weight of his rain-sodden fur made his paws stumble painfully over the stones. He felt as if he had been fleeing through the stormy darkness for moons. The whole world seemed to have shrunk to nothing more than rock, wind, and rain.

As he scrabbled up a broken rock face he realized that the rain was easing off. Soon it was no more than a spatter driven by the wind. The sky began to clear, the moon struggling to show its light between the clouds.

Brambleclaw halted, and the rest of the cats gathered around him. They were standing on a wide ledge; above them was a slope covered with scree, while below the rock fell away into darkness.

"I have no idea where we are," Brambleclaw admitted. "I'm sorry, I meant to bring you back the same way we came with the cave-guards, but I've never seen this place before."

"It's not your fault," Squirrelpaw meowed, with a glare at Crowpaw as if she expected the WindClan apprentice to say something rude. "The rain has washed all the scent away, and it's too dark to see anything."

"That's all very well," Tawnypelt pointed out, "but what are we going to do now? If we're not careful, the Tribe cats will catch us."

"Or Sharptooth," Feathertail added with a shudder.

Stormfur cleared his throat. He was feeling guilty and betrayed that he had ever thought of the Tribe cats as his friends, and he wanted to forget them and everything to do with them as soon as he possibly could. But they had taught him skills that could be useful now, and it would be mouse-brained not to use them.

"I think I can find the way," he meowed. "I hunted with the Tribe, remember, more than the rest of you."

"You lead, then," Brambleclaw responded immediately. "Just get us out of these mountains."

Stormfur warmed a little at the ThunderClan warrior's trust in him. He wouldn't have been surprised if he had lost all Brambleclaw's respect, after the way he had settled in among the Tribe cats. He knew now how much Brambleclaw's friendship meant to him.

"It'll take a few days to cross the mountains," he warned the tabby warrior, remembering the day Brook had taken him to the top of a high peak and shown him the towering folds of rock stretching endlessly ahead. At least they would have the rising sun to guide them when daylight came. "But I think I can get you out of the Tribe's territory."

"The sooner the better," muttered Crowpaw. He was standing so close to Feathertail that their fur touched. There seemed to be an unspoken connection between them, and

Stormfur wondered what had happened while he'd been held prisoner in the cave.

Stormfur took the lead along the ledge and then diagonally up the scree, his paws slipping on the loose stones. Reaching the ridge, he paused to figure out the direction from the way the moss grew on the rocks and the trunk of a gnarled tree. Guilt swept over him again as he realized how easy it seemed to use Tribe ways, as if he had allowed himself to become a Tribe cat instead of a warrior loyal to RiverClan.

"What's the matter?" Feathertail asked quietly, coming up to him and brushing her side against his. He should have known she would be able to sense how bad he felt.

"I trusted them." Stormfur choked over the words. "Brook and Crag and the rest. I never thought . . . And then they took me prisoner, and the rest of you risked your lives to get me out of there."

"We couldn't leave you." Feathertail let out a comforting purr.

"They never told me anything about the prophecy, you know, not all the time we were hunting together. It was just as much of a shock to me when Stoneteller told us about it in the Cave of Pointed Stones."

"Yes, we know," his sister murmured.

"But do we have to stand here talking about it?" Crowpaw demanded disagreeably as he joined them on the ridge. "Let's just get *moving*."

"They *must* have been wrong." Stormfur ignored the WindClan apprentice, holding Feathertail's gaze and trying to convince himself as much as her. "I *can't* be the promised cat, right? It doesn't make sense."

"No, of course not," Feathertail mewed. "Don't blame yourself, Stormfur. None of us realized what was going on. And the Tribe, they aren't bad cats—just desperate."

Stormfur hoped his sister couldn't see the guilt that clawed deep inside his belly. What if the prophecy were true, and the Tribe of Endless Hunting really had chosen him to help the Tribe cats? StarClan had chosen four cats to save the forest, but he was not one of them. He had come on the journey because he couldn't bear to see Feathertail leave without him. Now he wondered whether somehow the Tribe of Endless Hunting had influenced his decision so that he would be in the right place to destroy Sharptooth.

But then he had turned his back on the Tribe at the time when they needed help the most. He remembered watching Sharptooth leave the cave, his fierce jaws gripping Star as she yowled vainly for help. What if the next cat to die was Crag? What if it was *Brook*? A picture came into Stormfur's mind of the beautiful she-cat trapped in those savage teeth, and he desperately tried to push it away.

He shivered, hardly aware that the rest of his friends were waiting for him.

"Is there something wrong?" Brambleclaw asked.

Stormfur shook himself. "No," he meowed. "It's this way."

On the other side of the ridge, the ground fell away into a slope broken up by shallow precipices, low enough for a cat to leap down from one level to the next. As he crouched on the edge of one of these, he saw a roosting mountain bird just below him.

Squirrelpaw, at his shoulder, prodded him and pointed with her ears. To be on the safe side, Stormfur flicked his tail lightly across her jaws and signaled to the rest of the cats for silence.

"I'll get it," he whispered. "You stay here."

He was appalled by the way his new skills seemed natural to him, as if he had known them all his life. The bird was on a narrow ledge, so he could not leap down on it without risking a bad fall. In the forest, cats wouldn't hesitate to jump out of trees, but that was onto soft earth, not jagged stone that sliced open paws and jarred bones.

Instead he cautiously crept down a few tail-lengths farther on and worked his way stealthily back to the bird, using broken rocks for cover. When he was close enough he pounced, pinning the bird against the rock face, where it fluttered helplessly for a few heartbeats until he took its life.

"That was great!" Squirrelpaw exclaimed, curling her tail up in admiration. "You're just like a real mountain cat, Stormfur."

"I hope not," Stormfur mewed.

All six cats gathered around to eat their share of the bird. By the time they had finished, a thin rain had begun to fall and clouds were massing once more to cover the moon.

"This is hopeless," mewed Brambleclaw, swiping his tongue around his jaws. "I think we should shelter for the rest of the night."

"As long as the Tribe cats don't track us down," Tawnypelt warned. Stormfur noticed that her shoulder wasn't giving her trouble anymore; Stoneteller's herbs had worked well. At least that was something they could thank the Tribe cats for.

"I think we're far enough away by now," he meowed. "Brambleclaw's right. We can't keep going in this rain. Let's see if we can find a cave."

He took the lead again, this time looking for somewhere that would give them shelter. He found it soon enough, a dark hole leading into the mountainside from the base of a rock, overhung by a couple of scrubby bushes.

Cautiously he approached it and sniffed. "Stale rabbit," he reported. "It was probably a burrow a long time ago."

"Too bad," Squirrelpaw meowed. "I could do with a rabbit."

"Tribe cat scent, too," Crowpaw added, coming up beside Stormfur to sniff. "And that's fairly fresh. I'm not going in there."

"Stay outside and get wet, then," Squirrelpaw retorted, stepping forward.

"Hang on." Tawnypelt used her tail to bar Squirrelpaw's way into the cave. "Let me check it out."

She slipped down the hole while Squirrelpaw stared indignantly after her. For the first time that night Stormfur felt himself growing more cheerful, warmed by the ThunderClan apprentice's courage. She still couldn't bear to leave the dangerous tasks to full warriors.

A moment later Tawnypelt's voice came out of the hole,

echoing as if she were speaking from a larger space below. "Come on. Everything's fine."

Stormfur led the way down the cramped passage, his fur brushing the walls on either side. The opening narrowed until he had to breathe in, afraid of getting stuck, then suddenly grew wider. Though the darkness was unbroken, the echo of his pawsteps on the floor told him that he was standing in a fairly large cavern.

"This is great!" Squirrelpaw's voice came from just behind him. He felt her shake the raindrops from her pelt as she added, "All we need now is a good pile of fresh-kill."

Stormfur checked by scent that all six cats, even Crowpaw, had entered the cave. He was just beginning to relax when another scent washed over him and he froze with horror: It was a Tribe cat, yet somehow different from the Tribe cats he knew.

At the same moment a voice meowed from the shadows, "And who might you be?"

CHAPTER 18

🍀

All night the Clan had kept vigil for Dappletail, and now, in the pale dawn light, the elders were bearing her body out of the camp to be buried. The clearing was wreathed in mist and the leafless branches of the trees dripped rain from a sharp shower during the night. Leafpaw watched in silence. The old cat had been part of her life, and with her passing it seemed as if everything else she had known would slip away too.

As the elders departed through the gorse tunnel, the other cats gathered together in little groups, mewing urgently and casting anxious glances at one another. Leafpaw could not hear what they were saying, but she didn't need to. She knew they would be discussing the disappearance of Cloudtail and Brightheart. That made four cats that were missing from ThunderClan, but Leafpaw could not believe that StarClan had summoned Cloudtail and Brightheart away too—unless the others had already failed on their quest, and would never return. *If you can't help us, StarClan*, she thought desperately, *why are you taking our cats away?*

Cinderpelt broke into her thoughts, pushing her nose into Leafpaw's fur in wordless comfort, then limped forward a pace or two to meet Firestar and Graystripe. Leafpaw spotted Mousefur loping across the clearing after them with Thornclaw and Ashfur just behind her.

"I'm taking out the dawn patrol," Mousefur announced as she came up. "Do you still want us to look for Cloudtail and Brightheart?"

"Not that there's much point, if they left on purpose," Ashfur added darkly.

Leafpaw's heart sank even further as she remembered the Clan's efforts the day before to find the two cats. Patrols had covered the entire territory, picking up a scent-trail leading toward the place where the Twolegs had destroyed the forest. It had broken off abruptly near one of the huge tree-cutting monsters, and after that there was nothing.

"Keep your eyes open," Firestar replied. "That's all you can do."

"I wouldn't put it past Cloudtail to have gone back to the Twolegs," Mousefur growled. "With so little prey in the forest, even Twoleg food must look tempting."

"And he ate it often enough when he was an apprentice," Ashfur put in.

"Yes, don't forget the time he left us," Mousefur mewed. "Cats were put at risk, rescuing him from the Twolegs."

"That's enough!" Graystripe hissed.

"No, she's right." Leafpaw couldn't believe how tired her father sounded. "Cloudtail has always had a paw in the Twoleg world. But I thought he was loyal to his Clan now."

"Of course he is. You're not being fair to him." Cinderpelt's voice was sharp. "It's been a long time since Cloudtail ate kitty-pet food. He was young and stupid then."

"Besides, Brightheart would never do that." Graystripe supported his missing Clanmates with a flash of his amber eyes. "And Cloudtail wouldn't go off without her. We have to figure out why they're *both* missing."

"And why they left Whitepaw behind," Thornclaw meowed. "She's their only kit."

Mousefur grunted. "True. I wonder if they went over to RiverClan?" she suggested. "Stealing fish?"

"Now I wouldn't put *that* past Cloudtail," Cinderpelt agreed, but there was no hostility in her voice.

Graystripe thought for a moment, then shook his head. "No. If RiverClan caught them they'd just chase them off. There'd be trouble at the next Gathering, but our cats wouldn't just disappear."

Unless they fell in the river, Leafpaw thought, not daring to put words to the idea. She couldn't forget the surge of flood-water when she nearly fell off the stepping-stones, on her way to help Reedpaw.

"Their scent trail didn't lead toward RiverClan," Firestar pointed out. "I can't help thinking it's strange that it ended so close to the Twoleg monsters. Suppose . . ."

He let his voice die away, but Leafpaw saw the anxiety in his eyes, and she could guess what his thoughts were. She had seen how the first Twoleg monster turned from the Thunderpath and began to tear up the forest. If a cat got in its way it could be crunched in those powerful jaws without the monster even realizing it. She shivered, and her gaze met her father's. They were both fond of their wayward kin Cloudtail, and Leafpaw loved Brightheart fiercely for her courage in coping with the terrible injuries from the dog pack. The two cats would be a great loss to their Clan.

"Just carry on as usual, Mousefur," Firestar decided. "And report if you see anything odd."

"I always do." Mousefur hurried off with the two younger warriors behind her.

Firestar shook himself as if he was pushing useless thoughts away. "Cinderpelt, has StarClan shown you anything at all about Cloudtail and Brightheart?"

"No," Cinderpelt replied. "Nothing at all."

"Or any signs about more warriors going missing in the forest? It's . . . it's not all that long since Brambleclaw and Squirrelpaw disappeared." He choked the words out like half-eaten bones.

Again Cinderpelt shook her head. "StarClan is silent. I'm sorry."

Yet again, Leafpaw struggled with the urge to tell her father and mentor what she knew, that Brambleclaw and Squirrelpaw had been summoned away by StarClan to discover something that would help the forest. But she hardly knew what to say anymore. Whenever she tried to reach Squirrelpaw she had nothing but confused, terrifying impressions of rushing water, darkness, and raking claws—blood, rock, and water churned together. She couldn't reassure Firestar that Squirrelpaw was all right, nor give Graystripe hopeful news of his missing children from RiverClan.

"Perhaps I ought to make a trip to Highstones," Firestar meowed. "StarClan might speak to me, if—"

He broke off as Brackenfur came up, his apprentice, Whitepaw, just behind him. Leafpaw's heart went out to her. The young cat's head was bowed, and her tail trailed in the dust. She was obviously grieving for the loss of her parents.

"Firestar, I think you ought to have a word with Whitepaw," Brackenfur mewed worriedly.

Firestar's ears flicked up. "Why, what's the matter?"

Whitepaw looked up at him. "I want to be excused from training," she begged, her eyes burning with the intensity of her plea. "I want to look for Cloudtail and Brightheart."

"I've told her she can't go off on her own," Brackenfur continued. "But she—"

"*Please*," Whitepaw interrupted. "I'm only an apprentice. The Clan can do without me. I've *got* to find them."

Firestar shook his head. "I'm sorry, Whitepaw," he meowed gently. "Apprentices are important to the Clan, just as much as any other cat. Besides, Brackenfur is quite right. You can't go wandering off by yourself, especially now, when we don't know what the danger is. In fact, no cat should leave camp alone."

"We've searched already," Graystripe added. "We did everything we could."

"But it wasn't enough!" Whitepaw wailed. Leafpaw knew that Whitepaw would never have spoken to the Clan deputy like that if she hadn't been driven out of her mind with worry.

"StarClan will be with them wherever they are," Cinderpelt murmured comfortingly, pressing her nose into Whitepaw's fur.

"Brackenfur, take out a hunting patrol," Firestar meowed. "StarClan knows, we can use the fresh-kill. Whitepaw, go with him; you can keep your eyes open for Cloudtail and Brightheart as well. But you're *not* to leave your mentor, is that clear?"

Whitepaw nodded; she was looking a little more hopeful.

"I'll go with you," Graystripe offered, "and I'll get Sandstorm to come as well. If any cat can find them, she can." He hurried off into the warriors' den.

"Thank you, Firestar," mewed Whitepaw, dipping her head respectfully before following her mentor toward the camp entrance.

Leafpaw watched until Graystripe and Sandstorm came to join them, and all four cats disappeared into the gorse tunnel.

"We aren't safe in our own territory anymore," Firestar murmured. "But surely *four* cats can't go missing without—"

He broke off as a low, feeble wail rose up from the nursery. Leafpaw whipped around to see Dustpelt emerge. He staggered forward for a couple of tail-lengths and sank to the ground as if his legs would not hold him up.

With a glance at her father, Leafpaw dashed across to him, visions of disaster rushing through her head. Firestar and Cinderpelt followed, and came to a stop in front of Dustpelt.

"Are you hurt?" Firestar demanded.

The brown tabby warrior gazed up at his leader with eyes

as dull as pebbles. "It wasn't her fault," he whispered. "Fern-cloud did her best. But she hasn't been eating enough to keep herself alive, let alone three kits."

As he finished speaking, Leafpaw heard the wail break out again, echoing with enough grief for the death of a whole Clan.

"What is it?" she cried.

Dustpelt gave her a long, hopeless stare. "Larchkit is dead."

Instantly, Cinderpelt whisked past Dustpelt, on her way to Fecloud in the nursery. Firestar rested his tail-tip on the brown warrior's shoulder, in a vain attempt to comfort him. Dustpelt briefly pushed his nose into his leader's flame-colored fur. Leafpaw felt her throat tighten to see the two cats, who had never been friends, brought close together by their shared grief.

"What next?" Firestar meowed, lifting his head to the gray morning sky. "StarClan, what trouble will you send to ThunderClan now?"

CHAPTER 19

What was that? Every hair on Stormfur's pelt shot up in fear. He
and his friends were trapped in this dark hole; whoever had
just spoken was blocking the entrance, and there was nowhere
else to go. Desperately he tasted the air and picked out the
scents of several cats, all of them smelling of Tribe, and yet not
Tribe.

"Who are you?" he demanded.

For an answer he felt a powerful shoulder thrusting him
aside as the strange cat entered the cave. There was the soft
sound of pawsteps as the others followed.

Then he heard Brambleclaw's voice, tense but still calm.
"We are traveling to our home far from here and we took
shelter only for the night. We have no quarrel with you."

The strange cat spoke again. "This is our place."

"Then we'll leave," Tawnypelt mewed. She padded toward
the entrance, and the other cats shuffled around to follow
her.

Stormfur felt his fur begin to lie flat again. With any luck
they could get out of here without a fight. These cats couldn't
have come from the Tribe of Rushing Water, or they would

have known who he and his companions were. Yet they carried the Tribe's scent; Stormfur was puzzled, but he was content to leave the mystery behind him if they could just get away safely.

"Not so fast," the newcomer growled. "How do we know you're telling the truth? I don't know you, and I don't know your scent."

"Talon, we should take them prisoner." A soft hiss came from one of the other cats. "We might be able to use them as bait for Sharptooth."

"You know about Sharptooth?" Stormfur exclaimed.

"Of course we know about Sharptooth," rumbled the first voice, the one called Talon. "Every cat in these mountains knows about Sharptooth."

As he spoke, Stormfur realized that the darkness was no longer unbroken. Gradually the shapes of the strange cats were outlined in faint gray light as dawn filtered down the tunnel. Every hair on Stormfur's pelt prickled with fear as he looked at them.

The first of them, Talon, was one of the biggest cats he had ever seen, a dark brown tabby with massive shoulders and huge paws. His ragged pelt was bristling with hostility, and a deep scar stretched across one side of his face, curling his lip in a frozen snarl. His amber eyes were narrowed, his gaze flicking suspiciously over the forest cats.

Behind him were two other cats, a scrawny black tom whose tail was little more than a jagged stump, and a gray-brown she-cat. Both of them flexed their claws as if they could hardly wait to sink them into the Clan cats' fur.

Although the Clan cats outnumbered the strangers two to one, Stormfur didn't like their chances in a fight. They certainly wouldn't get away without serious injuries. He could see his friends were thinking the same; even the aggressive Crowpaw was silent, his gaze fixed warily on the strangers.

"We have seen Sharptooth and we know how savage he is." Brambleclaw was still trying to keep the exchange peaceful. "But we're on an urgent mission and we have to leave."

"You'll go when I say you can," Talon growled.

"You can't keep us here!" Stormfur winced as Squirrelpaw spoke up, her green eyes blazing. There was nothing wrong with her courage, but sometimes she hadn't the sense of a mayfly. "We've already escaped from the Tribe of Rushing Water."

Crowpaw let out a furious hiss, and for once Stormfur sympathized with him. Squirrelpaw needed to be a lot more careful about what she told these terrifying cats.

But to Stormfur's surprise, the suspicion in Talon's gaze seemed to fade. "You have been with the Tribe?"

"That's right," meowed Brambleclaw. "You know of them, then?"

"We know much, and too much," Talon replied, and the tabby she-cat added, "We were once Tribe cats too."

Stormfur stared at her in astonishment; he had assumed that these cats were homeless rogues. It would explain the puzzling scent, if they had once belonged to the Tribe, but he remembered how the Tribe had refused to turn the Clan cats out at night in case they met Sharptooth. If they had been that concerned about strangers, it seemed odd that they would let their own Tribemates live outside the cave. Unless they had committed a crime that outweighed the threat of Sharptooth. . . .

"Did the Tribe make you leave?" he asked.

"As good as," Talon grunted. Slowly his bristling fur began to lie flat. He flicked his tail at his two companions, which they seemed to take as an order to guard the entrance, for they settled down one on either side of it. "Sit," Talon said to the forest cats. "Sit and we will talk. But don't try to leave, unless you want to lose your ears."

Stormfur believed that he meant the threat. Cautiously he sat down; his friends did the same, making themselves as comfortable as they could on the bare sandy floor. As the light strengthened Stormfur made out his surroundings more clearly: The roof of the cave was thickly interlaced with roots, stretching above earth walls, with more roots and stones jutting out here and there. He could not see any bedding, any fresh-kill pile, or any other sign that these three cats lived here permanently. Yet Talon had said it was where they regularly came to shelter. It must be a harsh life that they led here.

"My name is Talon of Swooping Eagle," the huge tabby began, raising one paw to the scar on his face. "An eagle's talon did this when I was a kit, and gave me my name as well as a mark to remind me how close I came to losing my life. This is Rock Where Snow Gathers and Bird Who Rides the Wind." He pointed his tail at the black tom and the she-cat in turn.

Stormfur's fear began to ebb. Somehow knowing the strangers' names made them seem less like enemies.

"Many seasons ago," Talon went on, "the Tribe of Endless Hunting sent a sign to Stoneteller. They chose six cats to leave the shelter of the caves and go out into the mountains to face Sharptooth and kill him. We are three of that six."

"What happened to the others?" Crowpaw put in.

"Sharptooth happened," Rock snarled from his place by the entrance. "He nearly had me, too. How do you think I lost my tail?"

"So, wait," Tawnypelt mewed. "The Tribe sent you out to kill Sharptooth?"

Talon bowed his head. "Stoneteller ordered us not to come back without his pelt."

"But that's mouse-brained!" Squirrelpaw burst out. "How could six of you kill Sharptooth when the whole of the Tribe couldn't do it?"

The tabby looked up again, and Stormfur winced at the depths of bitterness in his eyes. "I don't know," he replied. "Do you think we haven't asked ourselves that question? I'd give the fur off my back to save my Tribe, but what can any of us do?"

Feathertail let out a comforting murmur. "Could you not go to Stoneteller and tell him you've done your best? He might let you back in."

"No!" Talon's eyes blazed at her. "I won't crawl to him and beg. Besides, what use would it be? We all obey the will of the Tribe of Endless Hunting."

Stormfur blinked. There were times when the words of his own warrior ancestors seemed harsh and difficult to understand, but he could not remember StarClan ever banishing cats to a lonely existence that could only end in their death. *Would I have the courage to obey if they did?* he wondered.

"I'm surprised we didn't hear about you before," Brambleclaw meowed. "They told us about Sharptooth, but no cat mentioned you."

Talon snorted. "They've probably forgotten all about us."

"Or they're ashamed," Bird added grimly.

"You've just left the Tribe recently?" Talon asked. When Brambleclaw nodded, he went on with longing in his voice. "There's a cat . . . her name is Brook Where Small Fish Swim. Did you see her there?"

Stormfur's ears pricked up. For a heartbeat, jealous fury swept through him at the obvious affection with which this ragged loner spoke of the prey-hunter.

"Yes, we met Brook," Feathertail replied.

"Is she all right? Happy?"

"She's fine," Tawnypelt told him. "And as happy as any of them are with Sharptooth breathing down their necks."

"Because we failed . . ." All Talon's bitterness was in the three words. "Brook's my sister," he went on, letting out an awkward *mrrow*, half amused and half embarrassed. "You'd not think a pretty cat like that was related to me, would you? She's from a younger litter, and when Sharptooth took our mother I wanted to be there to look out for Brook."

Stormfur relaxed. What was the matter with him? Why

should he care that Brook was Talon's sister, and not his mate?

"She would have come with me," Talon went on. "But it wasn't the will of the Tribe of Endless Hunting. I was glad. This is no sort of life."

Stormfur knew he was right. He flinched as he thought about the destruction that Sharptooth had brought to the Tribe: not only the cats he had killed for prey, but the lives he had destroyed in their desperate attempts to kill him. Cats driven into exile, separated from their kin . . .

And what if he really was the chosen cat, destined to save the Tribe from Sharptooth? Had he any right to refuse his destiny? The thought crossed his mind that he ought to go back, but the idea terrified him so much that he pushed it away. He and his friends had their own mission, to tell their Clans what they had learned from Midnight, and nothing must be allowed to interfere with that. They had to tell the Clans to leave the forest before it was destroyed by the Twolegs' new Thunderpath.

The light in the cave had grown brighter and turned golden, as if the rain had stopped and the sun had risen above the mountaintops. Feeling as if he could not bear to be trapped belowground for another heartbeat, Stormfur rose to his paws.

"Will you let us out to hunt? We need fresh-kill."

Talon glanced at his companions.

"We're not going anywhere," Brambleclaw assured him. "We're all exhausted, and we need to rest."

After another pause, the tabby shrugged. "Go, stay, do what

you want. It's nothing to do with us. We wouldn't feed you to Sharptooth, whatever Rock might say."

Stormfur pushed his way through the narrow tunnel and out onto the mountainside. The sun hovered over the top-most peak; that was the way they should be going, following the sunrise until they came home to the forest.

Squirrelpaw followed him out, and stood looking around alertly, as if she had not spent all night scrambling about on the mountain in the pouring rain. "Right," she meowed. "Where's the fresh-kill?"

In the rain and the darkness, Stormfur had seen very little of their surroundings before they found the cave. Now he saw that just below the entrance the rocks were broken up; thin soil had lodged in the cracks, enough for grass to grow and a few bushes. A trickle of water wound among them. "Down there," he suggested.

Squirrelpaw swept her tail back toward the hole. "The rest want to sleep, just as if they were hedgehogs in leaf-bare," she meowed. "Let's hunt, and surprise them when they wake up!"

"Okay." Stormfur was pleased to be hunting with the determinedly cheerful apprentice, away from the ThunderClan warrior who took up so much of her attention. But since the beginning of their journey home he had been aware of how close she and Brambleclaw had become. It would always be easier for them to be together than for her to have any connection with Stormfur. Besides, he was starting to realize that he felt about Brook in a completely different way from how he felt about Squirrelpaw.

He had kept a check on his feelings for Squirrelpaw because they were in different Clans, but he was drawn to Brook in a way that he couldn't ignore so easily. The sheen on her tabby fur, the glow in her eyes, her speed and skill, stayed with him even though he had escaped from the cave. Was that how Crowpaw and Feathertail felt about each other? he wondered suddenly, with a pang of sympathy he had never felt before. Would he cross boundaries like that to be with Brook?

Stormfur pushed the thought away. He would never see Brook again, so what was the point? He tried to focus instead on the sunny morning, and the pleasure of hunting with a skillful partner. It was good to have Squirrelpaw beside him as a friend, without the jealousy that might have threatened his friendship with Brambleclaw.

"Come on!" Squirrelpaw had already bounded down among the bushes. "I want you to teach me some of those new mountain moves."

As the sun rose higher they stalked through the sparse mountain vegetation, beginning to build a pile of fresh-kill on the ledge outside the cave. Squirrelpaw learned the new ways of hunting quickly, and couldn't stop herself bouncing like a kit with the delight of bringing down her first falcon.

"We need to teach this stuff at home," she meowed, flicking a feather off her nose with one paw. "We always hunt in the undergrowth, but like this we could hunt out in the open as well."

Bleak thoughts about the future of the forest rushed

through Stormfur's mind. Squirrelpaw clearly guessed what he was thinking, for her triumph faded and she added somberly, "We might need to."

When they returned to the cave with more prey to add to the pile they had started, Stormfur saw Talon crouched on the ledge, his eyes half closed as he let the sun soak into his ragged fur.

He opened his eyes as the two Clan cats approached. "You've hunted well," he meowed.

"Help yourself," Stormfur invited him.

"Thanks." He padded over to the pile and dragged out a rabbit.

Squirrelpaw trotted back inside the hole. "I'm going to get our lazy friends," she announced.

Stormfur noticed that Talon had stopped eating after just one bite, and was looking at him expectantly. Almost without realizing what he was doing, Stormfur pulled a falcon from the pile of fresh-kill, took a hasty bite, and shoved it toward Talon. The Tribe cat nodded and pushed his own piece of fresh-kill toward Stormfur.

"I see your Tribe shares as well," was all he said, and Stormfur looked down at his paws, suddenly feeling uncomfortable.

For a few moments, they ate their prey in silence. Stormfur was not sure how the exiled cats had changed from being enemies to something like friends, but he was certain that the Clan cats had nothing to fear from them now. He just wished that there were some way of helping them.

"I can tell you're worried about the Tribe," he began awkwardly, swallowing a mouthful of rabbit.

"Of course I'm worried." Talon fixed him with a piercing amber gaze. "And so are you, even though you're not one of us."

Stormfur nodded slowly. He had been trying not to admit that, even to himself. Were his feelings so obvious, even to a stranger?

"Every day they live in fear," Talon went on. "Every pawstep out of the cave is filled with terror, when every rock might be hiding Sharptooth."

Stormfur nodded, thinking of the cave-guards who went out with the hunting parties. He tried to imagine what it would be like never to run freely through your own territory, always to feel the threat of claws and fangs. Cold shivers ran through his pelt as he remembered hunting with Brook in the first days of their stay with the Tribe. She had told him that Crag and the others were there to guard the prey-hunters from eagles, but now he understood that they were watching for Sharptooth as well. He and the Tribe cats had been in as much danger as any of the prey they hunted.

"I wish I knew what to do," he meowed. "We made this journey because of a prophecy from StarClan—"

"StarClan?" Talon echoed.

"The spirits of our warrior ancestors," Stormfur explained. "Like your Tribe of Endless Hunting."

He went on to explain how StarClan had prophesied great trouble for the forest and chosen four cats, one from each of the Clans, to make the journey and learn what Midnight had to tell them.

"I wasn't one of the four," he finished, "but I came to be with my sister."

"And now you're going home," Talon meowed.

"Yes, but we don't know whether we'll be in time to help." Even while he was speaking, Stormfur reflected that at least they *could* go home; Talon and his Tribemates never could.

"Your Tribemate said that you'd escaped from the Tribe of Rushing Water." Talon looked puzzled. "Does that mean they kept you prisoner? That is not the Tribe I knew."

"It wasn't quite like that." Stormfur swallowed. If he wanted to earn the trust of this cat, he had to tell his story, but he didn't know how Talon would react. There was every chance that the huge tabby would try to drag him back to the Tribe to fulfill the prophecy and win the right to return to his home. "There was another prophecy," he admitted. "Stoneteller had a sign from the Tribe of Endless Hunting. . . ."

Talon listened to the story with his unblinking amber gaze fixed on Stormfur. "A silver cat?" he rumbled, when the story was finished. "Do you believe you are the one?"

Stormfur started to deny it, and found he could not. "I don't know," he answered honestly. "At first I didn't see how I *could* be, but now . . . The first prophecy, the one from StarClan, matters more than anything to me. But I'm not one of the chosen. I can't help wondering whether I'm meant to do this instead." He sighed. "But I can't follow *both* prophecies.

Which one of them is right?"

Talon was silent for a few moments. Then he meowed heavily, "Neither of them is right. And neither is wrong." He let out a soft growl from deep in his throat. "Prophecies are strange things. Their words are never clear."

Stormfur nodded, remembering how he and his friends had thought that "midnight" meant just that, until they discovered that it was the name of the wise badger who had told them what they should do.

"Everything depends on how cats interpret the prophecy," Talon went on. "And whether the prophecy is fulfilled depends on what they decide to do about it. It is up to us to choose the code we live by. Isn't that true for your cats as well?"

Stormfur stared in surprise at the older cat. He was right. StarClan and the Tribe of Endless Hunting made exactly the same demands on the cats they watched over, with the same promises of protection and guidance if only they knew how to read the signs.

"What do you *think* you should do?" Talon challenged him.

Stormfur shook his head. "I don't know."

"But you will." The big tabby rose to his paws. "Your faith and your courage will tell you." Amusement glinted faintly in his amber eyes. "Just don't take too long about it," he added as he squeezed back into the tunnel that led to the cave.

When he had gone, Stormfur let out an exhausted sigh. These mysteries were too much for him; he was a warrior, and all he wanted was to follow the warrior code. But what should he do, when the code did not speak clearly to him?

The sun was warm on his fur, and it was a long time since he had slept. His belly was comfortably full of prey. He yawned, and his eyes closed.

Hardly any time seemed to have passed before he realized that he was lying in a forest clearing, though he could not have said exactly where it was. The scent of green, growing things was all around him, and he could hear the soft murmur of a stream. He opened his eyes to see moonlight filtering through the leaves above his head.

He stirred, puzzled. This was a forest at the height of green-leaf, though by now leaf-bare should be well on its way. Then another scent tickled his nose, something sweet and reassuring and somehow achingly familiar, though he had no memory of smelling it before. A voice behind him mewed, "Stormfur."

He turned his head and for a heartbeat thought he was looking at Feathertail. No, this cat had a silvery gray pelt very like his sister's, but he didn't recognize her.

"Who are you?" he demanded, rising to his paws.

The cat did not reply, but padded over to him and touched noses with him. Stormfur saw the glitter of starshine around her paws. With a shiver, he knew that he was dreaming, and that a warrior of StarClan had come to visit him.

"Dearest Stormfur, I am so proud of you and Feathertail," the strange warrior began. "You have come through great trials and proved your courage and faith, time and again. You have obeyed StarClan in everything, and we are well pleased with you."

"Er . . . thank you," Stormfur mewed uncertainly.

"Yet the cats of the Tribe have courage and faith too, even though they follow different warrior ancestors. You should honor them and the Tribe of Endless Hunting."

"I know," Stormfur agreed with feeling. Whoever this StarClan warrior was, she understood exactly how he felt. "Please tell me what I should do—and tell me who you are."

The cat bent close to him so that her sweet scent flooded his senses. "Don't you know?" she murmured. "I am your mother, Silverstream. And as for what you must do—Stormfur, remember that a question can have many answers. . . ."

The light around her began to fade. Stormfur was left alone in the clearing.

"Don't go!" he pleaded.

He spun around, trying to see where she had gone. His eyes flew open, and he found himself lying on the ground outside the hole, with his friends dividing up the pile of fresh-kill a little way off.

He staggered to his paws. He had been sent a dream from StarClan! He had seen his own mother, who had died giving birth to him and Feathertail. But there was no time to mourn the fact that he had never known her alive. At last he knew what he had to do, although he had no idea how he was going to do it.

Feathertail looked up, her blue eyes startled. "What's the matter?"

"I . . . I have to go back," Stormfur rasped. "I have to fulfill the Tribe's prophecy."

"*What?*" That was Tawnypelt, leaving the mouse she was

eating to come and stand over him. "Have bees swarmed in your brain?"

Stormfur shook his head. "I spoke to Silverstream. To our mother," he went on to Feathertail. "She came to me in a dream."

Feathertail's eyes stretched wide. "And she told you to go back?"

"Well, not exactly. But she told me that a question can have many answers. I think one of those answers is for me to go back and accept the fate that the Tribe of Endless Hunting have laid down."

"But Stormfur . . ." Brambleclaw looked puzzled. "What about your duty to StarClan? What about *our* prophecy?"

"I was never one of the four chosen cats," Stormfur meowed. "And Silverstream said that the Tribe of Endless Hunting should be honored too. They are warrior ancestors, after all, even if they are not ours."

He could see that Brambleclaw was unhappy about his decision, and he hoped that the ThunderClan warrior would not try to order him to continue the journey. He respected Brambleclaw, and had been content to follow his lead, but now that he knew that he had found the right path, nothing would turn him aside, not even the friendship that had grown between them.

"What do the rest of you think?" Brambleclaw meowed.

The Clan cats looked uncertainly at one another. While he was waiting for one of them to speak, Stormfur noticed Talon sitting a little way apart with Rock and Bird. For the first time Stormfur thought he could see a gleam of hope in his amber eyes, but when Talon caught his gaze he looked away, as if he would not allow himself a voice in this debate.

"Well, I think it's a mouse-brained idea." Tawnypelt's tail twitched back and forth. "I'm staying with Brambleclaw and going back to the forest. Or have you forgotten about what's happening there?"

"I'm not asking any cat to come with me," Stormfur meowed hastily. "This is something that I have to do, but the rest of you can go on with the journey."

Feathertail got up and padded toward him, pressing her nose against his shoulder. "Stupid furball," she mewed. "You don't think I'm going to let you do this alone, do you?"

"Then I'll come too." Stormfur was not surprised that Crowpaw wanted to go with Feathertail, but he was startled as the WindClan apprentice went on, "Actually, Stormfur, I think you're right. Ever since we rescued you, you've been mooning around like a rabbit without its tail. It makes my fur ache, just looking at you. You're obviously going to be no use at all until you've tried to help these cats."

Stormfur gave him a nod of gratitude. Crowpaw's bad-tempered words couldn't disguise that he had just made a courageous offer. None of the Clan cats could be sure that the Tribe would welcome them, not to mention the danger from Sharptooth.

"I want to come too!" Squirrelpaw sprang to her paws, her green eyes blazing and her tail curled up with excitement. Turning to Brambleclaw, she pleaded, "Can't we all go? We *can't* let Stormfur face Sharptooth by himself."

"He isn't by himself," Brambleclaw mewed dryly. With a rueful glance at Tawnypelt, he added, "It looks as if we're out-voted. If one goes, we all go. I haven't forgotten about the forest—but we have to remember the warrior code, too."

Squirrelpaw let out a wordless yowl of triumph.

Tawnypelt's tail lashed once. "I think you're all as crazy as hares in newleaf," she growled. "But I said I'd stay with you, Brambleclaw, and I will."

Stormfur looked around at them, warmed to the roots of his fur by their loyalty. Except for his sister, none of them had any reason to support him apart from the bonds that had been forged between them on their journey. Midnight had spoken the truth when she said that four clans had become one. Stormfur could see nothing but good in the way that the old Clan boundaries were melting away, and he wondered if in the forest the Clans were learning to be friends as well while facing the Twoleg threat. Perhaps at last the ache of his half-Clan heritage could be soothed, and he would find a place where he could truly belong. "Thank you," he mewed solemnly.

"The Tribe of Endless Hunting will honor your courage," Talon meowed. "But what exactly do you mean to do?"

"I have an idea!" Squirrelpaw looked almost ready to leap out of her fur.

Every cat looked at her. Talon let out a hiss of disbelief.

"Go on," urged Brambleclaw.

"What Silverstream said," Squirrelpaw began, "about

every question having many answers. Well, lots of cats have tried to kill Sharptooth and failed, over and over again. Even fighters like Talon. So we have to find another answer, and I think I know what it is."

"What?" Crowpaw's voice was dry. "Are you going to go up to him and ask him nicely to go away?"

"Mouse-brain!" meowed Squirrelpaw. "No, if we can't kill Sharptooth by ourselves, we have to find something else to do it for us."

CHAPTER 20

✿

The mouse's tail slipped between Leafpaw's outstretched claws, leaving her to glare in frustration at the crevice where the tiny creature had vanished. She had left the camp to collect more herbs for Cinderpelt, and following Firestar's order that no cats were to go out alone, Sorreltail was with her.

"Bad luck," the tortoiseshell warrior meowed sympathetically. "But it was pretty scrawny to start with."

"It was prey," Leafpaw retorted. "I'd have caught it if I weren't so hungry that I can't see straight."

She began backing out from underneath the bush. Suddenly she noticed its familiar dark green leaves for the first time, and the red berries that clung to its branches and lay scattered around the trunk.

"Mouse dung!" she hissed. "And I've got the filthy stuff on my paws."

"What's the matter?"

Leafpaw backed out the rest of the way and pointed at the berries with her tail. "Deathberries," she meowed. "I was so keen to catch the mouse that I never saw them."

Sorreltail shivered. "Let's find some water and wash it off, quick."

Leafpaw was puzzled to see the look of horror in her friend's eyes. Deathberries were pretty bad, but only if you ate them. Sorreltail was one of the bravest cats she knew, yet she looked thoroughly spooked by the sight of the berries, her ears lying flat and her fur bristling.

"Are you okay?" Leafpaw asked as they padded on into the forest, keeping a lookout for a puddle where she could wash off any poison that might have gotten onto her pads.

"I'm fine." Sorreltail blinked. "Did you know that I once nearly died from deathberries?"

"No!" Leafpaw stopped, her eyes wide with shock. "What happened?"

"It was when I was a kit, before you were born. I'd followed Darkstripe into the forest—you won't remember Darkstripe; he was Tigerstar's biggest ally in ThunderClan. When I spotted him talking to Blackstar— he was Blackfoot then, Tigerstar's deputy—on *our* territory, he gave me the deathberries so I couldn't tell any cat what I'd seen."

"That's terrible!" Leafpaw pressed her muzzle against Sorreltail's side.

"It's thanks to Cinderpelt I survived," Sorreltail meowed. "Still, it's all over now. Whatever the Twolegs are doing to us, at least we don't have Tigerstar to worry about anymore." She spun around, her tail held high in the air. "Come on; let's get your paws clean. A deathberry poisoning is the last thing the Clan needs right now."

Dark thoughts flew into Leafpaw's mind as she followed her friend deeper into the undergrowth. If Tigerstar really was the father of Hawkfrost and Mothwing, then perhaps that trouble *wasn't* all over.

The roar of the Twoleg monsters grew louder as they approached the Thunderpath. At last they found a small pool in a hollow where Leafpaw dipped her paws several times and rubbed them on the grass until she was sure all traces of the deathberries were gone. All the same, she knew she would feel uneasy about licking her paws for many days to come.

"There," she mewed. She had to raise her voice to make herself heard above the growling of the monster. "That should be okay. And look, there's a huge clump of chervil over there. Cinderpelt will—"

She broke off with a terrified gasp as the roar of the monster grew suddenly louder, as if the whole sky were splitting apart with thunder. A vast, glittering shape broke through the undergrowth, crushing the chervil she had just spotted. Sorreltail let out a startled yowl and fled for the nearest tree, clawing her way up the bark and coming to rest in the first fork, her fur fluffed up until she looked twice her size.

Leafpaw flattened herself in a hollow in the ground. She watched in frozen horror as the monster seized a half-grown ash tree and ripped it out of the ground with no more effort than she would have taken to dig up a burdock root. It lifted the tree high in the air, turning it in a huge, twisting limb as it stripped off the branches. Debris began to rain down around Leafpaw, pattering on the ground like hail.

"Leafpaw!" Sorreltail's yowl cut through her fear. Her friend had leaped down from the tree, perhaps realizing there was no safety there anymore. She pelted across the open ground and nudged Leafpaw to her paws. "Run!"

Leafpaw gave the monster one more terrified glance, to see it beginning to slice the tree into pieces. Then she was dashing through the forest behind Sorreltail, blundering into brambles and through deep troughs of mud in their mad rush to escape.

When the roar had died to a faint rumble behind them, the two cats halted, panting.

"They're taking more and more of our forest," Sorreltail gasped. "Soon there'll be nowhere left for us."

Leafpaw stood trembling, looking back and half expecting the monster to burst through the trees in pursuit. "I hate them!" she spat. "They've no right to come here. What did we ever do to harm them?"

"That's Twolegs for you," Sorreltail mewed. She was growing calmer, the fur on her shoulders beginning to lie flat again. After a moment, she touched Leafpaw's ear with her tail-tip. "Come on, let's go and look for herbs near the RiverClan border. We'll get as far from those horrible monsters as we can."

Leafpaw nodded, suddenly too scared to speak. She followed the tortoiseshell warrior through the forest, grief surging through her at the thought of the peaceful places that would never be peaceful again, the trees that would never again grow green in newleaf and cast their shade on the forest. StarClan must be grieving too, she realized, especially if they could do nothing to stop the destruction.

"What are we going to do?" Sorreltail asked after a few

moments. "I can't remember the last time I was full-fed . . . or any other cat in the Clan. Look at Ferncloud. She blames herself because Larchkit died, but it's not her fault at all."

Leafpaw thought of gentle Ferncloud, grieving over her dead kit, and Dustpelt's misery as he tried in vain to comfort her. She thought of Dappletail, dead because hunger had forced her to eat the tainted rabbit. Frostfur had become too feeble to leave the elders' den, and she had started to cough. Cinderpelt was waiting every day for an outbreak of green-cough, which could so easily turn into fatal blackcough.

"Sometimes I think the Twolegs won't stop until we're all dead," Leafpaw mewed softly.

Sorreltail let out a murmur of agreement. "It's as if StarClan has abandoned us. Leafpaw, haven't they spoken to you, or to Cinderpelt? Why didn't they warn us? Don't our warrior ancestors care about us anymore?"

Leafpaw shut her eyes. She desperately wanted to tell her friend that StarClan had prophesied all this, though not to the medicine cats or their apprentices. But she had promised to keep the secret of the chosen cats, and if she was to break her word it must be to tell Firestar or Cinderpelt before any other cat.

And more than this, she was starting to think that wher-ever the cats had been sent by StarClan, they weren't coming back. It was days now since she had been able to reach Squirrelpaw in her mind. Leafpaw's heart ached at the thought that she might never see her sister or Brambleclaw again. There was no point in dangling hope in front of

Sorreltail and then snatching it away.

As they approached the RiverClan border, where the ground sloped down to the river and the Twoleg bridge, Leafpaw began to feel calmer. The sound of the Twoleg monsters did not reach this part of the territory yet; everything was so peaceful that she could almost imagine the forest was just as it used to be.

Tasting the air, she caught the scent of rabbit, and spotted the creature hopping between one clump of bracken and the next. Her paws itched to pursue it, but she remembered Firestar's order and Dappletail's dreadful death.

"Infuriating, isn't it?" Sorreltail muttered, with an angry flick of her tail. "I'd swear the stupid creatures are laughing at us."

Leafpaw nodded, water flooding her mouth at the prey-scent. She couldn't help wondering how long it would be before they were all so desperate that, like Dappletail, they would take the risk of eating the rabbits.

Just ahead of her, Sorreltail dropped into the hunter's crouch. Cautiously, so she didn't disturb her friend's concentration, Leafpaw edged her way forward until she could see what Sorreltail had spotted: a squirrel, moving slowly across an open space. *Yes!* Leafpaw thought. Prey that was fit to eat, to take back to the camp for Ferncloud and Frostfur . . .

Sorreltail leaped. Though she made no sound, the squirrel fled a heartbeat before the warrior's front paws hit the spot where it had been. Sorreltail let out a yowl of frustration and hurled herself after it as it made for the nearest tree.

"Sorreltail, no!" Leafpaw called out as she realized that the tree was on the other side of the border.

But Sorreltail was deafened by the hunger in her belly, fixed on chasing the squirrel. As it ran up the tree she launched herself up and managed to snag a claw in its tail, but the squirrel twitched itself free. Sorreltail fell to the ground, spitting fury.

"Come back!" Leafpaw cried. "You're on RiverClan territory!"

Sorreltail scrambled to her paws, bits of grass clinging to her fur. "Fox dung!" she snarled. "I nearly had it."

Before Leafpaw could call to her again, a familiar scent swept over her. A tabby shape appeared from behind the tree, and as Sorreltail spun around a huge paw slapped her to the ground and pinned her there.

"What's this?" Hawkfrost growled. "ThunderClan cats trespassing on our territory?"

CHAPTER 21

Sorreltail glared up at Hawkfrost. Twisting under his paw, she raked her claws over his leg, but days of hunger had taken the edge off her fighting skills. The warrior didn't flinch as he cuffed her over the ear with his other forepaw.

"You're coming with me to Leopardstar," he snarled. "Let her decide what to do. ThunderClan have no right to ignore our borders."

"Let her go!" Leafpaw meowed. "She's only a couple of tail-lengths inside your border."

Hawkfrost gave her an unfriendly stare. "Oh, it's you again."

"Yes, me again." Leafpaw drew herself up and met Hawkfrost's icy blue eyes, summoning all her courage. "You were glad enough that I was there when Reedpaw had his accident." Persuasively, she added, "You owe ThunderClan a favor. Let Sorreltail go."

Hawkfrost's lip curled in a sneer. "Clans do not owe each other favors. The warrior code says we should respect boundaries, which she"—he gave Sorreltail a contemptuous flick with his tail—"clearly does not."

Leafpaw felt her fur bristle and her muscles tense, as if her body were telling her to fight with Hawkfrost. Together she and Sorreltail had a chance of beating him. . . . But she forced herself to stay calm and not move from where she stood on the border. She could just imagine what Firestar would say if he found out she had attacked a cat from another Clan on his own territory.

It was hard to beg such an obnoxious cat, but she had to make one more effort. "Please—it's not as if she was doing any harm."

Hawkfrost's blue eyes were chips of ice. "She was stealing prey."

"She was not!" Leafpaw's eyes flew wide. "That was a ThunderClan squirrel."

Sorreltail, who had been lying limp under Hawkfrost's paw, suddenly heaved herself upward. Hawkfrost let out a screech as her teeth met in his leg. For a moment they writhed together on the ground, but for all her bravery Sorreltail was no match for Hawkfrost's size and strength. Soon she lay panting under his paws again.

"Okay, take me to Leopardstar," she spat. "But I'll fight you every step of the way."

Hawkfrost looked bored. "Fine. You do that."

Desperately Leafpaw looked around; why wasn't Firestar or Cinderpelt here? They might be able to persuade Hawkfrost. There were no cats at all on her own side of the border, but she caught sight of a flash of gold in the reeds on the other side of the river, and a heartbeat later saw Mothwing running across the Twoleg bridge. The RiverClan apprentice bounded up the slope and halted beside her brother.

"What's going on?"

"You can see for yourself." Hawkfrost tapped Sorreltail with his tail. "I've caught a trespasser. I'm going to take her to Leopardstar."

"She didn't mean it," Leafpaw pleaded, feeling more hopeful now that Mothwing had turned up. "She was chasing a squirrel—one of ours—and she didn't realize that she'd crossed the border."

Mothwing looked from her brother to Leafpaw and back again. "Let her go," she meowed. "It's not important. She didn't catch anything. If you take her to Leopardstar you could start a war between our Clans."

Hawkfrost fixed his cold blue stare on his sister. "And why is that such a bad thing? Every cat knows that ThunderClan is in trouble. This could be our chance to move in and take their territory."

Leafpaw gasped. Was that what Hawkfrost really wanted?

Mothwing returned her brother's stare. "Don't be mouse-brained," she mewed frostily. "Remember what Leopardstar owes Firestar. He gave the Clan back to her when Tigerstar tried to take over. She'll never go to war against him."

"She will for a good enough reason," Hawkfrost argued. "This isn't about old favors; it's about the warrior code. The borders between the Clans have to count for something!" His voice was becoming high-pitched with desperation, and he took a deep breath before growling, "And you watch your tongue, Mothwing. Remember you could be talking to the next Clan deputy."

"*What?*" Leafpaw blurted out. "What about Mistyfoot?"

"Mistyfoot is a coward," Hawkfrost snarled. "She couldn't face what's happening in the forest, so she ran away."

"No cat has seen her for a whole day," Mothwing explained to Leafpaw, her eyes wide and anxious. "Not since she went to patrol the border near Fourtrees. We don't know what has happened to her."

"Even if she comes back, she won't be deputy anymore," Hawkfrost growled. "Clan deputies can't just go wandering off when they feel like it."

Leafpaw's head spun. She couldn't believe it. Mistyfoot was no coward; besides, she had assumed that RiverClan wasn't affected by what was happening to the other three Clans, because their territory was the only one the Twolegs hadn't touched. But now Mistyfoot had disappeared.

How many more had gone? Had *all* the Clans lost cats? A chill crept bone-deep into Leafpaw; these disappearances couldn't be related to the prophecy from StarClan. Even if the first cats had failed, StarClan wouldn't send out more and more to a nameless fate. Somehow the Twolegs and their monsters must be responsible.

She said nothing of this to Mothwing and Hawkfrost, and to her relief Sorreltail did not tell them about the disappearance of Cloudtail and Brightheart. The less RiverClan knew about ThunderClan's affairs the better, especially if Hawkfrost was spoiling for a fight because he thought ThunderClan was weak.

Instead, it was Mothwing who broke the silence. "You know, you're a fool, Hawkfrost," she mewed.

Her brother bristled. "What do you mean?"

"If you want to bring down ThunderClan, you're going about it the wrong way."

"And you know the right way, do you?" Hawkfrost sneered.

"Yes, I do." Mothwing's tone was cold. Leafpaw could hardly believe what she was hearing; she suddenly felt as if she didn't know this cat at all.

"Go on, then, enlighten me."

Mothwing turned her head to give her shoulder a couple of quick licks. "Be kind to them. Make them grateful to us. That should keep them quiet while they get weaker and weaker. Why fight and risk injuries to our Clan? Let the Twolegs do the job for us. *Then* we move in and take their territory."

Hawkfrost's eyes narrowed thoughtfully. "You could have a point," he grunted. "Okay." He stepped back and let Sorreltail get up. "Leave, and don't come back."

Sorreltail shook herself and glared at him before taking the few steps that carried her back into her own territory. Leafpaw studied her closely as she crossed the border, but apart from a couple of superficial scratches, Hawkfrost hadn't hurt her.

"I'll tell Firestar what you said," she meowed to Mothwing, striving hard to keep her voice level. "He'll take it up with Leopardstar at the next Gathering."

Two pairs of eyes, ice blue and amber, turned their gaze on her.

"Sure, tell him," Hawkfrost invited. "Even if he believes

you, what can he do about it? Don't you think Leopardstar will back me against a ThunderClan cat?"

Sorreltail nudged Leafpaw's shoulder. "Come on. Let's go back to camp."

Leafpaw turned away, her tail drooping. She had liked Mothwing and trusted her, and now it seemed that her friend had betrayed her. Even if Mothwing's first loyalty was to her Clan, Leafpaw hadn't thought that she would be so coldly calculating.

She had not gone more than a few foxlengths when she heard Mothwing calling her name in a low voice. She stopped and looked back. Mothwing was standing on the border; Hawkfrost was nowhere to be seen.

"Leafpaw!" Mothwing beckoned with her tail.

"Ignore her," Sorreltail muttered. "Who needs friends like that?"

"Leafpaw, please . . ." Mothwing's voice was pleading now. "Let me explain."

Leafpaw hesitated, then took a few reluctant steps back toward the border. Sorreltail padded close beside her; Leafpaw sensed her tension and winced at the look of disgust she shot toward the RiverClan she-cat.

"I had to say that in front of Hawkfrost," Mothwing explained urgently. "Don't you see? He'd never have let your friend go otherwise."

Leafpaw felt relief flood over her. She hadn't wanted to think badly of Mothwing, not when they shared the bond of all medicine cats.

She could see her own relief reflected in the RiverClan

cat's eyes as Mothwing added, "You do believe me, don't you? We are still friends?"

"Of course we are." Leafpaw stepped forward to touch noses with Mothwing. She ignored a skeptical snort from Sorreltail just behind her. "Thank you."

Behind Mothwing, at the foot of the slope, she saw Hawkfrost emerge from the shelter of a bush and lope easily across the Twoleg bridge. She shivered when she remembered the cruel ambition in his eyes. Surely no other cat but Tigerstar had been so greedy for power?

"Mothwing," she murmured, unable to bear the uncertainty any longer, "who was your father? Was it Tigerstar?"

Shock flared in Mothwing's amber eyes. For a moment she hesitated, and then replied, "Yes."

CHAPTER 22

❧

This was madness, sheer madness. The words echoed to the thud of Stormfur's paws as he allowed Crag and another cave-guard to escort him back into the cave behind the waterfall. The other forest cats were ushered in close behind him, with more guards on either side, while Talon and his fellow outlaws brought up the rear. A patrol had spotted them as soon as they reached the river; Stormfur was pretty sure they were prisoners now rather than guests, and he did not know what the Tribe cats would do to them. They had fought their way out two nights before, so it was reasonable to expect hostility. Talon and his friends were taking an even bigger risk, because they had been ordered not to come back until Sharptooth was dead.

The first rays of glimmering moonlight were creeping through the sheet of water at the cave entrance, and soon Sharptooth would be on the prowl. Stormfur was not even sure that he could make the Tribe listen to Squirrelpaw's plan. As he sought inside himself for courage, Silverstream's scent drifted faintly around him. Stormfur glanced back, wondering if Feathertail could sense it, too. His sister was just behind him, her blue eyes troubled. But none of them had flinched when the cave-guards swarmed out from behind the rocks, as well hidden as ever by their mud-streaked fur. Stormfur felt humbled by his friends' bravery, by their loyalty to him and to the warrior code even this far away from the forest. He knew they would do whatever it took to help the Tribe, or die trying.

Stoneteller had clearly been warned of their arrival, and was waiting for them in the middle of the main cave. Under his coating of mud, Stormfur could see that a slice of his fur had been torn away in the fight against Sharptooth, and he had a raw wound across one ear.

Stormfur strode over to him and laid at his feet the piece of prey he had carried all the way through the mountains: a mountain hare, its pelt just beginning to turn white for leaf-bare.

"What's this?" Stoneteller's voice was cold, and his eyes were hostile. "Why have you come back?"

"To help you defeat Sharptooth," Stormfur replied.

His heart began to pound even faster when he saw neither welcome nor relief in the Healer's expression. "And just what do you think you can do?"

His gaze swept around the cavern; following it, Stormfur saw the Tribe creeping out of the shadows. They looked curious but wary. The friendship they had begun to show toward the cats had been scorched by the shock of Sharptooth's attack, and Stormfur's failure to save them in spite of their warrior ancestors' promise. Like Stoneteller, many of them bore raw scars or limped heavily from fresh wounds. Stormfur searched for Brook, but could not see her.

"Sharptooth took Star yesterday," Stoneteller growled. "Many cats were injured as we tried to drive him out. One has already died, and two others lie on the border of the Tribe of Endless Hunting. You didn't help us then. You ran away."

His contempt struck Stormfur like a claw. Even worse was the murmur of agreement from the gathering Tribe, as if they had felt betrayed by his flight, just as he had felt betrayed when they made him a prisoner. He heard a hostile hiss from one of the Clan cats—he guessed it was Crowpaw—and hoped that the apprentice would keep quiet.

"I didn't believe I was the promised cat," he meowed honestly. "And I didn't like being trapped in the Cave of Pointed Stones. But since I escaped, I've been thinking . . . and I've come back freely. Even if I'm not the cat who was named in the prophecy, I'll do all I can to help."

"We all will," Brambleclaw added, coming to stand at Stormfur's shoulder.

The Tribe's Healer began to relax. There were more murmurs from the cats around him, and some at least sounded approving.

Then he heard Brook's voice behind him. "Stormfur! I knew you would come back."

Stormfur turned to see her slipping through the crowd. A shiver ran through his pelt as he looked at her shining eyes and heard the welcome in her voice.

"We should listen to him," she urged Stoneteller. "The

Tribe of Endless Hunting has sent him to help us. Why else would he come back, after seeing what Sharptooth can do?"

Stoneteller looked as if he lacked energy to believe anything anymore, but he bowed his head. "Very well," he said. "But what are you going to do that we haven't tried before? Sharptooth has killed the best fighters in my Tribe as if they were puny kits."

Stormfur flicked his ears to beckon Squirrelpaw forward. She carried a wad of leaves in her jaws. "Show Stoneteller what you have," he mewed, and added into her ear, "I hope you haven't swallowed any."

Squirrelpaw dropped the leaves. "I'm not mouse-brained!" she muttered indignantly.

Turning back to Stoneteller, Stormfur prodded the hare with one paw. "This prey is for Sharptooth," he meowed. "And inside it, we'll put these." Delicately he unwrapped the leaves to reveal a small heap of glossy red berries.

A kit who was crouched with its mother at the front of the tribe took a step forward to sniff them curiously; Squirrelpaw thrust her tail in its way and guided it back to its mother.

"Don't touch," she mewed. "Even one of those would give you the worst bellyache you've ever had—if you survived."

The kit stared at her with huge eyes and said nothing.

Gazing at the berries, the Tribe's healer let out a faint hiss and took a step back. "Night-seeds?"

"You know them?" Stormfur asked. "In our Clans, we call them deathberries."

"I know all the herbs and berries that grow in these

mountains," Stoneteller responded. For a moment a gleam of interest showed in his eyes; then he bent his head again and when he spoke his voice was defeated. "And none of that knowledge is any use to protect my Tribe. Sharptooth is too strong. Not even your deathberries will defeat him."

"Three will kill the strongest warrior." Squirrelpaw spoke up boldly. "I think what we have here would be enough even for Sharptooth."

Stoneteller looked surprised. "Are you sure?"

"Even if they don't," Stormfur added, "they'll weaken him so we can finish him off."

Stoneteller still looked undecided. His shoulders were bowed as if the whole weight of the mountains rested on them.

Then Stormfur heard a stir among the Tribe cats, hostile muttering that swelled to furious yowling. Talon was thrusting his way forward to stand before the Healer; thanks to the shadows that darkened the cave most of the Tribe had only just noticed that the outlaws had returned.

Talon stood stone-still, while his former Tribemates hurled accusations at him.

"You were supposed to kill Sharptooth!"

"You failed us!"

"Stoneteller, he's disobeying you by coming here. Kill him!"

Instinctively, the Clan cats gathered around Talon, ready to defend him. Crowpaw's neck fur stood on end, and Tawnypelt had unsheathed her claws. Even the gentle Feathertail lashed her tail from side to side. Stormfur felt as proud of his warriors as any Clan leader.

Stoneteller lifted his tail for silence, but it was several heartbeats before the clamor died away. "Well?" the Healer growled. "I hope you have good reason for coming here."

"The best reason," Talon replied. "You can kill me if you like, but that won't make you any stronger against Sharptooth. Your enemy is outside this cave, not inside. The silver cat has come, and it is time to believe the prophecy of the Tribe of Endless Hunting. If we fail, then you can kill us."

The Tribe fell silent. Their hostility had changed to uncertainty; Stormfur let his neck fur lie flat again.

"We cannot kill the creature in its lair," Talon went on, "since we do not know where it lives. So we must bring it here to die."

"Here?" Brook exclaimed, one voice among many cries of outrage. "In our cave?"

Stormfur reached out with his tail and rested it on her shoulder. She had to trust him, however dangerous their plan seemed.

"Yes, here," Talon growled. "This is the place we know, where we have somewhere to hide, and where the whole Tribe can wait to ambush Sharptooth if we need to give him the death blow."

"And how do you propose to bring him here?" Stoneteller asked icily.

"With blood."

Talon lifted one huge paw and sliced it open with his teeth;

scarlet drops spattered to the ground like rain. Then he
raised his head and let out a ferocious yowl that echoed
around the cavern, louder than the waterfall outside. He spun
around and dashed out of the entrance, Rock and Bird racing
on his heels.

They left behind them a dizzy, echoing silence, apart from
the sound of water. Stormfur let out a long breath. The plan
had begun. The trail of blood was being laid.

Brambleclaw was the first to speak. "Squirrelpaw and
Stormfur, you stuff the hare. Be sure you don't get any deathberry juice on your fur, and if you do, wash it off right away."

"Yes, O medicine cat." Squirrelpaw bowed her head with
mock respect, her green eyes flashing. "We know what to do!"

Stormfur listened while Brambleclaw and Tawnypelt discussed the best place to leave the hare. Stoneteller was giving
orders to his cave-guards, and sending the kits and kit-mothers
to the nursery. Guards were placed at the entrance to that
tunnel, while more of the cave-guards and the prey-hunters
scrambled into places on the rocks around the cave walls
where they could spring down on Sharptooth. Their mud-
streaked fur blended into the walls so that Stormfur could
hardly see where they were hiding.

All the while a sense of dread was growing inside him.
Somehow he felt like something terrible was going to happen. But why, if this was what the Tribe of Endless Hunting
wanted him to do? He drank in the air, but he could scent
nothing of Silverstream now, nor sense her reassuring presence.

"It will be all right." Feathertail came up to him and pressed her muzzle against his. "I know you're scared, but StarClan sent you here as well, with your dream about our mother. We have to do this."

Crowpaw, a gray-black shadow hovering at Feathertail's shoulder, nodded but said nothing.

An icy paw gripped Stormfur. Something was wrong; he knew it. There was something they had not understood, something they had not planned for. He looked around for Brambleclaw, wanting to share his fears with him, and saw him dragging the hare across the floor to lay it in front of the entrance, a few tail-lengths inside the cave. Tawnypelt watched, measuring the distance between the bait and the entrance, while Squirrelpaw made helpful gestures with her tail.

Stormfur padded over to them, feeling the eyes of the hidden Tribe staring at him from every corner of the cave. But before he could say anything, a screech split the air outside. Talon, Rock, and Bird dashed into the cave and skidded to a halt.

"Sharptooth!" Bird gasped.

"He's here!" Rock yowled, his voice rising to a wail. "He's coming!"

CHAPTER 23

🍀

Stormfur froze. It was too soon!

The outlaws dived for the cave walls, and the Tribe cats who had not already taken up their positions pelted down the tunnel to the Cave of Pointed Stones. Stormfur and his friends were left in the center of the cavern, staring around in panic.

Their moment's hesitation was a moment too long. A ferocious snarling sliced through the noise of the waterfall. A shadow fell across from the entrance, etched in moonlight. Then Sharptooth burst upon them.

Just as the Tribe had said, he looked like a lion from the elders' tales, but without the fiery mane around his head. Lean muscles rippled beneath his short-haired pelt, and his massive gold head was lowered, following the trail of Talon's blood. When he entered the cave he looked up. He saw the hare, and swiped it aside with one vast paw.

"No!" Squirrelpaw yowled.

Her screech brought the huge head swinging around, the round, thick-furred ears twitching with interest.

"Get back!" snarled Brambleclaw. "All of you, hide!"

He leaped toward the lion-cat, lashing out with both front

paws and rolling aside before Sharptooth could turn on him. Stormfur saw Squirrelpaw dash in from the other side and spring onto Sharptooth's back, sinking her claws into the base of his tail.

"Squirrelpaw!" Brambleclaw yowled. "What in StarClan's name are you doing?"

As the lion-cat twisted, trying to dislodge her, Squirrelpaw leaped down and fled for the boulders that lined the cave wall. With a roar of fury, Sharptooth launched himself after her, but she was too fast for him, scrambling out of reach to stand hissing on a jutting piece of rock, her ginger fur fluffed up.

Stormfur fled to the opposite cave wall, following Feathertail up a series of cracks in the rock until they reached a tiny ledge tucked under the roof. Crouching in the narrow space beside his sister, he looked down at the cave floor.

The Tribe cats were all in their hiding places, too scared to move. Brambleclaw had gained safety too, on another ledge just below Squirrelpaw. He was snarling up at her, looking almost as furious as Sharptooth himself; Stormfur couldn't hear what he was saying, but he could guess.

For a moment Stormfur could not see Tawnypelt; then he spotted her head poking out of a cleft halfway up the cave wall near the entrance. That just left Crowpaw. Then Stormfur felt Feathertail tense against him and heard her murmur, "Oh, no!"

Sharptooth was scraping at the cave wall almost directly below them. Stormfur caught a terrifying glimpse of his eyes, glaring black in the moonlight, and his lips drawn back to reveal savage, dripping fangs. Crowpaw was trapped in a crevice at floor level that was too shallow to shelter him, desperately trying to press himself against the rock and escape the vicious claws. A cry of terror escaped him.

Stormfur felt his belly flip over. Everything was going wrong. Sharptooth had ignored the baited hare and pursued the cats instead. Within heartbeats he would have Crowpaw, and StarClan's mission would be ruined. How could four Clans become one if the WindClan cat were killed? Stormfur cursed himself under his breath; there was nothing that he could do, because he was not the cat the Tribe's warrior ancestors had promised. His stupid, thoughtless pride had gotten it wrong.

Beside him, he heard Feathertail whisper, "Crowpaw." She gave Stormfur a long look, filled with love and sorrow, her blue eyes glowing in the moonlight. "I can hear the voices clearly now," she murmured. "This is for me to do."

Then Stormfur felt her muscles bunch. Before he realized what she was doing, she leaped—not down, but up toward the cave roof, digging her claws into one of the narrow talons of stone with a grating noise that sent shudders along Stormfur's spine.

"No!" he yowled.

The rock split and broke away under Feathertail's weight. With a terrifying wail she plummeted down, straight at Sharptooth. The lion-cat looked up. His throaty growl changed to a scream as the spike of rock plunged into him; he fell writhing to the ground. Feathertail plummeted to the floor of the cave beside him.

Stormfur hurled himself down the wall, slipping on the rock and feeling his claws rip, until he reached his sister's side. Feathertail lay without moving, her eyes closed. Sharptooth was still twitching, but as Stormfur scrambled to a halt the lion-cat gave one massive shudder and died.

"Feathertail?" Stormfur whispered.

He was aware of Crowpaw creeping out of the rock to crouch beside him. "Feathertail?" The WindClan cat sounded desperate. "Feathertail, are you okay?"

Feathertail did not move. Stormfur lifted his head and saw the other Clan cats gathering around him, along with cats from the Tribe, creeping fearfully from their hiding places. He dropped his gaze back to his sister, and saw the faint rise and fall of her chest as she breathed.

"She'll be fine." His voice cracked. "She's got to be. She . . . she has a prophecy to fulfill."

Crowpaw crept forward until his nose touched Feathertail's fur. He breathed in her scent, and then began to lick her gently. Blood from a slash on his shoulder smudged against her pelt. "Wake up, Feathertail," he whispered. "Please wake up."

There was no response. An achingly familiar scent wreathed around Stormfur, and he looked up. "Silverstream?"

Near the entrance to the cave, where moonlight rippled through the sheet of falling water, he thought that he could see a silver cat. She was nothing more than the faintest sliver of light, but her voice sounded clearly in his head, filled with grief. "Oh, Feathertail!"

There was a gasp from Crowpaw and Stormfur snatched his gaze back to see that his sister's eyes were open. Trembling, he spoke her name. She shifted her head and blinked.

"You'll have to go home without me, brother," she murmured. "Save the Clan!"

Her eyes focused on Crowpaw, and Stormfur saw in them a lifetime of love for the difficult young apprentice, enough to sweep their Clans' rivalry away forever. "Think you have nine lives, do you?" she whispered. "I saved you once. . . . Don't make me save you again."

"Feathertail . . . Feathertail, no!" Crowpaw could hardly get the words out. "Don't leave me."

"I won't." Now her whisper was scarcely audible. "I'll always be with you, I promise."

Then her eyes closed, and she did not speak again.

Crowpaw threw his head back and let out a wail. Stormfur crouched beside his sister with his head down, grief freezing his limbs. Around him he heard the voices of his friends rise in sorrow. Squirrelpaw huddled close to Brambleclaw, murmuring, "She can't be dead—she can't be!" Brambleclaw bent his head to lick her ear. Beside them Tawnypelt stared at Feathertail with misery in her amber eyes.

The Tribe cats started whispering to one another. Somewhere deeper in the cave a yowl of jubilation broke out. "Sharptooth is dead! We are free!"

Stormfur flinched. The price had been too high. He turned his head toward the mouth of the cave, where the faint outline of the silver cat still stood in the moonlight.

Silverstream's voice came to him through the roar of the water. "My dear son, try not to grieve too long. Feathertail will hunt with StarClan now. I will take care of her."

"*We* took care of her," Stormfur replied bitterly, and then he realized that he was lying. They had failed. If they hadn't, she would not be lying there, dead, her fur glowing silver in the moonlight.

"She came," whispered Brook. "The silver cat came."

"No," Stormfur growled. "I brought her."

Crowpaw turned his head, a terrible blank look in his eyes. "It's my fault." His voice was a hoarse whisper. "If I'd refused to come back to the cave, she would have stayed with me."

"No . . ." Stormfur murmured, reaching out one paw, but Crowpaw bowed his head.

A gentle voice said his name. Brook had drawn close to him, with Stoneteller behind her. Shyly she touched her nose to Stormfur's muzzle. "I'm sorry," she whispered. "I'm so sorry."

"The Tribe of Endless Hunting spoke truly," Stoneteller meowed. "A silver cat has saved us all."

But it wasn't me, thought Stormfur. *I wish it had been.*

He turned away from where Crowpaw lay beside Feathertail, his nose pushed into her fur, and looked at the sheet of falling water. Just for a heartbeat, he thought that he saw two silver cats there shimmering in the half-light, side by side, watching over the shattered remnants of the questing Clan cats.

He blinked, and they were gone.

CHAPTER 24

"No! Help them!" A wail of sorrow and fear broke from Leafpaw. She opened her eyes with a jump and saw that she was in her nest outside Cinderpelt's den. The morning sunlight was pale and cold. The rumble of monsters from her nightmare had reached the camp in the waking world, too, and their stench hung in the air.

Shuddering, Leafpaw curled deeper into the moss, trying to find comfort in its warmth while the last wisps of her dream hung in her mind like mist. She had been standing near the Thunderpath, watching the Twoleg monsters as they roared through the forest, crushing cats under their huge black paws. Blood had run like a river across the forest floor. Spottedleaf had stood beside her, and Leafpaw had turned to her with a desperate plea. "Save them! Please! Why don't you save them?"

Spottedleaf's eyes had rested sadly on Leafpaw's dying friends. "There is nothing more StarClan can do to help," she murmured. "I'm so sorry."

Then she had faded away, and Leafpaw had woken up.

She rose to her paws, staggering, and padded across to

Cinderpelt's den. The medicine cat was not there; Leafpaw could see an empty heap of bedding at the back of the cleft and wondered if some emergency had called her away, and whether there was yet another disaster they would have to face. A whimper rose at the back of her throat, and she firmly closed her jaws on it. Whatever fate was coming, even if their warrior ancestors were helpless, she would go on helping her Clan while she had the strength.

A rustle behind her made her turn to see Cinderpelt brushing her way through the fern tunnel. The medicine cat's tail was drooping, though she tried to brighten up when she saw Leafpaw.

"What's happened?" Leafpaw asked, bracing herself.

"I've been to see Frostfur," the medicine cat replied. "Don't look like that; she isn't dead. In fact she's a little better. I'm pretty sure she hasn't got greencough."

"That's good." Leafpaw tried to sound pleased, but she couldn't help adding, "It's hunger, not greencough, that will be our real enemy this leaf-bare."

Cinderpelt nodded. "True. And if more cats disappear, there won't be enough warriors to provide food for the kits and elders, even if they could find prey." She let out a discouraged sigh.

"Shall I try to catch something for Frostfur?" Leafpaw offered. "I could join a hunting patrol, unless you want more herbs."

"No, we're pretty well stocked now. That's a good idea, Leafpaw—though I'm not sure you'll find much out there."

Leafpaw didn't argue. She padded through the ferns into the main clearing, and for a moment she felt as if she had stepped into the camp as it used to be. Sandstorm and Rainwhisker had just appeared at the mouth of the gorse tunnel, both with fresh-kill in their jaws. Spiderpaw and Shrewpaw were lying in a patch of sunlight outside the apprentices' den, while Dustpelt and Ferncloud shared tongues at the entrance to the nursery. Firestar and Brackenfur were talking together at the base of the Highrock.

Then Leafpaw realized what she was really seeing. Her father and Brackenfur both looked worried. The two apprentices lay still, instead of scuffling playfully as they used to. The fresh-kill pile where her mother and Rainwhisker dropped their prey was pitifully small. As Leafpaw padded past the nursery, she watched Dustpelt push a mouse toward Ferncloud. The she-cat's appearance horrified Leafpaw; she was little more than a skeleton, every bone visible under her dull fur.

"You must eat," Dustpelt meowed. "Hollykit and Birchkit still need you."

The reek of monsters hung over the clearing, and their roar sounded even louder to Leafpaw. Her eyes filled with a vision of them breaking through the wall of thorns that surrounded the camp, the sun glittering on their bright pelts as they crushed the terrified Clan. She blinked, forcing the images away. She could not stop the Twolegs from doing what they wanted, but she could do something small to help her starving Clan.

As she headed toward Firestar and Brackenfur, she remembered her encounter with Hawkfrost the day before. So far she had not told any cat about his plans to take over ThunderClan's territory, and she had asked Sorreltail not to say anything either. She hardly knew how to load more trouble onto Firestar's shoulders, when he had so much to bear already. How could she tell him that his greatest enemy, Tigerstar, lived on in Tigerstar's son Hawkfrost, in a Clan not weakened by hunger or ravaged by Twolegs? She knew she had to find the words, but she wanted more time to think.

Drawing closer to her father, she heard him meow to Brackenfur, "You could try a hunting patrol near Twolegplace. That's about as far as you can get from the monsters."

The anguished cry of a cat in pain interrupted him. Leafpaw spun around to see Graystripe and Mousefur stumbling out of the gorse tunnel. Graystripe looked anxious, and Mousefur was limping along on only three legs, one of her forelimbs hanging useless. Her brown fur was sticking up as if she had been in a fight, though Leafpaw could not see or scent any blood.

Firestar bounded across to her, and Leafpaw followed.

"What happened?" Firestar demanded. "Who did this?"

Mousefur was in too much pain to answer. Her teeth were gritted, and she let out a wordless moan of agony.

"Twolegs," Graystripe spat, terror stark in his eyes. "We went too close to the monsters, and a Twoleg grabbed her."

Firestar stared in astonishment.

"Come and see Cinderpelt," Leafpaw meowed before her

father could delay them by asking more questions.

She padded close to the injured she-cat on the way to Cinderpelt's den. Mousefur's eyes were glazed with pain; though she struggled along bravely, the effort of making it back to camp had obviously exhausted her. Leafpaw tried to help by letting her lean on her shoulder.

Behind them, Graystripe walked beside Firestar. "The Twolegs usually stay inside their monsters," he meowed. "But today they were swarming all over the place—StarClan knows why. One of them yowled at Mousefur and she ran, straight into the paws of another one."

"This is mouse-brained." Firestar sounded utterly confused. "The Twolegs have always ignored us."

"Not anymore," Graystripe mewed grimly.

"At least I gave him a few scratches to remember me by," Mousefur gasped.

Leafpaw raced ahead to alert Cinderpelt, who was sitting at the mouth of her den with her eyes raised to the sky as if she were trying to read some message from StarClan in the movement of the clouds.

"It's Mousefur—she's hurt!" Leafpaw gasped.

Cinderpelt leaped to her paws. "Oh, great StarClan!" she exclaimed. "What next?" She squeezed her eyes shut as if she could barely brace herself to carry on, but her voice was as calm as ever when she meowed, "Come and lie down here, and I'll take a look."

Mousefur lay down in front of the den, and Cinderpelt ran her nose along the injured leg, sniffing carefully at the shoulder. "It's dislocated," she meowed at last. "Cheer up, Mousefur. I can put it right, but it's going to hurt. Leafpaw, fetch me some poppy seeds."

Leafpaw obeyed, and Mousefur licked them up. As they waited a few moments for the seeds to dull the she-cat's pain, Leafpaw listened to her father and Graystripe talking together near the mouth of the tunnel.

"I'll have to forbid cats to go anywhere near the Twolegs," Firestar mewed. "Soon there'll be nowhere safe outside the camp. Already some of the cats are too scared to go out on patrol."

"We're not finished yet," Graystripe retorted stubbornly. "StarClan won't let us be destroyed."

Firestar shook his head, and stalked back down the tunnel into the main clearing. After a moment Graystripe, with a worried glance at Mousefur, followed him.

"Okay, Leafpaw," Cinderpelt meowed. By now the brown warrior was growing sleepy, her head lolling forward onto her paws. "Let's do it. Put your paws there," she went on, pointing to Mousefur's other foreleg. "Hold her still while I put her leg back. I don't want to be clawed to death. And watch carefully what I do," she added. "You haven't seen this before."

Leafpaw carefully positioned herself as her mentor had shown her, while Cinderpelt took Mousefur's injured leg firmly in her teeth, bracing one paw against her shoulder. Then she pulled; Leafpaw heard a sharp click and Mousefur jerked, letting out a furious yowl.

"Excellent," Cinderpelt muttered.

She examined Mousefur's shoulder again while the she-cat lay limp and trembling. "That's fine," she mewed, nudging the brown she-cat to her paws. "See if you can put your weight on it."

Mousefur tried; she staggered, more from exhaustion and the effects of the poppy seeds than from her injury, Leafpaw thought, but stayed on her paws.

"You'd better get some sleep." Cinderpelt began guiding her to the ferns at the edge of the clearing. "I'll check you again when you wake, but I don't think you'll have any more trouble." Glancing back at Leafpaw, she added, "You did well there. I can manage now if you want to go and hunt."

Leafpaw paused while her mentor settled Mousefur among the ferns. "Are you sure you don't need me?"

Cinderpelt shook her head. "There's nothing more to do. There's nothing any of us can do," she added in a lower voice. "StarClan is silent."

Her despair appalled Leafpaw. Amid all the chaos caused by the Twolegs, she had always believed that Cinderpelt's faith would stand firm. And worst of all, there was nothing she could say to lift her mentor's spirits—not when Spottedleaf herself had admitted that StarClan was as powerless as the cats in the forest.

"I'm not going hunting," she meowed firmly. "I'm going to find out what happened to our missing cats."

Cinderpelt stared at her, puzzled. "What?"

"Don't you see? If Mousefur hadn't struggled free, the Twoleg would have taken her away. We might never have known what happened to her. That must be what happened to Cloudtail and Brightheart too."

The medicine cat's expression cleared. "Yes, I see that. But Leafpaw—what if *you* don't come back?"

Leafpaw gazed at her, half regretting that she had told Cinderpelt her plan. What if she refused to let her go?

"This is the first clue we've had about the disappearances," she meowed. "We *must* try to find out the truth."

To her relief, after a moment's hesitation, Cinderpelt nodded. "Very well. But be careful. And find another cat to go with you." As Leafpaw turned to go, she added, "You're a brave cat, Leafpaw. Remember that the Clan can't afford to lose you."

Leafpaw dipped her head, embarrassed by her mentor's praise, and slipped through the ferns. Back in the main clearing, she could sense that a change had fallen over the Clan. News of the attack on Mousefur had clearly spread; the air was full of the scent of fear and despair. Leafpaw wanted to spring up onto the Highrock and call out to her Clanmates, to make them realize that they mustn't give up. As long as they were alive, there was still hope. But who would listen to an apprentice? And what words could she find that would make a difference?

Taking a deep breath, she made up her mind. She would go to Firestar and tell him everything she knew about the cats who had been sent away by StarClan. Even though she had no idea where they were now, or if they would ever return, the news might at least give Firestar and the rest of ThunderClan reassurance that StarClan was not indifferent to what was going on in the forest. She would tell him about Hawkfrost too, and his plans to take over ThunderClan's territory. She was sick of secrets; it would be a relief to unburden herself after so long.

But first she would go and look for the missing cats, in case Firestar punished her for not telling him sooner by confining her to the camp. Quickly she made her way to the outside of the warriors' den and called, "Sorreltail!"

Her friend peered out through the branches. "Leafpaw? What is it?"

Leafpaw thought back to the morning not so long ago when she had called Sorreltail out to visit WindClan. Then there had been hope; Sorreltail had been bright and lively, eager for action. Now her tortoiseshell fur looked dull, and her eyes stared blankly at Leafpaw.

"I want you to come with me," Leafpaw began, and explained her plan to investigate the disappearances.

To her relief, Sorreltail's eyes brightened as she spoke. "Okay," the tortoiseshell warrior meowed. "It's better than lying around the camp all day. Let's go."

She threaded her way out between the branches of the den, and both cats headed through the gorse tunnel.

Leafpaw followed Graystripe's and Mousefur's scents back toward the scarred section of the forest where the Twoleg monsters rampaged. She had been this way the day before, when she and Sorreltail had watched the monster uproot the tree, but she was astonished to see how much more destruction the Twolegs had created in such a short time. The ground had been churned into mud, with monsters crouched here and there, or roaring across the ground with a horrible slow movement as if they were creeping up on prey.

There were Twoleg nests there, too, roughly made of wood rather than the hard red stone in Twolegplace. The cats crouched in the shelter of one of them, peering out at the Twolegs walking around. Leafpaw could feel Sorreltail quivering, fear-scent coming off her in waves; she felt just as terrified, but there was no way she was going back now, not when she was so close to finding out what happened to Cloudtail and Brightheart.

"What's *that?*" she murmured to Sorreltail.

She pointed with her tail at what looked like a miniature Twoleg den, made of wood and open at one end, set underneath one of the few surviving trees. It was far too small for a Twoleg to get inside.

Sorreltail shrugged. "Dunno. Some Twoleg thing."

"I'm going to look."

Warily glancing from side to side in case a Twoleg tried to grab her, Leafpaw crept across the open ground. Behind her she heard Sorreltail meow, "Be careful!"

As Leafpaw drew closer, she picked up the scent of food coming from the den. Though it was unfamiliar, not the fresh-kill scent she was used to, water flooded her mouth. She needed all her self-control not to dash forward and start eating. She knew that whatever it was, Twolegs must have put it there, and that meant danger.

Outside the small den, Leafpaw blinked as another scent reached her. Cat scent, familiar but very faint and stale, and at first she couldn't figure out which cat it was. Certainly not from ThunderClan. Then she remembered, and her paws tingled with excitement. Mistyfoot! The RiverClan deputy had been here, as well.

Cautiously Leafpaw peered into the den. It was empty except for a white, hollow thing that held the food. Mistyfoot was not there now, and there was nothing to tell Leafpaw where she had gone.

The food scent was even stronger inside. Slowly, one paw at a time, Leafpaw crept into the little den. The white thing held small brown pellets like rabbit droppings, smelling strangely of food and Twolegs at the same time. Leafpaw wondered if this could be the kittypet food Firestar had told her about. Kittypets ate it without being harmed, didn't they? She took a mouthful, shivering as it slid into her empty belly, and wondered if there were any way she could carry some back for Frostfur.

"Leafpaw! Get out!"

A deafening chorus of voices suddenly seemed to yowl in Leafpaw's ears. Sorreltail's was there, but there were many more that she did not recognize, and Spottedleaf's was loudest of them all.

She choked on her mouthful of pellets. Spinning around, she caught a glimpse of Sorreltail, staring at her in horror. Then the open end of the den slammed shut, and Leafpaw was left in darkness.

EPILOGUE

❧

Squirrelpaw was trapped in a small, dark space that rocked violently from side to side. Her head spun, and she swallowed the bile that rose in her stomach. Her paws scraped frantically on something smooth and solid. She let out a terrified yowl: *"Leafpaw!"* Then her eyes flew open and she found herself scrambling in a shallow dip in the ground.

"What's the matter? Yowling like that, you'll scare all the prey."

Tawnypelt was standing over her; she had dropped a plump, fresh-caught vole so that she could speak. The five Clan cats had left the mountains last night and were traveling across open moorland. The rising sun, relentlessly showing them the way they must go, had just cleared the horizon.

Squirrelpaw heaved herself out of her nest and shook scraps of grass from her pelt. "Nothing. It was just a dream." She gave her chest fur a few licks to try to hide how shaken she was. Her sister was in terrible danger; she knew that the dream had taken her to wherever Leafpaw was, and shown her the terror she was feeling, but Squirrelpaw guessed that the practical Tawnypelt wouldn't understand her fears.

Tawnypelt was looking faintly interested. "Was it a sign from StarClan?"

"No." Squirrelpaw knew she could share some of the details of her dream, without telling Tawnypelt it had connected her with Leafpaw. "I . . . I felt like I was trapped somewhere dark. I didn't know where I was, and I couldn't escape."

Awkwardly, Tawnypelt stepped forward and pressed her muzzle against Squirrelpaw's side. "I think we've all had bad dreams," she meowed. "Ever since Feathertail . . ."

Squirrelpaw nodded. Like all of them, she found it hard to believe that they would never see Feathertail again. The Tribe cats had helped them to bury her, beside the pool where the waterfall fell endlessly, churning up spray that made the ground soft enough to dig.

"She has a place of honor here," Stoneteller had meowed. "We will keep her memory alive for as long as our Tribe survives."

That had been small comfort for the Clan cats. Crowpaw in particular was shattered by grief, spending all the next day crouched beside Feathertail's grave. Stormfur kept vigil with him, racked by guilt that he had done nothing to save Feathertail, and had not even imagined that she might be the chosen cat. Her silver fur had been slicked black with water when they first emerged from the waterfall, which was why the tribe cats hadn't paid any attention to her. At last Brambleclaw had ordered them both inside the cave to rest.

"We're leaving at dawn," the ThunderClan warrior had

told them. "You'll need all your strength. Our Clans need us."

The journey had begun again. The Tribe cats had escorted them part of the way through the mountains, and they soon came to easier country with flat green grass and hedgerows to provide prey. But they felt no sense of hope or relief that they would soon be home. Their hearts stayed with Feathertail, in the land of rocks and water.

Squirrelpaw soon recovered enough from her nightmare to help with the hunting so that they could get going and make the most of the rapidly shortening days. Though no cat wanted to eat, they forced themselves to gulp down the fresh-kill. Once or twice Stormfur caught himself looking around to ask Feathertail something, before he remembered that he would never speak to her again.

All that day and the next they traveled on, until their paws were cracked and bleeding. It was as if the horrors they had seen had numbed them to everyday pain. The sun was going down behind them again as they came to the top of a rise. Their shadows streamed out ahead of them, pointing toward a hill with a jagged crest. It seemed to smolder in scarlet fire from the rays of the setting sun.

"Look!" Tawnypelt's voice was an exhausted croak.

For a few heartbeats no cat spoke. Then Squirrelpaw's green eyes flashed with a fire that had seemed dimmed forever by Feathertail's death.

"Highstones!" she exclaimed. "We're almost home."

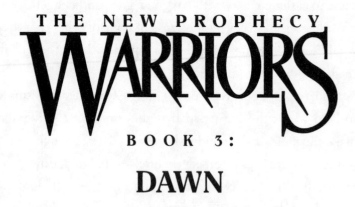

The questing cats finally return to the forest, only to discover that their part in the prophecy is far from over. Now they must convince the warring, starving Clans to travel mysterious paths to find a new home . . . but how can they leave when so many cats, including Squirrelpaw's beloved sister, Leafpaw, are missing?